WHEN IT RAINED AT HEMBRY CASTLE

MEREDITH ALLARD

When It Rained at Hembry Castle

Cover design by Jenny Quinlan

ISBN: 9780692631409

When It Rained at Hembry Castle/Meredith Allard – 1st paperback edition 2016

{1. Victorian England—Fiction. 2. Victorian Historical—Fiction. 3. Victorian Romance—Fiction. 4. Historical British Romance—Fiction. 5. British Historical Literature—Fiction. 6. Literary—Fiction.} I. Title

Copperfield Press

A FUNERAL AT HEMBRY

The mourners lined the village roads as far as the castle, their umbrellas pointed like black wreaths at the crying sky. There were hundreds of them, from the village of Hembry, from across the county of Berkshire, from London 60 miles away. They bowed their heads, tipped their hats, or curtsied as the hearse passed on its way toward the church, the black-draped driver keeping his four black stallions with their glossy fake tails moving in time to the slow-falling rain. The onlookers tried to see through those at the front, the shorter on their toes, straining their necks, while fathers held their children on their shoulders to see the white lilies on the polished oak casket. There were few dry eyes as the body of the 8th Earl of Staton passed. The women hid their sorrow behind their handkerchiefs while the men insisted they weren't crying, it was rain on their faces, after all.

The escort to the church was a well-orchestrated affair. Ten men acted as pages, four were feathermen, and two mutes in black gowns and silk hatbands acted out the family's sorrow in a lugubrious pantomime. The family's carriage jerked up and down, up and down over the mud-slicked road while the mourners trailed behind, following the 8th Earl on his final journey. As though the heavens had their fill of tears to shed that day, the closer to the church the mourners came, the harder the rain fell. The onlookers struggled to protect themselves from the warm June splashes until, in the space of a breath, the sky cleared and the sun peeked pink beneath the parting clouds. The air was heavy, you could hold it in your hands like warm dough, and the mourners dabbed with handkerchiefs at perspiring foreheads.

The mourners of a mind to converse remarked on the size of the crowd. It was rare that the death of a peer touched the lives of so many. Normally, when one died, people shrugged, muttering how it was too bad Lord Whatshisname or Lady Soandso had passed on, but you know how it goes. When you get to be that old you have it coming. The Earl of Staton had died in residence in his country seat at Hembry Castle, so some public display of grief was to be expected, and there were always those who turned out with expectations of pocketing whatever alms the family saw fit to bestow. But the 8th Earl of Staton prompted more than shrugging and greed for alms. Everyone knew the Earl as a good man, a compassionate man, and they mourned him. Many had already paid their respects by filing past as the coffin lay in state at the castle. They had all been there—the dignitaries, the aristocrats, the neighbors, the farmers, the tenants, the villagers, the tradesmen—but they came out again for the Earl's funeral. There are few truly good men in the world, and when one passes he should be acknowledged.

The hearse neared the church on a grassy hill dotted with yellow wildflowers and white budding bushes. The church itself was sun-bleached stone, its castle-like bell tower looming over the family. The stallions stopped, straining against their reins as though the slow pace had left them with energy to spare. The onlookers bowed their heads, praying for the eternal safekeeping of their beloved Earl, while the pallbearers lifted the coffin and carried the Earl inside. The onlookers waited in silence a respectful distance away while the family attended the church service. In time, the family reemerged with the white-robed, solemn-faced vicar.

Those lucky enough to get a view closest to the proceedings saw the eldest son, last week Richard Meriwether, today Richard, 9th Earl of Staton, as he passed the wrought iron gate to the crypt. He was only eight-and-forty, the new Earl, his long face handsome in an elegant way, his slim figure youthful and wiry, his chestnut curls peeking from under his black silk top hat and hiding the half-moon scar near his left temple. Every villager in Hembry could tell you how, when he was a boy, the Earl of Staton as is had fallen into the river when he tried to learn to swim. He lost his balance, slipped under the water, and nearly drowned as he cut the skin close to his left eye on a knife-like rock, leaving that half-moon scar still visible four decades later. There was no sign of the frightened boy that day, however. The new Earl of Staton looked fine in his close-fitting black mourning suit, his frock coat buttoned to his chin, his top hat his only protection against the wet. There was something in the new Earl's eyes, some misgiving, perhaps, and the onlookers pressed forward for a closer look. Normally, there would be a whisper or two about the new Earl's unmarried state, especially at his age, but on this solemn day the gossips let it rest.

As the family made its way to the cemetery gates, children and a few of the shorter adults elbowed their way closer for a view of the 8th Earl's widow, Agatha, Countess of Staton, who was hidden in black by a billowing dress and a heavy veil which left her featureless, like a storm cloud floating toward the gravestones. Necks strained higher when other members of the family appeared. The 8th Earl and his Countess had been unusually lucky since all three of their children were sons —Richard, the eldest, now Earl, behind him the Honorable Frederick Meriwether, at five-and-forty the second son, known as "the wayward" around the village (and possibly the castle itself) since it was common knowledge that he hightailed it to America the moment he completed his studies at Oxford. Everyone knew everything in a rural village like Hembry, and they knew Frederick was a widower, his wife having died nearly five years before. For this sad occasion, Mr. Frederick had brought with him his only daughter, his only child, to England for the first time. There were rumors that Mr. Frederick's daughter was a Beauty, as her mother had been (because who else could entice the son of a peer to stay in America but a Beauty). The golden-haired young woman appeared near the cemetery gate, and though a thin black veil covered her features, those close enough could see the sadness on her lovely face and they nodded, thinking, yes, she is indeed a Beauty.

The 8th Earl's youngest son, the Honorable Jerrold Meriwether, nine-and-thirty, and his wife, Hyacinth to family and friends (age withheld), had just arrived from London where they lived with their two young sons, Harold and Xavier, the boys somber in their small black clothing. Jerrold Meriwether, though he was the youngest son, looked older than his brothers with his thinning hair brushed to one side, an unfortunate pretense obvious even beneath his top hat. He wore a mustache over a protruding lower lip, which gave him the appearance of a lopsided mouth, too thin on the top, too thick on the bottom. He waited near the wrought iron gate looking at no one, especially not his wife, who was most certainly not looking at him. If they cast their eyes in opposite directions, they were also turned away from each other, he to the right, she to the left, and their backs would have had an easier time conversing than their fronts. Though the space between them was a few steps, it could have been miles for all the attention they paid to each other. Their two small boys, taking their cues, stood in the gulf between their parents and watched their grandfather's burial with detached glowers, as though this were the funeral of any poor sod they might have happened upon in the street. The only sign of emotion from anyone in Mr. Jerrold's family was from Mr. Jerrold himself, and that was when an infant child of one of the onlookers cried. At the sound of the wail, Mr. Jerrold snapped around, his neck growing longer, his lank hair blowing out from under his top hat as though Medusa's snakes were crawling from his head, ready to discover the unfortunate child who dared to make a noise. But there were no snakes to aid him, it was only his thin strands of hair blowing about, so Mr. Jerrold cast his eggshell glare over the crowd and grew small again. When his mother, the Countess, gestured for him to join her near the mausoleum, he walked to her side, leaving his own family near the gate.

After Mr. Jerrold was inside, the family's physician, Mr. John Hough, appeared. The new Earl pointed his walking stick toward Mr. Hough, and they found their way toward each other, the tall, lanky, chestnut-haired Earl and the nearly as tall though not so lanky doctor with glints of silver in his black hair. Mr. Hough whispered to the Earl and nodded toward Mr. Jerrold, who was too busy scrutinizing everyone else to notice. Did Mr. Jerrold expect a specter to jump out from behind a gravestone? The onlookers noted Mr. Jerrold's odd behavior, though some insisted that his behavior was no stranger than usual. He always looked like a little boy caught with his hand in the sweets jar. The golden-haired Miss Meriwether touched her Uncle Jerrold's arm, gently, and the man seemed to come to himself. He nodded at his niece and followed her.

Edward Ellis was among those watching the funeral proceedings, and he was struck, like many others, by the lovely young woman recently arrived from America. It was some time before he remembered to exhale. He wanted to press past the bodies and yell "Get out of my way!" like a churlish old woman knocking everyone aside with a walking stick until he could see Miss Meriwether up close. She couldn't truly be that lovely. After all, her features weren't clear under the black lace veil. If he saw her without the veil she wouldn't make such a strong impression. Would she? Then he saw the line of servants from the castle making their way into the graveyard, the female servants in their simple black dresses and bonnets, the male servants with their black armbands. He saw the butler and housekeeper at the head of the line, arm in arm, heads bowed. They didn't need to feign their sadness, Edward knew. He caught the housekeeper's glance and she nodded. She nudged the butler and gestured toward Edward. The butler looked over the top of his round spectacles and smiled in a muted way. Edward returned the solemn greeting and watched them walk more slowly than he had ever seen them. When the butler and housekeeper broke their staffs of office over the dead Earl's coffin, Edward knew their hearts would break too.

From outside the gates the melancholy voice of the vicar was heard reciting the burial rites: "I am the resurrection and the life, saith the Lord: he that believeth in me, though he were dead, yet shall he live: and whosoever liveth and believeth in me shall never die..."

The family was hidden behind bushes, trees, and ancient gravestones, and not much could be seen outside the gates. Some of the onlookers began to drift away while others remained until the end.

"I heard a voice from heaven, saying unto me, Write, From henceforth blessed are the dead which die in the Lord: Even so, saith the Spirit, for they rest from their labors..."

Edward wanted to stay. He wanted to see the golden-haired girl again. He wanted a glimpse of her without the veil. He wanted to be certain. He remembered the untouched paper in his carpetbag, and he knew he should be writing down everything he saw, but he trusted his memory not to forget this scene. Certainly, he wouldn't forget the girl. He pulled his fob from his pocket, saw the time, and sighed. He had to leave now if he were to make it to the train and back to London before nightfall. Edward Ellis looked once more at the cemetery, saw a smattering of black dresses, armbands, and top hats, but that was all he could make out. Since there was no glimpse of Miss Meriwether, he walked at a brisk pace from the cemetery. At the end of the field where horses grazed on grass and wildflowers shimmied in the humidity he heard the death knell. The old Earl had been entombed. Edward looked to his left and there in the distance, perched on the tallest hill, looming large above the village, bursting out beneath the darkening clouds, was the sand-colored limestone of Hembry Castle. Edward was certain he saw the chimneys bow toward the church in reverence for their lost lord, wondering if anything at Hembry would ever be the same again.

THE DAILY OBSERVER

*E*dward Ellis stood on the newly constructed Victoria Embankment looking down into the gray River Thames. He spent many hours in that spot, near the Houses of Parliament, daydreaming while he watched the lapping water wind its way from the Tower of London, past London Bridge, the gateway to the city, past the dome of St. Paul's, there near the Palace of Westminster and the Abbey, continuing further west past Hampton Court where it flowed through Oxford, Reading, and Windsor. Edward remembered how, when he was 12 and his family had first moved to London from Portsmouth, the Thames was a great pot of stink. There had been efforts to clean the water since then, and now, on certain days, it was as pleasant a river as any. Edward admired the view, the pea-soup-like London fog held at bay. The rain had gone and the sun was high, and he paused for a moment, hoping for a breeze to soothe the humidity that weighed him down from the top of his chocolate-brown hair to the bottom of his polished boots. He looked toward Westminster Abbey, its Gothic towers watching over London like the patient angel

9

it was, and he continued along the embankment, staying near the river until he reached Savoy Street and then the Strand, which he followed until it became Fleet Street near his destination on Gough Square—the offices of the London Daily Observer.

As it neared nine a.m. the streets grew from merely active to heavily congested as omnibuses released clerks, lawyers, and agents by the hundreds. Edward watched the men on the knife-board seats at the top of the buses disembark down the ladder as soon as the vehicle came to a halt (some before the wheels had completely stopped and he laughed when they had to unravel themselves—an arm over here, a leg under that fellow there—after they hit the ground). The men dispersed in whichever direction their employment lay, walking quick-step to offices of commerce, finance, or government. It was a morning ritual Edward found amusing. These were men who rode the same buses with the same men day after day, week after week, year after year. They passed the same faces on their daily travels, and still they hardly acknowledged one another, as if they couldn't be bothered with the effort. I'll see you again tomorrow, won't I, so I need hardly bother with you today. The difference between the older workers and the younger workers was striking. The younger workers looked shiny, new, excited for the day. They had a spring in their step and they walked with glint-filled eyes toward wherever they were expected. The older workers had lost their sheen altogether, their radiance faded into something between dull and dead. In their downcast glances Edward guessed these men had decided that this is all there is, this is all there would ever be, their demeanors matching their yellow neckcloths and brown-black coats.

Edward stepped quickly along the rounding streets, past the shops and taverns, past the Royal Courts of Justice, near the offices of the Daily Courant, the Mitre Tavern, and St. Bride's Churchyard, the dome of St. Paul's Cathedral watching with its giant green eye. He stepped around newspaper men going in and out of the public houses while two-wheeled Hansom cabs, barouches, and broughams filled the narrow streets as each vehicle attempted—some more successfully, some less—to bring their passengers to and from wherever they needed to go while carts and drays carried goods and people too poor to afford other forms of transportation. Everywhere was sound: wheels growling, hooves clopping, and horses neighing mingled midair amidst shouts from the drivers, bells from the muffin man, cries from the street peddlers, and too-loud conversations shouted over the din.

Normally, London made Edward's heart pump with the fascination of being alive. He had lived there half his life and he considered the city home. Still, at that moment he found himself yearning for the melodic bird songs in the quiet country village that was Hembry. Edward shook his head. If he was anything, he was honest with himself (most of the time) and he knew it wasn't the birds at Hembry he dreamed about. He shook his head again, hoping to rattle awake any sense he might have left between his ears. Nothing could come of the particular interest he had in Hembry, he knew, and he was mad to devote one more moment to such thoughts. It's a month already since the funeral, he reminded himself, and she never even knew I was there. Besides, she's returned to America by now, certainly. The fact that she's the niece of the Earl of Staton doesn't bode well, either. Whatever would his grandparents have to say about that! And then, Edward reminded himself, there's that other matter, so he dropped the thought entirely. Or he meant to.

He was so caught up in his daydream of the beauties of Hembry that he nearly passed the offices of the Daily

Observer, located in a brick building within the L-shaped court of Gough Square, where Dr. Johnson lived in his day. He stopped, realized his mistake, turned back, and walked into the building and up two flights of stairs. Somehow he ended up in the correct office. He nodded at a fellow reporter as he sat at his desk near the window. He knew he should begin transcribing his notes from the parliamentary hearing he attended the night before, but the political mumbo jumbo meant nothing to him then, his shorthand notes looking like sketches of fireworks instead of symbols for sounds and words.

He turned his attention to the window, as he often did, watching the faces of those passing below. He was fascinated by people, Edward. He had a quick eye and rarely missed a thing as he studied others for the truth they tried to hide—the silence within their words, the secret shiftings of their gestures, the meaning behind every expression. He couldn't help but notice the impressive-looking older woman who carried her vast self with great ceremony while a young man in midnight blue livery followed several steps behind. The young man opened the door of a brougham almost as impressive looking as the woman, while a driver, also in midnight blue livery, waited with the reins in his hands.

Edward watched as the woman attempted to lift herself into the brougham with some difficulty, then with assistance from her servant. Edward was joined in his spying by two fellow reporters, Thomas Roberts and Oliver Wellesley. The three young men pressed their faces against the glass as they watched the woman struggle to slide her ample bottom half onto her seat while maintaining some semblance of dignity. Edward snickered when he realized that the woman was lodged with her top half in the carriage while the bottom half remained stubbornly out.

Wellesley tapped his nose with his index finger. He

unlatched the window and pushed the pane up, letting in a thick brush of summer air. Then he reached into his trouser pocket and removed a fistful of peanuts in their shells. The three young men cracked the shells and ate the peanuts, admiring the half-in, half-out woman still floundering below. When the young men had their fill of nuts and the shells were empty, Wellesley began dropping them one by one out of the open window. Some of the shells dropped onto the parasols of passing ladies (you never did know what might fall onto your head in London). Other shells dropped onto men's bowler hats, the wearers unaware of Wellesley's attack. When the peanut shells started pummeling the fine-looking lady still not entirely within her carriage, Edward laughed so hard he walked away from the window to avoid being heard on the street below. Wellesley, dark eyes small in concentration, remained intent.

"Oh!" they heard. "It rains peanuts now, does it, Chester?"

A voice, which must have belonged to Chester, answered dutifully, "Yes, my lady."

"Well then! We must exhibit due diligence in such matters, mustn't we, Chester? We will not allow peanuts to spoil our day."

"No, my lady."

Wellesley nodded, pleased he had accomplished his goal. He dropped the remaining peanut shells into his trouser pocket, presumably for use at another time. He knocked the peanut dust from his hands as he turned to Edward. "I'm covering Parliament tonight. Are you off to the by-election, Ellis?"

"Tomorrow," Edward said. "I have the night off for once."

"They don't like to let you sit idle," said Roberts. "They say you're the best political reporter in England."

Edward shrugged.

"He wants to be like his hero, Mr. Dickens," said Wellesley.

"They say Mr. Dickens was the greatest political journalist in his day. He also used to travel across the country to report on the speeches and elections. Ellis here even moved to Fetter Lane to be near Furnivals where Dickens lived when he was a parliamentary reporter."

"It's a good place and it's close to here," Edward said.

"I've heard of worse reasons for living somewhere," said Roberts. He looked out the window and waved as the brougham carrying the great lady lurched away. "I still can't believe Mr. Dickens is gone. I'm half-expecting the next edition of Drood to come out and now it will never be finished. Can you imagine? Writing his book one day, dead as a doornail the next. So how would it have ended? Drood, I mean. Who killed him?"

"The uncle, Jasper," Wellesley said. "Dickens had to have meant for it to be the uncle. Dickens shows where Jasper goes to the graveyard and discovers the quicklime, all the better to decompose the body with. Later Edwin is told that Ned is in great danger, and Edwin was known as Ned by Jasper. And what about the way Jasper reveals himself to Rosa Bud? Such meanness! Certainly, he had the temperament to do away with his nephew, especially if he thinks that nephew is a threat by being engaged to the woman he loves."

Edward nodded. "But keep in mind that the most obvious answer may not always be the best answer. A master like Dickens may have wanted us to believe that it was Uncle Jasper, set him up perfectly, and then surprised us in the end. There are some hints that Datchery is in disguise. Disguised as whom? Why disguised? Datchery is a suspect, surely."

"As one Ned said to another," said Roberts. "At least there are two more numbers to be published, so there may be more clues yet to come. Mr. Dickens certainly seemed preoccupied

WHEN IT RAINED AT HEMBRY CASTLE

with mysteries toward the end. What about the mystery in Our Mutual Friend?"

"What mystery was that?" asked Wellesley.

"The mystery of John Harmon."

Edward shook his head. "That wasn't a mystery, just a misidentification. Harmon wasn't dead, he was presumed dead and living as John Rokesmith."

"Harmon was supposed to have drowned in the river," said Roberts. "Edwin Drood's watch and shirt pin were found by the river. I should stay away from the river if I were you."

"I wasn't planning on drowning any time soon, thank you, Roberts." Wellesley pressed his face against the window again, either looking for a new mark or trying to find some coolness on a stifling day. "Poor Mr. Dickens. Poor us! Never to know how his final tale should end. Wherever you look you see people still wearing their black for him and it's been over a month since he died. Did you go to his funeral, Ellis?"

"I didn't. I went to Westminster Abbey to pay my respects after the crowds died down."

Roberts nudged Edward with his elbow. "Ellis here got a little weepy, didn't you?"

"I didn't."

"You did. I was there. I saw you. A lot of people were sniffling and dabbing their eyes with handkerchiefs. I mean, I did like his books, I liked them quite a lot, actually, but it wasn't as though any of us knew him. Tell me, Wellesley, have you ever heard of people mourning a man they never met?"

"Many people who never met the Earl of Staton mourned him," said Edward.

"Speaking of," said Wellesley. "I've been away covering speeches, Ellis, and I haven't seen you since you returned from Hembry. How was the funeral?"

"Well attended. Many dignitaries were there, but it wasn't

just the toffs. I think the entire village of Hembry turned out. My grandmother said the funeral itself was low-key with no great ornamental displays, which is what the Earl wanted. He never cared much for grandiose funerals even if they are the fashion. Lord Staton believed in celebrating people while they were alive so they knew they were appreciated."

"How are your grandparents taking it?"

"Rather hard. They knew the Earl for more than 40 years."

Randall Tewson, the copy editor at the Daily Observer, wagged a crooked finger at the loitering young men. "You fellows might want to get some work done today. The new editor will be here any moment."

Tewson squinted at them, a poor man's evil eye. The copy editor shook his head and barked orders at others who laughed when he said the new editor was expected. Edward watched Tewson stomp toward his desk, still wagging a crooked finger at some invisible adversary.

"It hasn't been the same since Mr. Barden left," said Wellesley.

"What happened?" Edward asked. "I was away at Hembry when he resigned."

Wellesley looked back toward Tewson to make sure the copy editor's attentions were elsewhere. When he spoke he whispered. "Barden walked in one morning and announced that he was leaving to edit an English language newspaper in Spain and his friend from Oxford would be taking his place. It just so happens that friend is one Mr. Frederick Meriwether, or should I say the Honorable Frederick Meriwether, younger brother to the new Earl of Staton."

"I saw him at the funeral," Edward said. "I didn't realize he was taking over here."

A flash of golden hair danced behind Edward's eyes. He

shook his head with that snapping motion again, casting the vision aside.

"Why would the younger brother of the Earl of Staton be in newspapers?" asked Roberts. "Seems he ought to be well set up in life."

Wellesley, the man of confidences, whispered again. "I overhead Tewson say that Mr. Meriwether studied literature at Oxford. When he arrived in America he took a job at the New York Times. He started as a reporter and worked his way up, and now that he and his daughter will be staying in England for a while he decided to help his old friend Barden and take over here until someone permanent can be found."

Edward stopped listening at "...he and his daughter will be staying in England for a while ..." She was still in England then. He remembered his promise to stop thinking about her, but knowing she was still in England pleased him very much.

Wellesley and Roberts drifted back to their desks. Edward looked at his notes again, only now he was distracted by the knowledge that the beautiful American girl was still in England and he was working for her father. The window drew him again, and he watched the movements of the city as though the sights and sounds spoke to him. He studied the faces, wondering who the people were, where they were going, and what they were thinking. With typical July abruptness, the sky darkened and rain fell. The men pulled their hats closer to their chins, the women shifted their parasols, and everyone continued on their way.

Edward knew he should pull his attention from the panorama outside to the work on his desk. He still had to turn his notes into some cohesive narrative. That's the odd thing about being a writer—when you have something pressing that needs to be written, everything and anything seems more interesting than the writing you have to do. In the corner of the L of Gough Square Edward saw a flower merchant with his barrow of violets, lilies, dahlias, and daffodils in reds, yellows, and pinks, calling "Alla-growin', alla-blowin'!" Next to the flower merchant stood a round man in a top hat that fell to his eyebrows, wearing a too-long frock coat and too-short trousers that left the tops of his boots visible for public inspection. The man pulled on his watch chain every ten seconds or so, tapping his foot in exaggerated impatience for whomever he waited for. As Edward watched the man he thought to call on Wellesley for a few peanut shells. He was certain he could hit his target with extraordinary precision even from that distance.

Drawn as though by the man's impatience, Edward looked at the time. Nearly 11 a.m. No more dilly-dallying. He had to work. As he was turning from the window he saw her. At first, he thought his eyes deceived him. Certainly, he only thought he saw her because she had been so much on his mind since the Earl of Staton's funeral, but no, it was her.

Miss Daphne Meriwether stood near her father, whom Edward recognized from the funeral. Though she was still in full mourning, she was a vision, her pale skin set off by the crinkled black crepe that fell in ripples from her waist. Edward memorized every detail of her—her gold hair pulled back in a simple knot at the base of her neck, a few strands loose beneath her black bonnet. She wasn't wearing a veil, and Edward was able to focus on the heart-shaped face with the same kind smile as her father, who wore his mourning as a black band around his arm. As Mr. and Miss Meriwether crossed the street, the cab drivers pulled their horses to a halt and doffed their hats in the young woman's direction. Her father doffed his hat in return, and the Meriwethers crossed unmolested by man, vehicle, or beast, a near miracle on the busy London streets. As they walked, Mr. Meriwether gestured toward the building from where Edward watched them. Edward felt embarrassed suddenly. He wanted to hide, but where? Under his desk? Should he run up the stairs to the next floor? He couldn't possibly let her see him. She would know at a glance that he had been thinking improperly about her—well, not improperly, perhaps, but not entirely properly either. But he didn't run. His feet wouldn't move. She was too lovely, after all, and who knew when he would see such a sight again.

As father and daughter were about to enter the building, a ruddy, plump-cheeked boy raced across the street, dodging vehicles, horses, and low-flying birds, causing shouts from annoyed pedestrians. The boy held a small bouquet of yellow calla lilies toward the golden-haired young woman, and Edward saw the ruddy, plump-cheeked flower vendor wiping his hands on his apron and laughing at his son. The boy stopped short, nearly running father and daughter over in his haste to get to them before they disappeared inside. The boy, shy suddenly and pulling his slouch cap over his eyes, grinned sheepishly as Miss Meriwether kneeled next to him, took the bouquet, inhaled deeply as though the flowers smelled of ambrosia, and kissed the boy's cheek. The boy clasped his hand to his face as though he meant to keep the kiss forever. He looked back toward his father and beamed. He had won his prize. Mr. Meriwether reached into his coat pocket and handed a few coins to the boy, who was clearly in love. Edward leaned close to the open window and heard the boy say, "Oh, no, sir. My pa says the flowers are a gift for the pretty young lady in black. To cheer her from her sadness."

"That is a most generous gesture," Frederick Meriwether said. "Where is your father, young man?"

"Just there, sir." The boy pointed to where his father waited by the flower barrow.

"How very kind," Miss Meriwether said. "You see, Papa,

people in London can be as considerate as people in New London."

Edward watched as Mr. and Miss Meriwether walked the boy back to his father and Frederick Meriwether and the flower vendor began talking. The younger brother of the Earl of Staton speaking to a flower vendor in the street, where anyone could see? Edward wondered what Mr. Meriwether's mother, the Countess of Staton, would have to say about that. He realized too late that Roberts and Wellesley were beside him.

"Whatever has your rapt attention, Ellis?" asked Roberts.

"Ahhh..." Wellesley pointed to where Mr. and Miss Meriwether still chatted with the flower vendor and his son, who was now partially hidden behind his father while he stared at the young woman as though she were the goddess Aphrodite come to earth.

"You have excellent taste, Ellis," said Roberts. "The young woman is in mourning. Perhaps she needs a shoulder to cry on."

As Mr. and Miss Meriwether left the flower vendor and his son, the rain picked up again. Suddenly, as though she sensed someone watching her, Miss Meriwether looked up and Edward knew he had been seen. Then she smiled. It wasn't a perturbed smile, which Edward would have expected from a well-born young English woman, a "How dare that strange man have the indecency to notice me!" sort of aggravation. It was a friendly smile, an acknowledgment—hello, I see you— and it made Edward's heart stammer. Then he did the unthinkable. He smiled back.

"I see you're acquainted with the young woman," said Wellesley.

"That's Mr. Meriwether and his daughter," Edward said.

Roberts looked toward the door. "Here they come."

Edward stood. He cursed the fact that bright colors had gone out of fashion because he suddenly thought his black frock coat and brown waistcoat were too dreary. He ran his fingers through his hair, brushing it first to the right, then to the left, then away from his face, then to the right again. He sat at his desk, crossing his right leg languidly over the left. He leaned back as though this were the most ordinary thing in the world. He was at work where he belonged and it was a daily occurrence for beautiful young women to visit there. Why shouldn't it be?

Roberts grinned. "You're prettying yourself up for the daughter of the brother of the Earl of Staton?"

"I am not prettying myself up."

The door opened and there were Mr. and Miss Meriwether. The office went silent. Mr. Meriwether smiled in a fatherly manner at the scrutinizing faces, though the young men brightened considerably when they noticed Miss Meriwether. Randall Tewson hurried from his desk as quickly as his short legs would carry him and he nearly prostrated himself in front of the new editor as though Mr. Meriwether were the Duke of Somewhereorother. In Mr. Meriwether Edward saw a tall, straight-backed man with the upright stature of an aristocrat and the manner of a friend. Mr. Meriwether's chestnut-colored hair was graying at the temples, and he was clean-shaven, as Edward was—a contrast to the style of the day since only men and very old women could grow beards properly. Though on another man his small blue eyes and refined features might look cold, Mr. Meriwether didn't appear disagreeable at all. With introductions led by Tewson, Mr. Meriwether made his way around meeting the men who would work for him. Edward noticed the way Mr. Meriwether looked everyone in the eye and asked everyone's name and their responsibilities at the paper. Yes, he spoke in the swanky tones of the aristocracy, but otherwise he could have been anyone from anywhere. If Edward didn't know better he would never have guessed that Mr. Meriwether was reared in the ancient halls of Hembry Castle. Then Frederick Meriwether stood before Edward as Tewson introduced them.

"I can't believe we haven't met before, all things considered," Mr. Meriwether said. Edward struggled to keep his eyes on the father, and he succeeded in looking at the daughter only twice. "I believe you know Mitchell Chattaway?"

"I do," Edward said. "I worked for him at the beginning of my career."

"He's a good man to know if you're in the newspaper business. My daughter and I dined with Chattaway and his family when we first arrived in England. Allow me to introduce my daughter. Daphne, this is Edward Ellis, the young man I've heard so much about. Mr. Ellis, my daughter Miss Meriwether. I've been telling everyone in my family about you, young man. Mr. Barden told me of your talents as a reporter as well as an editor, and he showed me some of the short pieces you've had published. I must admit, I'm rather impressed."

Miss Meriwether smiled, and Edward forgot why he was standing there. Mr. Meriwether had just said something nice about him—he was sure of it—but he couldn't say what and he couldn't guess how to respond. He nodded until Miss Meriwether rescued him.

"Is it true you're the fastest shorthand transcriber here? And the most accurate?"

"That's what Mr. Barden has been saying about him," said Mr. Meriwether. "Mr. Ellis, you'll be running this place before long if I have anything to say about it."

"Thank you, Mr. Meriwether."

Frederick allowed Tewson to escort him to the men he hadn't been introduced to yet. With Mr. Meriwether gone,

Edward was at a loss. He tried to look everywhere but at Miss Meriwether, though he could feel her watching him. She wasn't being indiscreet, staring like a coquette at men she didn't know. She was curious, and she was, after all, American. No well-born young English woman would dare be caught in a place where people performed work. To be associated with a trade? Never! Yet here was Miss Meriwether, unembarrassed, curious, and her father didn't appear concerned with exposing her to something as common as a newspaper office.

When Edward could no longer ignore the fact that Miss Meriwether's full attention was on him, he had to resist the urge to hide in the supply closet. Though his left foot was turned toward the door, his right foot stayed stubbornly in place. He realized, after some thought, that he needed to either stay where he was or trip over himself in his haste to get away, looking even more ridiculous in Miss Meriwether's eyes than he was sure he already did. He decided to stand strong, so he scanned himself—trousers fastened, boots on the correct feet, waistcoat right side out. Was his hair a mess? He wanted to run a hand through it again, but he didn't want to seem vain so he resisted.

"I saw you looking out the window," Miss Meriwether said.

"I saw the flower boy give you that bouquet." Edward gestured to the yellow calla lilies she held in her black-gloved hand. Her eyes were so blue they appeared violet, and those violet eyes watched him like two amethysts.

"He was a sweet little boy." Miss Meriwether watched her father speaking to several men across the room. "You needn't worry, Mr. Ellis. You're in good hands with my father. You won't find a fairer employer anywhere, and he already thinks you're so talented."

"That's good to know." Edward wanted to say something bright, something witty to make her laugh, but, as it always happens in moments when you most want to sound impressive, his grasp of the English language eluded him. Finally, seeing her mourning dress, complete sentences formed and he even managed to speak them aloud.

"I'm sorry about your grandfather. I've had the privilege of meeting him on more than one occasion, and I know he was a kind man, a magnanimous man, respected by everyone who knew him. I was at his funeral, covering it for the paper. That's where I saw you the first time." Edward pictured himself with his pen running a delete line through that last sentence.

Miss Meriwether was about to respond when Mr. Meriwether called her to join him and Mr. Tewson at his desk. Edward tried to work for the third time that day, but now his thoughts were consumed by wishes for a glimpse of the golden-haired, violet-eyed beauty. Whenever he looked in her direction all he saw was the backside of Randall Tewson.

"Look!" cried Wellesley. "He keeps looking in Miss Meriwether's direction. Ellis is in love."

"Don't be daft," said Edward. "I'm thinking of my article and how little time I have to finish it."

"And longing for a glimpse of the radiant Miss Meriwether."

Edward grimaced at Wellesley before fastening his eyes onto the notes with the dots and doodles. He picked up his quill, filled it with ink, and began working. All around him were the manic scrapes of feather tips on paper as others scrambled to meet their deadlines. Edward thought of the beautiful young woman on the other side of the room as he translated those dots and doodles into English.

Finally, as Edward readied his copy, he heard snickering. He was about to say something rude to Wellesley and Roberts, but he realized Mr. Meriwether was standing near his desk and caught himself in time.

WHEN IT RAINED AT HEMBRY CASTLE

"Is your piece ready to go?" Mr. Meriwether asked. Edward handed the editor his work, which somehow he managed to finish. Mr. Meriwether scanned the piece. "This looks quite good."

"Thank you, Mr. Meriwether."

"Your attention to detail was so highly praised by Mr. Barden I was afraid he was going to try to carry you off to Spain. Did I mention I had a chance to read the pieces you've had published?" Edward nodded. "You have quite a grasp for storytelling, young man. I'd even go as far as saying you're the next Mr. Dickens."

"Exactly what our Ellis is longing to hear," said Roberts with a wink.

Edward pretended he didn't hear. "You're very kind, Mr. Meriwether."

"Kindness has nothing to do with it. Your stories are moments in time—humorous, perceptive, they make people think differently—and that's no small task, young man. As a matter of fact, I'd like you to write a few original pieces for this paper, that is, if you're interested."

"Yes, Mr. Meriwether, I'm interested."

"And you'll be able to write the stories while keeping up with your other duties?"

"I'm not afraid of hard work."

"So I've heard." Mr. Meriwether looked at his daughter. "A young man with talent and ambition. Those qualities are not so easy to find these days. I'm happy to have you on my staff, Edward Ellis. I know your grandparents are very proud."

"I hope so."

"As I'm sure you're aware, we've had a death in the family."

"I'm very sorry about your father."

"Thank you, yes, it was very sudden. None of us were quite prepared, though I dare say one is never prepared for such a thing. I should be home at Hembry now, but I felt I needed to come and meet everyone before I started messing things about. I've left Mr. Tewson with instructions about how to help things run a tad more efficiently, and I know from Mr. Barden that he can be trusted. My daughter and I are returning to Hembry today, and I'll be there for a while. I'd like you to join us for luncheon so we can discuss those original pieces you'll be writing for us. I know your grandparents will be happy to see you."

"What about the Earl?"

"My brother would be happy to have you as our guest at Hembry, as would I."

"Even though…"

"Even though."

"Then yes, I would like very much to come for luncheon."

"Excellent. We'll settle the date soon."

Mr. Meriwether gathered Edward's work and went into the office that held the long wooden editor's table where the pieces of the newspaper were laid out like a jigsaw puzzle. When Mr. Meriwether closed the door, the tittering began. Wellesley poked Edward in the back.

"What did he say?"

"He invited me to Hembry Castle for luncheon."

"They're having you for luncheon?" Roberts exclaimed.

"They invited me to luncheon, to eat it, you fool, not to be luncheon."

Wellesley pointed at Edward. "Why do you get to go to Hembry Castle? I've been here longer than you. I've covered Parliament longer than you, and I wasn't invited."

Roberts sat on Edward's desk, his arms crossed over his chest, a disapproving expression on his face. "And what about Miss Chattaway? What would she think of your dining at

Hembry Castle, casting lovelorn glances at the beautiful Miss Meriwether?"

Edward cringed. Miss Chattaway. In the month since he had laid eyes on Miss Meriwether he had not once thought of Christina. He had certainly not been to visit her, and there were her unanswered letters waiting less patiently by the day. Whenever he glanced at the unopened envelopes lying in a haphazard pile on his desk at his lodgings, he felt them tapping their fingers, stamping their feet, demanding acknowledgment.

"There's nothing she needs to think about," Edward said. "I work for Mr. Meriwether. He wants to discuss some original pieces he wants me to write for the paper. He invited me to Hembry Castle so we can eat luncheon while we have the discussion. That's all."

"And Mr. Meriwether's beautiful daughter will be there too," said Wellesley. "That's all."

Yes, Edward thought. That's all.

DOWNSTAIRS AT HEMBRY CASTLE

*I*n south-central England near the River Enborne are the North Hampshire Downs where the chalk hills rise and the green land rolls and the coral-colored field poppies, pink orchids, and yellow buttercups sprout haphazardly around grazing sheep and a startled deer or two. If you listen, you can hear skylarks singing and woodpeckers pecking in the plentiful trees. If you're traveling from London, you'll pass first through Slough, then the tall-tree woods of Bracknell Forest, and further on you'll pass villages like Woolton Hill, Burghclere, and Highclere within the surrounding region of Staton. In the sprawling countryside of the North Downs you'll find the village of Hembry. You'll know you're in Hembry when a farmer, or the postmaster, or the vicar tips his hat to you. As you continue into the village, the cottages bid you welcome with open doors and fires at every hearth. You'll pass the plots of land cultivated by the tenant farmers, and the farmers' families will wave as you pass.

Over there is the village pub, the Staton Arms, and over there is the post office—the center of village life where everyone congregates, most to gossip, others to insist gossiping is wrong though they may have overheard a tidbit or two they feel obliged to share. If you want to know what Mrs. Montrey said to Mrs. Kents about the burgundy dress with the embossed sleeves and the blooming flower at the high collar that Lady Staton wore at the latest village fête—the one held only a month before the 8th Earl died—then you should stay close to the post office. According to Mrs. Montrey, her lady-ship's dress featured the newest fashion—a protruding bustle at the back—and how does one ever sit in such a contraption, Mrs. Montrey wondered? When you've had your fill of village chatter, you'll cross the common square where the aforemen-tioned fête is held and arrive near the stone church, the sun-bleached one commissioned by the first Earl of Staton. And there, on the highest hill, is Hembry Castle.

In 1596, Blackfriar's Theater opened in London, Shake-speare's The Merchant of Venice was performed for the first time, and Her Majesty Queen Elizabeth named Horace Meri-wether the first Earl of Staton for his role alongside the Earls of Essex and Nottingham when British forces destroyed 32 Spanish ships and captured the city of Cádiz. Immediately, on the vast gift of land Her Majesty most graciously bestowed upon him, the new Earl began building a home worthy of his title. He was lucky, Horace Staton, formerly Meriwether, since he began his life as your lordship with wealth—his family had made their fortune as shipbuilders in Southampton—and his country seat was impressive from day one. The house had changed quite a lot over nearly three centuries. The castle's fortifications—the stone walls, the keep at the center, the towers on the four corners, the outer curtain wall—were knocked down by the fourth Earl when he became convinced that the first Earl's fear of barbarian attack was largely over-rated. Now, the Countess' Garden is built over what used to be the moat. Now, the castle features had largely disappeared, though a fragment or two could be found in the parklands so the name Hembry Castle remained.

Edward Ellis admired everything he saw as he walked at his usual brisk pace through the village of Hembry. He enjoyed wandering the winding roads, nodding at the friendly, curious faces, laughing at the gossip in the post office, watching the sheep loiter, and admiring the green patchwork farms dotting the landscape. You could hire a wagon (driver included) to take you up the hill, but Edward preferred to walk. It gave him a chance to take in the country scenery along with the quiet calm that can only be found in nature and birdsong—two things Edward missed when he was in London. He was born and had spent the first half of his life in Hampshire, in Portsmouth, and he loved the sweeping hills of the northern part of the county as much as he loved the southern coastline. It was a steep climb toward the castle, but Edward didn't mind. He loved the green pastures that stretched as far as he could see, and the closer he came to the great house, the more clear its features became, the more he was struck by its steadfast stance, like a patient parent watching over its children.

On the outskirts of the grounds were the follies, the decorative mock castles (more reminders of the house's earliest incarnation), and the Greek temple façades, which made Edward chuckle with their extravagant uselessness. He passed the rotunda and the statues from Ancient Greece and Rome, added to the family's collection by previous Earls. He stopped to admire the rainbow spray of colors in the Baroque-style Countess' Garden, then walked the tree-lined avenue toward the house. He marveled at the dignity of the old place, how the sand-colored limestone blended gracefully into the green hills, the winding river, and even the sky above. The exterior of the castle was as eccentric as some of the Earls who had lived inside. The pitched roof pointed skyward with seventeenth-century gables while the south-facing exterior was designed in the Palladian style by renowned architect William Kent. Edward paused to admire the Corinthian columns, the cornices, the triangular Tympanum above the entrance. He stepped toward the door, changed his mind, and walked down the slope to the other side.

JEMIMA WAS the newest housemaid at Hembry Castle, and she screamed in a manner most unbecoming when she dropped a silver tea service and sent the pieces clattering to the floor. Fortunately, the empty pot bounced so there was only a splash of tea that she and Ruth, another housemaid, had to wipe away. They giggled nervously as they glanced for the housekeeper, but when they realized Jemima's clumsiness had passed unnoticed, their giggles became laughter.

"You're a lucky one," Ruth said as she wiped away the remnants of her ladyship's tea. "If that pot had been full it would have been a disaster to clean up."

"At my last place the butler could hear anything from anywhere in the house, though it was a much smaller house, of course. He loved to dock our wages for time wasted, and he was such a mean old brute he would have considered this time wasted."

"Housemaids are under the housekeeper's orders."

"Supposed to be," said Jemima. "The butler and the housekeeper were always arguing about his ordering her staff around."

Ruth gathered the tea things and set them back on the tray. "You don't need to worry about that here." She winked at the cook, Mrs. Lainie Graham, who had come to see what all the racket was. "Our butler and housekeeper get along quite well."

"Most of the time," Mrs. Graham said.

Ruth carried the tray and Jemima followed with the wet cloths, setting them down in the washing sink in the scullery. Mrs. Graham was so busy with the pigeon pie for that afternoon's luncheon—slicing the ham, melting the butter, beating the eggs, and laying the puff pastry over the mixture in the baking dish—that she hadn't noticed the girls admiring her work.

"Something smells good," Ruth said.

"The family's having a few guests for luncheon," Mrs. Graham explained.

"I thought they were still in mourning," said Jemima.

Mrs. Graham wiped her hands on her apron. "It's nothing fancy, her ladyship said. Just some friends of his lordship and Mr. Frederick's for a simple meal. Her ladyship isn't very happy about it, I gathered, but his lordship said his father liked to have friends nearby and he wouldn't have wanted the family sitting around like wet sacks feeling sad all day."

"His lordship never did like mourning," Ruth said. "God bless him in Heaven. I do miss him."

"Who is 'her ladyship?'" Jemima asked. "His lordship never married."

"He isn't married yet," said Mrs. Graham, "though I fear he may be soon enough. Since there's no wife, his mother remains Countess for now."

Ruth leaned closer to the cook. "Is his lordship going to speak out?"

"There's been some chatter about Lady Lily Carter-Marsh as the next Countess of Staton, but I don't think anything is settled yet. I don't think it will ever be settled for him, poor soul." She checked her menu, then stirred the suet and candied peel for the baked plum pudding. She shook her wooden spoon at Jemima. "You should hear the rumors they spread about his lordship. Mr. Lannow, Lord Tilling's valet, told us. They like to say his lordship is quite the ladies' man. Of course his lordship doesn't help matters, traipsing off to who-knows-where with his band of merry men like he's Robin Hood, disappearing for weeks at a time. His lordship is suspected of having female companionship in London, if you know what I mean. That's why he disappears as often as he does, they say, to visit her in Covent Garden. They say he sends her money too." She dropped her voice to a whisper. "They say there's a child. But you listen to me—there's no truth in that." She winked at the plum pudding as she pressed the mixture into the baking pan.

"Mr. Lannow should know what his lordship is up to," said Ruth. "After all, his lordship and Lord Tilling are friends."

"What else did Mr. Lannow say?" asked Jemima.

"That his lordship goes about with the Prince of Wales."

"I don't know," said Ruth. "His lordship doesn't seem the type to involve himself with such a crowd. His other friends like Mr. Hough aren't from aristocratic families."

Jemima spun across the kitchen floor, her hands out as though she were dancing with a gentleman. "His lordship is so handsome, isn't he? His eyes are a little small, and his face a little long, but there's something about him that makes him so pleasant to look at. He has such a nice smile. Is he as kind as he seems?" Jemima swooned at the thought. "He asked my name my first day. I don't think my last employers knew my name the whole year I worked for them."

"Yes, he is every bit as kind as he seems," said Ruth. "His brother, Mr. Frederick, seems much the same, though the goodness must have skipped over Mr. Jerrold. He's too much like his mother." Ruth pressed her hands over her mouth, stopping herself from saying more, though the downstairs walls stood stoic as ever, used to such gossip.

"Rachel said she was dusting the sitting room this morning when she heard his lordship and her ladyship arguing," Jemima said. "Rachel said her ladyship told his lordship she wants him married by the end of the Season."

"She's been saying that for five-and-twenty years," said Mrs. Graham.

Jemima curtseyed, dipping toward the floor in the manner of a great lady. "I should be most happy to marry his lordship."

Mrs. Graham threw her flour-covered dishtowel into the air. "The likes of you married to the Earl of Staton! Whoever heard of such a thing?"

Jemima stood with some difficulty from her curtsey and straightened her apron. "Why isn't he married already? Has his heart been broken? Is he pining over someone?"

"Who knows what goes on in other people's hearts?" said Mrs. Graham.

Ruth leaned toward the cook. "I know that smirk, Mrs. Graham. You look that way whenever you know something other people don't. What do you know?"

"I get the meals around here prepared on time. More than that, I don't know."

Ruth peeked into the servants' hall where the footmen Henry and Colin sat at the table drinking tea and eating sandwiches. She sighed as though she wanted to join them. "Come Jemima. We have a lot more to get through today."

They were startled by a knock at the downstairs door. Outside Jemima found a good-looking young man of average height and slim build with chocolate-brown hair that fell over large hazel eyes, more gold than brown or green, that seemed to take in everything at once. The young man smiled.

"Good afternoon. I'm here to see my grandparents."

"Grandparents?" Jemima glanced into the hallway. "There's no grandparents here, sir."

Jingling keys grew louder. "I believe here comes a grand-parent as we speak," the young man said.

Mrs. Mary Ellis, the housekeeper at Hembry Castle, appeared. Edward Ellis took his grandmother's hands with the greatest affection.

"What are you doing down here?" Mrs. Ellis asked. "You're a guest today. You should have used the front door."

"I wanted to see you and Grandfather before I went up."

Mrs. Ellis kissed her grandson's cheek. "You look so hand-some today, Neddie, but a little thin. Aren't you eating? Don't they pay you at that newspaper? Heaven knows you work hard enough for them."

"They pay me well enough, Grandmother, and yes, I'm eating." He sniffed the air. "If luncheon tastes as good as it smells, I'll be eating plenty."

Mrs. Ellis opened the door wider so Edward could step inside. "Come in and sit down. I pressed and ironed the clothing you sent ahead and they're laying out in my sitting room, though you have time for tea and a chat before you change. Jemima, close your mouth and tell Mrs. Graham my grandson is here. Ask her to send Frannie with some tea."

"Yes, Mrs. Ellis." Jemima smiled at Edward as though she agreed with the housekeeper—her grandson was looking rather handsome that day. A stern look from Mrs. Ellis and the maid scurried away.

"Is she new?" Edward asked. "I don't remember her."

When Mrs. Ellis entered the servants' hall the footmen stood until she acknowledged them. She gestured for Edward to sit at the table.

"As a matter of fact, she is new. She's never worked in a manor like this before, so she has a lot to learn." Mrs. Ellis looked at the whitewashed walls decorated with paintings of Queen Victoria in various stages of her life—from young ingénue to fleshy widow. The sunlight cast pink-yellow shadows on the wall, leaving the tea-drinking footmen under two spotlights as though they were on the stage. It was, Edward noticed, the only color in the room. "I can't complain, though. I know what those first months in a big house are like. I remember when I first came to Hembry more than 40 years ago. I was lucky that my sister would watch your father when I couldn't have him down here." Edward shrugged, and his grandmother didn't press him. "Fortunately for me, your grandfather had already been here some time so I had an easy enough adjustment. But there's so much to learn in a big house like this."

"And you learned it quickly, my dear."

Edward marveled at how his grandparents hardly changed as the years passed. Augustus Ellis, butler for one of the most respected families in England, was a medium-statured man like his grandson, his slim frame hunched forward, Edward guessed, from his perpetual downward-looking stance, as though he were always trying to sneak up on something that needed improving upon, his round, wire-rimmed spectacles dipping from the tip of his nose. Edward's grandmother had grown stouter through the years, and her hair was more white than gold now, but she still had that motherly smile that put everyone at their ease. With the appearance of Mr. Ellis the footmen stood, and again, after acknowledgment, they sat.

Edward nodded at the footmen. "Being in service is similar to calisthenics, isn't it? Sitting and standing, sitting and standing."

Henry Horrocks, the peacock of a first footman, was about to respond though he stopped after a swift kick under the table from Colin Pratt.

"Yes, it is, sir," Colin answered.

Clattering was heard from the kitchen, and then Mrs.

Graham bustled into the servants' hall with a tray of tea and cakes. "Ned! Let me have a look at you." She put the tray on the table, then her hands on her hips as she squinted at Edward. She was a tall, broad woman, Lainie Graham, with her sharp eyes and dark hair swept haphazardly under her cook's cap. She nodded with approval at what she saw. She poured some tea and handed Edward the cup and saucer.

"You didn't need to do this yourself, Mrs. Graham," Edward said. "You should have sent one of the maids."

"I wanted to see you before you disappeared upstairs."

Edward sipped his tea. "You don't have to stay, any of you. I know you're busy."

"I think everything is settled for the moment," said Mr. Ellis. "I wanted a moment to speak to you before you went upstairs, Edward. There's something I need to tell you."

"It sounds serious, Grandfather."

"Not too serious, I hope. But I do want you to know that Mr. Frederick discovered that you're my grandson because I told him so. At the time I didn't think anything of it, but I realize now it may have been a lapse of judgment on my part. If I did wrong, I apologize."

"If I weren't your grandson, then apologies may be in order, but as it stands…"

"Thank you, Edward, though I feel I ought to explain. I knew Mr. Frederick had agreed to take over the editorial duties at the Daily Observer, and in a burst of pride I blurted out the fact that you worked at that same paper." Mr. Ellis gave a hard stare in the direction of the footmen, both of whom appeared not to notice anything but the teacups in their hands. "I'm very proud of the work I've done for this family, Edward."

"As you should be, Grandfather."

"Your grandmother and I have put our all into Hembry Castle, and we consider it an honor to be in service for such a respectable family. And yet I understand how a young man like yourself, who has chosen a different path in life, might not want it known by his employer that his grandparents are in service for said employer's family. You needn't acknowledge me in front of the others upstairs. In fact, it wouldn't be proper if you did."

"Grandfather, as you carry off every fine detail of this luncheon to perfection, as you always do, I'll point to you and say loudly enough for everyone in the castle to hear, 'That great man is my grandfather. I learned my work ethic from him. I learned how to work hard, take pride in my work, and always perform to the best of my ability from him, and my grandmother as well.'"

"Thank you, Edward, though I don't know how well the family will take to such a display of familiarity between us." He nodded, his butler's duties overtaking his family feelings. "Now if you'll excuse me. Henry and Colin, I believe luncheon should be attended to?"

The footmen marched single-file up the stairs. "Henry and Colin will get everything in order," said Mr. Ellis, "but I should be there to supervise."

"Of course, Grandfather."

"Perhaps you should reenter at the front door. You're an invited guest of Mr. Frederick's, after all."

"Mr. Meriwether is perfectly aware that I'm your grandson. I doubt he'd be the least surprised to see me coming from down here."

Mrs. Ellis looked at the clock on the mantelpiece. "You ought to change, Neddie."

Edward disappeared into his grandmother's sitting room, emerging a quarter of an hour later in his freshly pressed coat and trousers, wing collar shirt, and blue and green plaid waist-coat. Mrs. Ellis tied her grandson's cravat into a fancy-style knot, then reached into her apron, pulled out two repoussé cuff links, and slid them into place. "Your grandfather and I thought these would look nice."

"Are these Grandfather's?"

"They were a present from the 8th Earl. We know it's only luncheon, but still, how often do you dine with the family?"

Edward admired the gold at his wrists. "Thank you, Grandmother. I look as fine as the Earl of Staton."

Mrs. Ellis led Edward to the staircase. "Are you ready?"

"You sound like I'm about to be sacrificed to the lions."

"There's a whole other world up there, Neddie, one I hardly understand and I've been here a long time. You already know Mr. Frederick is a good man, and his lordship is much the same. Her ladyship is…her ladyship is…"

"I've heard she's quite deaf."

Mrs. Ellis turned her sternest expression onto Jemima, who was yanked into the kitchen by a disembodied arm.

"Is she deaf?" Edward asked. "I thought it was more of a selective hearing."

"You'll see for yourself soon enough. Just remember that Mr. Frederick wants you here, his lordship is happy to have you, and that's all you need to know. Your grandfather will be there to help you."

"Will I need help, do you think? After all, I have eaten luncheon before. Perhaps not upstairs, but I am familiar with the meal. Will I be dragged away by my ear for using the wrong fork or for speaking to someone on my left when the Countess is looking to her right? Besides, I thought luncheon wasn't as formal as dinner." Edward brightened. "Will Miss Meriwether be there?"

"Do you know Miss Meriwether?"

"I met her briefly at the newspaper office."

Mrs. Ellis eyed her grandson with the observant look he

inherited from her. "Yes, Miss Daphne will be joining you for luncheon. I understand her ladyship has big plans for Miss Daphne."

"I'm sure she does."

Mrs. Ellis pointed at the staircase. "All right, then. Up you go."

"I feel like I'm being dropped down the rabbit hole."

"In this case Wonderland is upstairs."

Edward grinned as he climbed toward the Wonderland of Hembry Castle.

UPSTAIRS AT HEMBRY CASTLE

*C*ertainly, Edward had spent many carefree days as a child at Hembry Castle running through the servants' hall or hanging onto his grandmother's skirts or Mrs. Graham's apron. He always knew there was a different world through the green baize door, though he never had any great desire to know that world better. He had always found the nobility amusing with their odd manners, strict rules, and monotone voices, and he had never felt any burning desire to see them in their natural habitat. Edward knew from his grandparents that the people upstairs weren't so different from anyone else though they (and anyone else) believed they were. Certainly, the aristocrats had land, a manor house, sometimes even money, but they also had the same problems as people anywhere. Sometimes their problems were magnified because of their position. Perhaps it was because of his proximity to Hembry Castle that Edward was never particularly impressed by any of it. He wasn't worried about what the Countess of Staton thought of him, or what the Earl of Staton thought of him, or what anyone else thought of him, except for his new editor. And the editor's daughter.

Edward stepped through the green baize door and stopped. It was the first time he had entered the castle proper and he had to admit he was dazzled. It was as though the sun shined brighter on the other side, and Edward laughed to think that the Earl of Staton and his family would certainly think so. It was only that the sun had finally prevailed against the rain and the windows upstairs were floor to ceiling whereas downstairs there were only a few glass eyes at the top of the walls to let light through. But we'll allow the family to think the sun shines only for them, Edward thought.

He closed the door and heard nothing from downstairs. The door was a barrier, a clear sign to the servants from the family—you are there and we are here. You are allowed into our space to make our lives easier, but we will rarely stray into yours. Edward stood near the foyer near the front entrance with long halls stretching away from him in three directions, the walls perfect showcases for an art collection nine generations strong. There were masterpieces from Raphael, Titian, and Tintoretto. Wherever Edward looked were portraits of Meriwethers, beginning with flat, two-dimensional figures painted during the Renaissance to a Gainsborough from the 18th century. One in particular that caught Edward's eye was called "The Earl's Daughter" by Thomas Lawrence, the portrait artist for George III. Without looking at the title, Edward could have guessed that this was another family portrait. The young woman, wearing a flowing canary-yellow dress and holding the leash of a pointer dog, had the same heart-shaped face and the same violet eyes as Miss Meriwether. In fact, with a few minor differences (Miss Meriwether's nose was not so long and her smile not so coquettish as the young woman in the painting, who looked certain she would capture some appropriate suitor's eye soon enough), it could have been Miss Meriwether.

Edward's heart beat faster and he dried his palms on his trousers. The thought of his editor's daughter was enough to make him palpitate. There were pretty girls all around if one deigns to look, but with Miss Meriwether, it was...what? Her smile? Her friendliness? American girls were known for their friendliness—that's the first reason young American heiresses were all the rage in London (the second being they were heiresses). Edward had spent many hours daydreaming about that moment outside the Daily Observer when Miss Meriwether knelt beside the flower vendor's son. No well-born young English woman would chat in the street—it's so common, you know, chatting in the street—but she would most especially not stop to chat with a flower vendor and his son. Miss Meriwether was fascinating in comparison. That's it. Edward snapped his fingers. He was fascinated by her. Fascinated, and nothing more.

He heard a stout "Ahem!" and turned to see his grandfather with his hands clasped behind his back, hunched forward, looking over the top of his spectacles in his usual manner.

"Grandfather! You'll scare someone to their death one of these days."

"Disappearing and reappearing when one is needed is a butler's greatest talent."

"You don't need to appear like a genie out of Aladdin's bottle on my account." Edward nodded toward the portrait. "Do you know who this is? It only says 'The Earl's Daughter.'"

"That is Lady Rowena Meriwether. She was the fifth Earl's daughter."

"She looks like..."

Mr. Ellis squinted at his grandson. "Yes?"

"It's not important. Is it time?"

"It is. The family will be going into luncheon shortly."

Edward followed his grandfather through a maze of rooms and hallways. "How does anyone remember their way in this house? All the passages look the same."

Mr. Ellis pressed his spectacles against his nose. "If you pay attention you can learn the ways of the house. Whispers are telling you everything you need to know if you listen." He stopped outside the drawing room. "Mr. Edward Ellis," he announced. He nodded toward the door, indicating that Edward should go in. Edward exhaled, feeling like he had, perhaps, been sacrificed to the lions after all. Once he was safely in the room, he scanned the occupants, hoping to see Miss Meriwether. Frederick Meriwether rose from his chair.

"Young Mr. Ellis. I'm so happy you could come. Welcome."

"Thank you, Mr. Meriwether."

Frederick gestured to a fine-looking older woman in black bombazine for her deceased husband, her gray hair pulled into a simple chignon, sitting in state with her back to the hearth. "Mamma, this is Edward Ellis. He's a reporter at the Daily Observer."

Edward bowed. "How do you do, Lady Staton."

The great lady tugged at the chain around her neck, found the silver ear trumpet attached at the end, and held the device to her ear. "What did you say?"

Frederick spoke louder. "Edward Ellis, Mamma. From the Daily Observer."

"Mainly over, did you say? Mainly over where?"

"EDWARD ELLIS FROM THE DAILY OBSERVER!"

"I heard you, Frederick. There's no need to be rude in front of our guest. Isn't the Daily Observer that dreadful paper you're working for? For the life of me, I can't fathom why you insist upon it when you should be here with your family."

Frederick sighed. "That's right, Mamma. That's the newspaper I'm editing and young Mr. Ellis here works for me."

Lady Staton repositioned the ear trumpet to better effect. Her youngest son, Jerrold, and his wife, Hyacinth, stood near, watching with great interest. Both Jerrold and Hyacinth were tall, thin, and frigid-looking, as though the thickest blanket in England wouldn't warm them, and they appeared more like brother and sister than husband and wife. They stepped closer to the conversation, stopped, stepped closer again, and stopped once more when they were close enough to hear the proceedings. Jerrold gestured to the empty wing chair closest to his mother, which Hyacinth took without as much as a glance at her husband. Mrs. Meriwether reached down, and Edward thought she would come up with an ear trumpet of her own. Instead, she flourished a filigree monocle. She held the glass to her eye and examined Edward, though Edward was more amused than concerned, thinking of "Little Red Riding Hood" —all the better to hear you with, my dear. All the better to see you with. Perhaps he hadn't been sacrificed to the lions but to the wolves. If Edward knew anything from his grandparents, he knew aristocrats didn't like anyone they weren't used to, so he was hardly surprised at being studied like a wax figure at Madame Tussaud's. Besides, while they were busy studying him he could return the favor. He noticed that the Countess of Staton was not a beautiful woman. In her later 60s, she didn't have the radiance of a woman who had been beautiful in her younger days and was lovely still. She seemed as though she had withered too young, perhaps before she ever bloomed. Finally, she nodded.

"Our butler is named Ellis."

"What a coincidence," Edward said. "I have a grandfather named Ellis who is a butler here."

When Lady Staton didn't seem to hear, Frederick said

47

loudly, "I told you that young Mr. Ellis is Ellis' grandson, Mamma."

"Ellis? Our Ellis? Is the young man lost?"

"No, Mamma. He's here for luncheon."

"Is he serving? Someone find him some livery."

Frederick shrugged at Edward. "I do apologize. I told her last week you were coming."

"She must have not had her ear horn at the time," Edward said. "Besides, I quite understand her confusion. What would the grandson of the butler be doing here except to serve at table?"

Frederick turned away—in an attempt to hide his smile, Edward thought. "Indeed." Frederick stepped closer to his mother, found her trumpet on the chair, and handed it to her. The Countess nodded with great dignity and held the device to her ear. "Mamma, young Mr. Ellis is here as a guest. He'll be dining with us."

"Pining with us?"

"Dining with us!"

"I heard you, Frederick. You needn't shout. Why is the butler's grandson dining with us?"

"Because I asked him to."

"I see."

The Countess' expression darkened, and Edward guessed that she finally understood. She rose from her chair, she was taller than Edward expected, and tugged at her gloves, bringing attention to the egg-sized jewels she wore even to this small afternoon gathering. "Frederick," she called. Frederick joined his mother by the window. Edward couldn't make out the Countess' words and he wished for an ear trumpet of his own. Still, he didn't need to hear to understand her meaning. Lady Staton released Frederick and called her youngest son and his wife to her, after which the three stood close in commiseration, their eyes darting toward Edward.

"Don't pay any attention to them," Frederick said. "My brother and I are most glad to have you." As if on cue, the Earl of Staton entered the drawing room. "Richard, this is Edward Ellis, the young man I was telling you about. He's one of the finest reporters we have at the Daily Observer and a talented author in his own right. I invited him this afternoon to discuss some writing he's going to do for the paper. And I thought Ferguson and Wately might like to make his acquaintance. Are they here?"

"Ellis told me they've just arrived."

"Excellent. Edward, my brother, Lord Staton."

Edward bowed. "How do you do, Lord Staton."

Richard Staton smiled in a manner as friendly as his brother Frederick. With this closer view than he had at the funeral, Edward saw what his grandmother had been telling him for years—the new Earl was a handsome man in his refined, languid way.

"I'm happy to know you, Mr. Ellis. I've heard wonderful things about you." The Earl noticed his mother, brother, and sister-in-law watching from the corner. "I see Mamma understands that this fine young man is the butler's grandson."

Frederick nodded. "I don't know why it's such a surprise. I told her Edward was coming last week."

Lord Staton stood next to Edward. "Remember that you are my guest, and I want you to feel welcome."

"I do, Lord Staton. Thank you."

"Now." Richard nodded toward the doorway. "Here comes Hough, my dearest brother." A man about Richard's age, in his later 40s, with graying black hair and a square face that retained his urbane handsomeness, entered the room. Edward recognized him from the funeral.

Frederick gestured to Edward. "Mr. Hough, I'd like you to meet Edward Ellis. Young Mr. Ellis works at the Daily Observer. Mr. Ellis, this is Mr. John Hough, our family physician."

They were distracted by the arrival of more guests. Mr. Ellis tried to reach the door before they did to announce them, but the three men created a wide rank and they were in the room before the butler. Frederick clapped when he saw them. "Poppers, wonderful to see you. Carlton! You haven't changed in 20 years." There was another guest, a young man around Edward's age with his fair hair tucked behind his ears, his eyes darting around the room.

"I don't believe you've met Mr. Palmer, Freddie," said Lord Staton.

Mr. Palmer looked at the juniper-green curtains, the embossed wallpaper, the damask chairs, the tapestry foot-stools, stopping on the Countess of Staton who stared at him like she didn't know what he was—animal, vegetable, or mineral. The young man nearly jumped from his boots when he noticed her daughter-in-law watching him as well, her left eye a squint while her right eye pierced him through her monocle.

"Palmer here had never been to Hembry, so I thought this would be a good time to visit. What do you think so far, Palmer?" The young man shook his head, nodded, shrugged, then shook his head again, all the while staring at Mrs. Meri-wether, whose monocle pointed accusations his way. The Earl laughed to fill the space. "We've been friends for years, haven't we, Palmer?" Palmer winked in response.

The Countess of Staton condescended a nod in the men's general direction. She was granted a reprieve from small talk when Mr. Ellis appeared in the doorway.

"Mr. Ferguson and Mr. Wately."

Edward chuckled at the relieved look on his grandfather's face, as though the day hadn't been a complete loss after all. The two newcomers received the same scrutiny from the corner, though they were good-natured about it and even managed to engage the taciturn Jerrold in light banter. When Jerrold had exhausted his topics of conversation, which took all of three minutes, Ferguson and Wately gestured toward Edward.

"So tell us, Mr. Meriwether, is this the young genius you intended to introduce to us?"

"The very same," said Frederick. "Young Mr. Ellis' pieces are among the most widely read at the Daily Observer, and he's had a few stories printed in various publications. I sent them to you last week."

"Yes," said Ferguson. "We've read them. That's why we agreed to come."

Edward stopped breathing, only for a moment, but it was enough to leave him feeling faint. He leaned close to Frederick and whispered, "Mr. Ferguson and Mr. Wately of Ferguson and Wately Publishing Limited?"

"Indeed. I thought perhaps they might like a personal intro-duction to an up-and-coming literary talent such as yourself."

Edward wanted to say something that expressed the depth of his gratitude, but then his grandfather announced Miss Meriwether. Edward marveled at how Daphne's asymmetrical black silk dress flowed downward from her waist and gave her the appearance of floating. Even in black she's lovely.

Miss Meriwether joined her father by the window. "I'm not late, am I, Papa?"

"Not at all. Ellis hasn't...well, there he is."

Mr. Ellis bowed toward the Countess. "Luncheon is served, my lady."

Everything happened in such an orderly fashion, and it

occurred to Edward that life at Hembry Castle was rather like those stage performances he loved to watch at Covent Garden or the Theatre Royal, Drury Lane. Everything unfolded as though it had been rehearsed to perfection, with the actors and actresses learning their roles and their stage business, reciting their dialogue with impeccable timing, keeping the performances running smoothly, day after day, night after night, for centuries. Following her script, Lady Staton rose, her ear trumpet left to dangle behind her. She whispered something to Richard, who shook his head.

"This isn't a grand dinner party, Mamma. It's simply a few friends who have come to luncheon. We don't need to sashay into the dining room two-by-two like animals herded onto Noah's Ark."

The Countess nodded her acquiescence. "You're the Earl now, Richard. However, your father…"

"My father isn't here. Besides, if I remember correctly, and I think I do, he was never one to harp on formality when it wasn't necessary. At this moment, it isn't necessary." Richard the Earl smiled at his guests. "My dearest Daphne," Richard held his arm out to his niece, "allow me to escort you."

Edward heard Lady Staton say, behind her fluttering fan, "I do wonder about your brother sometimes, Jerrold."

To which Jerrold, his face a thin-lipped mask like his mother's, replied, "We did always wonder about Richard."

The dining room was grand in its simplicity, painted daffodil yellow per the 7th Earl's decree to add some sunshine inside. Three chandeliers hung from the white ceiling with moldings of flowers and birds. The marble Greek-style fireplace was set off by white-framed family portraits and a painting of a beautiful blue-eyed cat. Mr. Ellis directed his grandson to the left of Mr. Frederick, while to Mr. Frederick's right sat Miss Meriwether. Lady Staton conducted herself with all graciousness, though Edward noticed the eye darts intended for her eldest son, of which Lord Staton appeared not at all aware, or, more likely, not at all concerned. Mr. Hough, the doctor, and his lordship's other friends were seated to Edward's left since there were not enough ladies to complement the number of gentlemen. Young Mr. Palmer sent forlorn winks Lord Staton's way, to which the Earl nodded in commiseration while struggling through a one-sided conversation with his sister-in-law. Mrs. Meriwether began her midday meal by running her white glove over the back of her chair, wiping the flatware on the napkin, and sniffing the wine before she tasted it (only partaking in these activities when the Countess' head was turned, of course). Mrs. Meriwether removed her gloves with the utmost reluctance, as though, Edward thought, she was afraid of touching anything because nothing at Hembry Castle met her meticulous standards. Mr. Ellis watched Mrs. Meriwether, as did Lord Staton, though Lord Staton seemed amused where Mr. Ellis was not.

Ferguson and Wately (pronounced Fergusonandwately) seemed quite at home at the table of Lord Staton. They caught Mr. Ellis' attention quickly and often for refills of the Chateau Lafite Rothschild they pronounced "Superb!" If Edward hadn't known his grandfather was standing in the shadows he would hardly have known he was there. The servants were, under Mr. Ellis' direction, wisps of movement, neither seen nor heard. They stayed back if they were not needed, and when they were required they stepped out, accomplished the deed, and disappeared again. Jerrold Meriwether appeared to be eating alone. He spoke to no one and kept his eyes on his plate, holding up his wine glass when needed. Occasionally, he'd sneak a glance at his wife, who was oblivious to him. Mrs. Meriwether tilted her long neck toward her mother-in-law and the ladies leaned close in conversation. They looked, Edward thought, like a two-headed gorgon. Meanwhile, the discussion for the others turned to the state of the publishing business, which Fergusonandwately lamented as precarious indeed. Lady Staton held up her ear trumpet to listen.

"Are you discussing books again?" She turned to her daughter-in-law. "Your brothers-in-law have always spent too much time in books."

"Books are preferable company to most people I know," Frederick said.

Lady Staton turned away as though she hadn't heard, which she might not have since her ear trumpet was now dangling behind her. Frederick whispered something to his daughter, who laughed. Edward struggled to stay focused. He heard a cough and saw the shadow of his grandfather.

"More wine?" asked Mr. Ellis.

"Thank you, Grandfather."

The room fell silent.

The Earl of Staton held up his glass. "Ellis, have I told you how impressed I am with your young man? I believe Fergusonandwately here are considering publishing a collection of his stories—at least, that's what I've gathered from our conversation. Isn't that right, gentlemen?"

Ferguson, looking somehow ruddier and less steady than he had when he arrived, nodded.

"Quite correct, Lord Staton. We've been speaking to young Mr. Ellis here, and we're impressed. Am I right in saying so, Mr. Wately?"

Mr. Wately nodded. "Very true, Mr. Ferguson. Very true. We had already read the young man's pieces in The Daily News and The Fortnightly Review. Tonight was simply to see if the young man himself showed as much promise as his stories, and we believe he does. Don't we, Mr. Ferguson?"

"We do," said Mr. Ferguson.

"As you can see, Ellis," Frederick said, "I was quite right to invite your grandson this afternoon. He has made a fine impression."

Mr. Ellis bowed and backed into the shadows.

"Congratulations, Mr. Ellis," said Miss Meriwether. "I think you're going to be a famous author. Papa enjoys helping rising literary talent. He has an eye for spotting the best." Miss Meriwether took a sip from her glass, and Edward noticed how the red wine stained her lips.

"I'm fortunate to have your father's confidence so soon after our acquaintance."

"Papa told me you remind him of himself when he was your age. Isn't that right, Papa? Driven to be the best, determined to succeed. Papa wanted to be an author himself."

"It's true enough," said Frederick. "I'm afraid I let the dream slide away after I began working as a journalist. Now I find enjoyment in helping new authors succeed."

"I predict only good things for you in the future, Mr. Ellis," Miss Meriwether said.

Edward wanted to pause the moment there. He was speaking to Miss Meriwether, and despite the stuttering, he thought he was succeeding well enough. But then their time together was done. Though it was luncheon and not dinner, Lady Staton still excused herself and the other ladies. She was certain the men had important business to discuss, she said. Edward couldn't decide if she sounded sarcastic or not. With the women gone, Lord Staton waved his hand in the air.

"Well, Ellis, since the ladies have left we may as well have the brandy and cigars." He looked at his guests. "Gentlemen, would anyone mind terribly if we indulged in some nighttime luxuries this afternoon?" The men laughed since none of them minded in the least.

With Miss Meriwether gone, Edward turned his attention

to Lord Staton's friends. They were an eclectic group of men and hardly the sort you'd expect the Earl of Staton to roam about with. Mr. Hough was deep in conversation with the man called Poppers, who had black hair, a white complexion, a red carnation in his buttonhole, and a blue neckerchief rolled under his collar. His lordship whispered something to the one called Carlton, whose long mouth pulled wide whenever he smiled. Poor Mr. Palmers appeared to be completely over-whelmed. All he could do was nod at everything anyone said.

The footmen placed glasses next to each of the men, and Mr. Ellis reappeared with the brandy and the cigar box. After all the men had been served (both Edward and young Mr. Palmers passed on the smokes), the one called Carlton pointed his cigar in Edward's direction.

"So tell me more about yourself, Mr. Ellis. Lord Staton tells me you're a reporter at the Daily Observer. What else should I know about you? I mean, if Fergusonandwately here are considering publishing your stories, you must be someone I should know."

"Young Mr. Ellis is quite the talented writer," said Frederick.

"Are you?" Carlton squinted as he leaned across the table. "And what is it you write about with such talent?"

Edward felt heated, either from the brandy or the weight of everyone's attention. "For the newspaper, I write about poli-tics. For myself, I write about life."

"Life! A worthy topic indeed. And what sort of life do you write about?"

"Whatever I notice around me. About people and the way they behave..."

"They behave in a most ill-mannered way if you ask me," said Jerrold. He drained his brandy and Poppers slid the bottle in his direction. "They make out like you're the only one in the world, you're the only one they need, and then they take advantage when you're in a weakened state. Whoop! And they finish you off. Then they want you to clean up the mess like the whole disaster's all your damn fault and…"

The Earl shook his head. "My brother is getting broody. You'd think I'd never done a thing to help him." If bullets could shoot from eyeballs, Jerrold Meriwether would have sent a bullet or ten in his eldest brother's direction. As it was, Lord Staton remained unscathed. He nodded at Edward. "Please excuse my brother's interruption. You write about people and…?"

Frederick placed his hand on Edward's shoulder. "I told you, Richard. This young man is the next Mr. Dickens."

"The next Mr. Dickens!" Carlton squinted again, this time with a sly smile. "That's quite the compliment. And I noticed you're clean-shaven." He gestured toward his friends, including the Earl. "We're all clean-shaven, aren't we, gentlemen?"

Jerrold wagged his finger vehemently in case anyone missed the straggly excuse for facial hair protruding like undergrown grass above his lip. Fergusonandwately featured well-grayed beards, one full and luxurious, the other adorned by muttonchops. Frederick laughed as he patted his own newly growing gray-flecked beard. The rest of the men were indeed clean-shaven, which Edward had to admit.

Carlton scratched his naked chin as he considered. "Yes, you are a very handsome, very clean-shaven young man who is being touted by the Earl's brother as the next Mr. Dickens. I must know more of you."

"Carlton, please." Mr. Hough shook his head. "Don't bother the young man."

"I'm not bothering him. I'm simply curious. Mr. Ellis, have you ever gone to see the new prints at the printers' shops in London?"

Edward looked at Frederick, then the Earl, hoping they would let him in on the joke Carlton must be playing. The Earl shook his head with an expression that said Don't pay him any mind.

The Earl turned his back on Carlton and faced the publishers. "And what do you think of our Prime Minister, Mr. Ferguson? You had a rather low opinion of him the last we spoke of it."

"My low opinion has sunk even lower." Ferguson spoke with the harshest tone Edward had yet to hear from him. "Her Majesty doesn't care for him, and neither do I. He wants Home Rule for Ireland, of all things. If that villain Gladstone wants Home Rule for Ireland, who knows what part of the Empire he would grant Home Rule to next? India? Preposterous!"

Wately nodded, his double chin wagging comfortably beneath his muttonchops. "I couldn't agree more, Mr. Ferguson. A liberal Prime Minster? In 1870? Who could have imagined such a thing!" He held out his hand as though pronouncing the death verdict on Gladstone. "Where is Mr. Disraeli when you need him?"

"Mr. Disraeli was defeated in the General Election," said Lord Staton. "It's Mr. Gladstone's turn. What do you think, Freddie? I should warn you gentlemen that my brother Frederick might very well be a liberal at heart."

Frederick puffed on his cigar as he considered. "I prefer to make up my own mind about such things. I don't care for propaganda from either side."

Lord Staton shook his head. "If he likes to make up his own mind then he's most certainly a liberal. Don't you agree, Palmer?" Young Mr. Palmer shrugged, the most he had contributed to any conversation that afternoon.

Wately turned to Edward. "So, young Mr. Ellis, grandson of the Ellis standing behind me, who will gladly refill my empty glass with more of that excellent brandy, won't you? Thank you. Good man." Wately drained his glass in one swallow. "Now, Edward Ellis, what do you think of Mr. Gladstone's liberal government?"

"I'm happy to have a liberal government in place, Mr. Wately. I hope it means good tidings are in store for the working-class people who have been neglected by previous governments."

"Indeed? And what do you think of the Irish Question? The Eastern Question? The Woman Question?"

"I think that for a country that insists it has all the answers there are certainly a lot of questions."

Everyone laughed, even Jerrold, though the exertion seemed to tire him. The Earl's friends held their glasses high, toasting Edward Ellis, the Next Great Thing in Literature. The Earl of Staton clasped Edward's shoulder, Frederick beamed as though he had discovered a great prize, young Mr. Palmer winked, Mr. Ellis smiled in the shadows, and Fergusonandwately nodded in unison. But all Edward could think about was seeing the American girl again.

THE 9TH EARL OF STATON

*L*ater that night, Richard, Earl of Staton, sat in his dark-paneled smoking room puffing on his fourth or fifth cigar of the day—he lost track of how many. Alone, puffing out the surly smoke, refilling his glass from the near-empty brandy bottle, he found his thoughts dissipating into smoke rings. Your Lordship. Lord Staton. Richard, Earl of Staton. No longer Richard Meriwether, no longer simply Lord Staton's eldest boy, the one who would inherit the title someday. He was the Earl. There was no getting away from it now.

He stamped the stub of his cigar into the ashtray and reached into the black lacquer box for a new one. It was dark, nearly midnight, with few stars to light the view outside. He was enjoying his solitude, basking in the absence of anyone but the former Earls who watched unimpressed from their hanging portraits while beloved hunting dogs, sitting like the good boys they were, panted in their portraits across the room. Richard liked the smoking room best of all because it was the one place in the house where his mother would never follow him. It was unnatural, to live with your mother when you were eight-and-forty and a man in your own right, but this was the life he had been born to, and what could be done? He wasn't married so he couldn't send his mother to the Dower House. Could he? He was the Earl, after all. His word was law in the land of Hembry, and if he wanted to send his mother to a quaint, comfortable cottage in the village he didn't see why he shouldn't. He sighed because he knew he wouldn't go through with it (it would be too much trouble) so he resigned himself to hiding in the smoking room whenever he could. For forever, he thought. I'm going to be tucked away in here forever. He cut the tip of the new cigar, lit it, then puffed until he coughed a cloud of smoke.

A knock caused him some worry—it couldn't possibly be his mother, not here, not at this hour—until John Hough appeared. The doctor was wearing his reading spectacles and held a book in his hand.

"Do you mind if I join you?"

Richard waved in welcome. John Hough shut the door, then sat on the brown leather sofa next to the Earl. The two sat in comfortable silence, John engrossed in his book, Richard staring as though he were having a conversation with the 4th Earl on the wall. Finally, John Hough put his book down.

"What's troubling you?" Richard shook his head like he hadn't heard. "Richard?"

"Must you ask?"

Richard leaned back into the sofa, crossed one leg over the other, and puffed on the cigar. Suddenly, perhaps because he had one smoke too many, he couldn't take another taste, which was sour now. He stamped the burning end into the ashtray, and for the first time that night he didn't reach for another. He offered the doctor the black lacquer box, but the doctor shook his head. Hough studied Richard through his reading spectacles.

"You're right. I don't need to ask. I thought…well, I thought now that it's happened you'd feel better about things." Hough smiled in a manner meant to be comforting. "Richard, Earl of Staton. It sounds good if you ask me."

Richard walked to the window. He looked to the left to the rolling hills, to the right to the river that flowed through the grounds, hoping to see some glimmer of moonlight on the water, but there was nothing.

"You may as well accept it. It's not like you didn't know it was going to happen."

"It's the first thing I ever consciously knew in this life." Richard kept looking to the left, still consumed by the invisible hills. "I knew I was going to be the Earl of Staton before I knew my name."

"Now it's come to pass. Far sooner than any of us hoped, of course. Your father should have lived many more years. He never as much as sneezed before this one illness. But your father is gone and you are Earl, and I say make the best of it."

Richard nodded. That had always been his father's advice, after all. You take whatever life gives you and make the best of it you can. "How many men have received titles they didn't want, do you think? How many reluctant earls or dukes or even princes have there been?"

"Honestly." John Hough walked to the window and squinted into the darkness. "Who wouldn't want to be an earl or a duke or a prince?"

Richard felt wobbly suddenly and he grasped the windowsill. An excess of cigars and brandy, he thought.

"Are you certain you're all right? I am a doctor, you know."

"Yes, Doctor. I'm perfectly aware of the talents of our family physician."

Richard felt his legs steady beneath him and he shook only a bit as he returned to his seat in front of the unlit hearth.

Looking at the portraits on the walls, he realized that it was time to have his father's portrait brought there. The smoking room had been his father's favorite room too, most likely for the same reason—to escape the Countess—and Richard knew his father would like to have his portrait among the other Earls and their dogs.

"Have you made your decision about Lady Lily Carter-Marsh?"

Richard looked at Hough for the first time that night. "I've made my decision."

"And?"

"I won't be marrying Lady Lily."

"Your mother will be crushed."

"She wants me married by the end of the Season."

"Then you better get going, Lord Staton, because there isn't much time. What about Ecchols' little sister? She isn't so little anymore. She's grown up to be rather pretty in a billowy sort of way. Or Lassen's sister Lady Bertina. Off the top of my head I could name a dozen suitable young ladies who would love nothing more than capturing the hand, if not the heart, of the Earl of Staton."

"Please." Richard covered his ears with his hands. "I can hardly stand speaking about this with Mamma." He yawned as he looked at the clock on the mantelpiece and saw it was nearly two in the morning. "Have you discovered where the Prince is these days?"

"At Sandringham House recovering from his testimony on the Mordaunt divorce suit."

Richard smiled for the first time since seeking refuge in the smoking room. "No one was too surprised to find that the Prince of Wales had visited Mrs. Mordaunt while her husband was busy with the House of Commons. Were they?"

"Hardly." Hough looked at the Earls' portraits as though

judging whether or not they would gossip amongst themselves when the room was empty. "So will you tell your mother you're going to see the Prince?"

"Norfolk is as good a place as any, and the Prince entertains so lavishly no one will notice much about anyone else. While mother thinks I'm in Norfolk I'll be in London."

"Your brother needs you to go to London again?"

Richard shrugged. "I don't think my brother cares. I'm going because I want to see for myself. If he won't handle the matter then I will. Besides, I've been around Hembry long enough. As much as I love this house, I can only be here for so long before it starts to swallow me whole. Right now I feel like if I stay another day I'll…"

"You'll what?"

"I'll go mad. That's all. I'll go mad."

"Things will get better. You'll see."

The Earl turned off the gas lamps, leaving the two men illuminated by candlelight. Hough snubbed out the flames and they stood in darkness. Richard paused with his hand on the doorknob. Was there something he'd forgotten? Was there something he needed to tell John? If there was, he couldn't remember. He was so tired, and it was late. Richard opened the door and allowed the doctor to pass, sighing as he left the smoking room.

THE AMERICAN GIRL

*D*aphne Meriwether's arrival at Hembry Castle had been a shock to her system, to say the least. It was wet the day she arrived, the dark skies sprinkling moisture all around. As the stately gray carriage and four drove down the tree-lined path she thought she had fallen into someone else's fairy tale. She had never seen a house so grand. Her father had been telling her about Hembry Castle her whole life, but nothing had prepared her for seeing it for the first time. The carriage stopped in front of the Palladian-style façade with the mismatched gables on the roof, and a handsome young footman in gray livery helped her down the carriage steps while a second footman held an umbrella over her head and followed her to the front door where a stoop-shouldered, gray-haired man with wire-rimmed spectacles bowed.

Eclectic. That's what Daphne thought during her first glance around Hembry Castle. Above her was a hammer beam ceiling, and she remembered her father telling her that the third Earl had it installed to resemble the one at Hampton Court Palace. The walls were dark-paneled wood while marble

Roman arches held the walls upright. The floors were covered in Turkish rugs, and the large windows let in a panoramic view of the peaks and valleys of the countryside. To her right, to her left, straight ahead, everywhere Daphne looked was some new treasure to behold.

"Those are the galleries," her father said. Daphne marveled at the paintings, the portraits, the bronzes, and the Greek and Roman statues. Frederick waited, giving her a moment to take it all in. "What do you think?"

"It's incredible, Papa. It's like a museum."

"It is very much like a museum." Frederick handed his hat and coat to the silent footman. "And you are?"

"Colin, sir."

"Thank you, Colin." Frederick nodded at the butler. "There are many new faces here, Ellis."

"Yes, Mr. Frederick. It's been too long since you've been home."

"That it has. How is my father?"

"Mr. Hough has just been to see him. His lordship isn't any better, I'm afraid."

"Take us to him."

Mr. Ellis led the way, down that hallway, through this passageway, into the other room, up those stairs, across one more hall. Daphne wondered how anyone remembered their way around. She thought of asking her father for a map of the house, but then they were with her grandfather and the thought of anything else escaped her. Her grandfather died the next morning surrounded by a loving family and well wishes from villagers, farmers, and many others besides. At least we had a chance to say goodbye, Daphne thought.

After the funeral, after the well-wishers had gone and the curiosity seekers drifted away, Daphne had time to acquaint herself with the old house, to wander its vast hallways, admire the paintings, and inspect the bronzes. While there was much to love about Hembry, and about England, she thought it rained too much. Her father had warned her about the rain, but he tried to frame it in a positive way. After all, he said, without the rain there wouldn't be the bountiful gardens, so it couldn't be all bad. Daphne, watching the dripping wet through the vast windows, wasn't convinced. The rain prompted her to stay inside, so she had hours to wander the halls. She was never sure which direction she was headed, but even when she was lost she discovered yet another treasure, like the music room with the gold harp and the Erard piano which she could play a little, or the nursery, now empty, where generations had been raised at the hands of nannies. How strange, Daphne thought as she handled the toy soldiers, the jigsaw puzzles, and the rosewood rocking horse, thinking how her father had been raised by a nanny and not his mother.

It took two weeks for Daphne to learn the way to the sitting room and the library, where she spent most of her days, reading or needlepointing or helping her father with editing and other newspaper duties. At home in Connecticut, she would have been bored with so little to do, but this quiet life-style was only temporary, she knew. She would return home soon. She wanted to get back to her own house, her own people, her own life, her own ways without feeling like an oddity to be examined through a monocle.

She was distracted from her thoughts by the giggling of two young girls in long calico dresses, white aprons, and white caps, neither of whom could have been more than 16 years old. When they saw Daphne watching them they vanished. Daphne sighed. She didn't think she would ever get used to the move-ment everywhere around her. Yes, the servants were silent, most of the time, but something about the proximity of so many strangers unnerved her.

It was her grandfather's greatest wish that she should visit Hembry Castle. He ended every letter to her with, "Won't you come see my castle, my most darling granddaughter?" And Daphne, being young and thinking she had all the time in the world, made excuses. Her father never seemed too keen on the idea of returning to his homeland, and Daphne never pressed him. It was her grandfather's illness that prompted them to make the journey across the ocean. The first thing the 8th Earl said when he saw her was, "Finally, you have come to see my castle." She knew he would have taken great joy in showing her around his ancestral home, and he would have told her how to get from the sitting room to the drawing room without getting lost.

Daphne was startled when Mr. Ellis peeked around the open door.

"Miss Daphne, his lordship wishes to speak to you."

"Of course, Mr. Ellis. Where is he?"

"I'm here." Richard stepped into the room. "Would you like some tea, Daphne?"

"I'm always ready for tea."

The Earl winked at his butler. "See, Ellis. I told you she was English at heart."

Richard sat on the blue settee and leaned back against the cushion. He was always handsome, Richard, leaner than her father, his chestnut hair showing only a shimmer of silver at the temples. His cat-like blue eyes, the same shade of aquamarine as her father's, left him looking more youthful than his 48 years. There was always a quickness to Richard, though since Daphne had arrived at Hembry his quickness had slowed. Of course he's feeling overwhelmed, Daphne thought. His beloved father has died and now he's inherited a vast estate with great responsibility. I'd be overwhelmed too if it were me.

"How are you, Uncle Richard?"

"Quite well, my dear."

Daphne sat next to her uncle. "I know you're expected to maintain a certain appearance, but you don't have to pretend for my sake. I've seen the sadness in your eyes since Grandpa died, and I don't think it's all from mourning. Is there anything I can do?"

Richard's long face brightened with a boyish smile. "You're a sharp girl, Daphne. Sharp young woman, I should say. I knew you had grown older, of course, but it didn't sink in until you arrived. Here was this lovely young woman standing before me, and how surprised was I to realize she was my own most darling niece." Richard looked toward the window to see the sunlight breaking into golden spirals. "Do you remember the first time I visited you in Connecticut?"

"How can I forget? I think I was seven at the time. We were sound asleep, and it must have been four in the morning when there was this banging on the door. I remember Mama and Papa coming out of their room, Mama hiding behind Papa, and Papa was nervous about answering the door because he couldn't think who it might be at that time. I've never been so surprised and so happy as I was when I saw you there holding your arms toward me. You never told us you were coming."

"I wanted to surprise you. The journey from New York took longer than we thought so we arrived later than we hoped. I couldn't wait to see you so I went to your house straight away. I had to bang on the door because no one heard me when I knocked."

"I remember having so much fun visiting New York City with you and showing you my little girl toys and my childish paintings. What a fuss you made over them, and what silly games we played. I always wanted you to come swimming in the lake with me but you insisted you couldn't swim."

"Still can't, I'm afraid." He pointed to the half-moon scar by his left temple.

"That happened when you were a boy. Really, Uncle Richard, you can't let a childhood accident keep you from swimming for the rest of your life."

"I did nearly drown."

"It was a long time ago."

Richard looked aghast. "Not that long ago, I hope."

"Of course not. You haven't aged a day. Those are my favorite memories, you know. Whenever you came to visit is one of my favorite memories."

"They're my favorite memories too. I never wanted to leave."

The sitting room was a Georgian vision in blue and white toile wallpaper with matching blue and white curtains swinging in the breeze from the open windows. Mahogany Queen Anne chairs with their knobby feet and a cream-colored chaise lounge were set just so over the Turkish rug. Blue and white Wedgwood vases filled with white peonies sat on the mahogany side tables, and decorating the walls were portraits of the same black spaniel in various poses. When the sun was out, as it was at that moment, it was a pleasant place for Daphne to read and write letters to her family and friends at home. Daphne tried to see the room through her uncle's eyes, and she wondered if the room was as pleasant to him after 48 years.

"Papa was always trying to talk you into staying in Connecticut with us."

"Which is what I wanted."

"It's what I wanted too." Daphne snapped her fingers when she remembered. "When you came to visit us that first time you came with a friend. When I was introduced to Mr. Hough

I thought he seemed familiar. Was it Mr. Hough who came with you to visit us?"

"One and the same."

Richard looked as though he wanted to say more, but Mr. Ellis appeared with the tea, poured the drinks, and disappeared again.

"How do you like Hembry Castle, Daphne?"

"I like it very much, though I still get lost."

"You can always ring for help when you can't find your way." He gestured to the tasseled rope hanging in the corner. "Every room in the house has one. Pull the rope and Ellis or another one of the staff will come."

"Everyone who works here seems so nice. It's just..."

"Is everyone treating you well?"

"Oh, yes. Many times they bring me what I need before I know I need it. It's strange to me to have so many people everywhere all the time. Sometimes I feel like I'm never alone, like servants are hiding behind the curtains or under the beds, aware of everything I do and say. Sometimes I feel a little paranoid, like I'm being spied on. That's silly, isn't it?"

Richard pulled the curtains aside, revealing only a blue and white toile wall. "There's no one hiding in the sitting room, at least. However, it is fair to say that when there are servants around the walls do have ears. It's also fair to say that the staff knows more about us than we know about them. The servants may be standing silently by, but you can guess they're listening to every word we say, and they report everything downstairs. If you ever feel as though you don't have any privacy, tell Ellis and he'll shoo them away. Remember, their job is to make you comfortable, not uncomfortable. Or you could always hide in the smoking room with me."

Daphne laughed. "I wondered where you disappeared to

every night. Papa never liked the lifestyle here, did he, Uncle Richard?"

"You're right. He didn't."

"It's why he needed to get away, and how he ended up in America. I always wondered if he ever regretted leaving the splendor of Hembry Castle for an ordinary life in Connecticut. He never complained about it."

"And I never will."

Frederick stepped into the room and kissed his daughter's cheek. "I didn't want any part of this life. Besides, it had been made quite clear to me when I was still very young that no well-born young woman would want to marry me since I was merely a younger son and would inherit nothing. I was expected to go into the military or become a clergyman. But I didn't want to be an officer or a clergyman. I loved reading and writing." Frederick shook his head at the memory. "Your grandmother hated all my books."

"I guessed that at luncheon," Daphne said.

"She was convinced that all that reading put odd notions into my head, and one time she threatened to light a torch first to my library, then to Father's. Well," Frederick snickered, "she threatened to have a servant light a torch to the library. The funny thing is, she was right. It was because of all my reading I knew there were other worlds, other ways of being. I learned that the way we lived here at Hembry wasn't my only option. I didn't want decisions made for me. I wanted to decide for myself what my life should be."

"And you did that," Richard said. "You studied literature and poetry at Oxford and not theology as Mamma wanted."

"I was fortunate. I had Father's support."

"And then you made the Great Escape across the sea."

Frederick took Daphne's hand. "Yes, I did, and it was the best decision I ever made. I married the most intelligent, most compassionate, most beautiful woman, and we had an intelligent, compassionate, beautiful daughter, and we were so very happy together."

"Do you ever regret it, Papa? Leaving all this behind?" Daphne gestured at the Georgian antiques. "I was telling Uncle Richard it feels a little close sometimes with the servants everywhere, but it's still lovely."

"Yes, it is lovely. It just wasn't for me."

"It's strange." Richard sounded far away. "I always felt as you did, Freddie, but I didn't dare to leave."

"You leave quite frequently, from what I understand," Frederick said.

"Ah, but I always come back. Father was born to his role, and he understood innately what he needed to do and how to do it."

"You're born to it too," Daphne said.

"I wonder." Richard poured Frederick a cup of tea. "Father tried to teach me everything, the business, the farming, how to handle the tenants, my other responsibilities, and I listened, I did, but somehow nothing ever sank in. Now I don't know where to start. It's just as Mamma and Pappa always said, Freddie. It was an accident of birth that made me Earl and not you. They believed you would have been so much better at it than me. I agree. You should have been the firstborn."

"Nonsense. I was the one who ran when he had the chance. I'm the wayward, remember? What good would I have been?"

"But I know you, little brother. You have a cleverness about you that allows you to see what needs doing, figure out how to accomplish it, and get it done with great ability. You're far more like Father than I'll ever be. Your astuteness. Your empathy. Father was just the same. It's why he was so beloved. You're the one with the courage, Freddie. I can't even help myself. How can I help anyone else? Do you know how many people are depending on me?"

"You've had a great responsibility set before you, Richard, but I know you'll rise to the challenge."

"I could always count on you, Freddie. You've always believed in me."

"Pappa believed in you too."

"Yes, he did. He wanted me to make the best of the situation. He knew the role wouldn't come naturally to me, but he believed I could make it work."

"You're one of the most capable people I know," Frederick said. "You can make this work."

The cold wind that was Lady Staton blew into the room, her ear trumpet swinging behind her. "I hope you've been talking sense into your brother, Frederick."

"And what sense might that be, Mamma?" Lady Staton shook her head and held the trumpet to her ear. "What sense, Mamma?"

"Need I say it again? He needs a wife. Now. Yesterday. Twenty years ago. Tell your brother he must marry. Tell him he must sire a string of sons."

"Should I tell him how as well? I would have thought you'd have had the talk with him by now, Mamma. Or at least you'd have ordered Ellis to have the talk with him."

Lady Staton dropped her earhorn as though it had grown hot. "Don't be impertinent, Frederick. Your brother is Earl now, yet he has no wife, no children. What has he done with the last twenty years? Your father is dead and Hembry needs an heir. It's time for him to stop gallivanting about and grow up." She turned her gaze onto her eldest son, who gripped the windowsill as though he would rip it away, then pressed her ear trumpet back into place.

"You know I travel across the country to attend the Prince

of Wales' social gatherings," Richard said. "You've never had a problem with that."

"I was hoping you'd find a wife among his acquaintances. Besides, when the Prince of Wales becomes King he'll need to grow up as well."

Richard looked at his brother, then his mother. "I was just reminding Freddie of what you've always said, Mamma, that this is all an accident of birth. Freddie is the one most suited to the running of this estate."

"It doesn't matter who is most suited. You are the eldest, Richard, therefore the task is yours. Now is not the time for you to complain of it."

Lady Staton's arm must have grown tired because her ear trumpet had fallen to chin level. Frederick shouted to be heard. "What if Richard simply doesn't want to be married? He's too old to be lectured about his marital state. Isn't that his right to make that decision for himself?"

"It is absolutely not his right. I told your father time and time again that we needed to get Richard married. Your father made excuses, saying that Richard would figure things out when the time was right. With all the young ladies coming out every year you'd think he'd find one to his liking." She shook her ear trumpet at her eldest son. "You only need to find one, Richard. One girl to your liking. I was a grandmother at your age. You cannot escape your responsibilities."

"I'm perfectly aware of the fact that I won't be released from my responsibilities until I'm in the grave." Richard pulled his watch from his waistcoat pocket. "I have to go."

"Where are you going?" Lady Staton's ear trumpet was down to her throat.

"Sandringham House."

"Surely that isn't necessary," Frederick said. "There must be matters here that need your attention."

"You can tend to them, Freddie. I have all the faith in the world that you can handle whatever needs doing. I'm leaving for Norfolk in an hour."

"When will you be back?" Lady Staton asked.

"Friday in time for dinner."

The Countess waited until the door closed behind her eldest son. "You must talk to your brother about seeing to his duties, Frederick."

"I'm not sure I'm the best one for that, Mamma. I think Jerrold would be better suited."

"True enough. Though I know you and Richard have always been close, and it might be better coming from you. You know him better than the rest of us."

"And yet I don't know him at all. He's always been an enigma, even to me."

Daphne saw the stately gray carriage pull in front of the house, and the two footmen appeared with several bags of luggage. Her father noticed it as well, and he watched the preparations with a long expression. The Countess pointed her ear trumpet at her middle son.

"Richard needs your help, Frederick. The family needs your help. With Richard unwilling to assume his responsibilities, we need you to keep Hembry strong. We shall all be left with nothing if Hembry falls apart."

"Mamma, I've heard some things about Richard, worrying things. Please tell me they're not true."

"You must tell me what you've heard first."

"That he goes round with the Prince of Wales spending money like he hasn't a care in the world. And I've heard..." Frederick closed his eyes. "I've heard that he has a...friend in London. One he gives money to. And there may be a child?"

"Frederick!" Lady Staton squinted at Daphne. "Not in front of the girl."

"I'm not a girl, Grandma. I'm 20 years old, and Papa and I have talked a lot about Richard since we've been here. This isn't news to me."

"It should be news to you, hearing such things about your uncle. But I can only tell you what I know. Yes, there has been gossip about Richard's involvement in what you just named, but that's all it is—vile gossip. I have never seen anything in the way of proof. Whatever he does or does not get up to, he needs to understand that he has a duty to maintain the family line."

"If there is a child..." Daphne said.

"From marriage, Daphne. Richard needs a son from marriage."

"Just because someone gets married doesn't guarantee sons, Grandma. Not everyone has three boys like you did."

Lady Staton pressed her trumpet more firmly against her ear. "What about you, young lady?"

"What about me, Grandma?"

"Come here, child." Daphne allowed her grandmother to examine her as though they had never set eyes on each other. "Yes, I believe we can make something of you yet. I know several eligible young men from fine families who would be delighted to be introduced to the niece of the Earl of Staton. And the fact that your father has made a fortune of his own investing in American what-have-yous..."

"Bridges, Mamma."

"Midgets, that's what I said. The fact that your father has made a fortune investing in American midgets adds quite a lot to your value."

"My daughter doesn't need any help with her value."

The Countess grasped Daphne's arms and spun her around. "Yes, she'll do well enough, though she laughs too much. Why do Americans laugh so much?"

"Because we try to see the positive side of things as much as possible. A sense of humor helps make the days pass more pleasantly."

"You have the oddest notions. What do you mean by the positive side of things? Things are what they are, and it doesn't help to sugarcoat them. Still, despite your uncalled-for mirth, I know the first-born sons of three baronets, two earls, and one future duke who haven't found wives yet this Season. You haven't been presented yet, and that could pose a problem."

"Grandma, I don't think..."

"Most likely it's too late to have you presented this Season. We are still in mourning, after all. It would seem disrespectful to your grandfather, though he hated mourning, so perhaps we could say it was his wish that we only observe the wearing of black for six weeks."

"Grandma..."

"I believe I could make this work. Even if it is too late for you to be presented this Season, we must have the niece of the Earl of Staton presented at Court. If we have to wait until next year, then wait we must. After the dates of the Court Drawing Rooms are announced I'll write to the Lord Chamberlain to suggest your name for presentation. Then you could do the London Season and I'll be certain to extend invitations to the eligible young men you should meet. Daphne..." the Countess clasped her hands together "...what if you were to marry a duke!"

Frederick walked across the room, putting some space between himself and his mother. "Mamma, I know you mean well, I do, but Daphne wasn't raised to this way of life. I don't believe she would want to marry a man simply because of his position."

"Because you raised her as an American girl."

"I raised her as an American because she is an American. I married Daphne's mother for love, and Daphne will marry for love as well. Besides, I doubt the eldest son of any peer would be interested in marrying an American girl, as you call her, when the idea is to propagate future generations of noble English families."

"Frederick, one would think you were living under some sort of rock. What about all those American heiresses taking London by storm? There haven't been any matches yet, that I'm aware of, but there are several possibilities. Apparently our young men like the American girls' toothiness."

"You mean their smiles?" Daphne asked.

"And their Worth dresses from France are always noted by the most fashionable. Do you have any Worth dresses from France, my dear?"

"I have two. Papa bought them for me last year. I haven't worn them since we're still mourning Grandpa."

The Countess tugged on her black sleeve. "Very true. But we'll need to get those dresses aired out so they're ready after your presentation to the Queen."

"To the Queen?"

"Does she not even know about being presented to the Queen? What do you do with your daughters over there?"

"We tie them up in sacks and let them out when they're one-and-twenty."

Through the window, Frederick saw Richard and John Hough climbing into the carriage that would take them to Norfolk. The driver pulled the horses' reins, and the vehicle lurched toward the tree-lined path. Frederick turned to his mother. "This isn't why I brought Daphne to England, Mamma. She's been raised to make her own decisions, and it sounds as if you haven't the slightest care about her feelings in all this. You're already planning to auction her off to the highest bidder."

Daphne looked at her grandmother. "That's not what you mean, is it, Grandma?"

The Countess dropped her earhorn and patted the settee. Daphne sat next to her grandmother. "Don't you want to marry a marquess or a duke? You'd be the darling of Society. The most superior houses in England would be open to you. You'd be invited to the finest balls attended by the best people. Don't you want that?"

"I'd only be interested in marrying an earl, or a duke, or any man if I loved him. I don't need a title, Grandma. Uncle Richard has a title and that's enough for me. Hembry Castle is the only English house I need. As long as I have my family and friends, I'm happy."

"I don't know why I bother." The Countess glided across the room, leaving a whoosh of cold wind behind her.

THE WAYS OF HEMBRY CASTLE

*D*aphne sat on the edge of her father's bed while Henry Horrocks, the peacock of a first footman, packed some of her father's clothing into two leather satchels. She scanned the emerald-green room, the dark-paneled walls, the heavy curtains, the Turkish rugs, and the embroidered cushions on the Hepplewhite chairs. "Do you have to go to London, Papa?"

"I'm afraid I do, my dear. Newspaper business. But never fear. I'll be back in a few days."

"Can't I come with you?"

"I think it would be best if you stayed at Hembry. Get to know the house better. Discover the side aisles and secret passages. Richard and I used to hide in the hidden staircases when we were children. It drove Nanny wild, I can tell you. And you can get to know your grandmother better, and she you."

"I feel like I should call her Lady Staton."

"She does have that air about her. Even I've called her my lady once or twice. But the little-known truth is that under all that propriety is a woman who cares for her family. I want you to get to know that woman while you're here, Daphne. We won't be here much longer, and you may never have the chance again." Frederick looked through the window at the rolling green expanse that stretched toward the farmlands. "I wish we had come sooner. I wish I had taken my father up on his many invitations to spend our summers here."

"No one expected Grandpa to die. He was never sick a day in his life until the end."

"That's the way of it, isn't it? We walk about as though everything will always be the same, the people we love will always be there, and we put off the important things for when the time is right. And then, out of the blue, something changes, someone goes away, and then we realize how we let so many opportunities pass unheeded. In the end, what do we have but those who loved us and those we loved in return? Even the fact that your grandfather was the Earl of Staton—all the land and the houses and the wealth, none of it mattered in his final hours. All he wanted was the people he loved. I wish we had come sooner, that's all."

Daphne grasped her father's hand. "Grandpa came to America to see us as often as he could. We exchanged letters at least once a week. It wasn't as though we weren't in touch."

"He doted on you, you know. You were his only grand-daughter, and you were the light of his life. I think after Richard was born and your grandparents sighed with relief that their familial duty had been done, your grandfather wanted a daughter. Instead he had two more sons. Other noble families were envious of his surplus of boys, but your grandfather wanted a girl."

"Grandpa loved you dearly," Daphne said.

"Yes. And I him. Yet I never thought it was important to come back to England to see him. All I thought about was why

I needed to get away. I don't regret one moment I've spent in America with your mother and you, but I realize now I didn't need to turn my back on everything that helped shape me into who I am."

"It's all right, Papa. I understand why you want me to stay."

"It's only for a few days. Your granny can't have you married off by Friday."

"It won't be for lack of trying." Daphne kissed her father's cheek. "I'll be fine. I know how to say no if it comes to it."

"I know you do. That's why your grandmother doesn't know what to do with you. Well-born English girls are raised to acquiesce to their parents' wishes."

"Luckily for me, I was not."

Henry huffed as he lifted the leather cases, and Frederick opened the door for him. Daphne put her arm through her father's and they walked to the centerpiece of the house, the regal staircase with the ornamental handrail. They went down and out the front door, opened by Mr. Ellis, and Daphne walked her father to the carriage and held his walking stick while he seated himself inside.

"Look at this as an adventure," Frederick said. "You'll have Hembry Castle virtually to yourself for four whole days. It's a beautiful day. The sun is shining, the sky is blue, and the birds are chirping happy songs. Go for a walk through the parkland. Read a book in one of the gardens. If you leave the grounds, though, ask Mrs. Ellis to send a maid with you. It wouldn't be proper for an unmarried young woman to be seen walking about by herself."

"Why not?"

"A young woman out by herself is a frail thing that may be preyed upon at any moment. Didn't you know that?"

"No, and it's a good thing I didn't or I might not have come. Besides, will I have time for all these walks and all this reading?

Won't Grandma expect me to entertain her while you're away?"

"I shouldn't think so. She has village business to tend to, and acquaintances will pay calls out of respect for your grandfather. I wouldn't expect to see much of her except at dinner." The driver waved in Frederick's direction. "I'm sorry, dearest, but I must go. I'll see you soon."

"Don't worry about me. You take care of your newspaper business. Don't work too hard like you always do. And say hello to Mr. Ellis." Daphne looked at the butler, who appeared not to hear. "I mean young Mr. Ellis."

Frederick smiled. The carriage lurched forward, and Daphne waved as the gray vehicle disappeared down the tree-lined path. When she turned toward the house she was startled to see the elder Mr. Ellis waiting.

"Miss Daphne, her ladyship will be detained for much of the day, though she would like to see you at dinner tonight. In the meanwhile, might I suggest some pleasant walks around the grounds? Or, if you'd prefer, I'd be happy to have Mr. Harvey, our gardener, show you the rose garden. Your father mentioned that roses are your favorite. The garden is quite lovely this time of year."

"Thank you, Mr. Ellis. Yes, I'd love to see the rose garden."

"Ellis to the family, Miss Daphne."

"I'm sorry. I'll catch on, I promise."

"Don't fret, Miss Daphne. It takes time, but you'll learn. I've been here 40 years and I'm still learning."

"I doubt that. You've helped me so much since I've been here." Mr. Ellis bowed. "I don't think I'll ever feel comfortable here. My grandmother dislikes me."

"Never doubt her ladyship's sincere feelings for you, Miss Daphne. She wants the best for you, even if her best is different than what you're used to."

"You're exactly right, Ellis. Thank you."

Mr. Ellis disappeared, leaving Daphne alone in the foyer, which suddenly felt cold and cavernous. It was always cold inside the castle. Even when it was warm outside, it was chilly inside the vast rooms. Daphne had to remember to always wear a shawl to protect her from the raw air, and at that moment, standing alone in the foyer, she pulled her shawl more tightly around her shoulders and shivered. She had accepted her father's challenge and now she must face up to it. She would know Hembry better. To begin her explorations, she found her way to the library with only a couple of wrong turns. In the dark-paneled room with the floor-to-ceiling shelves, she searched the titles and found one to her liking, pulling down a copy of Our Mutual Friend. A social satire was exactly what she needed. Mr. Dickens would make her laugh with the absurdity of those on an insatiable quest for Society. There were many details about life at Hembry Castle worthy of mockery, Daphne thought.

Mr. Ellis cleared his throat. "Mr. Harvey is here, Miss Daphne. He's come to take you to see the roses. Mrs. Graham is fixing a luncheon basket, and Henry and Colin are bringing a table and chair into the garden. I thought under the beech tree would be best since the leaves will shield you from the sunlight while allowing you to see the garden to the best advantage."

"Is there anything you don't think of, Ellis?"

"If there is, let me know and I'll have it seen to at once."

They joined Mr. Harvey in the foyer. The gardener looked uncomfortable, hopping from one foot to the other as though in fear of muddying the polished floor with his earth-worn boots. He was a middle-aged, sunburned man, Mr. Harvey, but he was polite to Daphne and deferential to Mr. Ellis. Mr. Ellis accompanied Daphne and Mr. Harvey down the exterior stairs and alongside the winding lake to the rose garden on the west side of the castle grounds. The stippled gold sunlight brightened everything it touched, and with the down-like clouds floating overhead, the chipper bird songs, the green hills, and the pleasantly warm weather, Daphne thought she had found a little piece of paradise in her father's childhood home.

"Here we are," said Mr. Harvey.

Daphne followed the mosaic path and found herself in a rose-filled paradise. She savored the damask and nasturtium scents that mingled easily with clove and citrus. She walked from bush to bush, admiring the romantic English roses, the floribundas, the grandifloras, the miniatures, the shrubs, the climbing roses that covered the fences. There were flowers in every shade from the palest pink to the deepest red to the brightest yellow, with white, lavender, salmon, peach, and cream for accent. Mr. Harvey explained the types of roses, and their scents, and Daphne, who dabbled in gardening at home, asked questions about how Mr. Harvey managed to prompt such glorious blooms. As they spoke, Mr. Ellis checked that the table and chair were set under the beech tree and the footmen had laid out Daphne's luncheon in an appropriate manner.

"Everything is in order, Miss Daphne," Mr. Ellis said. "Mrs. Graham made the orange custard pudding especially for you since she heard you enjoyed it so much. Mr. Harvey and I will leave you in peace now."

Daphne marveled at her surroundings. She had seen many rose gardens, certainly, and there were her bushes at home. But she had never seen anything so lavish, so perfectly designed, as though not one detail had gone unheeded. She looked into the wicker basket set neatly on the table and found cold salmon with mayonnaise sauce, a green salad with peas and asparagus, bread and cheese, and the orange custard. There was a flask with tea, already sweetened to her taste, and she enjoyed her luncheon surrounded by the natural beauty of roses. When she finished eating, she opened her book and immersed herself in the world of the Boffins and the unfortunate effect sudden wealth can have on anyone. Daphne thought of her situation, finding herself living in this lavish house with servants to tend to her every need. Would she become as diseased by her change in circumstances as Noddy Boffin? And what about John Harmon, allowing the others to believe he was dead, presenting himself as John Rokesmith, observing everyone's true natures without invoking the slightest suspicion about who he really was? Daphne shook her head. It was just as her Uncle Richard had told her when he read Oliver Twist to her when she was a girl—"Mr. Dickens would have his flights of fancy."

When the afternoon began to wane Daphne decided to return to the castle. It was easy enough to find. You couldn't miss it from anywhere in the region of Hembry, but she paused to admire the follies—the Greek-style temple, the obelisk, and the ruins of a stone tower with stair turrets. As she neared the house she turned to the right instead of the left and found herself in the courtyard by the servants' entrance. She knocked on the door and a young housemaid appeared.

"I'm so sorry. I was out in the garden and I must have made a wrong turn. Is Mr. Ellis here?"

"Mr. Ellis?"

Daphne heard keys clinking on the other side of the door.

"Jemima, why are you standing there like you've seen a ghost?" Mrs. Ellis opened the door wider. "Miss Daphne, what are you doing down here? Come in, please."

"Thank you, Mrs. Ellis. I was in the rose garden and somehow I ended up at your door. I feel a little foolish, to be honest. My sense of direction seems to elude me here."

"If you pay attention you can learn the ways of the house,

Miss Daphne. Whispers are telling you everything you need to know if you listen."

Daphne looked down the hallway, painted white with dark wood beams overhead. It was such a contrast to the lavish living upstairs. She walked to the kitchen at the far end and saw Mrs. Graham standing over the stove stirring two pots, one with her right hand and the other with her left. "Mrs. Graham?"

Lainie Graham started when she heard her name. "Miss Daphne! Was something wrong with your luncheon?"

"Not at all. I wanted to say thank you. Mr. Ellis said you made the orange custard especially for me."

"Her ladyship mentioned how much you enjoyed it so I thought you might like one this afternoon."

"I did like it, very much." Daphne noticed the kitchen maids stealing glances at her as they chopped vegetables. "I know you're busy. I'll let you get back to work."

On the other side of the green baize door, Daphne walked into the sitting room, expecting to find it empty, but there was her grandmother in the wing chair near the window embroidering flowers onto the canvas in her round frame.

"Daphne, my dear, how nice of you to take some time for your Grandmamma. Ellis said you were picnicking in the rose garden. How did you find it?"

"It's beautiful, Grandma. It's the most beautiful rose garden I've seen."

"I'm glad. Now listen to me, my dear. I know your father has plans to return to America soon. He wants to leave before the winter weather makes crossing impossible, but I'm hoping I can convince you to stay." She gestured with her round embroidery frame at the settee. "Sit, Daphne. I want to talk to you."

At that moment, with the two of them alone in the sitting

room, Lady Staton seemed less formidable. Perhaps this was the woman her father was referring to, the woman he wanted Daphne to know. Threading yellow silk into daisies, the Countess of Staton deflated from a grand lady to a normal woman doing an ordinary thing.

"How are you enjoying your stay at Hembry?"

Daphne spoke loudly since the ear trumpet was nowhere to be seen. "I'm having a wonderful time, Grandma. I've listened to Papa tell stories about this house my whole life, and I'm glad I finally get to see it for myself."

"And you're finding England to your taste?"

"It does rain a lot, but other than that I am."

"Very good." Lady Staton put down her embroidery. "Daphne, I want you to know that I don't mean to cast you aside."

"That's good of you, Grandma."

"I want to help you."

"Help me?"

"With protocol. With our way of life. You understand we're a very old family, don't you?"

"I thought everyone's family was as old as everyone else's."

"Not in England, my dear. In England only aristocrats can be said to have old families."

"I see."

"You're the niece of the Earl of Staton, and we have a place in Society to uphold. There are expectations for a family like ours, and everyone's eyes are always upon us. We're required to be models of behavior at all times. And I'd like to help you learn our ways."

"Certainly people would understand that I wasn't brought up to your way of life. Certainly..."

"What I can guarantee, Daphne, is that none of that is true. As long as you are in England, and as long as you stay at

Hembry, you will be scrutinized as we are all scrutinized. After your presentation to the Queen the scrutiny will magnify a hundredfold." She leaned close to Daphne, squinting as though she were looking through her daughter-in-law's eyeglass. "Was your mother blond?"

"She was."

"And you have no suitors?"

A vision of chocolate-brown hair, lively hazel eyes, and a friendly laugh struck Daphne. She was startled by it, but she swept it swiftly back to wherever it came from. "I do not."

"No one?" Daphne shook her head. "That's surprising, but it is good news. It suits our purposes. I've written to the Marchioness of Carrington, and she agrees that you must be presented at court next Season. You're old for it at 20, but better late than never."

"I'm sure that's not necessary, Grandma. Besides, is that even allowed? I'm not sure Her Majesty would want an American presented in her court."

"American girls are presented before the Queen all the time. Besides, you're not any American girl. You're the niece of the Earl of Staton. I'll submit your name for consideration, and I may neglect to mention the fact that you were raised in Honeynut in America."

"Connecticut."

"That's what I said. Then, once you're presented, I'll find all manner of eligible young men to introduce to you. We'll find you a husband very soon afterward, I'm certain of it. Why, I wouldn't be surprised if you were engaged by the end of the Season. Even if your father isn't the heir, it is still correct for you to make a suitable match."

"What would be a suitable match?" Daphne asked.

"A young man from a suitable family, of course."

"What constitutes a suitable family?"

"Believe it or not, Daphne, I understand why you ask the question. You wouldn't have suitable families in America, would you? The country is barely old enough to hold its head up. A suitable family is one with a history as old as ours."

"Other aristocrats?"

"Yes."

"Rich aristocrats, I assume."

"They're aristocrats."

"But what if I don't like any of the men who are from suitable families? What if I like someone else?"

"Who else?"

Daphne thought again of chocolate-brown hair and an amiable smile. "I only meant, what if I found a wonderful man who was a doctor or a lawyer? Or a journalist?"

"That sort of thing might do well in America, but here we have standards. The niece of the Earl of Staton will not marry a journalist. The niece of the Earl of Staton will not become involved in a mésalliance. You may as well marry the muffin man."

"Who lives in Drury Lane?"

The Countess shook her head. "You are much like your father. I do not mean that as a compliment."

"I'm sorry, Grandma. I'm trying to understand."

"I take full responsibility, Daphne. I should have brought you to England long ago. I asked your father, I pleaded with him to send you after you were born. Even if he and your mother insisted on staying in America, there was no reason we couldn't raise you properly here at Hembry. But he refused. Neither he nor your mother could ever be made to see the sense in it. I'll never understand American mothers. How can the nanny do her job if the mother can't bear to be without her children?" Daphne said nothing, and her grandmother continued. "We must prepare you to be presented to the Queen. When is your birthday?"

"May 12th."

"You'll be one-and-twenty on the 12th of May? That is cutting it close. Still, we've come back from worse in this family." Again, Lady Staton studied Daphne as though she were a scientific specimen. "Do you wear your hair like that intentionally?"

"Don't you like it, Grandma?"

"I want my maid, Rowland, to begin styling your hair. Then, after Mrs. Ellis has trained her, we can take the new girl Pamela as a maid for you. She seems a well-intentioned creature, and she's about your age so I think it would be a good match. We need to make sure you look the part of the niece of the Earl of Staton."

"I've always done my own hair, Grandma."

"So I can see." Lady Staton sighed and the hard line of her mouth softened. "I know this is an adjustment for you, Daphne, I do. But this is the way our family has done things for a long time, and you are part of this family. I can see you have a bright spark, much as I did when I was your age. Your shortcomings are not your fault, but the fault of your parents for bringing you up in America when you should have been raised here."

Daphne had to restrain her smile. "Whatever shall be done about me, Grandma? I seem to be past hope."

"No Meriwether has ever been beyond hope. Now, our first task is to begin accepting callers. The silver tray in the entrance hall is overflowing with cards left by those who have come to pay their respects. We didn't see them, of course. It wouldn't have been correct so soon after your grandfather's death, but now I've sent back our cards to indicate that we're ready to receive visitors."

Lady Staton gestured to the writing desk near the window. Daphne opened the top drawer and found a stack of scalloped-edged cards with a thick black border and the name The Countess of Staton written in calligraphy in the top corner. Daphne traced the embossed white dove with a pink rose in its beak with her finger.

"Grandpa would have hated this. He hated any sign of mourning."

"Yes, my dear, you're right. He would have. But this is the way we do things, so this is the way it must be done." Lady Staton picked up the round wooden frame of her needlework and worried out a thread that had become unraveled in the canvas. "I'll expect you to help me receive our callers. Our first guests should arrive tomorrow after luncheon."

Whatever softness had relaxed Lady Staton's demeanor vanished, and she was the grand dame once again. She nodded at Daphne, dismissing her, and resumed her needlework.

PAYING CALLS

*D*aphne forgot her father's warnings and wandered to the village alone, taking some time for herself before that day's calls were expected. Of course she and her mother had paid calls at home in Connecticut and, when the occasion required it, New York City, but here Daphne was afraid she'd get it all wrong. She stopped near the old stone church, watching the gray sky brighten to pale blue as the sun rose higher and the songbirds nestled in the trees. She walked around to the graveyard and saw the headstones with dates going back generations, wondering how much life had changed, or if it had changed at all, in the centuries since her father's family first inhabited this land. It was her family too, she reminded herself, even if it didn't always feel that way.

She pushed open the cemetery gate, listening to the crunch as the old iron scraped against itself. She found her way to the mausoleum where her grandfather had been laid to rest, sat beneath a downy birch tree, and wept. She felt more lonely than she had since arriving in England. She knew her grand-mother meant well, as Ellis had said. Perhaps there was a correct way to do things in New York Society as well, but Daphne had never been part of that scene. Her parents, and she, had been invited into the inner circle often enough since it was known among the fashionable set that Frederick was the younger son of a peer and the leading ladies of New York were always looking to add another English aristocrat to the guest lists for their candlelight suppers. But Daphne's mother never showed any interest in Society, calling anyone in those circles too high-handed and small-minded for their own good. Add to that the fact that her father nearly choked on his tea whenever such an invitation was extended, and you can see why the Connecticut Meriwethers preferred their comfortable cottage hearth to any upright, uncomfortable salon in fashionable Manhattan.

Daphne dropped her head into her hands, still feeling the ache brought on by her grandmother's lecture that morning. After breakfast, Daphne had been beckoned to her boudoir by Rowland, her grandmother's maid. Daphne was directed to sit at the mahogany table while the gray-looking, stern-faced Rowland brushed her hair and pulled it into an elegant chignon at the base of her neck, leaving a few curled tendrils floating by her ears. With her hair perfectly coiffed, Rowland helped Daphne into a lovely lilac silk taffeta tea gown with embroidered crepe, bows at the sleeves, and pearl accents. Lady Staton arrived in time to squint at the dress.

"This is the dress you wanted to see Miss Daphne in, my lady?" Rowland asked.

"Yes, that is the one, Rowland. Thank you for asking after Miss Daphne has it on."

"I only thought…"

"Thinking. What a wonderful idea. You were thinking. And what were you thinking?" Her ladyship held up her ear trumpet as though to be certain to catch every word of the imaginative thoughts that popped unwarranted into her maid's mind.

"I was thinking the dress has pearls, my lady, just the small ones down the front, but they're still pearls."

"Our callers won't arrive until after luncheon so the pearls will do very nicely." Lady Staton turned to Daphne. "We couldn't have you wearing pearls before luncheon, but after luncheon will be fine, especially since they're small accents."

"No more black?" Daphne asked.

"It's only been two months since your grandfather died, but I'm certain you can get away with half-mourning by now. You lived in America and didn't know your grandfather at all."

"Grandpa came to visit us many times, Grandma."

"No one else knows that. I don't want our callers to see you in dull black when they meet you for the first time. I want them to know you're a force to be reckoned with."

Lady Staton sat straight-backed on the settee in front of the window watching the proceedings with narrow eyes, inspecting every movement Rowland made, clucking her tongue when she thought Rowland made a mistake, which was often. Rowland handed Daphne a pair of pearl earrings which perfectly matched the accents on her dress. Rowland looked at Lady Staton, who nodded in approval.

"There are a few things you must know, Daphne. When our visitors arrive, you must never notice anything peculiar about the person or comment on anything such as a deformity or defect of any kind."

"I wouldn't normally do that, Grandma."

Lady Staton replaced her trumpet by her ear, her arm must have grown tired, and Daphne repeated herself.

"I should hope not. You are a Meriwether even if you were raised in Cumberbuns in America. Remember that the point of any conversation is to entertain, though since we are still in mourning you'll find that most of our visitors will confine their topics to the decorations in the drawing room and the weather. Do not discuss politics for any reason, and do not ever gossip. Only the lower classes gossip."

"I see."

"Our callers may tiptoe around the topic of your grandfather. If they see they can mention him without causing pain to us, or embarrassment to themselves, then they may speak of enjoyable moments they shared with him."

"I'm happy to speak about Grandpa with anyone who knew him. I'd like to hear what others have to say about him."

"That's all fine and well, Daphne, but as you're acquainting yourself with our callers, never pry into their affairs. And even if they behave stupidly, which they often do, especially when calling after a bereavement and they don't know what to say, never show your impatience. Smile, Daphne. That is our greatest weapon—our smiles. Not those ridiculously wide grins that show every tooth in your mouth the way you Americans do it, but a sedate parting of the lips. As aristocrats, we're known for our impeccable manners. We put people at their ease while they are in our presence."

"And then we talk about how badly they behaved when they're gone?"

"Precisely. Now, when our callers arrive Ellis will show them into the drawing room where they will wait until we are ready to show ourselves. We are fortunate to be receiving our guests in the country where it's less ceremonial than London. Here we don't have as many rules." Lady Staton nodded as Rowland added the finishing touch, a simple pearl bracelet around Daphne's wrist. "Come here, child. Let me look at you."

Lady Staton's lips pulled apart into what Daphne decided was that smile her grandmother had just described.

"The half-mourning lilac suits you. Yes, you're perfectly

acceptable as the niece of the Earl of Staton. Remember, when we receive our callers this afternoon, you must be certain to do everything exactly as I've taught you. There can be no room for mistakes today."

"I thought there weren't as many rules in the country, Grandma."

"There are certainly fewer rules, my dear, but there are still rules."

Afterward Daphne made her escape from the house. She passed through the rose garden, but that day the blooms held no magic for her. She continued through the parkland, past the castle ruins, and down the steep hill until she reached the church where she sat near her grandfather's grave. She touched the mausoleum, a neoclassical stone structure with Egyptian pylon towers on either side, the monument smooth against her hands. She bowed her head as she spoke.

"Your home is beautiful, Grandpa, but it's lonely without you, and with Papa gone I feel like I don't have a friend in the world." Daphne stepped back from the iron-trimmed door as though expecting her grandfather to push it open from the inside. She waited, but when only the shushing melody of the breeze answered her she sighed. She brushed some fallen leaves from her dress. "Grandma will scold me if I get my dress dirty. I probably shouldn't be here now." She opened the gate and looked back toward the mausoleum. "Say hi to Mama, Grandpa. I love you both so much."

Daphne walked from the graveyard, pausing at the sight of the castle on the hill. She knew she should return—it would be luncheon soon and their callers would begin to arrive. She walked up the green hill, past the tradesmen's cottages, past the workshops, past the stables, through the gardens to the main door where Mr. Ellis let her in.

For the rest of that day and days afterward, Daphne was

held captive in the drawing room while she witnessed an endless parade of only the finest ladies with only their finest daughters. Daphne met three marchionesses, four countesses, two viscountesses, and one baroness (it couldn't be helped). Even a duchess arrived to pay her respects. After the first three calls the visitors all blended into one polite smile and one long conversation about how Daphne was finding England (The weather must seem dreadfully wet to you, Miss Meriwether). One noble mamma (a marchioness) mentioned that her daughter Adeliza, a waif of a girl who appeared to be no more than 15, thought the new Earl looked positively dashing the last time she had the pleasure of his acquaintance. Adeliza squealed "Mamma!" with such force Daphne was afraid the poor thing might fold in on herself, she was so slight. Another marchioness (Daphne lost track of their names the moment after they were introduced) asked after Frederick, inquiring, in an all-too-innocent tone, "He's a widower now, isn't he?" When the Countess replied in the affirmative, the mamma, and her three daughters, could hardly contain their delight.

Daphne was amused by the interest in her father as a potential match for the unmarried daughters. She knew her father would simply laugh at the thought of being a potential suitor for girls younger than she was. Whenever the conversation turned to the eligibility of Richard or her father (sadly, Jerrold Meriwether was married), Lady Staton held her back a little straighter, flashed her eyes a little smaller, spoke her words a little slower, enunciating every syllable, and then she steered the conversation back to the weather.

The callers that stood out in Daphne's mind were the young Americans. A viscountess brought along two American sisters—the Miss Cadwalladers (Morena was 18 and Twilla 21). The Viscountess Meddleham had met the young women in London at one of the premiere balls of the Season, and she had enjoyed the girls' buoyant personalities and ready laughter so much she couldn't bear to part with them. She brought them home to Kent and kept them there ever since. The Viscountess spoke to the sisters as if there were no end to the amusements they could provide, as if the young women were toy poodles, leashed for her entertainment. While the Viscountess Meddleham and the Countess of Staton discussed polite topics over the top of their steaming teacups, Morena and Twilla pulled Daphne to the settee near the window. The sisters giggled over this handsome baronet's son or that duke's heir who was already engaged, sadly, but what a prize he would have been! Daphne nodded at appropriate intervals, and Miss Morena declared that Daphne was the world's greatest companion, she truly was.

"You must visit us at Elwyn House in Kent," said Miss Morena. "Viscountess Meddleham doesn't like to brag (such a funny thing about the English, don't you think?), but her son Reginald is so debonair, so elegant. It's worth a visit to Kent to meet him!"

Miss Cadwallader shook her head and said, perhaps too loudly, "I'm sure Miss Meriwether doesn't need to be introduced to any more young men, Morena. I'm certain Miss Meriwether has been introduced to more than enough young men already."

Miss Morena shook her finger in her sister's face. "Don't be silly. Everyone needs more friends. Isn't that right, Miss Meriwether?" Before Daphne could respond, Miss Morena said, "Besides, don't forget only one of us can marry the Viscountess' son. Miss Meriwether's uncle is the Earl of Staton," she dropped her voice to a whisper, "and he still needs a wife."

Miss Cadwallader studied Daphne from the top of her gold curls to the bottom of her satin boots. Miss Cadwallader took her time examining Daphne's dress, the lilac silk taffeta tea gown that Rowland had helped her into earlier. "Pearls. How charming." Miss Cadwallader may have grimaced—Daphne wasn't sure—and when she spoke she had that sugary inflection Lady Staton used whenever she was putting someone down in her most genteel manner. "Why haven't we met before, Miss Meriwether? I don't recall seeing you at any of Mrs. Vanderbilt's soirées or with Mrs. Astor at the opera. Perhaps you've been to Newport?"

"Nowhere so grand, I'm afraid. I'm from Connecticut."

"Greenwich? Our parents have a home there."

"New London. We haven't met in fashionable New York because my family never went out in Society."

Miss Morena's hand covered her mouth to stop her squeal of surprise. "Never went out in Society? But why not? Especially with your pa the son of an English aristocrat, you would have been eaten up by all the important people—the Beekmans, the Rhinelanders, the Stuyvesants, the de Peysters, the Schermerhorns. They would have had an all-out war to see who could catch you first."

"That's exactly what my father was afraid of," Daphne said. "He saw New York Society trying to imitate everything he disliked about English Society and he didn't see the point of it."

Miss Morena shuddered. "Didn't see the point of it! My goodness gracious, Miss Meriwether. Our ma was always on about how to get to the right people, how to get into the right balls, how to meet the right young men. They didn't like us much in New York—we were new money and all—so our mother brought us here." She nodded toward Viscountess Meddleham. "We were lucky to meet her. She brought us to live with her at her big estate. And she introduced us to her handsome son."

"What a dreadfully boring life she must have led before we arrived," said Miss Cadwallader. "Everything is so dull in the country, everything so ordered, and everyone does the same things at the same times every day. We help to liven things up for her."

"But isn't that the sort of life you'll have if you marry an aristocrat?" Daphne asked. "If you marry the Viscountess' son you'll spend the rest of your life living like that."

"Once you're married you can do what you want," said Miss Morena. "And if you're firm enough you can train your husband to your liking."

Daphne looked at the ceiling in response.

Fortunately, the calls were not a complete waste. One caller was a young widow who was less than 30 if she was a day. Her name was Mrs. Gibson, and she was simply lovely, Daphne thought, with her dark hair pulled into a long braid that was wrapped into a bun while her mourning dress fell away from her in ripples of silk. Mrs. Gibson's sister has been married to Lord Landerson, a baronet. Her sister had recently died, and Mr. Gibson passed soon after. Despite her double dose of sorrow, Mrs. Gibson was a gentle soul who spoke in soothing tones about her great respect for the 8th Earl of Staton and how he had done so much to help her husband begin his life in business. Because the young widow had nothing but the highest praise for her late husband and conducted herself in only the most genteel manner, the Countess liked Mrs. Gibson immensely. Daphne liked Mrs. Gibson as well. After Mrs. Gibson left, Lady Staton pronounced, loudly enough for the servants to hear, "She'd make a wonderful wife for Richard. After all, she's already produced one son. She has a daughter too, but that couldn't be helped, I'm sure."

"That's not why she came to call today. She wanted to pay her respects to Grandpa."

"But that's precisely it, my dear. The fact that she didn't

arrive fangs bared and claws out eager to catch a husband means she knows how to conduct herself."

"I was under the impression that husband-searching here was a fang-bared, claws-out affair," Daphne said. Lady Staton waved her ear trumpet at her granddaughter but said nothing.

The idea of paying calls was further redeemed when Daphne's only friend in England, Miss Christina Chattaway, arrived. Her father knew Miss Chattaway's father through the newspaper business, and the Chattaways had been kind enough to host Daphne and her father for dinner shortly after they arrived in England. Daphne would always be grateful for the warmth with which Miss Chattaway greeted her. Daphne and Miss Chattaway had become friends at first sight, and they exchanged frequent letters since. That afternoon only Miss Chattaway and her mother arrived at Hembry, the younger Chattaway girls left with their father in London. Mrs. and Miss Chattaway had come to the country at Daphne's invitation since Miss Chattaway wanted to pay her respects to the old Earl. Miss Chattaway had met the old Earl once, only briefly, but he had been kind to her and she wanted the Countess to know.

Mr. Ellis showed Mrs. and Miss Chattaway into the drawing room with more deference than normally reserved for guests, and Miss Chattaway smiled shyly in the butler's direction. The callers curtsied at the Countess, who acknowledged them in her grand manner and lowered herself onto the settee as regally as the Queen ever lowered herself upon the throne. Mrs. Chattaway didn't seem to notice that her ample figure left little room on the sofa for her daughter, who was all manners as she squeezed into the small space allotted. Miss Chattaway said what she wanted to say to the Countess, who accepted the tribute with great courtesy. Miss Chattaway was such a sweet-natured, amiable young woman that even the stern Lady Staton was won over. Miss Chattaway was pretty too, with her hair nearly the same spun gold color as Daphne's. With her apple-like cheeks and bright blue eyes, Christina Chattaway looked to be exactly what she was—a young woman who was all friendliness and charm.

"I can't get over how pretty you look today, Daphne. That lilac suits you."

"I loved my grandfather dearly, but I'm happy to be out of black."

Mrs. Chattaway began speaking too loudly, as though she wanted everyone in the castle to hear. "Oh, yes, your ladyship. My cousin's first wife was related to a baronet through marriage, and we take that connection to the aristocracy quite seriously."

Christina shook her head. "Mamma, we don't want to bother Lady Staton with such trivialities."

"Trivialities! Why, I watched the Countess of Bergeron drink her tea once, and don't forget the time when I bumped into Lady Blarkins and she said 'Pardon me' as though we had been the greatest of friends all the livelong day. Now I forget precisely when I saw Lord Constance. Are you acquainted with Lord Constance, Lady Staton?"

Lady Staton nodded once. "I am."

"Mamma." Christina's complexion matched the dusky rose of her silk taffeta dress.

But Mrs. Chattaway did as her name suggests, and she chatted away about every time she had been within a ten-mile radius of anyone remotely connected to the aristocracy. Daphne admired her grandmother, who was nodding at the blathering woman with great patience. Daphne nearly laughed aloud when she realized her grandmother's ear trumpet was lying unused on the settee. So that's how she manages these trying conversations, Daphne thought. While the older ladies continued their one-sided conversation, Daphne leaned close to Christina.

"How is your engagement coming along? Have you set a date?"

Christina blushed dusky rose again. "Not yet. He wants to be financially settled first."

"And so he should be. But why haven't you told me his name? You're so mysterious about him, Christina."

"It's just…"

"Yes? You can tell me. I see it's causing you some worry."

Christina Chattaway whispered. "I'm worried about his feelings for me. I haven't seen him since the beginning of summer."

"I'm sure he's just busy. Does he write?"

"Oh yes. The most wonderful letters."

"Then I wouldn't worry."

Christina caught Colin's attention, and the footman refilled her teacup. She helped herself to a strawberry petit four and finished it in one bite. "They're delicious," Christina said.

"Yes, Mrs. Graham does wonders with desserts. Now tell me what your fiancé does again?"

"He's a journalist. He used to work for my father, but he's moved on since."

"A journalist! How funny. Both of our fathers are journalists, your fiancé is a journalist, and I've met the most engaging young man who's also a journalist—he works for my father at the Observer. It's such a coincidence that his grandparents work here at Hembry Castle."

Christina paused as she sipped her tea. Her cup empty, she set it on the side table. "And how well acquainted are you with this engaging young journalist?"

"Not well at all. But my father speaks so highly of him, and I've read some of his writing and I think he is as talented as my father says." Daphne smiled. "He's certainly handsome to look at."

"And would you like to know this handsome-to-look-at journalist better?" Christina teased.

Daphne laughed so loudly that she garnered a rude glance from her grandmother. "Of course not. Papa and I will be returning to America soon, so it hardly pays to form an attachment here. Except for you, my dear Christina. I know we'll be lifelong friends. Once Father and I have returned home I hope we can convince you to come visit us. Maybe that's where you could go on your honeymoon—Connecticut!"

"I would like that very much," Christina said, though she looked subdued, if not downright sad, for the remainder of her visit.

SHORTHAND

Downstairs, Mrs. Ellis found her husband hunched over his desk in the butler's pantry. It was dark in the room, the oak wainscoting dull and uninspired, the only light flickering from the flames in the hearth. Mr. Ellis' desk stood before the locked shelves with the family's silver, as though it had been commissioned to guard the valuables and took its job seriously. Mrs. Ellis watched her husband of fifty years fiddle with two telegrams, and when he read the first he muttered to himself, his mouth thin, his eyebrows a flat line over his spectacles. When he finished he turned the telegram face down on his desk as though the offending message needed a reprimand. As he read the second telegram his shoulders dropped from his ears.

"What is it?" Mrs. Ellis asked.

Mr. Ellis' head snapped up. "My dear, you mustn't sneak up on me like that."

"You're not the only one around here who can appear at will. What is it, Gussie?" She glanced at the telegram in her husband's hand.

"Mr. Frederick has sent word that his business in London will detain him longer than expected. He asks Miss Daphne to join him."

"What is that?" She pointed to the naughty message face down on the desk.

"You don't want to know."

"George?" Mr. Ellis nodded. "How much?"

"Fifty pounds."

"Lord." Mr. Ellis handed her the telegram and she read it for herself. "What on earth could he have done that's going to cost us fifty pounds? You'd think we were the family upstairs instead of the servants the way he's always asking."

"He's always asking because we always send it. Perhaps..." Mr. Ellis stopped. He had that thin-lipped look again, the one he wore whenever he carefully chose his words. "Perhaps it's time we stopped sending him money."

Mrs. Ellis sat in the empty chair across from her husband. "You know what's happened every time we haven't sent the money. Besides, I'm not thinking of George. I'm thinking of Edward. He's on his way, Augustus. Those stories of his, they're wonderful, and people love reading them."

"I know, my dear."

"And now those publishers are thinking about publishing a collection of his stories. His very own book, Gussie! Our little Neddie may have his very own book! He's already been invited upstairs for luncheon, and it won't be the last time, I'm sure of it." Mrs. Ellis grasped her husband's hand across the desk. "I don't want anything to get in his way. And what about Kate and Nathan? They're still young enough to be at home. Where will they be if George falls into trouble again?"

Mr. Ellis wiped his spectacles on his handkerchief. "Should we tell Edward, do you think?"

"Absolutely not. You know Neddie will take it upon himself

to get things sorted, and heaven knows the boy can't afford fifty pounds. We can barely afford fifty pounds." The housekeeper sighed when she stood, and an uncomfortable silence filled the room. They had had this conversation too many times. Finally, she said, "Have you told Miss Daphne about Mr. Frederick's telegram?"

"I've only just received it myself."

"I'll have Pamela pack Miss Daphne some clothes."

"How is Pamela working out?"

"Very well. I was worried at first, the way his lordship insisted I find a place for her. She has no parents, poor girl, only a sister in London. We can always use an extra pair of hands around here, but there was something about the way his lordship took such an interest in the girl. It made me wonder, or worry, I'm not sure which."

Mr. Ellis replaced his spectacles onto the permanent groove at the top of his nose. "How does his lordship know her?"

"He never said. But Pamela's hardworking and eager to please. And her ladyship is already talking about pulling Pamela as a maid for Miss Daphne, which won't make the housemaids who have been here longer very happy, but if it's what her ladyship wants it's what her ladyship will have."

Mrs. Ellis watched Colin, the footman, as he passed the open door. "I should probably send Pamela with Miss Daphne to London. Otherwise Miss Daphne will be traveling alone."

Mr. Ellis walked to the door and called "Colin!" When the footman reappeared, he said, "Find Pamela and tell her to pack some things for Miss Daphne and to pack a bag for herself. She'll be accompanying Miss Daphne to London this afternoon. Make sure the carriage is brought round front. Then go to the kitchen and tell Mrs. Graham to put together a luncheon basket for Miss Daphne, and one for Pamela as well."

Colin disappeared, and Mrs. Ellis saw Jemima standing on

one foot as though she were ready to take flight. The young maid leaned close to the housekeeper. "Will Miss Daphne see your grandson while she's in London?"

Mrs. Ellis had a few harsh words with Jemima's name on them, but there was Pamela Escott, the young maid in question.

"Mrs. Ellis, Colin just told me about my trip and I was wondering how long Miss Daphne and I were to be in London?"

Mrs. Ellis looked at her husband.

"Mr. Frederick said he expects to return a week from Tuesday," said the butler.

"Pack enough for a fortnight to be safe," said Mrs. Ellis. When Pamela was gone, Mrs. Ellis turned to her husband. "So what do we do about George?"

"For now, nothing. Let's see if he can find his way out of this mess."

Mrs. Ellis' keys clinked as she walked to the door. "There's a first time for everything, I suppose."

DAPHNE WAS STILL GETTING USED to London, just as she was still getting used to Hembry. She loved the excitement of the city, and it felt the same yet different just as everything in England felt familiar and strange at the same time. The morning after she arrived in the city she was driven in the family's carriage from Staton House on Park Lane to the offices of the Daily Observer near Fleet Street. It was a bit of a drive, especially in the crowded afternoon hours when every possible obstruction—man, beast, or vehicle—blocked their way.

To pass the time, Daphne challenged herself to name the landmarks they passed—the Mall, Covent Garden, Drury

Lane—until they neared Lincoln's Inn Fields. The hustle of London was not unlike the bustle in Manhattan, yet it was different. A different rhythm, maybe. In New York, the people were impolite one way while in London they were impolite in another. In New York, they were too busy to notice you, too intent on where they were going to think about anyone else. In London, it wasn't that they were too busy to notice you. They simply didn't care. When Rogers, the family's coachman, pulled to Fleet Street, Daphne and Pamela were amazed by the passers-by who crossed the street in front of the moving carriage as though the carriage should know to get out of the way. If the passers-by weren't eluding the fast-moving vehicles then they were bumping into other people without the slightest acknowledgment that you were standing where they wanted to go. Even after they stepped on you they kept walking, eyes forward, as though they didn't realize they had stepped on a person instead of a lamppost. If Daphne happened to make eye contact with the bumper, he might murmur a quick "Sorry" as he continued past.

Finally, Daphne and Pamela arrived at the newspaper office. Daphne looked at herself, then Pamela, and exhaled with relief when she was certain they had crossed Fleet Street into the relative calm of Hough Square in one piece. Daphne slipped her arm through Pamela's—they were great friends by the time the train arrived in London—and they entered the newspaper offices together. A young man stood, unsteady on his feet, when he saw Daphne, then Pamela. He kept looking from one to the other as though he couldn't believe his eyes.

"Is Mr. Meriwether in?" Daphne asked.

"Who?" the confused young man asked.

"Mr. Meriwether?"

"Oh!" The young man tapped his fingers on the top of his

head, and his confusion must have cleared in the process. "He should be back any moment."

"Is it all right if we wait in his office?" Daphne asked.

The young man tripped over his own feet as he rushed to open the door for the young women. When he saw only one chair near the editor's desk, he came back with another, then vanished before Daphne could ask his name. She noticed Edward Ellis at his desk by the window, one hand scribbling quickly with an ink-stained quill while the fingers of his other hand skimmed the markings on another page.

"There's Mr. Ellis. I should say hello."

"We should wait for your father in here, Miss Daphne."

"It's Mr. Edward Ellis, you know, the Ellises' grandson."

Daphne watched Edward's brow form the same flat line as his grandfather's did whenever he was intent on something. Edward Ellis' writing hand flew across the paper, stopping only to refill his pen with ink. Daphne stepped closer to the young man, intrigued. His chocolate-brown hair fell like a feather across his forehead, his expression emphatic, his wide hazel eyes steady on his work. He looked handsome when he was engrossed in his work like that, Daphne thought. Self-conscious suddenly, she realized she shouldn't disturb him while he was busy. Then Mr. Ellis must have noticed her because he jumped to his feet, knocking his chair over and gaining the interested stares of everyone in the office as a reward.

"Miss Meriwether." His voice faltered. "I didn't see you there. Forgive me."

It was warm in the office, the August humidity sticking to London and everyone in it. Daphne felt the heat on her cheeks and wondered if she looked as pink as she felt.

"No, Mr. Ellis, the fault is mine. I didn't mean to disturb you. I can see you're busy."

"I've been very clumsy."

"You were involved in your work."

Mr. Ellis gestured to the papers on his desk. "Racing to meet a deadline, as always."

Daphne stepped closer to inspect the papers. "What are you working on?"

"I'm transcribing my notes from the parliamentary debates last night."

"What are they debating now?"

"The Education Act."

"Is that a good thing?"

"It may be the best thing to happen to education in England. Finally, they're talking about providing education on a national scale."

"Do you agree with the bill?"

"Absolutely, though more needs to be done. There's still nothing to make schooling compulsory for all children, so it does nothing to help the abuses of child labor."

"Is education an important issue to you, Mr. Ellis?"

"Everyone deserves an education. Everyone deserves a chance. I was fortunate since my grandparents made sure I was well educated."

"I know how proud they are of you, as they should be."

Mr. Ellis' cheeks reddened. "The education they provided for me has given me opportunities to press forward in the world where I might not have had a chance otherwise. Everyone deserves the same chance."

"Where are your parents?" When Mr. Ellis turned away to straighten the writing quills in their stand, she added, "I'm afraid my American curiosity is getting the better of me. I apologize if I've offended you."

"I'm not offended. There's no great secret, I assure you. I spent a portion of my childhood at Hembry with my grandparents. My parents...my parents..." Mr. Ellis faltered. He looked through the window as though the right words would appear in the bright white clouds. Daphne wanted to take his hand, but that was a definite faux pas in England. Maybe in Connecticut it wasn't entirely acceptable, either. She stayed her impulse by imagining her grandmother shaking her head, a vigorous "No!" accompanying each shake.

"I'm writing a piece about the Education Act," Mr. Ellis said. "Your father has graciously agreed to publish it in the Observer. People need to understand why education is so important. They need to see why the bill must be passed, and then they must push for the next bill to go even further."

"Are there people who doubt that everyone deserves an education?"

"I don't know how things are in America, Miss Meriwether, but here there are too many toffs who believe the lower classes are best left ignorant, as though the quality of life for the upper classes will somehow be lessened if everyone is equally well educated."

"This may be a silly question, but what's a toff?"

Laughter came from two desks over, and a young man she recognized from her previous trip to the office stood.

"If you'll allow me to explain, Ellis," the young man said. "A toff is a snobbish rich person, you know, an aristocrat for example."

Daphne grinned. "Like my family, perhaps?"

Mr. Ellis went from sallow to crimson. "That will be all, Roberts."

"I was only explaining..."

"Goodbye, Roberts."

Roberts shrugged. "Miss Meriwether, if I caused offense I didn't mean to do so."

"Not at all, Mr. Roberts. Based on your description, my

grandmother is the definition of a toff. My uncle may be the Earl of Staton, but I wouldn't call him snobbish in any way. Not everyone with a title is the same, just as not everyone without a title is the same." Mr. Ellis visibly exhaled when Mr. Roberts tucked himself back behind his desk.

"I apologize for any impertinence," said Mr. Ellis.

"I'm not interested in whether Mr. Roberts was being impertinent or not. I'm interested in this piece you're writing. It makes me glad to know you're committed to such important matters, Mr. Ellis. I'm glad to know that some good people care about what's happening in the world, people who are determined to make things better."

"If we don't take measures to help ourselves, Miss Meriwether, then there's no one else to do it." He looked at the pile of papers on his desk. "I'm afraid I do have to get back to work."

"Can I be of any assistance? I often help my father with his newspaper duties." Daphne shock her head. "I'm sure I shouldn't have said that. I'm too forward, or at least that's what my grandmother is always telling me. I know in England young ladies aren't expected to do much but sit still and keep out of the way."

"And in America?"

"I prefer being useful."

Daphne noticed the silence. Where before there had been chatter and quills scratching paper, now there was nothing. Everyone else had stopped what they were doing to listen in on her conversation with Mr. Ellis. Mr. Ellis shook his head at Roberts and Wellesley, who were standing across the room, smirking as though they shared a secret joke in which he and Daphne were the punch line.

"Thank you very kindly, Miss Meriwether, but my notes are in Pitman shorthand and wouldn't make sense to anyone who hadn't studied it. People speak rather quickly, so journalists use shorthand to keep up with what the speakers say while covering speeches or debates."

Daphne sat in Mr. Ellis' chair, leaned over the dabs and scribbles of his notes, and read:

"My Lords, it is a satisfaction to me and a circumstance which will very much shorten the observations it is my duty to make, that in moving the second reading of a Bill, the object of which is to establish a system of national education throughout England and Wales, I need not, in the present political and social position of the country, detain your Lordships by any arguments as to the importance of the spread of education, or as to the advantage to be derived not merely by those immediately affected..."

She picked up his quill, filled it with ink, and began writing. Mr. Ellis watched over her shoulder.

"Where on earth did you learn shorthand?"

"From my father. He was always busy transcribing his notes when he worked for the New York Times so I asked him to teach me so I could help him. Like I said, I prefer being useful." She finished transcribing the page she held. "I don't understand how my grandmother lives the way she does. It must be so tiresome to have a brain in your head and no cause to use it."

"I wouldn't go so far as to say your grandmother doesn't use her brain. Lady Staton is one of the most formidable women I've ever met. Even with her ear horn." Edward mimicked holding an ear trumpet to his head and said, in his best Lady Staton impersonation, "I heard you, Frederick. You needn't shout." Daphne laughed so loudly that the others stopped again to listen. "But I do see your point, Miss Meriwether. Lady Staton would be of no use to me at this moment, whereas you may be helpful. Are you sure you don't mind? It wouldn't please your grandmother to know you spent an after-noon in London transcribing notes in a grubby little office instead of at the dressmakers or the milliners."

"I wouldn't have offered if I minded, and my grandmother isn't here." She straightened up and spoke in a thin voice, as Mr. Ellis had, echoing Lady Staton's elongated vowels as well as she could. "Is that a thought in your head? Heavens, child, put that away this instant before you harm yourself!"

Mr. Ellis doubled over in laughter, as Daphne had after his Lady Staton impersonation. He stepped closer, perhaps aware of the prying eyes everywhere in the office, and whispered, "I think the thoughts in your head are quite grand, Miss Meri-wether, and I would never tell you to put them away." He picked up the chair he had knocked over, stood a second chair in front of the empty desk across from his, sharpened a pen, filled a second inkwell, and set them on the desk in front of Daphne. "If you're certain your father won't mind, I gladly accept your offer of help."

"I promise you, my father won't mind."

Daphne and Mr. Ellis settled down to work, and Daphne only needed to ask Mr. Ellis' meaning once or twice (Was that a dot for an ing or a crumb of toast? A crumb of toast? Very well. Was that a slash for an it or did your pen slip? An it? That's that I thought.). When they finished, Daphne realized her father and Pamela were watching her. Daphne kissed her father's cheek.

"I was helping Mr. Ellis transcribe his notes."

"So you were." Frederick smiled at Mr. Ellis. "My daughter is rather handy to have around, isn't she?"

"You should hire her as an editor here."

"Even my father isn't that forward thinking," said Daphne.

Frederick shook his finger at his daughter. "You never know what ideas I have lurking in this creaky brain of mine.

For example, I was going to invite young Mr. Ellis here to Staton House for dinner, but when I saw Mitchell Chattaway earlier he said you were dining with his family tonight."

"I didn't know you were going to see Mr. Chattaway, Papa," Daphne said. "I would have gone with you so I could see Christina." Again, Mr. Ellis' complexion faltered from pale white to ruby red. "You do have an engagement with the Chattaways, Mr. Ellis?"

Mr. Ellis staggered as he had when he knocked over his chair. "An engagement with the Chattaways. Of course, yes. I was so busy I had forgotten."

Frederick clasped the young man's shoulder. "I shouldn't worry. There will be other opportunities for you to visit Staton House, and you'll have a pleasant time with the Chattaways. Chattaway is an agreeable man, and his daughters are pleasant company. His wife is...shall we say enthusiastic...but she means well when all is said and done."

"You'll come to dinner some other time then?" Daphne asked.

"I would love nothing better," said Mr. Ellis.

Frederick looked at his daughter and smiled.

MISS CHATTAWAY

*E*dward arrived at the Chattaways' home on Theobalds Road near Gray's Inn in a state of panic. Normally, he crossed the street and knocked on the door in hopeful anticipation of the company inside. The happy laughter in the Chattaway home had always been music to his ears since it was too quiet in his solitary bachelor's flat. But that night Edward paced the pavement in front of the house, looking at the door, walking toward the door, changing his mind, walking away for good, walking back for good, standing still, leaving again, too confounded to think one complete thought from beginning to end. Of course he should have his dinner with the family as he was expected to, but the obvious answer was no longer the simplest answer, or the right answer, for Edward. Since he first saw Daphne Meriwether at her grandfather's funeral nothing was simple or right. When the Chattaways' curtains fluttered as though they had been lifted and dropped, he forced himself to the door, though he stood with his curled fist hanging midair for the longest time. Suddenly, the door flew open and

Maribel, at 12 the youngest Chattaway, grabbed his hand and led him inside.

Maribel took Edward's coat and hat and led him into the parlor, a busy-looking room with cream damask curtains, French country chairs, and short tables with vases of sun-colored lilies. In the corner stood a Broadwood boudoir piano on which Felicity, the second oldest at 17, was playing an upbeat tune Edward couldn't name. Standing next to the piano and turning the sheet music was Julia, 14. Edward looked for Christina, the eldest, but didn't see her.

"Edward Ellis, you naughty boy! Where have you been hiding?" Mrs. Chattaway rolled into the room, her wide mauve dress forming a full circle around her ample figure and giving her a ball-like appearance. She clasped her hands under her chin. "Christina! Mr. Chattaway! Our dearest Edward has come!"

When Edward turned Mitchell Chattaway was there to shake his hand.

"It's been far too long, that is true. I hear they're keeping you rather busy at the Observer. I never will forgive Barden for stealing you away from the London Quarterly Review. You were a great loss, Edward."

"You're at The Times now. I think you've done quite well without me."

"Yes," interposed Mrs. Chattaway, "but Christina may not be doing quite as well."

"Now, now, Mrs. Chattaway," said Mr. Chattaway, "we ought not to make Edward feel guilty. He's been hard at work from what I gathered from Mr. Meriwether."

"I think Mr. Meriwether ought to be more mindful of our dearest Edward's time. Mr. Meriwether ought to be more respectful of Edward's duties here. What kind of person is this Mr. Meriwether that he impedes so on our Edward?"

"Mr. Meriwether is brother to the Earl of Staton, my dear. You know that."

"You're quite right, Mr. Chattaway, quite right. Why, when I had tea with the Countess of Staton we discussed how you helped Mr. Meriwether settle into his role as a London editor. 'Lady Staton,' I says, 'Lady Staton, my husband Mr. Chattaway was invaluable to Mr. Meriwether as he settled into his newspaper duties in London. I don't know how Mr. Meriwether would have got on without my Mr. Chattaway.'"

"And what did Lady Staton say?" Edward asked.

"She nodded in the most genteel manner. You can always tell breeding." Mrs. Chattaway waved frantically toward the empty stairs. "Christina, I said come! Edward is here!" When silence ensued, Mrs. Chattaway went in search of her eldest daughter.

"Edward!" cried Maribel. "Come and see the new sheet music. Felicity wants to know what you want to hear."

Edward joined the girls by the piano, and as he read over the titles on the sheet music he heard Mrs. Chattaway speaking sharply to someone, who must have been Christina, the only Chattaway unaccounted for. In a moment, Miss Chattaway was there, and from her downcast eyes, he guessed something was wrong.

Mrs. Chattaway prodded Christina's shoulder. "Say hello to Edward, dear. He's come to see you."

"He's come to see all of us, Mamma," Christina said.

Christina's gold hair was pulled into two braids wrapped around her head and left to fall down her back like a two-tailed serpent. She wore a brown silk dress trimmed with light blue faille and silk fringe, and she was very pretty in her way, Edward thought. He had certainly been struck by her when he first met her. Now there was a heaviness about her, a sadness perhaps.

Mrs. Chattaway pressed Christina closer to Edward. "I saw you admiring our Christina's new dress, Edward. Isn't it lovely?"

"Mamma…" Christina shook her head.

"Now, Christina, Edward ought to see that only the very best for our eldest daughter will do. It's from Worth, you know, in Paris. This slimmer look is all the latest fashion, though I," she gestured to the ball-like dress she wore, "prefer the older silhouette."

"Thank you for that, Mrs. Chattaway," said Mr. Chattaway. "We were dying to know."

A simple dinner of pheasant soup, mixed game pie, curried rabbit, and braised ham was presented, and afterward Edward helped himself to one more cup of boiling-hot punch than he should have. He had come to feel at home with the Chattaways, but at this moment they seemed such strangers, even Christina, who should have been anything but a stranger to him. He found himself at a loss for what to say to her, or any of them, which left him filling his mouth with almond cake and another cup of punch. Mr. Chattaway asked him questions about his work, and Edward answered by rote, struggling to disguise how ill at ease he felt.

"I hear Fergusonandwately are considering publishing a collection of your stories," Mr. Chattaway said.

"How wonderful!" exclaimed Mrs. Chattaway. "You're going to be famous, Edward. That's excellent news, isn't it, Christina?"

"Nothing has been settled," Edward said.

"And to think," said Mrs. Chattaway, "we'll be practically family with the Countess of Staton now that dear Christina is going to be married to the grandson of her butler."

"Now Mrs. Chattaway," said her husband, "I hardly think Lady Staton would see it that way."

But Mrs. Chattaway would not be deterred. While Mr. and Mrs. Chattaway debated the point, Edward sat on the settee next to Christina.

"Are you feeling well?" he asked. "You don't seem yourself this evening."

"I am very much myself, Edward." Christina looked him in the eyes for the first time that evening. "Pappa said you were invited to Staton House."

"I was, but I had already made arrangements to come here."

"Do you want to be here?"

"Whatever do you mean?"

Christina spoke to the rug beneath her feet. "I met them when they first arrived in England, Mr. and Miss Meriwether. Mamma was beside herself, having the son of the Countess of Staton in her very own home, dining at her very own table, even if he is, in Mamma's words, only the second son. Mamma's been boasting of it to anyone who will listen, just as she boasts of paying a call to Lady Staton."

Mrs. Chattaway overheard them. "Why shouldn't I boast about having the man who is now brother to the Earl of Staton to my very own home? Why shouldn't I boast about having tea with Lady Staton? Now we're going to have a man of letters in the family, and I'll boast of that as well. Why shouldn't people know about our good fortune? Of course, you realize that Edward wouldn't be the first man of letters in our family. I had an uncle who was a man of letters (or was it litters?) who brought great honor upon the family. He once attended a garden party where he saw Lord Littleworth playing cricket!"

Mrs. Chattaway's eyes were thin glints as she studied Edward and Christina. She stood and nodded at the door. "Let's leave Edward and Christina so they can have a quiet conversation without everyone hovering about."

"That isn't necessary," Edward said.

"I wonder if it's proper, Mamma," said Christina.

"Nonsense! You're engaged, after all, and it's been too long since you've visited, Edward dear." Mrs. Chattaway rolled toward the doorway. "Mr. Chattaway and I will pop back in a moment."

Christina watched her fingers twist in her lap. "I think she's lovely."

"Who?"

"Miss Meriwether. I think we were lifelong friends by the time Mamma and I finished paying our call at Hembry Castle. Mamma thinks she's too forward, but I think she's simply being friendly. She has such an easy way about her. They do things differently in America, don't they?"

"I believe so. I didn't realize you knew Miss Meriwether so well."

"You saw her when you went to Hembry Castle to meet the publishers?" It was a statement disguised as a question. Edward nodded. Christina twisted her fingers into such knots he wondered if she would ever free them. "You haven't come here to visit since you went to Hembry for the funeral. Was that the first time you saw her?"

"Yes."

"She's interested in you, you know."

"Interested how?"

"She mentioned you, not by name, but I knew she was speaking of you. I think she's intrigued, but she is returning to America soon."

"You didn't tell her we're engaged?"

"She knows I'm engaged, but I didn't say it was you. Should I tell her?"

"I think...I mean..." He sighed.

"She wants us to visit her after she returns home. She said we should honeymoon in Connecticut."

"I've always wanted to visit America."

Edward wished he could guess what Christina was thinking, but for whatever reason the hearts and minds of those closest to us are often the hardest to understand. Where we can guess what a stranger is thinking or feeling with relative ease, often those we know best are shut off to us like a door slammed in our faces. But Edward was as guilty of closing himself down as anyone, he knew. Christina was such a nice girl, sweet and kind in her way, never pressing him. Things were the way they were, and that was enough for her. It was this simplicity Edward had been drawn to, thinking he would have a quiet, comfortable life after he married her. Now she surprised him with her astute judgment on the subject of Miss Meriwether. His grandmother had always told him that women had a sense all their own concerning matters of the heart. Now he knew that was true.

Edward took Christina's hand. 'I could have gone to Staton House tonight, but as you can see, I've chosen to be here with you. Besides, what would the niece of the Earl of Staton want with me? I'm a journalist who's the grandson of her family's servants. Lady Staton wants Miss Meriwether to make a grand match, which excludes me. Not," he kissed Christina's hand, "that I needed exclusion. Miss Meriwether is nothing to me."

Christina clutched Edward's hand. Her pulled brow relaxed and her shoulders dropped. She smiled, and a pretty smile it was too. Edward sighed. He had convinced Christina that Miss Meriwether was nothing to him. Now he only had to convince himself.

STATON HOUSE

The next day when Edward arrived at the offices of the Daily Observer he found a note on his desk from Mr. Meriwether. Edward was expected at Staton House that afternoon for luncheon. Staton House! It was less than a day since he promised Christina that Miss Meriwether was nothing to him. Already the memory of that promise was slipping away.

Wellesley and Roberts, one over each of Edward's shoulders, read the note and snickered.

"You're invited to Staton House for luncheon," said Wellesley.

"Apparently so," Edward said.

Wellesley snatched the note from Edward's hands. "First you win over the brother of the Earl of Staton, now the Earl himself. Soon it will be the Prince of Wales, and then Her Majesty the Queen."

Roberts sat in Edward's chair, legs crossed, face expressionless. When he spoke he pronounced his words in elongated tones this side of nasal.

"I say! Egads! Crikey! Blimey!" Roberts mimed holding a teacup with his pinky finger stretched toward the ceiling. "You see, my good man, I went round to Hembry Castle for a spot of tea with the Earl of Staton, and the Earl was quite well when I saw him, quite well. We had a laugh with the old boys Jiggy and Beaker while we were out shooting things and then we ate them for dinner. That's the things we ate for dinner, not Jiggy and Beaker. What!"

Edward grabbed his note from Wellesley, laughing despite himself. "If you must know, it wasn't Lord Staton who invited me but Mr. Meriwether."

"Mr. Meriwether or his pretty daughter?" Roberts winked at Edward.

"I don't think Miss Chattaway would approve," said Wellesley.

"Not that it's any of your concern, but I saw Miss Chattaway last night and she's perfectly at ease with my acquaintance with Miss Meriwether. She and Miss Meriwether are great friends."

"Miss Chattaway has never seen your face when Miss Meriwether is near."

Without another word, Edward stomped down the stairs, pushed through the exterior door, and stopped near the L of Gough Square, struggling to pull air into his lungs, his throat was so tight. He was blinded by the late summer sun, realizing too late that he had left his hat at his desk. He wasn't going back now. He wouldn't be mocked by the likes of Roberts and Wellesley about something as innocuous as a simple luncheon. Edward used his hand to shield his eyes as he watched the people jostle toward the drivers who blocked the main thoroughfare with their cabs. Though Edward could find his way around London blindfolded, he was suddenly at a loss about where to go. He felt naked without his hat, which, to be fair, he nearly was. Only the working classes went without hats, and then only when it couldn't be helped. Edward knew he should go back to get the offending article, but he was stubborn. Perhaps he should deny the accusations, giving Roberts and Wellesley a good telling-off, but it was too late now, and he knew everyone in the office was having a good laugh at his expense. Oh well. He had had enough laughs at theirs. Hatless, he turned down St. Dunstan's Court and walked toward Fleet Street. He wondered if he had a moment to go home for a new hat but decided against it. He didn't want to be late to see Mr. Meriwether. Then, in a panic he realized he didn't know where he was going. He pulled the note from his pocket and saw the West End address on Park Lane.

Edward decided he had time to walk the three miles if he kept a brisk pace, which was good since he needed the exercise to clear his head. He headed west along the Mall, past St. James' Park, past Buckingham Palace to the east side of Hyde Park and Park Lane. Edward stopped at the edge of the green expanse, looking at the people out for a drive, indulging in their moment to see and be seen. The women inside the carriages looked straight head with great dignity, feigning not to notice the women in the other carriages as those inhabitants did the same. He found Staton House easily enough, Number 10 Park Lane, the white Georgian with its arched doorway and the large windows that let in the green of the park. Edward laughed when his grandfather opened the door.

"Hello, sir," said the elder Mr. Ellis. "May I take your coat and...? Might I inquire after the location of your hat?"

"It's at the office. Don't ask." He grasped his grandfather's hand. "I didn't know you were here, Grandfather."

"I arrived last night. Come in."

Edward walked into the reception room where his grandfather took his coat. With the high, molded ceilings, white walls, and large windows, there was a brightness to Staton House that Hembry Castle lacked.

"What brings you to London, Grandfather?"

"I had some pressing news for Mr. Frederick. Her ladyship thought it would be best if I told him myself."

"Is everything all right?"

"Mr. Frederick will have everything under control."

Edward grasped his grandfather's arm. "Is Miss Meriwether all right?"

"Miss Meriwether? Oh yes, she's perfectly well. It's his lordship."

"Is Lord Staton well?"

Mr. Ellis straightened his jacket as though he were reminding himself of his butler's duties. "For now, let's say that Mr. Frederick is doing everything he can to help his lordship. I assume," Mr. Ellis looked sternly at his grandson, "that this news will not leave this room."

"I'll be the soul of discretion."

Mr. Ellis showed Edward into the sage-green sitting room with green and blue carpets and mahogany furniture. "Mr. Frederick asked me to give you his apologies. His business has taken longer than he expected, though he sent word that he'll return shortly. He asked Miss Daphne to keep you company in the meantime." Mr. Ellis gestured to the sage-green sofa. "Would you care for some tea?"

"Yes. Thank you, Grandfather."

Edward studied the paintings on the walls—regal-looking, well-dressed, long-nosed aristocrats, fine-standing horses, and one portrait of a golden retriever. The bookcase caught his eye, and he examined the volumes. He was startled when a maid arrived with the tea tray.

"Shall I pour, sir?"

"No, thank you. I can manage."

"Mr. Ellis says to tell you Miss Daphne will join you directly."

"Thank you…"

"Anabel, sir."

"Thank you, Anabel."

The servants at Staton House were as good at disappearing as they were at Hembry Castle, and before Edward blinked Anabel was gone. He poured himself tea, admiring the blue thistle Royal Worcester set, wondering how many years of salary such a porcelain luxury would cost. As he glanced at the crown-wearing stamp on the bottom of the saucer Miss Meriwether appeared, a vision in lavender which brought out the violet in her eyes. Edward tried to stand and smiled sheepishly when he realized he was already standing and had only succeeded in making himself look a half-inch taller. He was enthralled at the sight of her until he gave himself an internal lashing. Hadn't he just seen Christina the night before? Besides, the lovely young woman standing there was Daphne Meriwether. She lived in this grandeur, and he lived—well, he didn't live at Staton House. She was the niece of the Earl of Staton. He was Edward Ellis, grandson of the butler and housekeeper of the Earl of Staton. Again, he thought of Christina. It was always a surprise how easily he could forget her when Miss Meriwether was there.

"I'm sorry to keep you waiting," she said. "I was downstairs showing Mrs. Bucket, our cook, how to make American-style biscuits."

"Are American-style biscuits so very different than our biscuits?"

"What you call biscuits we call cookies."

"Cookies? That's a great word. Cookies."

"It comes from the Dutch word 'koekje' or so I've been told."

"You're a linguist as well."

"Hardly. When Americans say biscuits we mean something more like a scone, though maybe a bit heartier. Come to the kitchen and you can try one."

Edward followed Miss Meriwether down the stairs. He passed the servants' hall, more compact than the one at Hembry Castle, and saw a footman and a maid huddled too close for propriety near the table. Miss Meriwether must have seen them as well because she turned to Edward with a conspirator's grin which he found positively endearing. Edward smelled something comforting coming from the oven, and Mrs. Bucket, the Staton House cook, shook her graying hairs, the ones sticking out from her cap, at Edward.

"Are we on parade now?" Mrs. Bucket asked.

"This is Mr. Ellis," Daphne said. "He works for my father at the newspaper. I invited him down to try an American-style biscuit." Daphne opened the oven, took two oven towels, and pulled out the tray.

Mrs. Bucket shook her head. "Too much flour if you ask me. Looks like you're baking bricks."

"If I've done everything correctly they should be flaky and light." Miss Meriwether held her index finger in front of her mouth. "Ssh," she whispered. "Don't ever tell my grandmother you saw me doing this. You're both sworn to secrecy. Lady Staton would die of fright if she knew I baked my biscuits."

"Don't matter a toss to me," said Mrs. Bucket.

Edward bowed. "Your secret is safe with me, Miss Meriwether." He watched as she lifted a golden biscuit and set it on a white porcelain plate. "Do you enjoy cooking?" he asked.

"As a matter of fact, I do. My mother taught me. I cook for Papa all the time at home."

"Ohhh…" Mrs. Bucket slapped a white-floured hand to her

forehead, leaving a pasty ring above her eyes. "Ellis? Are you...?"

"My grandson."

Mr. Ellis stood in the doorway. "If you're going to be the guest of Mr. Frederick, Edward, then you should behave like the guest of Mr. Frederick and not like the grandson of the butler."

Miss Meriwether stepped between the butler and his grandson. "I'm sorry if I did wrong, Ellis. I asked him to come down to taste a biscuit." Miss Meriwether spooned some freshly churned butter into a bowl and set it on a platter. "Would you like to try one, Ellis?"

"No, thank you, Miss Daphne. And you need never apologize to me. You're still learning our ways, and I don't fault you at all. My grandson, on the other hand," he turned a sharp look onto Edward, "knows better."

The maid who had brought Edward his tea appeared. "Mr. Ellis, Mr. Frederick is home."

The senior Mr. Ellis waved Edward and Daphne toward the stairs. "You mustn't keep him waiting."

Miss Meriwether added the rest of the baked biscuits to the platter and led the way upstairs. Mr. Meriwether was in the sitting room pouring himself some tea from the pot Edward left behind. He kissed his daughter's cheek when she appeared.

"Uncle Richard?" Miss Meriwether asked.

Mr. Meriwether shrugged and left it there. He nodded at the platter of biscuits, grabbed one, slathered it with butter, and took a bite. "A taste of home."

"Is America home?" Miss Meriwether asked.

"It's my chosen home. It's strange to think of now, but for a long time I thought of myself as an Englishman living in America with his beautiful American family. But since we've been back I realized I'm more Americanized than I knew. I feel as though I'm a visitor here."

"Is it better in America?" Edward asked.

"Not better," Miss Meriwether said. "Different."

"Different how?"

"There's no aristocracy in America, at least not officially. There are no lords and ladies, no House of Lords, no rules of etiquette, or if there are they aren't as pronounced as they are here."

"That might not be entirely true," said Mr. Meriwether. "Those in New York Society have their rules of etiquette, surely. I've heard Mrs. Rhinelander and her lot are rather strict about following rules, even more so than we are here, if that's even possible."

"Fortunately for me, I was not part of that scene. My mind spins in confusion every time Grandma corrects me."

Mr. Meriwether gestured to the sofa. "Sit down, both of you, please." When everyone was comfortable, Mr. Meriwether rang for a fresh pot of tea. "Thank you for coming this afternoon, Edward. May I call you Edward?"

"Of course."

"And you will call me Frederick." When Edward tried to protest Mr. Meriwether waved his hand. "Please, Edward, I insist that we must be equally on a Christian name basis. Having lived in America for as long as I have all this formality is wearing on me."

"If you insist, then I'll certainly concede."

"There you are. Good man. Now, you're probably wondering why I asked you here this afternoon. As it happens, recent events concerning my brother the Earl lead me to believe I'll be detained at Hembry Castle for some weeks, and I need to know that I leave the newspaper in capable hands. I want you to take over as acting editor." Frederick paused, allowing Edward a moment to take in the news. "As acting editor, you'll be in charge of day-to-day operations, and all final decisions will be yours. I know this is very sudden, and I've only been at the Observer a short time myself, but you were the first person I thought of when I realized I wouldn't be able to come to London as often as I'd like. Will you do it?"

"It's a great opportunity," Miss Meriwether said. "To be the acting editor of the Daily Observer? At your age? It will help your prestige, and maybe even encourage Fergusonandwately to publish that collection of your stories."

Edward sipped his tea as a way to allow himself time to think. Finally, he said, "I'm certain there are those who have been at the paper longer than I who should be considered first."

Frederick finished the rest of his biscuit in one bite and helped himself to another. "The truth is, Edward, you and I have been working closely together, and I know that of all the staff you're the one with an eye for the bigger picture. You have your finger on the pulse of what people want to read. And the original stories you've written are among the paper's most widely read. Circulation has gone up since your stories started appearing. Of course, if you don't feel comfortable taking on the assignment, I certainly understand, but I want you to know I have no doubts about your ability. I know you'll keep the ship sailing smoothly." Frederick turned to Mr. Ellis, who was standing silently by the tea tray. "What do you say, Ellis? Do you believe this young man would be capable as the editor of the Daily Observer?"

"I believe that young man can do anything he sets his mind to, Mr. Frederick."

Miss Meriwether leaned toward Edward. He was distracted by her rosewater fragrance.

"There, you see. We all know you can do it. What do you say?"

Edward wanted to kiss her hand, at the very least, though he restrained himself since his grandfather and Mr. Meriwether were watching. "I'm most grateful for your offer, Mr. Meriwether. I'm happy to accept. I won't let you down."

"I know you won't. And it's Frederick, please."

Luncheon was ready, and Edward laughed when Frederick carried the plate of biscuits with him to the dining room. While the meal—the soup, the salad, the ham—were all delicious, the part that stood out to Edward was the biscuits baked by Miss Meriwether's own hands. They were indeed light and flaky, yet hearty, as though one biscuit would make a meal unto itself. He nodded after every bite.

"So you approve of my American-style biscuits?" Miss Meriwether asked. Something about the way her jewel eyes sparkled and her lips parted took his breath away.

"I approve heartily, Miss Meriwether."

Frederick helped himself to another biscuit. "Sitting here reminds me how awkward I felt when I first arrived in New York. As much as I had always longed to leave Hembry, I found myself out of place in America. For a while I thought I had been too impulsive in my haste to leave England. I thought it would be easier in America than it was. I was so frustrated I began looking for any excuse to return to England. Then, one day I was leaving the office on Park Row and I saw the most beautiful young woman—fair complexion, golden hair, eyes like amethysts. Sound like anyone we know?"

Yes! Edward wanted to leap out of his chair, but he felt his grandfather drilling a hole into the back of his skull with the intensity of his butler's glare.

"I was as struck by the young woman's beauty as it's possible to be, and then, as I had the chance to get to know her,

I realized her physical beauty was merely an external manifestation of the beautiful person she was inside. In that one moment of happenstance, I found my reason to stay in New York and I never looked back." Frederick took his daughter's hand and beamed at her with fatherly pride. With luncheon finished, he stood from the table. "If you'll both excuse me, I have some business to tend to before we leave for Hembry."

"I should be leaving as well," Edward said.

Frederick stopped by the door. "Edward, I'll come to the office later to tell everyone the news. If they give you any problems, tell me and I'll see to it at once."

Edward bowed to Frederick, then followed Miss Meriwether from the dining room. He stopped when he saw a stack of crates labeled 'Daphne's Room' lined up against the wall.

"Are you returning to America so soon?" He gestured at the crates.

"These are arriving, not returning. Some of my things were misplaced somewhere along the journey. They finally arrived this morning. Should we see what's inside?"

Mr. Ellis stepped from the shadows. "Shall I get the envelope opener, Miss Daphne?"

"Certainly, Ellis. Thank you."

Edward watched his grandfather leave. "I apologize for my grandfather, Miss Meriwether. I can see you're still disconcerted by the way he appears suddenly, out of the mist it seems."

"I'm getting used to it. And must it still be Miss Meriwether? If you can call my father Frederick, then you can call me Daphne, surely. We're much quicker to use first names, or Christian names as you say, where I live."

"Doesn't that lead to a false sense of intimacy? As though you're close to someone you hardly know?"

"I've never thought of it like that. We don't have the

distinction of rank the way you do here, so most people are Mr. or Mrs. or Miss so it isn't as necessary to acknowledge someone's title. I think my father was right about New York Society. They're certainly prim and proper about using titles and following rules, but in my quiet town where everyone knows everyone else we call each other by our first names. I hope you and I are good enough friends by now that I'm not being too forward if I said I'd prefer it if you called me Daphne."

"And you must call me Edward."

Mr. Ellis returned with the envelope opener on a silver tray. Daphne sliced the top of the crate and Edward saw the books inside. Daphne pulled the volumes out and smiled as though they were long-lost friends.

"I'm so glad these finally made it. I was sad to think I had lost them forever."

Edward sat on the floor beside Daphne to see the titles better. He helped pull the volumes from the crate—Ivanhoe by Sir Walter Scott, The Swiss Family Robinson by Johann David Wyss, and Tales from Shakespeare by Charles Lamb and Mary Lamb. Everything by Shakespeare. Everything by Dickens. "You have excellent taste. These are among my favorite books."

Daphne pulled a tattered volume from the bottom of the pile, and Edward saw the title, A Vindication of the Rights of Woman by Mary Wollstonecraft. "My mother gave this to me, as her mother had given it to her. Education is an important issue to me as it is to you. Wollstonecraft talks about how women have the right to an education if for no other reason than they are the first educators of their children. She also said women who are educated are better partners for their husbands instead of mere property or ornament. Do you find her ideas shocking?"

"Not at all. In fact, I quite agree. It goes back to when we were speaking about education—everyone has the right to be educated, rich and poor, male and female."

Daphne nodded, and Edward guessed she liked what he said. He had to pull his eyes away from her, his grandfather was standing behind them, so he looked back into the crate and saw the gold writing on the green-pebbled cloth, One Thousand and One Nights.

"It was one of my favorites," Daphne said. "I think 'Aladdin's Wonderful Lamp' and 'Ali Baba and the Forty Thieves' are the best stories in the collection. Have you read it?"

"Read it? I think this book saved my life when I was a child. I could escape into it and forget about..." He looked at his grandfather, whose right eyebrow was raised in caution over his spectacles.

"What did you need to forget about?" Daphne grimaced. "It's none of my business. I apologize for my American curiosity."

"Curiosity is important, I believe. It keeps you interested in life."

"You must be interested in life since you're a writer."

"I am, as it happens. Watching people, trying to understand why they make the choices they do, why they act as they do, why they say what they say and why they don't say what they mean, is fascinating. My desire to write stories stems from the many books I read as a child, I suppose. Those books became more real to me than the world I lived in. How much more fulfilling it was to be part of Sinbad's world or the Swiss Family Robinsons' than to be where I was. I always had crazy daydreams floating through my brain at any and all times of the day. I was always making up stories about the people I saw, and when I began working as a journalist I decided it was time to start writing down those odd imaginings."

"I understand exactly what you mean," Daphne said. "I

wasn't unhappy as a child, not at all, but I think all children want to have their imaginations stirred. And look at what a fine writer you've become, Edward Ellis. All because you loved books as a boy."

The desire to kiss her burned his lips, but a stout "Ahem!" from his grandfather returned his thoughts to more appropriate places.

"What have you been reading lately?" Edward asked.

"I've been rereading Mr. Dickens mostly. I still can't believe he's gone. Have you read the final number of Drood yet?"

"I have. What did you think?"

"I wish he had lived long enough to finish it."

Edward turned a copy of David Copperfield over in his hands. "So who killed Drood? Roberts, Wellesley, and I had quite a conversation about it at the office."

"How do you know Edwin Drood is dead? As far as we know, as far as we'll ever know, he may be murdered or he may be missing. Maybe he grew tired of it all and ran away. As my Uncle Richard says, Mr. Dickens would have his flights of fancy."

"Unfortunately, it seems The Mystery of Edwin Drood is destined to remain a mystery. What else have you been reading?"

"Since I've been here I've been reading about British history. That's one thing England has over America—your history is so much more fascinating than ours. England has such a long and extraordinary past with all your battles for the crown. Some of your history sounds like fairy tales to me. You have such riveting stories, kings like Henry VIII. Our history hardly compares."

Edward's grandfather chuckled in the shadows.

"Didn't your Civil War end fairly recently?" Edward asked.

"I try not to think about it," Daphne said. "It wasn't easy, listening to the death tolls, watching the black wreaths go up on the doors, learning of the loss of young men we knew. I thought I was trapped in a nightmare whenever I read about how horribly both sides behaved toward each other. Americans versus Americans, and they were so cruel. My father was running the New York Times when the war broke out, and he'd come home looking like he'd seen a ghost, he was so full of bad news from the front. Half the time he didn't even want to tell me what he heard. My mother died near the end of the war. From consumption."

"I'm very sorry," Edward said. Daphne looked so far away suddenly, and Edward wanted desperately to bring her back. "Our wars were much the same. They fought for kings and queens, but otherwise war is war. All wars are senseless in their own ways."

Edward thought Daphne looked very young and very wise at that moment, as though he could sense her joy but he could feel her sadness too. We all have our sadnesses, he thought. It's the way we handle them that makes us or breaks us. If he hadn't admitted to himself that he was in love with her before, now Edward was helpless against his feelings. I am in love with Daphne Meriwether, he thought. I cannot hide from it any longer. He looked up from the book in his hand to see his grandfather watching him, the accusatory eyebrow still hanging above the spectacles.

DINNER AT HEMBRY CASTLE

*E*dward took over the editorial duties at the Daily Observer with fervor, keeping everyone on task and making sure the printers were on time. He put out word that he was hiring for his reporter position, and a few names had come his way. He was good at this, Edward, as Frederick Meriwether had predicted, and there was some satisfaction in being the youngest editor in London (he was still only four-and-twenty). Yet no matter how well he handled his tasks, no matter how well oiled his newspaper machine, no matter that Fergusonandwately had very nearly said yes to publishing a collection of his stories, there was still a whinging inside his brain, some want he was afraid to name. He was used to longing for things. When he decided to make his way in the world through his own volition he became stubborn, working harder than everyone else, faster than everyone else. He was the first to arrive at the office and the last to leave, writing his own stories in whatever spare time he could scrape together. He had a complete vision for his life, including whom he would marry and how they would live. Now here was Daphne, and she was no inchoate concept of the future. She was real, she was there, and though he still convinced himself there was no way, he wanted to be near her. At that moment she was in the country at Hembry Castle, and though it wasn't so very far, it was far enough, and he had to fight the distraction that thinking of her brought on. He had to be on his toes at the newspaper since everyone's eyes were on him.

Frederick had left him in charge over others who were older and more experienced, and the others who were older and more experienced didn't hide their animosity. Men can gossip as well as women and with equal vehemence. That whippersnapper Ellis is nothing but an upstart—the grandson of servants! How can this boy (who hasn't even grown a beard) tell me what to do? Edward handled the men with patience and humor, the way Mr. Meriwether had, and after a few weeks, the jagged agitation settled to a mildly irritated hum as the men found Edward knowledgeable with an eye for detail and able to handle the demands of the job. Occasionally, Edward still heard a mumble or two directed his way, but he focused on his work, not the approval of others, and soon even the mumbles died away.

Of everyone in the office, Wellesley was the one who seemed to take Edward's advancement the hardest, as though Edward's promotion was a personal insult directed at him (people are not always happy for you when good things happen). Two months after Edward had taken over the newspaper, Wellesley walked into Edward's office and fell haphazardly into the chair on the other side of the desk. Edward didn't know what to make of Wellesley. Some days Wellesley had nothing but clipped words, and other days he was full of high spirits—talkative, easy to laugh, and there were glimmers of their friendship from days gone by. What mood was

Wellesley in today? Edward held his breath while he waited. Wellesley rested his boots on Edward's desk and smiled.

"How are things, Mr. Ellis?"

"I can't complain, Mr. Wellesley."

"And how is the Earl of Staton?"

"I wouldn't know. I haven't seen him. How is the Queen?"

"Still in mourning, poor old girl. You'd think she'd be past it by now, but there it is. How is Miss Meriwether?"

"As far as I know she's well. I haven't seen her either. You're asking because…?"

"Just wondering. You know pretty girls like that are usually grabbed up by some Lord Howdeedo."

Edward sighed. "Is there something I can do for you?"

"Not at all. I just wanted a word with my best mate."

"Are we best mates?"

"Perhaps. How is Miss Chattaway?"

"She's well, thank you."

"And you've set a date?"

"A date?"

"For the wedding. Certainly, you haven't forgotten about the wedding where you'll marry Miss Chattaway?"

"I haven't forgotten about the wedding, and the date is none of your business. I apologize, Mr. Wellesley, but I'm rather busy at the moment."

Edward opened the door, and Wellesley bowed and left. Edward's head pounded, so he poured himself a glass of water and held the glass to his forehead. When his racing heart settled he called to the others since it was time for the edition to go off to the printer's. After the edition was sent there was a ten-minute lull, and then the bustle began for the next edition. Several important decisions were looming, and Edward had a sudden thought. He felt perfectly capable of making those decisions, though he decided the others would accept his decisions more easily if Mr. Meriwether approved. Edward could send a telegram, but no. After all, Hembry wasn't so very far by train, and he could be there and back before anyone missed him. He didn't need a lot of Mr. Meriwether's time, just a quick signature or two.

Edward told Tewson to keep an eye on things while he was gone. When Tewson agreed, Edward grabbed his hat and left at a sprint, walking from Gough Square to Red Lion Court to Fleet Street until he hailed a hansom cab. Since the cab was unoccupied, Edward waved at the driver and shouted directions, to no response. Edward realized the man was soothing his whinnying horse, who appeared dazed by the London traffic, as though he, the horse, couldn't believe how busy the streets were that time of day. As the driver spoke babyish words, Edward grew impatient.

"If you're not able to take me to King's Cross, then I'll..."

The driver turned to Edward. "Did you need to get somewhere, young man?"

Edward sighed. "King's Cross."

"Why didn't you say so? Hop in!"

The horse took off at a bolt before Edward was seated. The cab raced down the street, dodging every person, every vehicle, every stray dog or cat, as though its wheels were on fire and it was racing toward Hell itself. Edward fell against the seat with a painful thud and held on for dear life, watching Gray's Inn Road with only one eye. So it's true, Edward thought as the cab thundered down the street. You do see your life flash before your eyes when you're going to die. "Yoho!" the driver yelled, and the horse went faster. Ladies screamed and men cursed as they jumped out of the path of the wayward vehicle while the driver looked on, unconcerned, pressing the horse faster, as if saying this was the way it had to be and such is life. Edward, his fingers aching from grasping onto whatever he could hold, stared with his one eye through the window to see if the wheels were on fire after all. He saw no flames, though he was certain there were sparks from the feet of the people leaping out of the way. Suddenly, the cab screeched to a halt.

"King's Cross!" the driver yelled. The man turned to Edward and named his price. Edward would have gladly paid that and twicefold more in gratitude—after all, he did arrive at his destination in one piece. Edward steadied his legs and caught his breath, pleased to discover that he had survived the journey without any visible injuries.

When he arrived at the servants' entrance at Hembry Castle the little maid Jemima opened the door. She let him in, calling one of the other maids to fetch Mr. or Mrs. Ellis. In a moment, Mrs. Ellis arrived.

"Neddie! What a surprise." She eyed her grandson. "Shall I tell her you're here?"

"Her?"

"Miss Daphne."

"Don't be silly, Grandmother. I'm here to see Mr. Meriwether."

"Is he expecting you?"

"He…I…"

"I see."

Edward followed his grandmother into the servants' hall. Mrs. Ellis gestured for Edward to sit at the table. She spoke softly so no one could overhear. "She's beautiful, Neddie. She's a wonderful person, a kind person. In many ways, she's everything I would have wanted in a wife for you. But she's Lord Staton's niece. You know what that means."

"I don't believe Daphne would marry a man simply because her grandmother told her to."

"Daphne?"

"Miss Meriwether. She has her own mind, and I don't see her being particularly impressed with a man simply because of his lineage."

"I don't know, Edward. What about those American heiresses her ladyship keeps talking about? Those young women seem very happy to have an English husband with a title. They've come here solely to try to catch one."

"But Daphne's not like that. She was laughing about the way her grandmother has been trying to get her to behave. And Mr. Meriwether isn't like the rest of his family either."

"No, he isn't. Now…" She turned at the voices behind her and saw Jemima and Ruth huddled together. "Can I help you?" The girls scampered away. Mrs. Ellis sighed. "It just goes to show, if you don't want anyone to hear what you say, don't say it."

Mr. Ellis joined them in the servants' hall. "And to what do we owe this visit?"

Edward shrugged. "I came to ask Mr. Meriwether…"

"I've been speaking to him, Augustus. I think he understands."

"I can't help seeing her," Edward said. "She's the daughter of the man I work for. It would be extremely rude of me not to speak to her when she and her father are together."

"Your grandmother and I are concerned about you, Edward, that's all."

Mrs. Ellis took her grandson's hand. "I feel like you're about to do something foolish, and I want you to be on your guard. I'm afraid Miss Daphne may have given you the wrong impression. She's less formal in her manners, and I think you might be taking her ways as interest."

"Because she could never be interested in me."

"That's not what I mean. Any young woman would be lucky to have you."

"Christina said Miss Meriwether showed an interest in me."

"When was this?" Mrs. Ellis asked.

"When Christina and her mother came to call on Lady Staton."

"Well," said Mrs. Ellis, "at least you remember the name of the young woman you're engaged to."

The kitchen maid stopped by the door, waiting for permission to come in. Mrs. Ellis waved and the girl set the tea tray on the table. Mrs. Ellis poured Edward's tea.

"You and Miss Chattaway will be very happy together, Neddie. I'm sure of it." She put the steaming cup in front of Edward, but he didn't touch it.

"If you'll excuse me," Mr. Ellis said. "I need to check on his lordship."

"How is he?" Mrs. Ellis asked. "He's seemed a bit taciturn since he's been home."

"Mr. Frederick is with him now."

"Let's hope Mr. Frederick can talk some sense into him."

Edward and his grandmother sat in silence over untouched teacups. In a moment, Mr. Ellis returned.

"I told his lordship and Mr. Frederick you were here, Edward, and they were adamant you stay for dinner. It seems you made a good impression on his lordship the last time you were here."

"I didn't bring a change of clothes," Edward said.

"You can borrow what you'll need from your grandfather," Mrs. Ellis said. "You're nearly the same size. I should warn you that her ladyship has invited several young men to dine tonight."

"Why?" Edward asked.

"Miss Daphne will be one-and-twenty next year, and her ladyship was concerned that there will be many younger, more blooming roses on display next Season. Her ladyship decided it would be all right to bend the rules a bit and introduce Miss Daphne to some eligible young men. Her ladyship thinks she'll be giving Miss Daphne a head start this way. I wouldn't expect her ladyship to bend the rules, ever, but she believes the potential grooms and their families will overlook the lack of Miss Daphne's presentation since she spent her life in America where her ladyship had no control over her upbringing."

Edward took a crumpet from the tray, smothered it in strawberry jam, then left it untouched on his plate. "So the race to find the highest bidder has begun?"

"I wanted you to know before you went upstairs."

"You don't have to go," said Mr. Ellis. "I can make your excuses."

"No," Edward said. "I'll go."

"You should change then," said Mrs. Ellis.

After Edward changed he felt even more uncomfortable than he already did. His grandfather's dress coat was made of black superfine cloth and lined with black glace silk—very handsome-looking but slightly large on Edward's frame. The black poplin waistcoat hung a little lower than it should have, and the black cashmere trousers itched some. He straightened his white tie, exhaled, and followed his grandfather upstairs.

DINNER AT HEMBRY CASTLE was a more formal occasion than luncheon, and Edward was fascinated as he watched the night's drama unfold. Tonight, his lordship was present, having returned from London, or Paris, or Timbuktu, or wherever it was he had disappeared to (no one was certain so rumors abounded). Mr. John Hough was there, along with others Edward remembered from luncheon: the black-haired, white-faced Poppers, a red carnation still fixed in his buttonhole, and

Carlton was there, his long mouth still pulled into a perpetual smile. Young Mr. Palmers wasn't present—presumably because the poor fellow hadn't recovered from his winking fit the last time he was at Hembry. That night Edward was introduced to other young men as well, one known as Patrick Warren, and another known as the Honorable Eamon Fronmer. George Hartwick, the future Duke of Norley, known in polite society as Lord Darges since he carried one of his father's lesser titles, was also present, along with two of his sisters, Lady Lorelai and Lady Ariadne Hartwick. His youngest sister, Lady Gertrude, was not invited. She had not yet been presented so she was invisible to Society—as Daphne should have been but for her grandmother's bending the rules. Lady Lorelai and Lady Ariadne looked like twins, Edward thought, both fair-haired and green-eyed, holding their turkey necks at awkward angles, their frames thin to the point of frailty. The future duke was a young man about Edward's age who constantly brushed his long fair hair from his pungent green eyes, and Edward pictured the future duke twirling his walrus mustache like a villain in a melodrama. When Daphne entered the drawing room wearing a mauve dinner dress with gold trim and ruffles at the bustle, everyone in the room turned while the Hartwick sisters snickered behind their fans. Edward guessed the snickers hid the jealousy the two plain girls must have felt in the presence of the lovely Daphne, who lit the room the way the sun brightened the sky.

For that night's dinner, her ladyship had been able to secure enough ladies to complement the number of gentlemen. After Edward's grandfather announced dinner everyone followed protocol and entered the dining room two-by-two, looking, as the Earl had said when Edward visited for luncheon, like animals herded onto Noah's Ark. There was a seriousness about it all as Lady Staton paired off the gentleman with the highest rank with the lady of the highest rank and so on down the line. Each pair followed in procession into the sunshine dining room where their seating arrangements were denoted by calligraphy cards. Edward had been paired with a Miss Soandso, who may have been an Honorable Someoneorother, he wasn't sure. At table, Miss Soandso sat to his right, while to his left was Lady Lorelai Hartwick, the future duke's sister, and he soon discovered that Lady Lorelai's job for the evening was to make her brother a most appealing marriage option for Daphne. Edward wanted to cover his ears, and his eyes, with his napkin while Lady Lorelai jabbered on about her brother, how he lately finished his studies at Oxford, only two years behind schedule, how his athletic accomplishments had no equal in England, how he is much loved by his companions, and how he is simply the greatest, kindest, most attentive brother in the world. Edward's dinner companion, Miss Soandso, who may be been an Honorable Someoneorother, shrugged at whatever Lady Lorelai said, more occupied with the roast on her plate than anything else.

Of course, Edward was too enamored by Daphne to think much about Miss Soandso. Daphne was polite to Lord Darges, who talked to no end about hunting expeditions at all the great houses and his close association with the nobility who lived in those houses. Was Daphne impressed by Lord Darges? Edward couldn't tell. The future Duke of Norley was languid in an aristocratic way, speaking about himself as though, while others might find him fascinating, he had yet to impress himself. Though he loathed to do so, Edward had to admit the future duke was a good-looking young man. Add to that his inherited land and a manor that put Hembry Castle to shame, and perhaps Daphne might be tempted after all.

Edward was pulled from his reverie by his grandfather's "Ahem!" as he poured wine into Edward's glass. Edward felt his cheeks blaze when he noticed the Countess of Staton watching him. Was his grandfather trying to warn him? Were his feelings for Daphne that obvious? The painful realization struck Edward like smoke clearing from a fire—Daphne might be won over by an heir after all. The thought made him want to scream, or at least strangle George Hartwick by his turkey neck.

After dinner, when the ladies retired to the drawing room, the gentlemen stayed around the table with their brandy and cigars. Lord Darges lit Frederick's cigar.

"Tell me about your daughter."

"What would you like to know?"

"She was brought up in America?"

"She's American through and through. She's not at all familiar with our way of life."

"But she can learn, certainly."

Frederick puffed on his cigar, eyeing the future duke through a smoky haze. "My daughter is an intelligent young woman. She can learn whatever she puts her mind to."

"She knows Pitman shorthand," Edward added. "She learned shorthand to help her father with his newspaper work." Edward looked around the room, expecting a disapproving look from his grandfather, but Mr. Ellis wasn't there.

"What on earth would a well-born young woman want with Pitman shorthand?" When there was no reply, the future duke said, "She is certainly one of the loveliest young women I've seen. Americans are so..."

"Yes?" Frederick said.

The future duke cleared his throat. "It's a shame she hasn't been presented."

"I believe my mother plans to fix that next season," said Lord Staton, looking alive for the first time since dinner began. He had a curious expression as he studied Lord Darges, as though he were trying to piece together some puzzle only the future duke could solve.

Lord Darges blew a ring of smoke across the table as he considered. "All I can say is I'm certain Miss Meriwether will make some man a very decent wife after some instruction. Is it true she cooks?"

"American-style biscuits," Edward said.

Frederick grabbed the brandy bottle and refilled his glass. "I'm certain that you, as the heir to the Duke of Norley, have several potential wives at the ready who are far more well-versed in this way of life. You shouldn't need to worry about marrying someone who knows shorthand or bakes her own biscuits. To be honest, and I share this in friendship, I'm not certain my daughter is the best choice for you."

"I believe my brother may well be right," the Earl of Staton said. Lord Staton nodded as though he had solved the puzzle after all. "I don't believe my niece is the right choice for you."

Lord Darges sat up straighter, ready for the duel. "Don't you think Miss Meriwether is the best judge of who would or would not make a suitable match?" He glared at Lord Staton, who stared back unperturbed.

"Gentlemen." Lord Staton stood, brandy bottle in hand. "Is anyone else up for a game of poker?"

Frederick looked at his brother. "Perhaps that isn't a wise idea tonight."

"Nonsense, Freddie. I need a chance to win back that packet I lost to Warren here in London."

Lord Darges laughed as he crunched out his smoldering cigar. "Your luck hasn't held since you've become Earl of Staton, Dickie."

"He didn't have much luck before," snickered Warren. "You should also try to win back the money you lost to Stevenson, and then you should try to win back the money you lost to Cranston, and then…"

"That's enough," said the Earl. "You're making me sound like an easy target, and we don't want to give these gentlemen any ideas." Mr. Ellis entered the dining room. "Ellis, tell the ladies we're playing cards. Have the brandy and cigars brought to the smoking room."

As Mr. Ellis disappeared, Lord Darges noticed Edward for the first time. "Do you play cards?"

"I'm afraid not," Edward said. "I prefer sure things."

"That must be difficult since there are never sure things in this life."

"Then we must work hard to turn the tides of favor in our direction."

Lord Darges twirled his walrus mustache as he stepped closer to Edward. "And you are…?"

"The butler's grandson."

Lord Darges laughed. "Is he one of your young men, Dickie? You always did have a sense of humor about those you keep company with."

"Young Mr. Ellis here is a journalist and the editor of the Daily Observer," Frederick said. "And he's an author in his own right. I believe young Mr. Ellis here will be the next Mr. Dickens."

"The next Dickens?" Lord Darges spat the name out like spoiled soup. "Wasn't the first one bad enough? All that man ever did was make a mockery of our kind of people. He never showed the slightest understanding of our way of life."

"I believe that was the point," Edward said.

Lord Staton's friend, Poppers, stopped mid-sentence in his whispered conversation with Carlton, Warren, and Fronmer, and the four men watched the future Duke of Norley walk to the door.

"Forgive me, Lord Darges," Carlton called to the future duke, his long mouth stretched to his ears. "I thought you looked familiar, though I can't recall where we may have met. Was it watching Boulton and Parke in the shopping arcades of the West End?"

The future duke colored to a sunburned pink. "I may have seen them engaging in their shenanigans at the Oxford Cambridge boat race."

The Earl of Staton laughed heartily. "Come now, Darges. Surely you remember when you and I saw them at the casino in Holborn. I don't know how you could forget. They tried to kiss you."

Now the future duke was an unpleasant plum shade, and Edward thought this is what the hanged men must look like when it was over, discolored and swollen.

"They were arrested for their folly," Lord Darges muttered.

"But it didn't stick, did it?" Frederick held the door for the others as they made their way toward the smoking room. "They were arrested earlier this year but they were acquitted when no one would testify against them. They were two grown men in women's clothing. What harm did they do, really?"

"None at all, Freddie," said the Earl. Lord Staton grinned at the future Duke of Norley, who would not return the Earl's gaze.

Edward followed the others up the wide staircase to the smoking room that was most definitely a man's room with its dark-paneled walls and black and gold carpeting. Edward studied the gold-framed paintings and he realized that one wall contained the portraits of family hunting dogs. One dog even wore a white wig and a crimson House of Lords robe. As the peacock and Colin set out the card table, the chairs, the replenished brandy bottles, and the cigar boxes, Frederick leaned close to his eldest brother and whispered. When Lord Staton remained impassive, Frederick exhaled, nodded at the others, and left. Edward followed him.

"You don't need to leave on my account," Frederick said. "If you'd like to play cards, please do."

"As I said, I prefer sure things."

"I'm afraid Lord Darges was correct, Edward. Nothing is certain in this world." Frederick looked at the closed door of the smoking room. "Do you have everything you need for the Observer? Perhaps I should return to London. Or even better New York." They heard raucous laughter through the door. The glasses of brandy had taken their effect.

"Are you returning to America so soon?" Edward asked.

"I was going to, but my mother has asked me to stay a while longer."

"Perhaps you should stay." When Frederick smiled at him, Edward stammered. "I mean, that is, if you think it best. Your family needs you, and we certainly need you at the Observer. I can keep the paper afloat for now but only with your help."

"I've heard quite the contrary. I understand the men have come to respect you and they're following your lead, even if it was grudgingly at first. The truth is, Edward, I don't think you need me there as much as you believe you do."

"But everyone at the paper looks to you for guidance, including me."

Frederick looked at the closed door. "I can't deny that in many ways I've enjoyed being home. And I'm pleased that Daphne is finally getting to know England. I believe she may enjoy staying longer. What do you think? Should we stay or should we go?"

Edward was afraid of giving himself away so he nodded in

response. At Frederick's request, Mrs. Ellis had a guest room prepared for Edward, though Edward got little sleep that night, unable to stop thinking about Daphne. In the morning he was on the first train back to London, so he had no time to see her before he left, which was probably just as well.

HORROCKS

*I*n case you were wondering, historically footmen were hired for their good height and impressive looks. Flings with Footmen is both a potential title for a tawdry tell-all as well as the reality for a good many high-strung families. The peacock known as Henry Horrocks was well aware of this. The golden-eyed, bronze-haired first footman at Hembry Castle waited for his chance to cash in on his tall, slender figure any way he could. When he first arrived at Hembry it was slow going since the Countess of Staton was the only woman about. True, she was older than Henry's gran, but she was a rich old harridan and everyone looks the same in the dark. When the Countess didn't see him as anything other than a piece of furniture or the cart that brought the tea and cakes, Henry dropped her, moving instead to her daughter-in-law, Hyacinth, a rich (slightly) younger harridan. Henry spotted Mrs. Jerrold Meriwether eyeing him through her monocle on more than one occasion, but Henry had never been able to contrive a way to begin an acquaintance that went past opening doors or serving her tea in dainty cups.

Henry thought the heavens opened and the angels sang when Miss Daphne appeared. She was indeed a Beauty, nearly as pretty as he was. So far so good. Since she was American she wasn't constrained by social class the way the British were—in Britain, there's a place for everyone and everyone in their place, as Henry's father used to say. When no one else was about, Henry had gone as far as speaking to Miss Daphne, idle chatter about how she liked it in England, how dreadful the weather was, blah blah blah. She didn't seem to mind, and being American she wouldn't know it was improper for the footman to dare to speak to a family member before he was spoken to. Whenever she passed him in the hallway, instead of staring through him as though he were a tapestry on the wall, Miss Daphne acknowledged him. True, it was a simple, "Good morning, Henry," or "Good afternoon, Henry," but it was more than the rest of the hoity-toities ever said to him except when barking orders.

Even with her greetings, Henry hadn't been able to make much headway with Mr. Frederick's daughter. Henry was sitting at the table in the servants' hall musing over ways to lure Miss Daphne closer when he heard the voices of the butler and housekeeper drifting toward him from the butler's pantry. He thought nothing of it at first. When Henry heard the pulled tones of Mrs. Ellis' voice he began paying attention. He was too far to hear comfortably, so he moved to the seat at the farthest end of the table and listened harder. When he still couldn't make out their words he gave up being discreet and stood this side of the pantry door so he could eavesdrop with better efficiency.

"What do you mean he's gone?" Henry heard Mrs. Ellis say.

"I mean his lordship isn't here. He left behind a note saying he was with the Prince of Wales, so Mr. Frederick went to Sandringham House to ask his lordship to come home. His lordship has work to see to here. When Mr. Frederick spoke to the Prince's guests, even the Prince himself, they all insisted his lordship never arrived. Lord Tilling was there, and he told Mr. Frederick that his lordship was never expected to attend that party. The men were there for a swimming excursion, which his lordship would never attend. He can't swim."

Mrs. Ellis chuckled. "A swimming excursion? Can you imagine the Prince of Wales in one of those short-sleeved swimsuits that stop at the knees? That must be a sight to see."

"It may be of some interest to you to know that when men swim with other men and there are no ladies about they wear less than that."

"And how do you know this, Augustus?"

"So I've been told, my dear. So I've been told. When Mr. Frederick was at Sandringham House, Lord Stenfield said he hadn't seen his lordship in over a year. Lady Waltbury told Mr. Frederick she heard that his lordship had gone to London to visit a friend…"

"Yes?"

"But when Mr. Frederick arrived at Staton House the servants said his lordship hadn't been there."

Henry heard the creak of a chair as it scraped across the wood floor. He peeked around the open door as much as he dared and saw Mrs. Ellis sit across from her husband.

"What's to be done, Gussie?"

"Poor Mr. Frederick is caught in the middle. There's business that needs tending here at Hembry, and since his lordship isn't here her ladyship has asked Mr. Frederick to do it. He won't be returning to America any time soon, I can tell you that."

"What about Mr. Jerrold? Or Mr. Windhall, the agent? Surely it's Mr. Windhall's job to take care of things?"

"Someone from the family always has the final say over the

agent, and her ladyship wants Mr. Frederick to do it and not Mr. Jerrold."

"Hmm. And I always thought Mr. Jerrold was her ladyship's favorite. At least that explains why Neddie was offered the position as editor of the paper."

"Correct."

"I'm glad something good has come from this."

The chair creaked again and a dull light filled the room, spilling past the door into the hall.

"Looks like it's going to rain," Mrs. Ellis said.

"It always looks like it's going to rain."

"Not always." Mrs. Ellis sighed. "Has anyone contacted Mr. Hough?"

"Why? Is someone ill?"

"About his lordship. If his lordship is to be found Mr. Hough is the one to find him."

"No one has contacted Mr. Hough as far as I know." The second chair creaked and Henry heard Mr. Ellis' heavy footsteps. When you're a footman you learn to recognize people by their footsteps. "Is there something I should know, Mary?"

"Nothing at all. I was only curious."

Henry tiptoed away wringing his hands until they were raw. A goldmine! His lordship has vanished and he's never where he said he was going to be. Mr. Frederick is taking over the duties at Hembry. Miss Daphne wouldn't be leaving for America any time soon. Mr. Hough has the means to find his lordship, at least according to Mrs. Ellis. Henry's thoughts danced a jig. Which one of those nuggets should he focus on first?

He saw the time and knew he should be upstairs helping Colin with the dining room. But Colin was there, and he was such a hob knocker, Colin, always smiling, always running from there to here and back again, getting his work done first, acting like he was first footman when everyone knew better. Getting ideas past his station, Colin was. Henry passed the green baize door and stopped. Of course! His lordship's room. There must be secrets to be found in his lordship's room. He peeked into the dining room, saw Colin setting out the plates, and slipped unseen upstairs. When no one was looking Henry let himself into his lordship's bedroom. It was a handsome room befitting the Earl of Staton with its beige walls with gold moldings, a marble hearth with the logs laid in a neat pile, ready for his lordship's return. On the mantelpiece was a gold-framed mirror, a Baroque clock, and Baroque candelabras while two wide tapestry-covered chairs sat before the hearth. Across the room was the canopy bed, and near the window was his lordship's gold-plaited desk with teal enamel inlay and out-turned lion's feet. The curtains were drawn and the candelabras unlit, but Henry didn't need light to know his surroundings. He brought firewood to this room often enough.

He found his way to his lordship's desk and opened the long top drawer, which contained nothing but quills, pen knives, paper, and ink jars. There was a second drawer to the right, though that one was locked. How to unlock the drawer? A pen knife? Someone might see that the lock had been tampered with, but who knew what treasures Henry might find in there? There had to be something here to supplement his meager salary by a quid or ten or more. Henry reached into the drawer for a pen knife, but then the book on the bedside table caught his attention. He saw the title, Our Mutual Friend by Dickens. The only book Henry had ever read in his life was written by Mr. Dickens so the footman was interested enough to look inside. Henry opened the cover and found the book hollow, the pages cut away from the center, leaving a hole large enough to hide a packet of letters.

Henry pulled out the packet and separated the letters. He

chose one to read—a love letter! It was mushy as well-written love letters should be, with the appropriate "You are my light" and "I can hardly remember not having you in my life" and "Where would I be without you" and "You are my life's true companion" and other such nonsense. The letter wasn't signed, but it doesn't need to be, Henry thought. Someone loved the Earl, probably someone the Earl loved in return since he kept the letter in this secret place. A little digging may reveal the identity of the letter's author and possibly even the Earl's whereabouts. After all, where else would the Earl disappear to except to be with his beloved? Henry thought of the countless young women her ladyship had invited to the castle with the hope of enticing her eldest son into marriage. So one of them had caught the Earl of Staton's eye after all. Henry tucked the letter safely into the pocket of his livery waistcoat.

The second letter wasn't that interesting. It was a note to the current Earl from his father, though it didn't make much sense, talking about how the 8th Earl cared for his son no matter what, he would always be proud of him, more blah blah blah. Rubbish the letter was, too soppy for Henry's taste. He stuck that letter into his pocket too—after all, you never knew what would come in handy later—and he picked up the final letter.

Henry licked his lips as he read it, as though he could taste the fortune this one would bring. The note was from some woman asking for help, not for herself but for her poor innocent baby. Oh! Henry skipped across the floor, clasping the letter to his heart. So this is what it feels like to discover you've been left a fortune by a long-lost uncle. A secret love, a cryptic note from the old Earl, and an infant! Was the love letter and the baby letter from the same hand? Henry would decide later. He tucked the last letter into his protruding pocket and danced a sailor's jig. He wanted to rush down the stairs to the servants' hall and pass the letters around for everyone to see, but he couldn't. He heard voices outside the door and the light tread of two maids. He flattened his livery, patted his hair, and exhaled. He stood by the door, listened, and, hearing no one, glided away. He had every business being in his lordship's room this time of day and how dare you think otherwise.

MR. ELLIS FOUND his wife standing in the doorway of his lordship's room staring toward the bed.

"Is everything all right, my dear?"

"Augustus, you scared me."

"It's something we're equally adept at—sneaking up on people. It's an occupational hazard for the staff—the knowledge that we could be lurking anywhere at any time."

"That's more true than you know. Shouldn't you be in the dining room? It must be time."

"They're about to go in, but I wanted to let you know his lordship is expected home on Thursday. Her ladyship had word this evening."

"Thank the Lord. I'm afraid one of these days his lordship is going to leave and never come back."

"Let's hope not. Have Ruth and Jemima give this room a thorough going over before he returns."

"Good gracious, Mr. Ellis. How would I ever survive without you telling me how to do my job?"

Mr. Ellis looked both ways down the long hall, and when he saw no one he kissed his wife's cheek. He turned to leave but stopped. "What are you looking at?"

"Nothing at all. I was just wondering when his lordship would be returning home."

"Now you know."

"Yes." Mrs. Ellis looked at the table by the bed. "Now I know."

READY FOR THE QUEEN

There was more to learn about life at Hembry Castle than Daphne ever imagined. Her enthusiastic Americanisms weren't proper, as her grandmother constantly reminded her, not at Hembry, not with any other fine British family, and most certainly not at Court.

"Everyone will be watching," Lady Staton said from her throne-like armchair in the sitting room. "People would love nothing more than to see the Earl of Staton's American niece fail at Court, so we will do everything in our power to make certain that you shine far above everyone's expectations."

"What will happen if I do something wrong, Grandma?"

"You will do nothing wrong."

"What if…"

"It's not up for discussion, Daphne. You will be perfect."

"But the presentations don't begin again until spring. Is it necessary to start practicing in September?"

"You should have been practicing since the day you were born." The Countess squinted at her granddaughter and set her ear trumpet in place. "Rowland?"

Leslie Rowland came to life where she had been standing in the corner. "Yes, my lady."

"I'd like to begin getting my granddaughter's clothing ready for her presentation."

"Yes, my lady."

"You're familiar with what she'll need? The length of the train and such?"

"Yes, my lady."

"My granddaughter has informed me that in America she makes her own clothing, but that will not suffice here, will it, Rowland?"

"No, my lady."

"That is all."

Rowland disappeared. At that moment Daphne wished she could disappear as well, from Hembry Castle, from England altogether. She was ready to run up to her room, pack her bags, and set off for the ships in Liverpool and take her chances with finding passage home. She wasn't quick enough, and Lady Staton gestured for her to stand.

"We'll need to continue working on your posture, Daphne. Head high, shoulders back. Walk gracefully, confidently. You're the niece of the Earl of Staton. Your grandfather was one of the most respected men in the country, as your uncle is, or as he will be when he pulls himself together. Every movement you make, every turn of your head, every wave of your hand shows pride in your family. Now walk from here to the window."

"Grandma, I don't think..."

"Daphne." Lady Staton sighed. "Why did your parents insist on giving you such a common name? They couldn't have named you Elizabeth, or Victoria, or Charlotte?"

"My mother named me after her favorite aunt."

"Of course she did. Now do make your dear Grandmamma happy and walk to the window and back."

Daphne was tempted to skip like a little girl, but she was afraid her grandmother's squint would crack off her face if she did. She glided away in her most demure manner, moving as few muscles as possible as she had seen from her grandmother and other visiting ladies. When Daphne returned from the window, Lady Staton shook her head.

"How could your father raise you without teaching you the most basic mannerisms? We have so much to do and so little time. You will learn to act like the niece of the Earl of Staton if it kills me."

"Let's hope it doesn't come to that, Grandma."

"You still need to learn the concept of polite conversation. It won't do to share everything you've ever thought or felt with complete strangers. And you must learn to control your emotions whilst speaking. Americans are far too boisterous. What do you have to be so happy about?"

"What do you have to be so dour about?"

"I'm not dour, Daphne. I'm well-bred. Join me in the dining room."

Daphne followed her grandmother into the dining room, though even the bright yellow walls couldn't cheer her.

"Please sit, Daphne."

Daphne sat at the table. Mr. Ellis watched Henry Horrocks as the footman set a dinner place in front of Daphne.

"It isn't luncheon, is it, Grandma?"

"No, my dear, it's time to learn some etiquette. First, you must sit up straight. Sit a comfortable distance from the table so that your hands are level with the knife and fork. Do not ever put your hands on the table."

"We do in America."

"I've noticed." Lady Staton sat beside Daphne and took the knife and fork in her hands. "Hold your knife and fork in this way." She held her knife in her right hand and her overturned fork in her left. She gestured with her fork. "After you cut your food, do not stab it like you're attacking your enemy with a pitchfork. Why do Americans insist on holding cutlery in such an undignified manner?"

"I can say in all honesty, Grandma, I've never given a moment's thought to why we hold our forks the way we do. It does seem like more work, though, pushing the food onto the back of the fork with a knife. Why not just use the side of the fork that works?"

"Are children allowed to run wild in the streets in America?"

"I don't believe so, Grandma."

"If they don't run wild in the streets then they should not be allowed to use flatware like heathens. Now, don't begin eating until everyone has been served unless the hostess gives her permission. Never eat too fast or too slow, but observe your hosts and eat at the pace they've set. Never make noises of any kind."

"What if I have to burp?"

"You will save your slurping for your own time, in private. When you are finished, you will place your utensils with the tines facing up on your plate like so." The Countess nodded at her own elegant display.

Suddenly, Daphne understood her father. She understood why he ran from England, why he loved their comfortable life in Connecticut, and, most importantly, why he had been so reluctant to return. Hembry Castle was beautiful. The history contained within those walls, the art and the sculptures, and the very house itself, told stories of a past Daphne cherished since it was her family's past. But the way you had to conduct yourself when you lived there was wearying to her brain and burdensome to her soul, and she wondered how much longer she would stay in England. She looked at the Georgian clock on the mantelpiece and thought she could still make a dash for Liverpool and find passage for home if she were quick about it. Thoughts of home made her smile. She pictured the whitewashed two-story house by the river that she shared with her father, the sailboat at the end of their dock bobbing in the wind-blown ripples. Daphne exhaled loudly enough for her grandmother to hear without her ear trumpet. Then she realized this too shall pass. She would be going home soon. She was thankful when her father walked into the dining room.

Frederick kissed Daphne's cheek and then his mother's. "Hello, my darling. Hello, Mamma."

"Hello, Frederick. Daphne and I were preparing for her presentation."

"In the dining room?"

"You must begin somewhere." The Countess stood, returning her ear trumpet to a useful location. "You must tell me about Richard, Frederick. Have you made any progress?"

"Progress?"

"You must have located your brother by now and persuaded him to return home. Did you make him realize his duty is here now?"

Frederick dropped into a dining room chair and stared at the flower moldings on the ceiling. "Yes, I persuaded him to come home, but I can't say I've made any progress. I think he's hiding something, but he won't confide in me."

"I don't care what he's hiding," said the Countess. "He must be made to understand that he no longer has the option of leaving Hembry to go gallivanting with his friends. He is the Earl of Staton!"

Frederick paced to the window to watch the gathering storm clouds, such a contrast to the brightness of the summer-yellow room. "I don't know how to say this Mamma, but it's best to come out with it. I think there's something wrong with Richard."

"Oh no." Daphne joined her father by the window. "Is he sick?"

"Not ill, not exactly. I think he's terribly sad."

The Countess nodded. "He's certainly behaving in a bad way."

"Not bad, Mamma. Sad. Something is bothering him."

"Tiddlysquats!" The Countess swatted some invisible pest near her face with the back of her hand. "I'm sad too. I'm sad my eldest son isn't able to perform his duties after his father worked his entire life to preserve this estate for him, his children, and his children's children. Your brother must leave behind those ridiculous men he insists on carrying on with. They're silly, vain men and they set my teeth grinding whenever your brother brings them here. Why doesn't Mr. Hough tell him? Mr. Hough is a reasonable man. Even when they were at university together Mr. Hough was the one with common sense. You should make Mr. Hough talk to your brother, Frederick, if you refuse to do it."

"I'm not refusing anything, Mamma. I've been trying to talk to Richard for as long as I've been here but he won't hear me. And it's not my place to make Mr. Hough do anything. Besides, I don't know how commonsensical Mr. Hough is. After all, he accompanies Richard virtually everywhere he goes. It's a wonder he's able to keep up with his duties here."

"Do you know what I think, Frederick?"

"I do, but you'll tell me again anyway."

"I think the only thing wrong with your brother is the fact that your father coddled him. Your father should have kept Richard at home and made certain he learned his responsibilities."

"Do you think you can force Richard to stay any more than you forced me?"

The Countess heard him. She had her earhorn in place, and Frederick had all but shouted the words. Daphne waited, not sure what to do. Though she didn't often agree with her grandmother, she didn't want to return to Connecticut with hard feelings on either side. For a flash, before she could pull her features into her unyielding mask, the Countess looked beaten. Then, as quickly as the weakness came on, it vanished.

"I forbid Richard to see those ridiculous men ever again."

"I'm afraid that attitude isn't going to help, Mamma."

The Countess turned her most disapproving look onto her middle son, and an impressive disapproving look it was. "I have a mind to…"

"To what, Mamma? Unless you tie Richard down with rope and sailor knots, I don't see what can be done."

The Countess blew away on her icy wind, leaving Daphne and her father alone in the dining room. Frederick looked around as though he wanted to be certain they were alone and no servants were standing silently by or hiding behind the curtains.

"What do you think is wrong with Uncle Richard?"

"My guess is your uncle has more troubles than he's willing to admit to."

"So what do we do?"

"I don't know. He's so uncommunicative these days. I know there's always been a level of detachment to him. Even when we were boys I knew he had secrets he didn't share with me, or with anyone. When he met Hough when they were at Oxford I was grateful that he finally had a friend he seemed to confide in. But lately Richard seems resigned somehow, que sera sera, what will be will be. I told him I can't be of any help unless he tells me what on earth is going on."

"Maybe if I talk to him," Daphne said. "Maybe he'll tell me."

"It certainly won't hurt for you to try. Now let's move on to more pleasant topics. What did you think of Lord Darges?"

"Who?"

"The young man who was clearly smitten with you when he came to dine. The future Duke of Norley."

"He seemed nice enough. I didn't see we had much in common. All he talked about was hunting."

"He was trying to impress you with his physical prowess. Do you think you might come around to liking him if you discovered that you did indeed have things in common?"

Daphne shook her head. "You're starting to sound like Grandma. Are you trying to marry me off too?"

"Never. I'm merely interested in your opinion. I believe young Mr. Ellis is also interested in your feelings toward Lord Darges."

"Why?"

"For such a perceptive girl, my dear, you're blind when it comes to young men's intentions toward you. Edward Ellis is in love with you."

"Don't be silly. Edward and I are friends."

"Edward? Things must have progressed if you're on a Christian name basis."

"Nothing has progressed. I was tired of being Miss Daphne or Miss Meriwether to everyone. I'm Daphne to my friends and Edward and I are friends. After all, you and Edward are on a first-name basis."

"True enough. And you have things in common with Mr. Edward Ellis?"

"As a matter of fact, I do. Edward and I share a love of the same books. I admire his work as a journalist, which I happen to have some experience with, and he's a wonderful author in his own right. We both think education is important for everyone, not only the wealthy, and we both find people at Hembry rather odd." Daphne saw those bright hazel eyes that flashed between green and brown and gold. She mimicked her grandmother's sharp tone when she spoke. "Don't be difficult, Frederick. Young Mr. Ellis and I are friends, and that is all."

"Whatever you say, my dear."

"Besides, we're going home soon, and it doesn't pay to form any attachments here."

Frederick sat at the table and pulled out the chair beside him. "Come sit, Daphne. That's precisely what I wanted to speak to you about." Her father looked serious. "My dear, I know we planned on staying in England only for a short time, and I had wanted to leave before the winter weather started, but is there any way I could convince you to stay a while longer?"

"How much longer?"

"I can't say for certain. Your Uncle Richard is having a difficult time. As I said, I believe something is wrong. You see how your grandmother is about the situation. Your Uncle Jerrold is the same. They see only family duty, not the human being behind the expectations. Richard is struggling, and I think, I hope, I can be of assistance to him in some small way. Who knows? Perhaps we can even find him a nice wife who will help settle him down."

"Do you think a wife will fix him?"

"At this point, I'm willing to try anything."

Daphne watched the pink-light sun appear suddenly, as was its habit in England. In Connecticut, if it rained it rained all day. At Hembry it rained, it cleared, and rained again all in a matter of moments.

"Of course we can stay, Papa. I want to help Uncle Richard too. Although," she grimaced, "if we stay until spring then I'll have to go through with Grandma's plan to have me presented at Court."

Frederick laughed. "It might not be so bad. It will be something to tell your grandchildren about one day, that you were presented at Queen Victoria's Court. Does the fact that you'll be presented make you reconsider Lord Darges?"

"Absolutely not."

"Never fear, my dear. Your grandmother will have plenty more young men lined up before long."

"She can line them up all she likes. I'm not getting married unless I'm in love."

Frederick held his arm out to his daughter, and together they left the dining room and the day's etiquette lesson behind.

THE KISS

September passed well into autumn, and Daphne enjoyed the darker weather just as she did when she was home. She liked the feel as the humid heaviness faded into smoother, cooler air. Crimson, rust, and gold leaves fell from the red oaks and the full moon maples, and she was less homesick when she thought of her lakeside home where the foliage peeped so wonderfully you wanted to grasp hold of the trees, blessing them for their artisan-like handiwork, and never let them go. Daphne had gone outside to watch Mr. Harvey, the gardener, and his assistants rake the mountains of leaves to either side of the road, leaving a path for the carriages coming to and from the castle, though an hour later the path needed clearing again.

Daphne's father had gone back to London and the Daily Observer, needing something of his own while he tended to the duties at Hembry. Frederick assured his mother he could tend to castle business while still running the newspaper, and he thought, he told Daphne, that if he were in the city perhaps he could begin to piece together this puzzle that was his

brother the Earl. The best news that autumn was from Fergusonandwately. The publishing gentlemen had finally, after four
worrisome months, agreed to publish a collection of Edward
Ellis' stories. Mainly, Edward told her, the stories were to be
about how education was essential for everyone if they were to
have a truly strong Britain. The message was to be cleverly
disguised into stories about ordinary working folk who can
improve themselves, and those around them, because of the
opportunities education brings. Since Edward was busy
working on the stories for his collection, he was more than
happy to welcome Frederick back as editor of the Observer.

Daphne soon joined her father in London. There may have
been a chocolate-haired, hazel-eyed reason she wanted to
return to Staton House, though she still wouldn't admit it—
even to herself. She was there, she insisted, because she
enjoyed getting to know the city, often walking around Hyde
Park arm-in-arm with Pamela. Daphne liked watching the
Punch and Judy street artists in the West End, and she liked
visiting the Crystal Palace and the Cremorne Gardens (by day,
since no polite young lady would dare be seen there by night).
The River Thames itself provided endless hours of entertainment, and Daphne watched ships from all over the world glide
toward London Bridge, the cutters and the skiffs bobbing
between the paddle steamers and the merchant vessels, the
banks alive with the movements of sailors. Daphne would
walk with her father along the river's edge, admiring the views
near St. Paul's Cathedral or the Palace of Westminster, and
wonder about the constant presence of industrial warehouses
and cranes. That was the first thing Daphne thought of when
she considered London—cranes, and the persistent rebuilding
and revitalization of the city. Other times she and her father
would frequent the New Chelsea Theatre, where most recently
they had seen an adaptation of Mr. Dickens' Great Expecta-

tions, which wasn't as good as it might have been, Daphne thought. The adaptations of Mr. Dickens' work often caught the drama well enough while neglecting the humor. Who would have guessed Mr. Dickens was one of the funniest authors in the English language from watching that banal depiction?

Daphne was happy to have a break from the eavesdropping eyes in the shadows and the spying ears in the walls at Hembry Castle. She had no ill will toward her grandmother. In many ways, Daphne liked Lady Staton. But then the Countess would remember the presentation and all she could talk about was how everything had to be perfect. In London, Daphne had a reprieve from the worry. In London, she could read whatever she liked without her grandmother's comments about how the niece of the Earl of Staton should not be reading anything as common as novels. In London, Daphne was able to make herself useful again, accompanying her father to the offices of the Daily Observer, much to the amusement of the reporters, though they always treated her with respect. She was the editor's daughter, after all.

In November, the autumn grew colder. Pamela spent her days, when she wasn't out with Daphne or visiting her sister, refurbishing shawls. It wasn't until the wintry weather began that Daphne admitted to herself, and only herself, that she enjoyed her time at the Observer with Edward Ellis. Where at first he was simply a nice-looking young man who worked for her father, now, the more she had come to know him, the more she realized he was intelligent, perceptive, and kind. He was more than nice-looking, really, the way his chocolate-brown hair fell into his hazel eyes, and when he laughed, which was often, he was positively radiant. At what point she started thinking of him as more than a friend, she couldn't have said. Yes, Edward was Mr. and Mrs. Ellis' grandson. Yes, Edward hadn't an aristocratic bone in his body. Yes, Edward was working his way up in the world. But none of that mattered to Daphne.

Unfortunately, that wasn't the end of the matter. How young Mr. Ellis felt about her, she couldn't have said. She often caught him gazing in her direction, though to be fair she was gazing in his direction as well, and it may have been curiosity causing the stares on his part. When they first met, something in the way he responded to her, something in the way he leaned toward her when she spoke, made her think he found her more than simply interesting, but now she wondered if she had been wrong. Sometimes he shined bright as a lamp, laughing, teasing people, or making wry comments about whatever was happening around them. Then there were the times when he was quiet, troubled even, and though Daphne had learned not to ask the English questions about themselves, she tried to gently prod at whatever it was that furrowed his brow. If I can't tell how Edward feels about me, Daphne thought, then I must be mistaken and he isn't interested in me at all. But it's fine. After Uncle Richard is settled Papa and I will return to America. I don't want to bring a broken heart home with me, so it's better this way.

In the middle of November, her father was called back to Hembry on urgent village business. Richard was gone yet again, so Frederick had no choice but to return to the castle and handle whatever needed handling. When Daphne returned to Hembry with her father, she resumed her etiquette lessons.

"Good posture makes you appear confident," her grandmother reminded her. "When you walk, step lightly. Don't drag as though you have bricks on your feet. It's unseemly. Keep your arms and hips contained. You don't want to seem common, or worse."

"What is worse than common?" Daphne asked.

"If you don't know, my dear, I'm not going to tell you."

That week her Uncle Jerrold and Jerrold's wife, Hyacinth, returned to Hembry, leaving their young sons in London in the care of the nannies. The day after they arrived Daphne overheard her uncle's wife explain to Lady Staton (Hyacinth was shouting since Lady Staton did not have her ear trumpet) that Jerrold had been gone for some weeks assisting a political campaign in Abingdon, or was it Andover, or Ashford, or Morpeth? Jerrold is such a respected barrister, Hyacinth shouted, and his connection to the Earl of Staton means that his endorsement is highly esteemed by those seeking seats in the Commons.

"He often travels to the speeches to give his endorsement more credibility!"

Daphne was certain her Aunt Hyacinth was shouting loudly enough for the maids to hear through the green baize door. They'll have something to gossip about tonight, Daphne thought.

"How often is he gone on these trips?" the Countess shouted back, as though Hyacinth were the one who couldn't hear.

"Oh, quite often, you know, and he's gone for weeks at a time. He's so respected in political circles. Jerrold says they insist he should run for office himself. He's certain to win whichever seat he wishes."

"His eldest brother is in the House of Lords," Lady Staton said. "What other political affiliation does the family need? Make sure he's not embarrassing himself, or the family, Hyacinth. The family's endorsements are not for sale."

"Jerrold would never do anything unbecoming. He's the embodiment of honor, and he takes great pride in his family's reputation. I believe Jerrold is far more concerned about the family's good name than Richard. Where is Richard, by the way?"

"Let us not speak of Richard," said Lady Staton. "We have enough on our plate right now, like getting Daphne ready for her presentation. It's November already. Spring will be here before we know it."

From that day on Aunt Hyacinth assisted Lady Staton in the molding of Miss Daphne Meriwether into a fine lady, or at least the respectable niece of a peer. Even Uncle Jerrold had an improving word or two whenever they passed in the hallways. Daphne marveled at them, Jerrold and Hyacinth, with their long limbs and bulging marble-like eyes as if they existed in a perpetual state of surprised discomfort. Edward made Daphne laugh once when he said that both Mr. and Mrs. Jerrold Meriwether suffered from gout of the eyes. But Daphne wanted to get along with her English relatives while she was there, so she did her best to display the deportment they were determined to instill in her. She was still hoping that Uncle Richard would settle himself soon so she and her father could return home before April. The winter weather usually calmed enough by March to allow for smooth passage across the Atlantic. There was still hope that she wouldn't have to go through with the presentation after all.

Daphne and her father were at the castle when the weather turned from wintry cold to simply frigid. The sharp bite of the wind chilled Daphne to the marrow in her bones. One afternoon, in the beginning whispers of December, during the brief sunshine allotted that day, Daphne went outside for some air, which she desperately needed after two hours of etiquette lessons. She had been cooped inside for four days due to the shivery weather and she needed to feel even the faintest rays of sunlight on her face. She headed in the direction of the rose garden, knowing the blooms would be gone, pruned away to allow for new buds in the spring, so she continued instead through the tree-lined path known as the Countess' Walk. She trembled and thought she should go back inside, but the thought of further scrutiny from her grandmother gave her the courage to brave the cold. She passed the stone bridge and arrived at the shrubbery lining the parkland.

"Miss Meriwether?"

She knew the voice before she saw the speaker. "Hello, Mr. Ellis."

She smiled, and the young man seemed to take confidence from that. He doffed his hat as he bowed, then took two steps closer.

"I came to see your father about some newspaper business. As I was walking up from the village I saw you here alone and I thought you might like an escort back."

"That's thoughtful of you."

"What are you doing here in this weather?"

"I was enjoying the little bit of sunshine."

They walked toward the castle, lost in their thoughts. Finally, young Mr. Ellis said, "How are your etiquette lessons?"

"My grandmother is frustrated with me. Everything I do continues to be wrong. I talk too much. I laugh too much. I still don't walk correctly. I'm not reserved enough."

"Ah, yes. Don't you know that being reserved is the English's finest talent?"

"You'd think I would, having an English father, but he never seemed reserved to me. If it weren't for his accent I never would have believed he was English."

Mr. Ellis gleamed somewhere between a smile and a smirk. "You do realize that here you're the one with the accent."

"So I've been told. Now you must tell me how the English acquire this talent of reservation."

A lone blackbird, out of place against the darkening sky,

squalled overhead. Edward watched the wide wings glide past as he considered. "From the moment we're old enough to understand such things, we're taught to be reserved. If we speak too loudly, laugh too loudly, or heaven forbid play too loudly, we're scolded, then embarrassed, and we learn before long to keep our thoughts and opinions to ourselves. Seen but not heard, that's how children are reared. Never let anyone guess what you're feeling. Never embarrass others by imposing your personal concerns onto them. Keeping yourself to yourself is esteemed above all other traits. Stoicism is honored, you see."

"I guessed that. One evening over dinner I watched my grandmother and my Uncle Richard having a conversation, and they were so polite, talking about the weather, discussing the farmers and their crops, and making decisions about the village fête. It was like watching two strangers strike up a conversation about nothing in particular. It's odd to me that they have to contain themselves even with the people they're closest to—their own family. At home in Connecticut, we laugh and tell funny stories when we're alone with those we're closest to. My grandmother would die of embarrassment if I so much as told a joke."

Mr. Ellis had that gleam again. "Do you know many jokes?"

"Why is a four-quart jar like a lady's side-saddle?"

"Why?"

"Because it holds a gal-on. Get it? A gallon?" Daphne covered her face with her gloved hands. "It's silly, I know."

Mr. Ellis laughed. "You could be a comedienne at the new Vaudeville Theater in the West End."

"I'd be roped and dragged off the stage before I could get to my second joke. But there is comedy theater in London, and many English authors are very funny. Not everyone is reserved all the time."

"There's a time and place for humor, certainly, especially humor that pokes fun at our reserved nature. Otherwise, that reserved nature is expected. A man could have the very hairs on his scalp on fire, and he would say, so very politely, 'Does anyone happen to have some water about? Anyone? No? It's all very well, I do assure you. Don't mind me while I leap inconspicuously into that lake over there.'" Daphne laughed. "Any display of emotion is considered overly sentimental, embarrassing even."

"Even if you're on fire?"

"Even if you're on fire. Self-expression in any form is forbidden. Not overtly forbidden, mind you, but people are made to understand that they are expected to conform or else be cast aside from everyone you know."

Daphne nodded. "That's it exactly. My grandmother wants me to be the same as everyone else. In America, at least where I'm from, individuality is prized above all else. Being true to yourself is what we value. One of my favorite American writers is Henry David Thoreau, and in his book Walden he said to let everyone mind his own business and endeavor to be what he was made."

"The whole of English society would come crumbling down if Englishmen and women began thinking that way."

"I can see that. But here I feel like I'm playing a children's pretend game by acting the way my grandmother wants me to. She expects me to marry one of these titled aristocrats, who would then expect me to act that way. I'd be playing a role for the rest of my life." Daphne stopped walking. She looked up at the venom-faced storm clouds splattering the gray-black sky. "It's hard knowing that my own family thinks everything about me is wrong."

"That's how the English feel most of the time."

"Not you." Daphne looked into Edward's eyes. They looked

more brown now than green or gold, and she wondered if his eyes changed with the weather. "You always seem so self-assured. I used to think I was self-assured, but now I don't know. They're trying to change me."

"Don't ever change, Miss Meriwether. You're perfect as you are."

A blast of wind rushed over them. Daphne shivered and pulled her shawl closer around her shoulders. "It's Daphne, please. I don't want to keep reverting back to formality. I need friends in England, and I won't feel like we're friends unless you call me Daphne."

"As you wish, Daphne."

A murky blanket rolled out, covering the gray-black sky, and the rain fell fast and hard. The ground grew slick with mud, and when Daphne slipped Edward offered his arm. They raced through the parkland, passing the obelisk, the Corinthian temple, and the marble monument in honor of the messenger god Mercury, his wings pointed to the sky. They laughed from the exhilaration brought on by the deluge soaking them through their coats and boots. They stopped when the wide expanse of parkland ended near the castle ruin where two towers were connected by a Romanesque arch. Daphne touched one of the old stone towers, running her gloved hand over the timeworn ridges and the arrow loops.

"Sometimes, when I need to escape my grandmother, I sit on the steps there," she gestured to the front of the ruins, "and wonder how they lived in the past."

Edward ran his hand over the same weathered bricks. "So you'll concede that England isn't all bad."

"I never thought England was bad. When it's time to leave I'll miss it terribly."

The rain fell harder, hitting them like darts, and Daphne and

Edward pressed against the castle tower in an attempt to shield themselves from the attack. They looked over the rippling green hills, gray in the gloomy weather, and they watched the shrubbery wilt. When the wind picked up, Daphne was swept toward Edward, and he caught her in his arms, keeping her from falling face-first into the puddles. She realized, as the thunder cracked and the mad rain fell, that she wanted him to kiss her. She looked into his eyes, more green now, and she tried to decipher the message they relayed. Was he happy? Sad? Confused? She couldn't tell. Maybe he doesn't know how I feel about him, Daphne thought. She touched his arm.

"Edward..."

He took her hands, first one, then the other, and then he put his arms around her and pulled her into his chest as though he were trying to shield her from the sharp weather. Daphne felt the careful plaits Pamela had created that morning come undone so she took off her bonnet and shook out her hair.

"You must know that you're the most beautiful young woman I've ever seen." Edward shook his head and stepped away from her. Daphne pressed her hand into his chest and looked into his eyes. Then he kissed her. Softly at first, tentatively. When she didn't pull away, when she pressed her lips back onto his, he pulled her to him and they kissed until they needed air. As the clamber of the thunder and the hammer-like rain blew east with the wind, they looked out of the lowest arrow loop and saw the sky settle into fog.

Edward watched the water drip from the Romanesque arch that connected the two towers. "Forgive me. I don't know what came over me."

Daphne grasped his arm, and he started at her touch. "It came over me too." She stood on one of the stone steps so she could see more easily into his hazel eyes which looked cloudy now, like the sky.

"But aren't you marrying the Marquess of Darges or the Earl of Iforgetwhere?"

"I prefer people who forge their own path."

They kissed again. Daphne didn't know whose lips touched whose first, but it didn't matter. When the winter wind blew through the arrow loops they leaned into each other for warmth. Another shiver struck Edward, though this one seemed to come from within himself instead of the weather. He nodded toward the castle, and they laughed as they ran toward the old house, joyous like children, splashing each other in puddles and gazing into each other's eyes.

EDWARD LEFT Daphne by the front and excused himself to the servants' entrance. He had a change of clothes in his grandmother's sitting room, and besides, he didn't want to walk into the castle proper dripping onto the antique carpets. He knocked at the back door and waited, but when no one came he found the door unlocked and let himself in. He heard voices from the servants' hall, and when he heard his name he stopped to listen.

"No!" said Jemima, her squeaky voice an octave higher than normal. "Not Mr. Ellis' grandson! Holding hands with Miss Daphne?"

"Just now I saw them," said the peacock. "I was helping her ladyship from the carriage when I saw them running toward the castle together."

"Did her ladyship see?"

"She had her back to them. But I saw it, plain as day."

"I believe it," said Mrs. Graham. "Why, Mrs. Ellis told me

the other day she was worried about her grandson making a fool of himself over Miss Daphne."

Edward wanted to storm into the room, plead his case, and make them understand that he wasn't making a fool of himself at all. Daphne had feelings for him too. If he had any doubts before, their time near the castle ruins cleared those worries away. He peeked around the wall to see their expressions.

Jemima whispered, and Edward had to strain to make out her words. "He can't be serious about Miss Daphne. Mrs. Ellis says her grandson's already spoken out for some other girl."

"I'm sure he was only being polite to Miss Daphne, helping her back to the house," said Ruth. "It was quite a downpour. I could feel the thunder rattle the house from down here."

"That wasn't polite arm holding," Henry insisted. "They were holding hands and smiling. You know." He tilted his head and batted his eyelashes at Mrs. Graham, clasping his hands in front of his heart.

"I still don't believe it," said Ruth. "I don't believe he would willfully lead on another young woman when he's already engaged."

"Maybe he didn't mean to," said an older woman's voice, one Edward didn't recognize. "Maybe he became engaged to the first young woman, met Miss Daphne, and decided he liked her ladyship's granddaughter better."

"Who wouldn't prefer Miss Daphne to any other woman?" said the footman.

"Henry!" said the older woman's voice.

"Look from the distance, Footman," said Mrs. Graham, "because that's the only view you'll ever have of her."

"I'm not so sure about that." Henry sounded smug. "She says hello or good morning to me. She smiles whenever she sees me."

"She's American," Mrs. Graham said. "She smiles at everyone."

"Besides," added Jemima, "her ladyship is very clear about the fact that she wants Miss Daphne to marry an earl or even a duke."

Edward heard enough. His blood rushed like a fast-flowing river through his limbs, crashing painfully into his skull. He wanted to creep down the hall to his grandmother's sitting room, but he was so numb he tripped and knocked into the wall. He heard the servants mutter and guessed he would be discovered. But no one came searching. Then he heard his grandfather's voice.

"It must be unusually quiet at Hembry Castle for so many of you to be gathered here this time of day."

Then his grandmother's voice. "I'm certain I asked for the sitting room to be given a good going over while her ladyship was out. Now her ladyship has returned. Am I to guess that the room is scrubbed clean?"

Chairs scraped and footsteps quickened. When it was quiet, Edward walked into the room.

"I thought I saw you," said Mrs. Ellis. "Neddie, you're soaked through."

"I came down to see if you still had my change of clothes."

"You came all the way to Hembry for a change of clothes?"

"No, I..." Edward forgot why he had come to Hembry. Then he remembered. "I came to see Mr. Meriwether." He saw the way his grandparents watched him, and he felt like his clothing had melted away in the rain and he was left exposed for all the world to see. "As I was walking toward the castle I saw Miss Meriwether. It started raining and the ground was slippery so I escorted her back."

"Is that all?" His grandmother didn't sound upset, only concerned.

"Should there be more?"

"Henry seemed to think there was."

Edward slumped into a chair. His misery cracked his voice. "What am I going to do?"

Mr. Ellis nodded at Edward, his wife, then removed himself from the room. He was a compassionate man, Augustus Ellis, even if he preferred to leave the softer parts, as he called them, to his wife. Mrs. Ellis sat next to her grandson, brushing his chocolate-colored hair from his eyes the way she did when he was a child.

"I know you're aching, Neddie, and I'm sorry. But you already have an agreement with Miss Chattaway. That agreement is legally binding. You know that."

"Yes, I've read The Pickwick Papers."

"Mr. Dickens spoke of a broken agreement in comic terms. Bardell v. Pickwick makes for funny reading, but I don't think it will be so funny if the Chattaways take you to court. You could have to pay damages. They could muddy your name and ruin your reputation. You could lose your position at the paper. Your career as an author will be finished before it ever started."

Edward laughed. He didn't know why since nothing about this was humorous. It must have been an involuntary reflex. Perhaps it was the idea that anything in his life should play out in a similar fashion to a comic Dickens novel that tickled his funny bone. He could picture it now, Chattaway v. Ellis, and he would have to defend himself against the charge of breach of promise. Perhaps he could convince everyone that it had been a misunderstanding on the Chattaways' part, just as Mrs. Bardell had misunderstood Mr. Pickwick's intentions.

"This is serious, Edward. It's one thing for you to join them upstairs for dinner. It's quite another for you to marry her ladyship's granddaughter."

Edward's whole body felt heavy. He held onto the table and closed his eyes. It took him some time to find his voice. "I believe she loves me too."

"What makes you say so?"

Edward told his grandmother what happened by the castle ruin, the way Daphne looked at him, the way they kissed, twice. Mrs. Ellis sighed.

"Oh, Neddie. You didn't make any promises to her, did you? You don't have a second understanding with Miss Daphne?"

"Of course not. What kind of fool do you think I am?"

"At the moment I'm not sure."

Edward couldn't think of the words to make his grandmother understand. He made his living with words, he understood them, and he could bend them to his will and twist them until they did his bidding. But no matter how hard he tried he couldn't think how to explain the depth to which Miss Daphne Meriwether had touched his heart.

"I'm sorry, Neddie, but this won't do." Mrs. Ellis helped her grandson to his feet. "I wish I had some wise counsel for you. Will you call it off with the Chattaway girl and risk everything?"

Edward shrugged. "I don't know."

Mrs. Ellis pulled her keys from the chain around her waist and unlocked her sitting room door. She shook her head at her grandson as he walked inside.

THE UNHAPPY EARL

*I*t was late that December night, the moon receding in an arc to the other side of the world. Though it was frigid outside and icicles dripped from the glass, Richard kept his window open. He had been back at Hembry since early that morning, he and Hough having caught the early train from London. He argued with Jerrold the night before, and he wanted to leave the city at first light before Jerrold returned for another round. Poor Jerrold. Jerrold, who was always whinging that Richard didn't do enough to help him, though Richard had done, and was still doing, quite enough.

Hough needed to return to Hembry anyway. Ever the doctor, he needed to see a patient in the village. He had insisted that Richard didn't need to accompany him, though the doctor suggested, gently, that perhaps there was business at Hembry that needed tending? Richard already felt spasms of guilt. He wasn't doing his duty, and it wasn't fair to Frederick. Frederick, who had been a good, kind brother from their boyhood. Frederick, who was always the first to defend him when their mother began meddling. Frederick, who should have been Earl but for an unfortunate accident of birth order. Because that's all birth order is, isn't it—an accident? It had been six months since his father died, but Richard still missed him terribly. His father would know what to do. His father would know what to say. But his father wasn't there, and he was Lord Staton now. He would be Lord Staton until the day he died.

Richard hadn't left his room since he returned that morning, refusing every visitor, even Frederick, even Daphne, especially his mother. But the day hadn't been all gloom. He was sitting by his window eating his luncheon on a tray when he saw his niece running toward the castle with the Ellises' grandson. Richard hadn't seen Daphne light up that way since she was a girl and he used to dress her rag doll in her mother's undergarments and say, in his most feminine voice, "Who took my bloomers? Do you have my bloomers? Where are my bloomers?" Daphne laughed so hard she gasped for breath, and so had he. Now here she was looking like young Mr. Ellis had told her the old joke and she couldn't contain her joy. The grass was slippery, and they had to grasp each other to remain upright. The heel of Daphne's boot caught in a puddle and she nearly plummeted to the ground, but young Mr. Ellis caught her around the waist. If they were going to fall, young Mr. Ellis seemed to say, they would fall together. It was so charming, the two young people, stealing shy glances, holding hands. Richard was happy for Daphne. Of course, his mother would die of shock if anything more serious than a run in the rain were to come of Daphne's acquaintance with the young writer. But Daphne and Mr. Edward Ellis were well-suited, both with their inquisitiveness, both with their ready laughter. Richard noticed their connection when young Mr. Ellis came for luncheon. The differences in social station were not an issue for the Earl. He believed the young people should be together if that's what they wanted. Why, in 1870, are we still caught up in a feudal system where only the first-born sons inherit? Why are we still trapped in this nonsensical world of titles and heirs and property? If my niece wants to marry a nice young man who has caught her fancy and is working hard to make his way in the world without a family name or a trust, then she should. And she will. Richard would see to it. You should be able to be with the one you love no matter what anyone else thought. No matter how hard you had to fight for it.

The rest of the day passed and Richard did little enough. He chose a book from his shelf, though he couldn't have said which book it was for all the attention he paid to it. When it was well dark and the rest of the house was asleep, Richard sat at his desk with the out-turned lion's feet, opened the long drawer, and pulled out his pens, ink, and paper. He had a vague idea of a plan to set things right, but that was as far as it went. He wrote a few ideas onto the paper, but they wouldn't do. He crumpled the paper and threw it into the dancing orange flames in the hearth. Richard poked the fire, which crackled as it rose higher. He dropped onto his bed in a heap that looked like a pile of well-tailored clothing. Though it was too dark to see outside, he looked for the shadow of the river that flowed through the grounds. It was a serpentine river, curving along the grassy banks that sprouted white and yellow daisies in spring and summer. It reminded Richard of the River Thames on a much smaller scale. He was such a child when the family stayed at Staton House and he and Freddie wandered off from Nanny and ended up by the river. At first the low-tide water looked fun, like he wanted to take off his shoes and splash in the mud and search for trinkets as he saw the poorly dressed boys doing. When they fished out the body of a dead man, drowned in the river they said, he ran back to the safety of Staton House. A few months later at Hembry, Freddie tried to teach him to swim. He remembered the moment as clearly as if it had happened yesterday. He was trying to keep up with Freddie, who was already an expert swimmer. In his haste he slipped beneath the water and hit his head against the sharp rocks, slicing the skin near his left eye and knocking himself unconscious. He nearly drowned. Since then, no matter how hard anyone prodded him, he stayed away from the river.

He looked around the room with its beige walls, marble hearth, and Baroque accents. Anyone would be pleased by such a home, by such a life. He was the Earl of Staton. He was a peer. And yet he had so many questions. Why had he been born into this family? Why was he the firstborn? His life would have been difficult for him no matter what station he had been born to—of that he was certain. But at least as a shoemaker's son or a soldier he might have had a chance to find some happiness. As Earl, he had no chance at all. It's true, Richard thought. As Lord Staton I have no chance at all.

He picked up the book on the table by his bed and smiled. Our Mutual Friend was his favorite after all. The weight of the volume felt wrong, and he opened the cover with such force he nearly ripped it away. He gasped when he realized the book was empty. He stormed to the door, his hand on the knob, ready to scream bloody murder until his letters were found. Those damned servants! Of course it was one of them. How dare they invade his privacy that way! How dare they...

He staggered back to his bed and sank down, his head bowed over his knees, his gray-streaked chestnut hair brushing the top of his boots. How could he make a scene? Everyone will search for the letters, and the letters will be found (if they were still in the house) and then everyone will know. About his love. About his father's words. The baby! He had promised about the baby! What would happen if the contents of those letters became common knowledge? What would happen to him? What would happen to the family, and to those who mattered most to him in the world?

Richard opened his wardrobe and threw whatever clothes he could grab—shirts, waistcoats, trousers, underthings—into his traveling bag. He didn't ring for Feesbury, the neglected man who was supposed to be his valet who was left behind more often than not. Richard needed to get away. Now. He had only arrived back that morning, and he was certain there were things at Hembry that needed seeing to, but Freddie could handle it. Freddie, who should have been the first-born, who should have been Earl. I'll leave Freddie a note saying I had to go, it was urgent. Freddie has figured out that I haven't been about with the Marlborough House Set for over a year, so I'll say instead I've gone to Gladfellow House in Yorkshire.

As Richard wrote his hurried note he decided against mentioning Gladfellow House, knowing Frederick could very well show up there. He wrote Frederick's name in large letters at the top of the envelope so whoever found the letter on his desk would know who to give it to. People were good at finding letters in his room. Richard slipped on his overcoat and a heavy scarf, set his top hat low on his head, and grabbed his travel bag. He turned the knob as quietly as he could, opened the door, and saw no one. It was so late even the servants would be tucked away in the attics. Richard stepped into the hallway with a light tread, afraid of setting the old floorboards creaking. He closed his door and left down the dark spiral staircase.

CHRISTMAS AT HEMBRY CASTLE

*C*hristmas at Hembry Castle was glorious. The same rooms that felt cavernous and cold the rest of the year now glowed gold and warm while the hearth fires waved holiday cheer to all who passed. Every surface in every room was covered with berried evergreens while mistletoe draped the walls and baskets of clove-wrapped oranges scented the air. The centerpiece of the castle was a 15-foot-tall tree lit with white candles and decorated with paper chains, strung candies, ribbons, and tinsel, presents from the village children. Even the Countess of Staton was softened by the glee of the season. She seemed almost dreamy as she floated about the castle, her wind blowing a few degrees less coolly. She entertained Daphne with memories of her sons' first Christmastides, naming every gift her sons had ever presented her, every mischief they had found themselves in. In the darkness, descending early now, Lady Staton spent hours with Daphne by the hearth in the sitting room over steaming cups of tea and lemon cakes telling stories of Frederick's antics as a boy, like the time he meant to give his nanny a frog as a holiday gift and the slimy thing leaped first into Nanny's apron pocket and then down the front of her dress. Another time Lady Staton told Daphne how Prince Albert had brought his native country's Christmas traditions, including Christmas trees, to Windsor Castle in 1841. "And if Queen Victoria had a Christmas tree," the Countess said, "then all of England wanted a Christmas tree."

"We have Christmas trees in America," Daphne said. "They add such a festive feeling to the season. And the candlelight is so beautiful." When Lady Staton looked surprised, Daphne said, "Yes, Grandma, even Americans are civilized enough to have Christmas trees." To Daphne's surprise, her grandmother laughed. A Christmas miracle indeed.

The day itself was snowy, and iridescent light filtered from the quilted gray sky. The castle was full, as it was every year, with family, friends, villagers, farmers, tradesmen, and anyone else important to the castle and its people. They had gathered together, as was the 250-year-old tradition, to eat and drink to their heart's content, sing carols, and dance. Daphne saw two faces that made her particularly joyous: her Uncle Richard and Edward Ellis. Uncle Richard had done his disappearing act a few weeks before, leaving behind a cryptic message to her father about how he had pressing business but he would be back at Hembry for the holidays. When Richard turned up on Christmas Eve, everyone was so relieved they let his latest disappearing act pass without comment. Daphne saw her uncle smiling, easy, relaxed—as though some great weight, some strangulating albatross, had been removed from his neck once and for all and he moved all the lighter for it. She watched him mingle with his guests, chatting with the farmers and villagers, joking with the servants, and dancing with his mother. Then he danced with a ten-year-old village girl, who positively beamed at the Earl of Staton.

Edward Ellis' arrival had a very different effect. He arrived in the afternoon, apologizing for his tardiness, but he had wanted to spend some time that holiday with his parents and siblings in London. Mr. Ellis greeted his grandson warmly, then stood near the wall in his usual hunched manner with his hands behind his back. The butler contemplated the festivities over his round-rimmed spectacles and looked pleased with the turnout. Frederick clasped Edward's shoulder and steered the young man toward the punch bowl.

"I'm so pleased you've come, Edward, as is Daphne."

Frederick then excused himself to see about Mrs. Pearson, a village widow whose son, Joseph, had been ill. Frederick spoke to Mr. Hough, and the men approached the woman and her small boy, giving the lad some peppermint sticks and molasses taffy to put a smile on his face. Frederick led the boy to the sitting room where a pantomime put on by the village children was in full swing.

"Who is that?" Edward asked as he watched Frederick and the boy. Daphne explained, and Edward said, "That's good of your father to take such an interest. And you."

"At first, Joseph seemed better but then he was ill again. Mr. Hough isn't sure what's wrong with the poor boy. He doesn't have a fever, and he doesn't have the chills. He's just ill. Mr. Hough left a note with directions for how to care for Joseph while he was gone, and we followed his instructions to the letter."

"It must have worked. The boy looks well enough today."

"He does, doesn't he? Let's hope that's a good sign."

Edward and Daphne joined the singing carolers:

GOD REST YE MERRY, *gentlemen*
Let nothing you dismay

Remember, Christ, our Savior
Was born on Christmas day
To save us all from Satan's power
When we were gone astray
O tidings of comfort and joy,
Comfort and joy
O tidings of comfort and joy.

WHEN THE SONG WAS DONE, the string quartet began an upbeat tune and dancers filed into the center of the Great Hall to bow or curtsey at each other before taking off down the rows on their toes. It was a beautiful scene, Daphne thought, as family, villagers, and anyone else who wanted danced before the tall tree. Mothers danced with their sons and fathers danced with their daughters. The Earl of Staton danced with the baker's wife and the peacock danced with the Marchioness of Braddleton. Edward laughed when his grandfather took his grandmother for a swing around the room. He nodded toward the dancers.

"Miss Meriwether, may I have this dance?"

Daphne curtsied, and she joined Edward with his grandparents and the others. As soon as she started moving she forgot everyone else. She forgot the holiday decorations and the table of delicious food. She forgot the music and the very walls holding up the castle around her. She was with Edward, his left hand on her hip, his right hand holding hers. He looked nowhere but into her eyes, and she looked into his. His eyes were very green then, spring green, green like new life and green like hopes and dreams. She expected some comic comment from him as was his way, but he only smiled, and she smiled too. A space opened around them, and Edward twirled Daphne so her red velvet dress with the gold embroidered ruffles flared behind her. She felt as though she waltzed on air. When the music stopped and the others clapped, Edward and Daphne clapped too, though Daphne was still dizzy with the exhilaration.

When the next song began, Edward grabbed Daphne's hand and led her to an empty seat near the hearth. He opened his mouth, about to speak, but then he looked from the dancers to the Christmas tree to his grandparents, who were close in conversation and glancing in Edward's direction. Edward reached beneath his black frock coat, his green and red paisley cravat falling out from his green velvet waistcoat while he fumbled in his pocket. After an anxious moment, he pulled out a small green box. He looked around, and though the room was full everyone was so caught up in their frivolity they didn't notice the chocolate-haired, nervous-looking young man and the small box he handed to the golden-haired, glowing young woman.

"I wish you'd accept this in the spirit it's intended—a holiday gift between friends."

Daphne turned the box over in her hands. "May I?"

"Please."

She gasped at the garnet earrings inside. True, perhaps the gems weren't of the same quality as the heart-shaped ruby ring her grandmother had given her, but they were perfect—small, round, set in filigree gold.

"You're not offended?" Edward asked.

"Offended? They're beautiful. I love them. Come here." Without thinking of the hundreds of people in the castle, without thinking of anything but the present she had for Edward, she took his hand and led him around the dancers to the ceiling-high tree. She kneeled by the white-lace skirt at the bottom and reached around the back, pulling out a gold-wrapped box with a sprig of holly tucked within the red bow.

"It's from Papa and me." She handed Edward the gift and waited with clasped hands while he opened it—a copy of A Christmas Carol signed by Mr. Dickens himself.

Edward turned the book from front to back to side to front again. "You must have contacts beyond the grave."

"Not quite. My father and I found it in a bookshop on the Strand in London. As soon as I saw it I thought of you, the soon-to-be famous author. Your book will be out before long, and who knows? Maybe you really will be the next Mr. Dickens." She pointed to the inside flap of the book. "In case you were wondering, that is his signature. My father had it checked. Someone must have not known what they had."

Edward stepped closer to her, closing the space between them. "I know exactly what I have."

Daphne wanted him to look at her that way all the Christmas day, with an intensity she had never seen from him before. When the musicians played a waltz, Edward held out his hand. Daphne curtsied, and again he twirled her across the dance floor, and again her ruby-red dress fanned behind her, and again she felt lifted by the air.

This time, however, Daphne was aware of the others in the room, and she felt them following her every move. Her grandmother squinted at her while she held her ear trumpet in place to hear her Uncle Jerrold and his wife Hyacinth, who held her monocle close to her eye so she wouldn't miss a detail. Her Uncle Richard leaned close to John Hough and whispered. Her father watched them too, exchanging sly looks with Uncle Richard and Mr. Hough. When the dance ended, Uncle Jerrold stepped forward.

"Excuse me, but I haven't danced with my niece, and it is Christmas."

Edward bowed and excused himself. He joined Frederick by the refreshment table, and Daphne saw that even from the distance Edward couldn't take his eyes from her. Uncle Jerrold cleared his throat, shook his head, and cleared his throat again. Daphne guessed he was struggling for something to say, and she wouldn't help him. He asked for the dance so he gets to steer the conversation. Finally, after one more clearing of the throat, he said, "Hyacinth and I are returning to London after the new year."

"I'm glad the boys could come. They must enjoy Hembry at Christmas time."

"Certainly they do. It was always my favorite time of year."

"I heard you're doing some traveling to offer your support during the elections."

"Oh, yes. One can't do enough to help further our cause."

"Which is?"

"The cause of tradition. The cause of the correct order of things."

"You believe there's a correct order, Uncle Jerrold?"

"Of course I do. People are born into their station in life, and it is their duty to fulfill that station." He looked in Edward's direction as though he were jabbing the young man with the intensity of his glare.

"Surely everyone has their own talents and should be allowed to see those talents as far as they can."

Jerrold shook his head. His features, always forlorn, looked as though they might drop from his face altogether. "I forget sometimes that you're American."

"I'm surprised. Grandma never does." Jerrold didn't dance as gracefully as Edward, and Daphne spent most of the polka trying not to trip over her uncle's toes. His legs moved awkwardly, and Daphne checked to see if his boots were on the wrong feet. "Will you be traveling again soon?"

"Oh, yes. Richard is..."

Jerrold stopped moving as quickly as he stopped speaking, and Daphne nearly tumbled onto the dancers beside her.

"What is it, Uncle Jerrold? Do you and Uncle Richard have a trick card up your sleeves?"

Jerrold stepped away, his hands shaking. "How dare you insinuate that I'm up to something. An Englishman's first priority is to his own home!"

Daphne said a silent thank you to the conductor when the music stopped. She curtsied at her uncle, then joined her father and Edward by the tree.

"What was that about?" Frederick asked.

"Uncle Jerrold was rattled by something, but I couldn't tell you what."

"He probably didn't know what to make of you dancing with me."

Edward smiled in that friendly way he had, and for the first time, Daphne realized what she had done. By speaking so publicly to Edward, by dancing with him to the exclusion of everyone else but her uncle, and by sharing their gifts in this public space, she had made a choice. Most likely everyone in the castle knew how she felt about Edward by now.

So let it be, Daphne thought. While Edward hasn't made any declarations yet, she hoped that he felt the same for her as she did for him. She had to follow her heart, and her heart led to Edward Ellis.

A SERVANT'S CHRISTMAS

The Christmas guests continued dancing, holding hands as they skipped around the tree, while the children munched on cakes and marveled at how beautiful their handmade gifts looked in the glowing light of the grand house. The hot punch and Madeira eggnog were in full effect now, and everyone mingled even more freely than they had before, talking and singing and laughing. After all, most of the guests had known each other their entire lives. As the saying goes, if you're born in Hembry you'll die in Hembry, and then they'll carry you feet first to your final resting place down the road a stretch. Most of the farmers and other tenants were descendants from the families living in the area when the first Earl of Staton received his patent. Where they were shy of the 9th Earl when they first arrived that Christmas day, the villagers soon discovered him to be a friendly soul who spoke easily to everyone. Perhaps he was like his father after all. In truth, they hadn't seen much of the new Earl since the old one died. The new Earl had been too much in London and other places, they heard, to which they nodded and said, well, he hasn't a wife to hold him down so he still floats about.

As Edward danced the day away with Daphne, he noticed the glint-eyed stares from the Countess, her youngest son, and her youngest son's wife. He saw the scarcely hidden concern from his grandparents too, but he wasn't going to let anyone put a damper on this perfect day. He leaned close to Daphne, admiring the way the high collar of her velvet ruby-colored dress with the gold-embroidered pomegranates framed her heart-shaped face and brought out the yellow tones in her hair.

"What are you looking at?" she had asked him.

"You. I cannot stop looking at you."

Daphne blushed, and a beautiful blush it was, her cheeks matching the deep gem tone of her dress. Edward forgot the squinting Countess, her thin-lipped son, and his Cyclops of a wife looking one-eyed at the world through her monocle. Edward excused himself from Daphne, who was speaking with Mrs. Pearson and her little boy. The little boy beamed at Daphne the way the flower vendor's son had beamed at Daphne—as though she were the source of all light. Edward opened the green baize door and went down, the wooden staircase creaking beneath his boots with each step. While the merrymaking continued upstairs, the servants' celebration was in full swing below. Certainly, the servants were included in the family's holiday revelry, but they always stole a little time, a little food, and perhaps a little of the piping hot punch and Madeira eggnog for themselves. Edward heard the boisterous laughter, the shouted conversations, and the slurps as the punch bowls were dipped into again and again. Colin played an old violin, his grandmother played the piano, and everyone sang an exuberant version of "Good King Wenceslas."

Good King Wenceslas looked out,
On the Feast of Stephen,

When the snow lay round about,
Deep and crisp and even;
Brightly shone the moon that
Night, though the frost was cruel,
When a poor man came in sight,
Gathering winter fuel...

Edward joined in the singing—it was Christmas after all. Then the footmen took a punch-induced initiative and changed the next lines of the song into a bawdy public house ditty, reminding Edward of Fezziwig's celebration in A Christmas Carol. When they finished singing Edward accepted a cup of eggnog from Mrs. Graham and found his way to his grandmother.

"Neddie! I'm so glad you could come down."

"Glad he could tear himself from Miss Daphne, more like," said the peacock.

Edward glared at Henry but said nothing. He had noticed how the first footman seemed rather pleased with himself lately, grinning at everyone with an I have a secret leer, but Edward liked the footman little enough and didn't care about whatever it was that had Henry looking smug.

Mr. Ellis appeared in the servants' hall. "Henry, see that the punchbowl upstairs is full. Colin, bring up the mince pies Mrs. Graham set on the tray." Mr. Ellis sighed. He sat at the table and whispered something to his wife, who looked at Edward with a concerned expression.

"What is it?" Edward asked.

"Not today, Neddie," Mrs. Ellis said. "It's Christmas Day."

"You can't whisper to each other with those forlorn looks and then not tell me what's happening."

"True enough," Mr. Ellis said. "It's your father, Edward. I'm afraid he's in trouble again."

Edward drained the rest of his eggnog in one swallow. "What has he done now?"

"The same," Mrs. Ellis said. "It's always the same."

The door to the servants' entrance swung open and the festivities spread outside. Ruth and Jemima threw their hand-knitted woolen scarves around their necks, grabbed wooden boards from the shed, ran up the hill of the courtyard, and slid down the snowy mound. Others followed, and soon the court-yard was busy with merry, eggnog-filled servants singing carols, pulling on Christmas crackers, and eating the bonbons inside. Despite the Christmas joy surrounding him, Edward felt his holiday spirit evaporate like the fog on the breaths of those outside. He watched the servants making snowmen and waving angels into the ground.

"I saw them this morning," he said. "We had Christmas breakfast together. Kate and Nathan seemed fine, happy. My mother was her usual chattering self. Father seemed content. No one said anything."

Mrs. Ellis stood beside her grandson. "You don't need to worry, Neddie."

"How can I not worry? Besides, it's not my father that concerns me. It's Kate and Nathan. Kate's only 16, and Nate's only 12. Perhaps they should live with me."

Mr. Ellis shook his head so swiftly his spectacles fell to the tip of his nose. "No, Edward. You need to concentrate on your-self right now. You need to get those stories ready for your publishers."

"How can I concentrate on myself knowing Father is up to his old tricks? I have a little money set aside, and I have more coming after I send the copy to Fergusonandwately. Perhaps I should send some..."

"You will do no such thing." Mrs. Ellis spoke with more vehemence than Edward had ever heard her. "You'll never get ahead in the world if you're always held back by the past. Your father is a grown man. He needs to make out for himself for once."

Edward knew she was right. But he also knew his father couldn't resist shiny new top hats, brightly colored waistcoats, or gleaming gold watches. He couldn't shake the thought of his younger brother and sister at the mercy of his father's whimsies, and something would have to be done about it sooner or later.

Mrs. Ellis turned her attention to the snowball fight taking shape outside. "I should bring them in. The guests will be leaving soon and the family will want to get ready for their Christmas dinner. Oh!" She laughed as Miss Rowland threw a snowball at Mr. Feesbury's head. "They're having so much fun though." She looked at her husband, who watched the frolickers from the open doorway. "We can leave them another minute or two."

Mr. Ellis grunted as he bent over. When he stood he tossed a snowball at his wife's apron. Squealing like a girl, Mrs. Ellis ran outside to get away from her husband, and her husband ran after her, and the servants applauded as they watched the butler and housekeeper chasing each other and leaving their footprints in the snow. After he finished chasing his wife, Mr. Ellis called to the staff. They had to see the guests off, they had to clean up from the celebration, and they had to have everything for the family's private holiday dinner that night. As the servants trailed into the house, shaking their boots and loosening their scarves, Edward thought about Daphne upstairs. Suddenly, he was alone with his grandmother.

"Did you have a good time today?" she asked.

"I think this may be the best Christmas ever."

"Any particular reason?"

"The decorations, the tree, the food, the drink, the dancing…"

"The Earl's niece?"

Edward groaned. "I love her, Grandmother. I can't help the way I feel."

"Have you decided what you're going to do?"

"I haven't a clue."

Mrs. Graham's frustrated voice rang out over the clinging and clanging of pots and pans.

"Sounds like a panic back there, Neddie, doesn't it?"

"Mrs. Graham always panics, and everything always comes out perfectly well."

"That's true enough. I hope everything comes out perfectly well for you, my darling boy." Her brows drew close as she considered her grandson. "Edward Augustus Ellis, whatever am I going to do with you?"

HENRY HORROCKS STOOD at the base of the servants' staircase and listened. More secrets! And he was starting to see a plan, a way through the maze so he could profit and the mighty would fall. The housekeeper's grandson is considering leaving his fiancée for Miss Daphne. The cheek of it! That upstart nobody thinking he had a chance with the niece of the Earl of Staton! Ah, well, thought Henry. Let him try. Nothing will come of it. I'll see to that.

Henry turned at the sound of footsteps and saw Colin on the stairs above him.

"Mr. Ellis is looking for you, Henry."

"Hold your horses. I'm coming."

Heavy footsteps brought loud creaking on the staircase. Mr. Ellis stood over the footmen, glaring at the young men over the top of his spectacles. Colin took one step toward the butler. "I've found him, Mr. Ellis."

"Thank you, Colin." Mr. Ellis pressed his spectacles against his nose. "I'm pleased to see that at least one footman is working today."

Colin looked back at Henry, smiled as though everything was grand, and then followed Mr. Ellis up the stairs. When Mr. Ellis appeared back downstairs a few moments later, Mrs. Ellis was near the steps, her hands on her hips as she stared at the wood railing.

"What is it, Mary?"

"Henry is up to something. I'm sure of it."

"What makes you say so?"

"It's a feeling I have."

"I can say from experience your feelings are usually spot on. What should we do?"

"I believe some investigation is in order, Augustus."

"Tell me when and where my dear."

Mrs. Ellis grasped her husband's hand. "I never realized how fortunate I am to have such a willing partner in crime."

Mr. Ellis was about to reply when a loud crash came from the kitchen accompanied by staccato screams from the kitchen maids and legato growls from Mrs. Graham.

"Should you check on them?" asked Mr. Ellis.

"Mrs. Graham will get it sorted."

The Ellises walked upstairs together. They spotted Colin, who was standing inside the green baize door.

Mr. Ellis' voice dropped an octave. "I thought you were the one footman working today?"

"I'm sorry, Mr. Ellis. I was wondering what you wanted me to do with the chairs in the Great Hall."

Mr. Ellis opened the door and allowed Colin past. He rolled

his eyes to the ceiling and shook his head at his wife. Mrs. Ellis held her hand over her mouth in an attempt to restrain her laughter.

THE PRESENTATION, OR A GRANDMOTHER'S DREAM

*L*ives in Hembry Village, as in Hembry Castle, continued as they had for centuries. Whether the Earl of Staton was at his country seat or not, the farmers, the villagers, the merchants, the artisans, the postmaster, and the vicar had their concerns and someone had to see to them. Whether it was his lordship, a family member, or the stable boy getting things done, the people of Hembry didn't care. Increasingly, they were directed to Mr. Frederick, second son of their beloved 8th Earl, and in time they came to trust the man known as the wayward who had his father's aquamarine eyes, benevolent smile, and genial manner. The Honorable Frederick Meriwether insisted he was happy to assist however he could. Please do tell him of any matters that need tending and he will make certain all is handled to everyone's satisfaction.

The widow Mrs. Clements' cottage flooded? Whatever of her belongings could be salvaged were, whatever was destroyed was replaced, and she and her children were relocated to a dry, clean home bigger than their previous dwelling though the rent remained the same. She was even given three months of free rent while she recovered herself and her young children. Mr. Kimball cannot pay his rent on time? We will not turn you and your sickly mother out into the winter cold, Mr. Frederick said. Mr. Spreang is ill and cannot farm his land? Robust boys from the castle will help, and Mr. Frederick brought round Mr. Hough, the family's physician, to tend to the sickly man. Both Mr. Frederick and his lovely daughter visited many times over several weeks to help Mr. Spreang, the lovely daughter bathing the ill man's forehead with cool water and feeding him soup made by the castle's cook. Other times Miss Meriwether cared for Mr. Spreang's children so Mrs. Spreang could sit undisturbed with her husband for a time. Mrs. Pearson's son Joseph was sickly again? Mr. and Miss Meriwether brought their doctor there as well. Mr. Hough continued to care for the boy, and Miss Meriwether visited with special treats for mother and son.

By the time church bells tolled in the Epiphany in January, instead of asking for his lordship, the people of Hembry wanted Mr. Frederick. When women or children were involved, Miss Meriwether's gentle touch was requested. It was as if they had forgotten that there was an Earl, perhaps because the Earl himself seemed to have forgotten. When his lordship was at Hembry he sat in on meetings about village business with Mr. Frederick, his lordship looking very bored, very ill, very distracted, or some combination of all. Lord Staton nodded when appropriate, looked serious when required, laughed when the mood needed lightening, but always he was happy to allow Mr. Frederick to handle the situation. The rumor around the village, told and told again at the post office, was that during these meetings Lord Staton turned to his brother and said, "See, Freddie. Everyone knew you were better suited to this than me."

. . .

SUDDENLY, it was spring, and a bursting kaleidoscope of color bloomed everywhere around the castle. Green replaced gray, flowers flourished, and Daphne's presentation to the Queen was at hand. Between dress fittings, etiquette lessons, practicing walking backward without tripping, and rehearsing her curtsey so she could kneel to the floor without falling (there was no way to fall gracefully, Daphne discovered), there was little time for the American girl to think her own thoughts. There were other oddities as well, such as the time Lady Staton suggested Daphne practice speaking with the family's elongated aristocratic tones. Since Frederick had only rude words in response, the idea was dropped. Daphne was exhausted by her grandmother's constant demands, and as the weather grew warmer she began to steal moments to sneak to the parkland to sit under the trees and watch the grass grow.

There were reprieves. Whenever Frederick traveled to London on Daily Observer business he took Daphne along to give her a break from her grandmother, for which Daphne was grateful. Despite the worry brought on by her upcoming presentation, her days brightened whenever Edward visited, though his visits grew fewer while he dealt with demands of his own. The due date for his story collection loomed closer and he was increasingly fretful about getting everything finished on time, about whether or not the stories were any good, and any other number of concerns that kept him bottled up inside his London flat with sweat on his hands and ink in his hair. Some days Daphne received a letter from Edward dated at 3 o'clock in the morning. His letters were so long that once Daphne wrote back telling him to stop writing to her, to take that time to work on his stories, to which she'd receive a reply saying that his letters to her were keeping him sane—

after all, his stories stopped making sense to him weeks ago. To make his point, Edward began sending the stories to Hembry Castle or Staton House, wherever Daphne happened to be. Daphne and Frederick read the tales aloud to each other and they nodded, saying, "Yes, this young man may very well be the next Mr. Dickens." Where Mr. Dickens had focused on oddities and caricatures of London life, especially that of the poor, Edward wrote stories where Education was the star, Education the hero that could raise the low and rescue the downtrodden and give everyone the opportunity they deserved so they could live the very best life they could create for themselves. Edward Ellis was a kind, sensitive, thoughtful man unlike any Daphne had ever known.

So there it was. Daphne had fallen for Edward. Their day together at Christmas had only cemented her attachment. The young man with the wide hazel eyes and the hair that refused to stay out of his face, the easy laugh, and the friendly smile, he was the one for her. She did not doubt it now. But he still hadn't made a declaration about his feelings for her, and she still wondered about his intentions. When they were together, Edward was all attentiveness and exuberance. His letters to her were always confidences about how he felt not quite up to the task set before him by Fergusonandwately, how he feared he might let her father down by neglecting his duties at the Observer, how her friendship meant everything to him, and how she kept him going during those long, long hours when he stared into the creative abyss. Those weren't simply the words of a young man in want of companionship. He wouldn't share himself that way with just anyone (he was English, after all). Yet Daphne wondered what it would take for him to finally declare himself.

Back at Hembry, Daphne sat alone in her bedroom in the wing chair by the hearth. Though the weather was warmer, it was still cold in that big house and she was always seeking out the comfort of the fire. Her bedroom was a beautiful space painted pearl pink, and it was the one place in all the castle where she felt free from prying eyes. Known as the Rose Tree Room, the wall behind the bed featured a mural of a sepia-brown tree whose branches spread gracefully toward the ceiling. On the green sprouts from the branches bloomed white leaves and mauve roses intertwined with blue and yellow birds. At the end of the tree, directly above the bed, was a golden birdcage with one little blue bird peering from behind the bars. That's how I feel at Hembry, Daphne thought. Like a bird in a gilded cage where I can see everything beautiful around me but I can't reach it because I'm trapped. She ran her hand over the flower-embroidered silk bedcovers that were the same shade of pearl-pink as her walls and she marveled at how every detail in this room, as in the whole castle, was arranged to perfection, from the color of the walls to the matching bed set, to the green polished dressing table with rose trellises painted down the sides, to the chandelier with the white and pink baubles that reflected the light. Someone knocked at Daphne's door and Pamela Escott appeared, her ringlets of ginger hair falling out from under her white cap. Daphne grimaced at the gown in Pamela's hands.

"Another fitting?"

"Is now not a good time, Miss Daphne?"

"Now is as good a time as any. It's not like I have anything else to do."

Daphne walked behind the screen near her dressing table, removed her deep green day dress, and put on the gown she would wear for her presentation. She had tried the gown on so many times she felt like one day they would sew it up so tightly she might never escape the gown again. They'll have to bury me in this, Daphne thought. She walked around the screen and stepped onto the footstool. "No Rowland today?"

"Her ladyship wanted me to handle the final fittings. Miss Rowland will supervise my work, of course, but her ladyship wants me to do it. This way I'll be ready when it's time for you to have a proper lady's maid."

"When will that be?"

"When you're married."

Daphne laughed. "I think my grandmother has great expectations for the result of my presentation."

"I think she expects you to be engaged by the end of the Season."

"The end of the Season! That doesn't give me much time."

"Do you have someone in mind?" Daphne felt her cheeks blush hot. Pamela took a pin from the case on the dressing table and pinned the white satin hem. "Anyone you'd care to mention?"

"My grandmother would not approve, I can say that."

Pamela stood back and studied her handiwork. "I think this may be it, Miss Daphne. I'll fix the hemline, and then Miss Rowland will inspect. If everything is to her satisfaction, then I think we can say your gown is finished."

Daphne studied the white gown with the long train embroidered with blush-colored roses. "It's beautiful, Pamela." Daphne stared into the mirror, examining her reflection, hardly recognizing herself in this grand gown in this grand room in this grand house.

"Is there anything else, Miss Daphne?"

"I was just thinking how perfect everything is at Hembry. The house, the furnishings, the meals, this gown. I'm not a perfect person. I don't belong here."

"None of us are perfect, Miss Daphne, and rarely is anything what it seems."

Daphne closed her eyes. She was so tired suddenly. The sky had darkened to slate gray as a springtime storm closed in, which only added to her feeling that she wanted to sleep. Was there ever a time it didn't rain at Hembry Castle?

"Of course you're right, Pamela. It's this presentation. It worries me."

"Are you worried about your gown?"

"My gown is the one thing I know will be perfect. It's everything else: the protocol, remembering to curtsey three times, dipping to the floor without sprawling over, remembering what to say and what not to say, walking backward without knocking into anything. It's knowing that my Uncle Richard has left again and no one knows where he is. Life doesn't make much sense these days, I'm afraid. The presentation itself is a sham because it doesn't mean to me what it means to my grandmother and I'm just going through the motions. Contrary to my grandmother's wishes, I won't be marrying an heir or a spare. I love Edward."

Daphne's palms grew wet and she closed her fists instead of wiping the sweat on her gown. She had said it aloud: I love Edward. She would say it to no one but Pamela, though the maid didn't look surprised. She peered at Daphne's reflection in the mirror.

"May I speak freely, Miss Daphne?"

"Always."

"It's all right to go through with the presentation for the sake of her ladyship. It would be a nice gift to her if you went through with it. It's all she's talked about since you arrived. She might have certain plans for you afterward, but you and I both know that when the time comes to marry you'll choose your own husband."

"If he'll have me."

"Believe me, Miss Daphne, I've seen the look on young Mr.

Ellis' face whenever your name comes up. I've seen the way he stares at you when you're near him."

"Then why hasn't he said anything?"

"He has to…" Pamela shook her head. "Maybe he's shy."

"He isn't very shy when we're talking about everything else in the world."

"It's one thing to discuss books and the stories he's writing, but it's different to share the depths of your heart, especially with the person at the center. And don't forget, you're the niece of the Earl of Staton. You could marry the most eligible titled men in England."

"But what is the point of a title? What is the point of a social position? Is that all there is to life, making yourself acceptable to people you hardly know, jockeying for position, showing off the finest jewelry, carriages, clothing, and homes to people who only care about showing off back to you? All I need is the people I love around me, my family and friends. I need a simple, comfortable home, and I need some kind of purpose. I can't sit around like a dressmaking mannequin all day." Daphne sighed. "I'm sorry, Pamela. These things have been weighing on me since I came here. And now with the presentation so near…"

"I understand, Miss Daphne. But I think you should look at the presentation for what it is, a gift to her ladyship. It might seem small, even silly to you, but this is her ladyship's way. This is how she came of age to marry, and then she met her husband, your grandfather. It's a sacrifice on your part, I know, but it would make her ladyship so happy."

Daphne faced the housemaid. "How are you so wise, Pamela? We're the same age yet I always learn so much from you. I'm afraid I have nothing to offer in return."

"I wouldn't say that, Miss Daphne. I've seen a lot in life, as

I'm sure you have, and I've learned so much from you as well. It makes me think I might like America."

"I think you would love America. America..." Daphne shook her head. "Maybe that's where my Uncle Richard has gone."

"His lordship is in London."

Daphne grasped the maid's hands. "How do you know?"

"He's tending to..." Pamela broke off, her eyes wide.

"Tending to what? If you know anything about my uncle, where he goes, what he does, anything, I beg you to tell me."

Pamela opened her mouth to speak, but the heavy knock stopped her. The two young women stayed frozen as the door creaked open. First the spectacles, then the rest of Mr. Ellis peered into the room.

"Excuse me, Miss Daphne, but her ladyship requests your presence in the sitting room. She wants to go over the details of the banquet for your ball with you and Mrs. Graham."

"Of course, Ellis."

Daphne released Pamela's hand and followed Ellis away. She looked back at the young housemaid as she left, hoping to absorb some of what Pamela knew about her uncle through the air between them.

LADY STATON PULLED strings with royal contacts dangling at the end and she managed to get Daphne on the list for the Queen's first Drawing Room of the Season. They arrived at Staton House the day before the presentation, and they had been so busy preparing for the trip to London and settling last-minute details about the ball that Daphne hadn't been able to question Pamela further.

The morning of the presentation Daphne was woken at dawn and given a hearty breakfast since she wouldn't eat again until they arrived back at Staton House (Her Majesty didn't wish to feed the debutantes since that might encourage them to outstay their welcome). After breakfast, back in her birdcage bedroom, Pamela helped Daphne dress. First was the chemise, then the bloomers, then the corset, then the cage bustle, then the petticoat, and finally the iridescent white satin gown with the requisite 12-foot-long train embroidered with blush-colored roses. The gown shimmered like sunshine on icicles when it caught the light. After the gown was adjusted to perfection Miss Rowland swept Daphne's gold hair into an updo with curled tendrils framing her face. Lady Staton joined them while Miss Rowland set the white tulle veil into place.

"That was my veil from when I was presented myself, Daphne, many years ago. This fan was mine as well. I've saved them for you all these years. I didn't have any daughters so I wanted my only granddaughter to be presented in them."

"I love them, Grandma. I wear them proudly."

The Countess clasped Daphne's hands. Maybe Pamela was right, and all the hassles leading to this day were worth it if her grandmother was this happy. The Countess pulled Rowland for herself so she could get ready, leaving Pamela to help Daphne into her white satin shoes and elbow-length white satin gloves. For the finishing touches, Daphne wore a head-band with white feathers and carried a bouquet of white roses with pink peonies. When everyone was allowed to see the result, her grandmother fussed over her train, her father beamed, her Uncle Jerrold nodded, and her Aunt Hyacinth squinted through her monocle. Someone was missing, and Daphne looked toward the door.

"Where's Uncle Richard, Papa?"

Her father shrugged. Before Daphne could ask more questions, she was loaded into the stately gray carriage. As soon as everyone was settled—her ladyship, Daphne, Frederick,

Jerrold, and Hyacinth—the carriage lurched forward and the family was driven down the Mall toward Buckingham Palace. While they waited for the gates to open at 2 p.m. precisely, Daphne saw other carriages carrying young women tittering with excitement. The coachman showed Daphne's invitation to the guards at the gate, and they were allowed across the forecourt where they passed Blore's archway. Daphne had seen the palace many times before, located as it was along Constitution Hill and adjacent to St. James' Park. When Daphne saw Buckingham Palace for the first time she made her father laugh by saying it wasn't so very impressive. It reminded her of Hembry Castle in the simplicity of its façade with its neoclassical influence. Daphne had been much more impressed with Hampton Court Palace and Kew Gardens with their Tudor stylings. In the distance, she could hear the bands of the Second Battalion of Her Majesty's Life Guards playing lively tunes to keep up the spirits of the young ladies, some of whom had been waiting for hours. Finally, Daphne and her family were escorted into the palace.

"What's wrong, my darling girl?" Frederick asked.

"I have a terrible feeling I don't belong here."

"Why on earth not?"

"Those girls look like children to me. I know I'm only two years older than they are but I feel Grandma's age compared to them. And I look silly in this dress with this ridiculous train and these giant feathers. I feel like a chicken. Those girls, it's like I can see their dreams for their futures in their smiles and I don't feel that."

"This is indeed an important day for them. They've looked forward to this since they were children. Your doing this for your grandmother is so very generous of you. Don't forget, while you're standing there with all those young women, that your life began the day you were born. You don't need a nod from Her Majesty to know you're special. You're special because of the extraordinary young woman you've become."

Daphne kissed her father's cheek. "That's a very American thing to say."

"Some of it must have rubbed off after all those years."

Daphne scanned the sea of unfamiliar faces. "Still no Uncle Richard?"

"I'm afraid he isn't here."

Daphne considered how to tell her father what she knew. "Before we left Hembry Pamela told me she knew where Uncle Richard had gone."

"What did she say?"

"She said he had gone to London on business, but then we were interrupted and I've been so busy I haven't had a chance to ask her again. He wasn't at Staton House when we arrived, so who knows where he is now."

Her father's aquamarine eyes scanned the faces around him as though he were searching for Richard. "Well well. Pamela knew where your Uncle Richard was and I didn't. Another mystery. We'll have to ask Pamela how she knew."

"I had the impression she didn't want to reveal any more, and maybe she didn't intend to say even that much."

"But if she knows something she must be made to see that we need to know as well."

Jerrold wrung his hands as though he were twisting a great worry away. He looked back at his wife, elegant in her long-limbed way in her pale lavender dress, her bustle making her backside unusually wide for such a slender woman. Her attention was directed elsewhere as she guided her monocle over the giddy young women, looking for imperfections, Daphne guessed.

"What were you saying?" Jerrold asked. "Were you talking about Richard? And who else? That housemaid? What did she say? I warned Richard not to hire her at Hembry. I knew she'd be trouble."

"Pamela is no trouble," Frederick said. "We were simply wondering where Richard is."

Jerrold wrung his hands again. "Richard." He coughed up the name as though putting a curse on his eldest brother. "As if Richard cares about anyone but himself. I've never seen anyone with less regard for his family." When Hyacinth waved her fan and called a high-pitched "Jerrold!" he rushed to her side.

Daphne was startled when a young woman with ceiling-high plumes walked past. It must be quite a balancing act to keep those feathers upright, she thought. Daphne marveled at how the young women greeted each other like old friends, admiring each other's gowns, laughing at the obstacles of getting ready for the day, tittering about the balls and operas to come. She knew Edward would make her feel better by pointing out the absurdities surrounding them, of which there were many.

"What are you thinking, my dear?" Frederick asked.

"I wish Edward were here."

"He'll be at your ball."

Lady Staton pulled herself away from a heavily bejeweled acquaintance to help Daphne fold the unwieldy train over her arm (it must be the left arm) and arranged the white plumes sprouting from her headband (they must be large since Her Majesty did not care for little feathers). Daphne shivered from the cold since the staterooms in the palace were even more chilly than the rooms in Hembry Castle. When she wasn't shivering she felt suffocated by the crush of courtiers, royalty, nobility, pages, military officers, butlers, gentlemen ushers, and yeomen of the guard. Finally, it was 3 o'clock. Daphne waved goodbye to her father as she and a group of other young ladies were ushered up the crimson-carpeted Grand Staircase into the presence chamber. Lady Staton looked like the black sheep of the Drawing Room since her mourning wear contrasted strongly against the light-colored dresses of the others. While they waited, Lady Staton chatted with other escorts. Lady Staton in conversation was all kindness and ease, though as soon as she turned her back she'd shake her head.

"Lady Laughsom's bosom will explode when she curtsies before the Queen if she's not careful. And Lady Crestonham's manner reminds me of a spoiled child who needs a reprimand from Nanny." She puffed Daphne's feathers and flattened her train. "You, my dear, are perfection, as I always knew you would be."

Daphne's name was announced with her grandmother's. After a discreet "Ahem!" from Lady Staton, Daphne dropped her train as she passed the threshold of the Throne Room and waited while the train was spread out by the wands of the lords-in-waiting. Hearing her grandmother's sergeant-like directions in her head (Bow three times, Daphne...), she remembered to curtsey upon entering Her Majesty's presence, again midway down the room, and the grand finale, kneeling all the way down with her head toward the floor. When Daphne floated down and up again with all the grace she spent months rehearsing, she heard her grandmother's sigh of relief. Daphne exhaled too, grateful the hardest part of her day was over. As Daphne backed demurely out of the room, careful not to trip over her train, she was struck by the hard stare of the well-fed woman on the throne, in mourning like her grandmother though her husband had been dead nearly ten years. The Queen wore her crown two sizes too small for her head, which was fine, Daphne thought, since her head was two sizes too small for the rest of her. I wish Edward could see her, Daphne thought. He'd have something to say about the

Queen's stately dourness and make me laugh. Edward had said presentations were much ado about nothing, and now she knew he was right.

The deed done, Daphne breathed easily for the first time since Christmas. After she arrived safely in the Picture Gallery, Lord Darges, the future Duke of Norley, made a point of stopping to say hello. His sister, Lady Gertrude, had also been presented that afternoon.

"You will be at Daphne's ball, Lord Darges?" Lady Staton asked.

Lord Darges kissed Daphne's hand as he bowed. "I wouldn't miss it for the world."

Lady Staton slipped away, leaving Daphne to make small talk with the future Duke of Norley. She nodded as he spoke of the tediousness of the House of Lords and smiled as he praised his sister's grace as she was presented before Her Majesty. Daphne felt her grandmother's stare drill through her. Lord Darges continued to talk, something about a hunting expedition at Worthley Manor, and Daphne was thankful when her father announced that it was time for the family to return to Staton House.

"What is it, Daphne?" Frederick asked.

"I was wondering what Grandma will say when I tell her I'm not interested in Lord Darges."

"Your grandmother had today to her heart's content. Now she's going to have to come to terms with the fact that you'll choose your own husband."

"Let's hope it's that simple." Daphne put her arm through her father's. "Uncle Richard never arrived?"

"I'm so very sorry, my darling."

Jerrold shook his head. "Richard is off doing whatever he wants however he wants as always."

Frederick looked at his younger brother as though he

hardly recognized him. "Thank you, Jerrold, for always being such a bright light. Your concern for our eldest brother is touching."

Hyacinth's monocle was pointed in Jerrold's direction and Jerrold joined his wife near the door. Daphne leaned close to her father.

"What did Uncle Jerrold mean before when he said Pamela was a problem? I've never known anyone who was less of a problem than Pamela."

"I'm not sure. But we must find out what she knows, Daphne."

Daphne allowed her father to help her into the family's carriage, and she wanted to cry with relief now that the presentation was over.

DOWNSTAIRS AT STATON HOUSE

A week after Daphne's presentation was her ball, to be held at Staton House. Familiar figures in black dresses with starched white aprons or freshly pressed liveries bustled through the rooms with the marble floors, the Ancient Roman accents, and the cherub murals on the arched ceilings. Many of the servants from Hembry had been sent to London for the occasion, though Lady Staton wanted to be certain there was enough staff on hand so she instructed Mr. Ellis to hire local help as well. Chandeliers were dusted, furniture was waxed, and floors were scrubbed. Food was ordered, prepared, and cooked. The dining room was set up for the help-yourself buffet as well as the formal sit-down dinner. Clothing and hair had to be seen to, jewelry chosen and buffed, shoes mended and polished. No one downstairs had time to rest, or even to complain about the lack of rest, there was so much to be done. Mr. and Mrs. Ellis barked orders and directed traffic in staccato unison.

"See that Miss Daphne has everything she needs."

"Lady Braythe will be staying the night. She'll be in the India room."

"The tables in the dining room need straightening."

"The carpets in the assembly room must be rolled aside."

"See that Miss Daphne has everything she needs."

Mr. and Mrs. Ellis were so overwhelmed keeping the preparations on track they didn't realize that Henry Horrocks was watching more than he was working. The footman stood in the whitewashed kitchen near the cast-iron stove with the copper pans hanging above it, watching Mrs. Graham assist Mrs. Bucket, the cook at Staton House, with the myriad of soups, salads, savories, roasts, and puddings required for a feast. Occasionally, Henry felt a glare from Colin, Ruth, or any of the others rushing from here to there and back again, but he didn't care. He wouldn't be working for the Earl of Staton much longer. In fact, the Earl of Staton was his train ticket out of service and into a more leisurely life. Perhaps he would take up shooting.

Finally, it was time for the servants' dinner. The maids and footmen straggled to the table in the kitchen (at Staton House the servants' table was in the kitchen) and slumped into their chairs, exhausted. Henry condescended to his fellow servants enough to take his meals with them, though he said nothing, listening as was his way. You learn far more by listening than speaking, his father had said.

Jemima watched the Ellises as she slurped some soup. "Will your grandson be going to the ball?"

Mrs. Ellis' head snapped toward the young maid. "I beg your pardon?"

"Your grandson. Will he be joining Miss Daphne at her ball?"

"I believe that is none of your concern, Jemima." Mrs. Ellis scanned the faces eager for some gossip. "And it's no concern of anyone else's either."

When the butler and housekeeper left to take their meal in the housekeeper's sitting room, the maids and footmen chortled.

"I'm willing to bet five quid that their grandson will be here with bells on, wagging his tail for Miss Daphne," said Miss Rowland.

"I think it's romantic," said Jemima.

"Romantic?" Miss Rowland snorted back her soup. "She's the Earl of Staton's niece. She can't marry whoever she wants."

"Of course she can," said Jemima. "I think his lordship would support Miss Daphne. At least he arrived in time for her ball."

"It's a shame he missed her presentation." Ruth looked at Henry. "What do you think of Miss Daphne and the Ellises' grandson?"

"Miss Daphne's too good for the likes of that upstart."

"You think the Ellises' grandson is an upstart? What does that make you?" The questions came from one of the hired footmen. Henry looked down upon anyone not of Hembry origin and he never looked at the speaker. He wanted to make certain the hired hand knew he had been cut.

"Young Mr. Ellis is going to be a famous author someday," said Pamela.

Henry scoffed. "If Edward Ellis is going to be a famous author then I'm best mates with William Shakespeare. It's time for some people around here to learn their lesson."

The others looked at each other under hooded eyelids.

"What are you going to do?" Pamela asked.

Henry's face brightened. "You wait and see."

. . .

AFTER DINNER that night Colin Pratt excused himself from the discussion around the table. During luncheon, in snatches of conversation while working, during dinner, everyone had been talking about the same thing—Miss Daphne and the Ellises' grandson—and the topic tired him. Who cared who the Earl's niece married? Of course her ladyship cared, but she was such a shrew Colin hoped Miss Daphne would marry the writer just to make the old hag angry. It would be good for a few laughs downstairs, that. What piqued Colin's interest was Henry. Henry was always impudent in his way, but that night the first footman was particularly smug and practically begging people to interrogate him about his plans. Since no one liked Henry, no one cared what he was up to. Henry scowled into his shepherd's pie for the rest of the meal. Then he disappeared. Colin tried to follow him, but Mr. Ellis appeared with a list of tasks that needed seeing to so Colin had to put his curiosity aside.

After his work was done, Colin claimed exhaustion and went up to the male servants' quarters and the room he shared with Henry. As he climbed the stairs he realized that if Henry did have a trick card up his sleeve, the lazy git would most likely hide that card in the room they shared. Colin decided to search the room, which would only take a moment since it was such a sparse space, as all the servants' rooms were. It was windowless and bare-walled, with four faded wooden dressers beside four thin beds. Colin turned to the dresser closest to Henry's bed and grinned. He tilted his head toward the closed door, trying to gauge if someone, namely Henry, was close by. When he felt confident no one was near, he opened Henry's drawers until he found the neat pile of letters tucked into a hollowed-out book. Colin didn't bother reading the letters before settling them into his pocket. Colin shut the drawer and sat on his bed, leaning his head against the wall so he would look sufficiently exhausted should Henry walk in.

Then Colin had to think. If he kept the letters, Henry would discover they were missing, and the first person Henry would point the finger at would be him. They had always had an uneasy relationship, and Henry would love nothing better than to have Colin dismissed. But if Colin put the letters back and let Henry keep them, Henry could dispose of them before Colin had a chance to gauge their worth. Colin pulled the letters from his pocket and scanned them—a love letter to the Earl, a begging letter, a—but then he heard footsteps and slid them under his mattress. Obviously they were worth something or Henry wouldn't bother about them. And there were two other footmen in the room with them, two of the hired hands Henry spat at whenever their backs were turned, so it wouldn't be too hard to direct Henry into blaming them. No one would believe their protestations of innocence, Colin decided, because no one knew them from Adam. I'll hide the letters away, put the blame on the hired hands if it comes to it, and then I'll figure out what Henry is up to. I'll alert everyone to the plot, helping them spot the evidence the way Guy Fawkes' gunpowder plot was undermined, only instead of a bonfire I'll celebrate by getting some accolades, and perhaps a few pounds, for myself.

Colin collected the letters once again, opened the door, and looked down the dark hallway, seeing no one. He snapped his fingers when he knew. He would keep the letters in the loose floorboard near the staircase. It was an innocuous defect, and Colin had only discovered it by accident when he tripped coming up the stairs one night. He stood at the top of the stairs, listened, heard no one, and moved the floorboard slowly so it wouldn't creak. Colin slid the letters into the floor, pressed the wood back into its slot, and returned to his room. He didn't hear the heavy footsteps stop when he opened the floor. He didn't see the hands clasped behind the hunched shoulders or the round-rimmed spectacles gleaming in the slivers of moonlight penetrating the window, and he certainly didn't see the eyes squinting behind the spectacles. Which was probably just as well. Mr. Ellis wouldn't have wanted Colin's sleep interrupted by the knowledge that he had been seen.

THE BALL

The night of Daphne's ball Staton House was aglow with candlelight and lively bouquets of roses, peonies, and daffodils in silver epergnes. A cloakroom was set aside for the ladies, a hat room for the gentlemen, a separate room for tea and coffee, and the dining room, featuring three long tables covered in the same pale blue lace as Daphne's gown, was set out to perfection. One table overflowed with tasty morsels such as salmon au bleu, Bayonne ham, smoked haddock, radishes, prawns, raw oysters, anchovies, sardines, olives, and gherkins, among other delicacies. On a second table garnished with roses and leaves were fresh fruits, cheeses, nuts, sweet cakes, and chocolates, as well as the orange custard made special for Daphne. Strawberry sorbet, lemonade, and negus were available for those who grew heated with dancing, and champagne served as a sufficient coolant as well. The main courses—dishes of stewed hare trimmed with parsley, sole cooked in tomato sauce, and roast beef—would be set out at midnight.

Daphne watched the footmen, Henry and Colin, as they set

the refreshments out in the dining room under Mr. Ellis' watchful eye, and she listened while the string quartet tuned their instruments in the assembly room. She knew there were balls scheduled that same night for other young ladies who had been presented alongside her, and she worried that everyone had gone to such a fuss for nothing. Who would attend her ball when there were darlings of Society to attend to?

The Earl of Staton beamed glee itself when he saw his niece. He clasped her hands and told her how beautiful she looked. Look, Hough, he called to the doctor, isn't my niece the loveliest girl in the world? Look at the way the blue of her gown brings out the amethyst in her eyes and the rosy glow of her complexion. My niece has no equal. To which the doctor, who had always been kindness itself to Daphne, bowed and said, indeed Miss Meriwether, you will tower over every other young woman in grace, charm, and beauty, tonight and every night to come. Daphne was so happy to see her Uncle Richard in such good spirits, and she hoped it was a good omen. The people in the world who mattered most to her—her father, her Uncle Richard, and Edward—would be there, and that was all she cared about.

Daphne felt like Aschenputtel as she listened to the clocks chime 8 o'clock. She thought she should escape the ballroom before she transformed back to herself—a regular girl from Connecticut who dwelled in a regular house and lived a regular life. Pamela, who must have sensed Daphne's anxiety, whispered, "People will visit some of the other balls first, Miss Daphne, then they'll come. You'll see."

"But why?"

"A ball given by the Earl of Staton for his niece will be one of the most important events of the Season. They'll visit some of the lesser balls first to make an appearance, and then they'll come here, and once they're here they won't leave until dawn."

"I don't know how I'm going to entertain all these people I don't even know."

"I'm not worried about you, Miss Daphne. You have your father's way of putting people at their ease. Besides, you look beautiful." Pamela beamed as though she were admiring her own sister. Daphne was stunning in the sky-blue silk ball gown with off-the-shoulder sleeves and white embroidered accents. Flounces of sky-blue silk flowed from her waist giving her the appearance of a happy summer day. Pamela had been trusted to do Daphne's hair without the guidance of Miss Rowland, and Pamela had curled Daphne's golden locks and gathered them loosely on top of her head, holding everything in place with gold combs and a few dabs of lavender-scented pomatum.

Daphne checked herself in the mirror over the hearth, more from nerves than concern about her appearance. "Have you heard about Edward?"

"I heard Mrs. Ellis say he's on his way now." Pamela tucked one of Daphne's curls back into place.

"Pamela, before my presentation you said my Uncle Richard was in London. How did you know?"

"You should know that his lordship is a good man, Miss Daphne. Don't let anyone tell you otherwise. He's done a great kindness for my family."

Daphne heard the jingle of keys and there was Mrs. Ellis. Again, Pamela disappeared before Daphne could ask more.

"You look lovely, Miss Daphne. I know your ball will be a splendid success."

"I was telling Pamela I'm not sure I feel up to it."

"There will be jealous young ladies here tonight, but I say let them talk. Not one of them can hold a candle to you, I promise you that."

Mrs. Ellis jingled as she left. Daphne wanted to call Pamela back and ask her once and for all what she knew about

Richard. What kindness has he done? But there was no time. As Pamela promised, Staton House was full within the hour. Everywhere you turned were ball-gowned, bejeweled young women and gallant, finely attired young men only too happy to see and be seen at the ball for the Earl of Staton's niece. They were curious about the American girl, and they were curious about the Earl himself, who had been seen about Society little enough since inheriting his title. That night the Earl looked handsome in his sleek gray trousers, black double-breasted frock coat, and white bow tie. He was every bit the doting uncle, dancing the first dance, a waltz, with Daphne. Since the ball was Daphne's formal introduction to Society, after that first dance the Earl took her on his arm and introduced her to the other young ladies and gentlemen in attendance. Even with an errant Earl with questionable whereabouts, the Staton title still meant something, so an eligible niece was welcomed by aristocratic families, particularly those with one son too many, and even more particularly by those who heard that her father, the Earl's younger brother Frederick, made a fortune of his own investing in American midgets.

Daphne was indeed the star of the night, and she was called here and there by the young women who acted as though they'd known her their whole lives, they were truly the greatest of friends and shared secrets of every kind. You aren't personally acquainted with Miss Meriwether? More's the pity for you! As the night progressed, however, and the young men became increasingly captivated by Miss Meriwether, the young women, who had claimed the very closest of friendships with her at the beginning of the ball, were now no more than distantly polite. You find Miss Meriwether perfectly charming? I'm afraid I don't see it myself. Those Americans are exuberant in a way I simply cannot understand. When the future Duke of Norley arrived with his sisters, the Ladies Lorelai, Ariadne, and Gertrude, Lady Staton was all smiles as she led the young man to Daphne.

"Daphne, my dear," said Lady Staton, "you remember Lord Darges." The young man bowed. Lady Staton reached for the ear trumpet dangling from the long chain around her neck.

"Of course. How do you do, Lord Darges."

"How do you do, Miss Meriwether? I haven't had an opportunity to see you since the Queen's Drawing Room."

"It was just a week ago."

"Ah, but a week can seem a lifetime. My sister Lady Gertrude told me afterward you did quite well during your presentation."

"That was kind of Lady Gertrude to say. I'm afraid I felt very awkward."

"And yet I understand you conducted yourself as elegance itself. I hope your dance card is not full, Miss Meriwether. I was hoping I might have the next dance."

Daphne thought her grandmother looked giddy. "Of course, Lord Darges."

Lady Staton sighed as she watched the waltzers glide across the floor with smooth steps. "Balls nowadays aren't the same as they were when I was younger. Dancing was fun then, a way to get to know others, a time for chatting and flirting. The line dances we did then were a wonderful way to interact with others without being too informal. These closed dances you young people do, that salts, for example, what good is it if you can only interact with one partner at a time?"

"Interacting with one partner has its merits," Lord Darges said.

Fortunately, the next dance was a lively Polish mazurka so Daphne didn't need to speak much. When the dance was over, Lord Darges was pulled away by his sisters, leaving several other young men an opportunity to capture Daphne's attention. But then Edward arrived, looking handsome in his black suit and blue and green-checkered waistcoat, his cravat tied in a simple American knot at the base of his throat which he had told Daphne he would wear in her honor. Daphne joined Edward near the wall, and she saw her grandmother, her Uncle Jerrold, her Aunt Hyacinth, and her Uncle Richard watching them, her grandmother and aunt tittering behind their fans. In a moment, Uncle Richard stood beside her.

Edward bowed. "How do you do, Lord Staton."

"I'm so pleased you could join us tonight, Mr. Ellis. Now, if you don't mind, I'd like this next dance with my niece."

Edward bowed his acquiescence, and Richard steered Daphne toward the dance floor. It was a slow Viennese waltz, and Richard twirled her around in graceful glides. They must have danced well because others stopped to watch.

"I didn't know you were such a good dancer, Uncle Richard."

"There are a great many things you don't know about me, my dear." Richard dipped Daphne backward, and those around them clapped their appreciation. He whispered in Daphne's ear. "You should know that your grandmother has sent me here to ascertain your feelings for Lord Darges. She believes the young man is smitten with you. I tried to dissuade her for two reasons: one, you're obviously in love with young Mr. Ellis, and two, whatever Lord Darges' feelings of friendship toward you, he is not the man I would choose for you." Daphne nearly stopped dancing, but Richard held onto her and slid her across the floor so they didn't miss a step. "Do you have an agreement with young Mr. Ellis?"

"No. Nothing like that."

"But you do love him?"

Daphne nodded. "Are you surprised?"

"My dear, I've known you were in love with Edward Ellis

since the day I saw you two running toward Hembry Castle in the rain. I have a sense for such things, you know."

"And you don't mind?"

"No, Daphne, I don't mind. I've been much impressed with him, and anyone can see you're well suited."

The dance ended and Richard escorted Daphne from the assembly room. When they passed the curious Countess, Richard shouted (her ear trumpet was down), "I'm taking Daphne for some refreshments, Mamma. How does strawberry sorbet sound, Daphne?"

Daphne followed her uncle into the dining room crowded with those helping themselves to the fine food. Richard handed Daphne a bowl of strawberry sorbet, a spoon, and a napkin. After she finished her ices, Richard brought Daphne to the dark-paneled library and closed the door behind him. He stood on the red rug in the center of the room and stared at the frieze of the family's coat of arms carved into the mantelpiece. The flag that flew over Hembry Castle when the family was in residence was green and blue—representing hope and loyalty. The family emblems were a cornucopia for the bounty of nature's gifts, a heart for contemplation, a ram for authority, and a phoenix for resurrection, the coat of arms supported on either side by centaurs since the first Earl had proven himself in battle. Daphne never paid much attention to her family's crest before, but since her uncle was staring at it with such intensity she stepped closer for a better view.

It was cold in the library, the fire dwindling low since the servants had been paying more attention to the front rooms where the guests were socializing, and Daphne's dress was off the shoulder, providing little warmth. After the initial shock of the cool room she relaxed. She was getting used to being cold. It was part of life in England, she decided. Richard was still staring at the crest on the mantelpiece, still preoccupied with some thoughts, some secrets perhaps, and she wouldn't disturb him. Finally, he sat on the chaise lounge.

"Are you all right, Uncle Richard? Is something troubling you?"

"Not a thing, my dear."

Daphne waited, certain there was more. When Richard said nothing, she thought it might be best to change the subject.

"While we were dancing you said Lord Darges isn't the man you would choose for me. I have to admit, you surprised me. I thought the future Duke of Norley was exactly the kind of man you would choose for me."

"Lord Darges is your grandmother's choice, Daphne, not mine."

"Why not? I thought you had become friends with the future duke."

"Which is precisely why I wouldn't choose him for you. I know him too well, and I know he would not make you a good husband. If it comes to it, I'd say he wouldn't make any woman a good husband. If you want nothing more than to be a duchess, then it might be all right. If you want to be in love with your husband, and he with you, which is what I wish for you, then I tell you to run in the opposite direction of Lord Darges as fast as your bustle will allow."

"Grandma would blush to hear you talk like that."

"Your grandmother is easily vexed, I'm afraid. But heed my words, Daphne. Sometimes the answer to our most pressing question is standing right before us." Richard grasped Daphne's hands so tightly she felt the warmth of his skin through her silk gloves. "My darling niece, if you've found love, whomever you've found that love with, you must grab onto it, keep it, hold it close to your heart no matter the cost. True love, the kind that makes your heart swell, your knees weak, and your eyes glow whenever your beloved is near, why, what a blessing that is in this cold, cold world. Whatever makes you warm inside is worth any sacrifice. Do you understand?"

Richard's aquamarine eyes widened, but then his stoic mask slid back into place, his features flat again. Daphne was reminded of Edward's story about the Englishman who caught fire and jumped calmly into the lake so he wouldn't inconvenience anyone. Is that what Richard was doing—jumping calmly into the lake? Was he on fire inside?

"Uncle Richard..."

"Listen to me, Daphne. If I ever felt for someone what you feel for young Mr. Ellis, then I would do anything in my power to keep that person close anyway I could." He checked the time on his watch and tucked it back into his waistcoat pocket. "Your father gave me this watch, and it is one of my most cherished possessions. Now you must forgive me, my dearest, but I have to go."

"Now?"

Daphne wished she had a magic lock to Staton House that kept everyone she didn't need out and everyone she loved in. The library door opened and her father peered inside.

"Everyone is looking for you, Daphne. Why are you both hiding in here?"

"Uncle Richard said he's leaving."

Frederick shook his head. "You cannot leave now, Richard. I simply won't allow it. It's Daphne's ball, and it's nearly midnight. Where must you go at this hour?"

"Nowhere you need concern yourself with."

Frederick grabbed his brother's arms. "Tell me what's wrong, Richard. Tell me what you need. I'll do everything in my power to help you."

Richard held Frederick's hand close to his heart. It was an unusually affectionate gesture for the English, Daphne thought, and she saw a flicker of sentimentality in her uncle's eyes. She was certain now. Her uncle was suffering from some internal inferno and he was afraid to call attention to his pain. Daphne heard a cough, and she saw the doctor, John Hough, near the open door.

"Frederick," Richard said, "you needn't worry about me. Daphne." He held his hand out to his niece. "It has been my honor to introduce you to London Society, but I see now the only introduction you needed was to Mr. Edward Ellis." He kissed Daphne's hand. "Now, I insist that you both enjoy the rest of this night."

Richard held the library door and waited for Mr. Hough to follow. Uncle Richard looks happy, Daphne thought. He looks better than he has since we arrived in England. And yet she still felt her misgivings lingering like the dying embers in the hearth.

AN UNWELCOME SURPRISE

*D*aphne stood in silence near her father. For a moment she thought the entire night had been a dream, her whole trip to England had been a dream, and she was in her own bed in her own home in Connecticut where everything made sense. Footsteps passed the library and Henry the footman scurried past, bringing her back to the moment.

"Do you think you should go with him, Papa?"

"I don't think he would let me, my dear."

"What do we do?"

"All we can do right now is wait."

"It sounded like he was saying goodbye."

"So it did."

"Will you tell Grandma?"

"Richard is the Earl of Staton. He's a little old for me to go running to Mamma."

Daphne checked her hair in the mirror above the hearth, and her father smoothed down his black dress coat. They exhaled and joined the others in the assembly room, watching the dancers swirl across the floor in time to the quick-step waltz. Frederick squeezed Daphne's hand, then went to do his duty and mingled with the guests. Daphne saw the married mammas sitting near the wall scrutinizing their daughters as they danced with the eligible young men. She recognized one of the matrons, a young woman in mourning black who gazed at the dancers as though she wished she could join them. Daphne gestured for her father to join her near the young widow.

"How do you do, Mrs. Gibson," Daphne said. "I'm so glad you could come tonight."

"How do you do, Miss Meriwether? Isabella and I were honored to receive an invitation to your ball. This is a wonderful gathering."

Daphne turned to her father. "Papa, this is Mrs. Gibson. She was kind enough to pay a call after Grandpa died. Mrs. Gibson, my father, Frederick Meriwether." Mrs. Gibson and her father exchanged the appropriate greetings. "And how are your children? You have a little boy and a little girl, if I remember correctly."

Mrs. Gibson watched the waltzers whisk by. "They're still adjusting to life without their father, but we all have our challenges and we must rise to the occasion."

"I'm certain you've provided great strength for them," said Frederick.

"You're very kind, Mr. Meriwether. I've done my best. I want them to know that while they'll always miss their father, they're strong enough to go on."

It had been more than a year since her husband died, so Mrs. Gibson was allowed out into the world again, no longer left to decay in the dark in her home because her husband was no longer living. She was still in her mourning, though Daphne thought the pretty young widow looked none the worse for it. Her dark eyes sparkled, her dark hair gleamed, and her peaches and cream complexion glowed in the candlelight.

"How is your niece Miss Cuthbert?" Daphne asked. "She looks lovely tonight."

"I certainly hope so," said Mrs. Gibson. "She spent long enough getting ready."

The widow laughed, and Daphne laughed, and Frederick laughed. Daphne watched her father lean closer to the young woman.

"Your niece seems to be doing rather well for herself," said Frederick. He watched Miss Cuthbert glide gracefully across the dance floor with Lord Whoeverthatis.

"Oh, yes. Isabella is very pretty and she's quite amiable when she wishes to be."

"I imagine you'll do well for yourself when it's time to put away your widow's weeds," Daphne said.

"That's very kind of you, Miss Meriwether, but I imagine that life is over for me now. I was quite fortunate in my first marriage, and I don't imagine I'll be so a second time. I'm glad to come to Staton House tonight to support my niece, and it's always a pleasure to be reacquainted with you, but my place is home with my children. They're my happiness now."

Frederick nodded. "I know precisely what you mean, Mrs. Gibson. When my wife died I was certain that part of my life was over, never to be revived."

"If you'll both excuse me," Daphne said. "I was looking for..."

She left her father and the widow to work their way through the conversation. She glanced back at her father and Mrs. Gibson, her father with his hands behind his back, the widow waving her black lace fan before her face, not in a coquettish way, but as though she had grown too warm. It was far too soon to consider such a thing, but Daphne decided she would approve of a match between her father and the pretty widow. We shall see, Daphne thought. She crossed the room looking for Edward, thinking maybe he had gone to see his grandparents. She was on her way downstairs when she heard Mrs. Ellis speaking.

"I know, Neddie, but you can't keep leading her on like this. It's better to make a clean break. You should have done it by now."

"It isn't as easy as you make it out to be."

"I never said it was easy, but it has to be done."

Daphne found Edward and his grandmother in the kitchen. "I was looking for Edward."

Edward smiled. "And now you've found me." He offered Daphne his arm as they walked up. "Where did you disappear to?"

"My uncle wanted to talk to me, and now he's gone." Daphne dropped her face into her hands, unable to stop her tears.

Edward put a comforting arm around her shoulders. "What's happened?"

"I'm not sure. He seemed well enough before he left. Something isn't right, Edward. I know it."

"Do you know where he went? Perhaps we can find him."

"He didn't say."

"Let's see how he is when he returns. I'm sure it's nothing to concern yourself with."

Daphne liked where she was, close to Edward. She stayed a moment longer than she needed to, and Edward didn't press her away. When they heard two young maids giggling they pulled apart.

"My grandmother must be angry with me," Daphne said.

"She's more furious with your uncle, I think. My grandmother said Lady Staton had as many hopes for him finding a wife tonight as she did of your finding a husband."

Edward grasped Daphne's gloved hand. He stroked the smooth silk, then brought her hand to his lips. He looked as though he were about to say something until Daphne heard her grandmother's voice down the hall. They pulled away from each other, and Daphne found the separation harder the second time.

The grand lady stepped in front of Edward. "I thought Lord Darges could accompany you into the dining room, Daphne."

"Grandma, I don't think..."

The look on Lady Staton's face was not one to be trifled with. Lady Staton paired her granddaughter with the future Duke of Norley, and the young lord was gracious enough to ask Daphne what refreshment she wanted, and he plated it for her and stood near while she ate. While he waited, Lord Darges struck up a conversation with a rueful-looking young man with sad eyes. Daphne remembered what her uncle said, wondering why Richard wouldn't choose Lord Darges when every other young woman at the ball couldn't take their eyes off the future duke. He was good-looking enough in his languid, fair-haired way, Daphne thought. Lord Darges seemed delighted with the rueful-looking young man, who tapped his toe and sipped his champagne to the beat of the polka emanating from the assembly room while he waited for a giddy blond in a yellow gown to finish her ice cream. Daphne listened as the rueful-looking young man boasted (in a non-boastful way, of course, because outright boasting would be bad manners) about the number of birds he knocked out of the sky at Frimpworth House. Then the rueful-looking young man pointed out a tall, handsome man with a serious look about his countenance standing across the dining room.

"He's a future earl, you know," the young man said. "He'll

inherit a vast estate in Yorkshire. He has his eye on the lovely Lady Violet over there."

Daphne watched the serious-looking young man hand a plate to a striking young woman, a coquette in a sea-green ball grown who fluttered her eyelashes in a way that captivated the future earl. The Lady Violet spoke to the future earl, and the future earl nodded, but they were too far for Daphne to hear their words.

"I know Lady Violet," said Lord Darges. "She's a beauty and quite a wit. She'll be a challenge for him, but I think he'll appreciate that. She'll never bore him, that's for certain."

"I've seen her before," Daphne said. "We were presented on the same day." Daphne watched how the young Lady Violet used her expressive gunmetal blue eyes behind her sea-green lace fan to the greatest effect. There was a whole language in the way a lady used her fan, Daphne knew. While Lady Violet was speaking she presented her fan shut toward the future earl, asking silently, "Do you love me?" When the future earl nodded, she hid her eyes behind the open fan, indicating that perhaps, and only perhaps, she loved him as well. The future earl leaned close to the young lady and whispered in her ear, and the young lady let the fan rest on her right cheek, "Yes" in the language of fans. For the rest of the night, Lady Violet fanned herself quickly, meaning she was either too hot or engaged.

Daphne couldn't take her eyes off the young woman. She had a confidence about her, Lady Violet, even for someone so young, and Daphne wanted to ask her how she did it. Daphne could have used some of that confidence. She knew how she felt about Edward, but she still had misgivings about his feelings for her. She thought about the conversation she overheard in the kitchen. Who was Edward leading on, and why did he have to break from her? Daphne was certain Lady Violet would have the truth out of Edward in less than a minute. Daphne noticed the way the rueful-looking young man stared at Lady Violet.

"Are you a potential suitor of Lady Violet's?" the future Duke of Norley asked.

"Perhaps once, but no longer. Once she realized a future earl was interested I fell off the list."

Daphne felt sorry for the young man, and she didn't want to be the one to tell him that Lady Violet and the future earl had most likely become engaged before his eyes. Daphne excused herself, leaving Lord Darges in his conversation with the young man. She found Edward and they returned to the assembly room together.

"Did you enjoy your time with Lord Darges?" he asked.

"He's a good dancer, if nothing else."

"If nothing else?"

"I'll have to tell my grandmother that the future duke is not the man for me." Daphne watched the giddy blond girl and the rueful-looking young man take to the dance floor. Miss Morena and Miss Twilla Cadwallader glided past with their respective partners, the sisters appropriately coiffed and bejeweled, Miss Morena in green damask and Miss Cadwallader in periwinkle silk. When Daphne noticed Viscountess Meddleham sitting with the matrons near the wall she wondered if one of the young men was the Viscountess' much sought-after son. Daphne continued to scan the faces and frowned when she didn't see the one she searched for. "It's too bad Miss Chattaway couldn't come. I was hoping she'd be here."

Edward appeared to be fascinated by the fleur de lis pattern on the wallpaper. "Miss Chattaway, did you say?"

"I thought she could bring her fiancé tonight so I could finally meet him. Edward? Are you all right?" Edward's complexion was as white as his shirt, and he dabbed at his forehead with his handkerchief. "Do you need to sit?"

"No, no. I'm perfectly well." He held out his hand. "What do you say, Miss Meriwether? May I have this next dance?"

They danced the next dance, and the next dance, and the next, and if other young men wanted their turn with Miss Meriwether they were out of luck. The other guests watched curiously. Some unknown who didn't know his manners was keeping Miss Meriwether occupied. Who is he, they asked? Have you seen him before? I never have. Who are his people? I believe that's Lord Renfield's son, you know, he has that estate in Ireland. Daphne wasn't worried about their loud guesses, caught up as she was in twirling and laughing with her mystery man. As the sun awoke in pink-light layers the guests dwindled away. The Countess sent the most eligible young men home with offers to visit Hembry Castle. In fact, the Countess said, she would be hosting a grand dinner party at Hembry at the start of the grouse season. Daphne smiled as her grandmother issued the invitations but said nothing, her thoughts still consumed with Edward, who had excused himself with a kiss on her hand at dawn.

It was daylight by the time the last of the guests had gone and the family crawled half-conscious to their beds. Daphne was soon asleep, and she dreamed about her comfortable home on the river in Connecticut, also known as the Thames River, which made her laugh now. In her dream her Uncle Richard was swimming in the river outside their home, which struck Daphne as odd even as she slept. She was jolted from her dream by a loud conversation in the hallway outside her room. She pressed her ear to the door and heard panic in the speaker's voice, whom she recognized as Mr. Ellis. She opened her door and saw her father in his nightgown, his feet bare, his sleeping cap in his hands. Mr. Ellis was dressed much the same, as though he had rushed from the cottage he shared with Mrs. Ellis. Daphne already dreaded the news. Creaking footsteps made their way upstairs, and then Mrs. Ellis stood beside her husband, the housekeeper tugging her shawl closer around her nightgown.

"What are you saying, Ellis?" Frederick asked.

"It's his lordship. It's…" Mr. Ellis couldn't hide his sorrow. Where he was normally hunched, now he looked as if he would never stand straight again.

"Ellis, please, I must know. Is my brother all right?"

Mrs. Ellis brought a handkerchief to her eyes. "He's gone."

"Gone where?" Frederick asked.

"I'm so very sorry." Mr. Ellis had to settle himself enough to speak. "He's dead."

Daphne stepped closer to her father. "That's not possible." But the sorrow etched around the Ellises' features told her it was true. Whatever proof the Ellises had been given, they were convinced, and so was Daphne, and so was her father.

"What shall we do, my lord?" Mr. Ellis asked.

Daphne looked at her father, who stared at the Turkish rug beneath his feet as though the symmetrical pattern held hidden clues to the many questions he would never have answers to.

"My lord?"

Daphne touched her father's arm. "I think Ellis is speaking to you, Papa."

The 10th Earl of Staton stared at his butler as though he hardly understood.

A FAREWELL

He was thrown in the river by the men he played poker with, some said. He had too many women too many times, said others. He had some other man's wife too many times. He had a child too, perhaps from that other man's wife, and the cuckolded husband strangled him and tossed him into the Thames. That's what happens when you're supposed to be taking care of business at Hembry or seeing to duties at the House of Lords and you're off gallivanting instead. He was the Earl of Staton, after all. What right did he have to leave whenever he wanted? He had responsibilities. Now he's paid the ultimate price.

Frederick Staton stood outside Staton House, his hand raised but unmoving near the door. How could he tell them? How could he put their minds at ease when he himself would never be rid of the sight—his brother's drowned body, Richard's chestnut hair sheared away, his handsome face disfigured beyond all recognition. He heard horses' hooves clomping on the street and he turned to watch the fine-looking ladies in their carriages out for their afternoon drive around Hyde Park. The ladies glanced at the other ladies to see if their dresses were finer, their carriages bigger, their footmen better looking than what the others had on display. He saw the children with their nannies running across the grassy lawn, and he saw the young male laborers watching the nannies since the nannies were the only servants who could get away during the day. It was a wonder to him, that life continued, the day went on, people went about their business whilst his life was forever changed. He had been grieved at the loss of his beloved father, but this was a different grief. One expects to lose one's parents, hopefully not until they, or you, are very old, but still it falls into the correct order of things. The loss of his eldest brother, who should have had many years ahead of him, was an unexpected tragedy, and those are always the hardest to handle. Frederick exhaled, steadied himself, and went inside.

Mr. Ellis directed him to his family—his daughter, his mother, his brother Jerrold, and Hyacinth—as they waited in the sitting room, each staring into the distance, lost in their thoughts. Daphne stood when she saw her father.

"Did you identify him, Papa? Was it Uncle Richard?"

Frederick meant to say something profound, something that would set their minds at ease. I am the head of this family now, he meant to say. I will guide us through this terrible tragedy and we will rise above this and we will comfort each other in our grief. We will show everyone, in Hembry, in Staton, in all of England, that the Meriwethers are strong. He had practiced his speech as he walked along the banks of the Thames, but now when it mattered the words wouldn't come. He crumpled onto the settee and wept.

Daphne kneeled next to her father, taking his hands, waiting for his wave of misery to subside. When Frederick could contain himself enough to speak, he tried to explain. The police had arrived that morning to say that Richard's body had been fished out of the Thames. The face was badly disfigured, and though the poor soul looked ghoulish, as though it had never been human at all, Frederick was able to identify his beloved brother because of his clothing, his watch, his shirt pin, and the bloodied remnants of the half-moon scar near the left temple. The ultimate proof, however, was John Hough.

"Hough was with Richard last night when he fell into the river," Frederick said. "They were walking across London Bridge toward Southwark. Suddenly, Richard said he had something to do, some business that needed tending, and he told Hough to wait there on the bridge for his return. When Hough tried to question him, Richard became belligerent, insisting that he'd be back in a moment. Hough was afraid of angering Richard further so he did what he was told and waited. Richard returned staggering, as though he had a few drinks in his absence. Then Richard started laughing at the sky and yelling at invisible phantoms, a typical drunkard's scene, Hough said. It was so dark, no moon, and Hough said he could hardly make out Richard's form. It was well after midnight by then, and Richard talked about how he had been too afraid in his life, he should have learned to swim when he had the chance, but it was never too late to face your fears. Richard leaned over the side of the bridge, mocking the water as it sat at low tide. Then he pulled himself onto the railing. By now he was talking nonsense about how he would do what must be done, the way he should have from the beginning. Hough tried to pull Richard down, but Richard was unsteady and Hough was afraid that if he tugged too hard Richard would lose his balance and fall. Richard dropped into the river before Hough could do anything. Hough heard the splash, looked over the railing, saw Richard bobbing in the water, and ran for help. They pulled Richard's body from the river at first light."

"Fell my eye," said Hyacinth. "He was pushed."

"By Mr. Hough?" Daphne asked.

"It hardly seems likely," Frederick said. "Richard and Hough have been friends since their Oxford days."

"My son was not a drunkard," Lady Staton said. "Besides, if the man they pulled from the river was so disfigured, certainly it could be a case of mistaken identity."

Frederick shook his head. "Hough saw him fall, Mamma. He heard the splash when Richard hit the water. And that was Richard's scar, and that was the watch I gave him for his birthday last year. It was his shirt pin, and those were the very clothes he wore to Daphne's ball." He paced to the window and watched the green grass in the park reflect shimmers of sunlight. He shuddered, thinking an icy wind must have blasted through the room though it was well spring now. He reached into his coat pocket and pulled out the gold watch inscribed with his brother's name. "Perhaps I should have left this with the police, but I had to have it."

Lady Staton moaned and fell to the floor. Frederick and Daphne jumped to her rescue, Jerrold and Hyacinth not far behind. Frederick pulled his mother back onto the chaise lounge, comforting her with soft words. But Lady Staton could not be consoled.

"My boy. My poor, poor, dear boy."

Jerrold's thin lips puckered. "I dare say Richard's conduct…" One sharp look from Frederick and Jerrold stopped.

"Obviously he was murdered," said Hyacinth.

"Don't be ridiculous," said Frederick. "Of course he wasn't murdered. He was with Hough and no one else, and Hough of all people wouldn't murder him."

"How do you know?" Hyacinth spoke in the clipped tone she often reserved for Jerrold. "Richard and that doctor were always disappearing together at the drop of a hat. How do you know what went on between them? How do you know they didn't argue? How do you know the doctor wasn't using Richard for his own gain? Perhaps Richard wouldn't give Mr. Hough what he wanted and Mr. Hough finally had enough and decided to do something about it."

"What on earth could Mr. Hough want from Richard?" Frederick asked.

"Money. Power. A position. Richard was the Earl of Staton, after all."

Jerrold looked like he tasted a lemon. "You'll have to excuse Hyacinth. She's been reading too much of that American Poe and now she sees treachery and murder wherever she looks." Hyacinth focused her monocle on her husband. He would have to deal with the Cyclops later.

Daphne brushed some wisps of silver hair back from where they had fallen from her grandmother's chignon. "Do you want to lie down, Grandma?"

Mr. Ellis stepped forward. "Shall I fetch Miss Rowland, Lady Daphne? Miss Rowland will know what to do."

Mr. Ellis returned with Miss Rowland, whose eyes were slits, her lips so thin they disappeared. Lady Staton stood on her own accord and walked under her own power, though when she reached the door she buckled over again. Frederick wondered if this would break her. She had suffered before, certainly, as everyone does. A father who died young, a baby boy who died in infancy, her husband of 50 years having moved on from this world less than a year before. But this was her son, her eldest, the one she had set all her hopes on. Frederick watched Rowland lead his mother away with a gentle hand on the Countess' back. Rowland acted with great tenderness, as though she were the nanny and his mother the child.

Jerrold and Hyacinth followed them, leaving Frederick and Daphne to make sense of everything that had happened.

AGAIN, the mourners lined the village road as far as the castle. Again, it rained in Hembry, and again their black umbrellas pointed like mourning wreaths at the crying sky. Now the solemn-black hearse, its sides of glass so viewers could see the white roses draped across the casket, carried the body of the 9th Earl of Staton to his final destination. Again, the onlookers struggled in vain to protect themselves from the warm rain splashes, and again the rain stopped as suddenly as it started and the sun peeked pink beneath gray clouds. He would have been nine-and-forty in a fortnight, the 9th Earl, and the mourners were saddened at his sudden loss. Nothing official had been said yet by the family or the police. The 9th Earl had met with an unfortunate accident on London Bridge was all they knew, and quite an accident it must have been.

"How fortunate," said one unthinking marquess to Lady Staton, "that you had an excess of sons."

All eyes were now on Frederick, the man known as the wayward who was now their lord and master. He stood tall, and like his eldest brother before him, he looked about him with level eyes, shaking hands with those he came into contact with, comforting those overwhelmed by the tragedy of the loss of a young man. He spoke to everyone whether they were peer, gentry, farmers, cottagers, or tradesmen, all had something to say about the 9th Earl. Perhaps they didn't know him as well as they had known his father, but they wanted to speak kindly of him all the same. The 10th Earl leaned forward—he was a tall man and had to bend to be nearer the speakers—and listened, nodding in sympathy to all they said. His lordship's remaining brother was there, along with his wife and their two young sons. Necks strained when Miss Meriwether, now Lady Daphne, was helped from the family's carriage by a liveried footman. There was another young man, one the villagers recognized as Mr. and Mrs. Ellis' grandson. What was he doing with the family, some wondered? At the very least it was something to gossip about, which was always welcome at the post office in Hembry.

AFTER THE FUNERAL, Frederick and Daphne sat in the library. Frederick still searched for those wise words, but they remained stuck somewhere he couldn't reach. Daphne dropped her face into her hands and wept. Frederick waited silently, as she had waited for him. He handed her his handkerchief, which she accepted gratefully. When she could speak, she said, "You don't think Uncle Richard did it on purpose? You don't think he meant to jump?" She clasped her hands over her mouth as though to stop her own words.

"I don't, my dear. I know Richard was unhappy about the duty that lay before him, but I can't believe he was as desperate as that. Since that time when we were boys and he slipped and fell he avoided the water like the plague. He wouldn't willingly jump into the river when he knew he couldn't swim."

"Maybe he meant to drown, or maybe he meant to die from the fall."

"I can't believe that, Daphne."

"Then why would he stand on the railing? I agree with Grandma. Uncle Richard wasn't a drunkard."

"Hough said Richard had disappeared for some time. It's entirely possible that he went to a nearby public house for a few pints. If there's more to be discovered, the police will discover it. But Hough was there, and we have no reason to doubt his story. There will be an inquest, and it should be simple based on Hough's testimony. Daphne, I must beg you, don't mention anything about the conversation we had with Richard before he left. We don't want to give anyone the impression he may have taken his own life. It wasn't very long ago when suicides forfeited their possessions to the Crown. Even now they're not allowed a Church of England burial. We don't want to cast any more of a shadow on your uncle's memory than his actions brought upon him."

"Will we be staying in England now? If you're the Earl of Staton, then Hembry is your responsibility."

Frederick sighed. "Hembry has been my responsibility for some months now, but yes, the responsibility has been officially transferred to me. The truth is, I don't know what any of this means. I don't know if I'll stay permanently. I'm the middle son. I wasn't supposed to be the Earl."

"But now you are. There are a lot of people depending on you."

Frederick looked closely at his daughter. He wanted to see her first reaction, her genuine reaction, to his question. "Would it be so terrible if we stayed? I know you were looking forward to going home, but could you be all right here? I know your grandmother has been driving you mad, but what if I'm able to restrain her enthusiasm about indoctrinating you to our way of life?"

"I think she'd be even worse now that you're the Earl." Daphne looked at a sepia-toned photograph of her stern-looking grandmother on the side table. "I know how much she loved Uncle Richard even if she didn't always show it. She spent all her time worrying about whether or not he was married."

"There's the problem all over again. I'm not currently married either, and I have one child. The last I checked she was a daughter. You know the primogeniture law here says you cannot inherit."

"Then you'll have to remarry, Papa. You were making rather merry with the widow Mrs. Gibson at my ball. She's young and pretty. She even looks lovely in black, and that's not easy to pull off. Maybe she'd be happy to marry you and give you a son. She'd even become the Countess of Staton in the bargain."

Frederick scoffed, but he knew he couldn't hide anything from Daphne. He had, in fact, found the widow Mrs. Gibson quite attractive, but that was a concern for another time. He became serious again. "Could you stay, Daphne? Could you be truly happy here? Of course," his voice faltered, "you could go home if that's what you wanted. You know your Aunt Ginny would be happy to have you stay with her."

"If you stay, I stay too. We're a team, you and I."

Daphne smiled, and Frederick guessed he knew of whom she thought. "I believe your grandmother could be brought to accept a journalist in the family if we approach it correctly. After all, I'm a journalist myself."

Daphne blushed but said nothing. After a moment she kissed her father's cheek. "Poor Uncle Richard. He deserved so much better."

"He did, my darling. Perhaps the best way I can serve his memory is to become the Earl he never had the chance to be."

"And I want to be here to help you."

Frederick took his daughter's hand. "I couldn't ask for a better partner to take on this extraordinary challenge with."

The door opened and Mr. Ellis appeared. "Pardon me, my lord, but there's a visitor for you and Lady Daphne."

"Who is it?" Frederick asked.

"My grandson."

"Of course, Ellis. Show him in."

Edward winked at his grandfather. Mr. Ellis, still in character, struggled to restrain a smile, but he failed and laughed aloud. Edward bowed with great deference before the Earl of Staton.

"My lord."

"Don't you start that. Please, Edward, sit. I need some normalcy or soon I'll be as overwhelmed as Richard was."

"My grandfather said you believe your brother's death was an accident."

"The accident was his lifestyle, I'm afraid."

There was a commotion in the hallway, and Mr. Ellis said, more loudly than he needed, "You must allow me to announce you, sir."

"It ain't necessary, I assure you, my good man."

Edward, Daphne, and Frederick saw a round-faced, mustachioed man in a dark gray frock coat that fell to his knees. The mustachioed man let himself into the sitting room, followed closely behind by a sullen-looking young man with the same round face, minus the mustache. The older man nodded as he studied the room and its inhabitants.

"Forgive me, my lord," said Mr. Ellis. "This is Mr. Ruckson, a detective, and this is his son, young Mr. Ruckson, who is a sergeant. They've come on account of the inquest concerning the death of the 9th Earl. I asked them to wait but they pushed their way in."

"I'd hardly say pushed," said the elder Mr. Ruckson. "I'm sprightlier than you, is all. I got here first so why not come in and say hello?"

Frederick stood. "It's all right, Ellis. Both Mr. Rucksons are quite welcome." He gestured to the chairs across from him. "Would either of you gentlemen care to sit?"

"Oh no, thank you," said the elder Mr. Ruckson. "So you're the Earl of Staton?"

"I am now."

"Your father is recently deceased?"

"It's been nearly a year."

"And your eldest brother, deceased within this past week, was the heir?"

"He was."

Mr. Ruckson removed his bowler hat and nodded toward his son, who was too busy noticing Daphne to bother about anything else. The elder Mr. Ruckson took one giant leap across the room, and he was tall enough to stand nose to nose with Frederick. Frederick stepped back in alarm and Mr. Ruckson nodded as though he had discovered his first clue.

"As a matter of course, where were you the night your eldest brother, the momentary Earl of Staton, died?"

"I was at Staton House in London, as was all my family. My brother had given a ball in honor of my daughter, who had been presented to the Queen."

"And your brother was at the ball for your daughter?"

"He was."

"You know this for certain?"

"I spoke to him myself, as did my daughter, as did most of our guests."

"What did you speak about?"

Frederick's heart slammed into his ribcage. He didn't have time to think of imagined innocent conversations. All he could say was, "We spoke about how lovely Daphne looked and how well the ball was going."

"Is that all?"

"As far as I can recall."

Mr. Ruckson gestured toward Daphne. "And this is..."

"My daughter Lady Daphne."

"And this is..."

"Our friend Edward Ellis."

"Ellis like the butler over there?"

"Edward Ellis is Ellis' grandson."

"Do you think he should stay for our conversation?"

"Are you suggesting he needs to go?" Daphne asked.

"I'm simply asking your preference."

"There's no reason for either of the Ellises to leave," said Frederick.

"I see." Mr. Ruckson spoke as though that were another piece of the puzzle. "And the whole family was at Staton House that night?"

"We were," Frederick said.

"Who is we?"

Frederick thought a moment. "My daughter, my mother, the Countess of Staton, my younger brother Jerrold, and his wife, as well as our household staff."

"How many in the household staff?"

Frederick looked at Mr. Ellis.

"On that particular night staff from Staton House and Hembry Castle were present, my lord, as well as those hired to assist with the ball. That would be 20 servants in all."

"Have you discovered something new about my brother's death?" Frederick asked.

"Perhaps. I heard your brother used to disappear for weeks at a time and no one knew where he went or why he was going."

"I'm not sure what that has to do with my brother's death, but yes, he would leave on occasion, though he always returned."

"Well," said the elder Mr. Ruckson, "he didn't return this last time, did he? You didn't find it odd, that he would disappear without a trace?"

"My brother was a grown man. He wasn't a prisoner. If he wanted to leave he could leave."

The elder Mr. Ruckson tapped his triangle-shaped beard with his finger. "I saw that poor doctor after your brother's body was retrieved from the river. He was in quite a state when he gave his statement, I can tell you. He said what happened right well enough, then he became as incoherent as someone suffering from the plague—like all he saw was ghosts and all he could say was gibberish."

"Yes," Frederick said. "I saw him disintegrate into a muddled mess, not that one can blame him under the circumstances. Doctor Hough couldn't be consoled. It was as if he'd lost his only friend in the world."

"I agree," said Mr. Ruckson. "Now, to answer your question, at this time I don't have any evidence to suggest that anything other than Mr. Hough's account occurred that night. As you may have been told, we expect the inquest to move quickly. Still, it never hurts to poke around a bit. We need to make sure everything is in order. To that end, my son and I questioned some of your staff when we arrived." Mr. Ellis glared at the detective over the rim of his spectacles. "Standard procedure, of course. One of your groundskeepers said he's seen a man loitering around here within the past few days. The fellow comes as far as the river and watches the house like he's looking for someone. We talked to the gardener, and he said whenever the man knows he's been seen he runs away. No one has caught him. Yet."

Frederick looked at the butler. "Ellis, is this true?"

"It's the first I've heard of it, my lord. I'll see to it straight away."

Mr. Ruckson looked rather pleased with himself, as though it were his mission to discover something the hoity-toity people in the castle didn't know. "A suspicious loiterer hanging around Hembry grounds so soon after the death of the former

Earl of Staton? We have to follow through on any leads. I'm sure you understand, Lord Staton."

"Is the man dangerous?" Edward asked.

"Perhaps. I wouldn't leave the house alone, any of you, but especially not the young lady."

"Thank you," Frederick said. "We appreciate everything you're doing on behalf of my family. If you need anything at all, we'll make certain you have it."

The detective looked as though he were leaving but he stopped. "By the way, who had the most to gain from your eldest brother's death?"

And then he was gone.

LADY DAPHNE MERIWETHER

*E*veryone in Hembry, castle and village, were back in
full mourning—crepe for the women and armbands
for the men. What would happen next? Two earls dead before
the end of a year, the newest with a life in another country and
only a daughter to show for it. What if he went back to America? What if he neglected his duties as his brother before him
had? Even the household servants walked about on tiptoe,
afraid that one wrong move would plunge them all into chaos.

Frederick, without being told, sensed the awkwardness as
servants averted their eyes and villagers spoke to their feet
when he was near. After a long discussion with Daphne about
what to do, Frederick decided, as was his way, to address the
problem directly. He gathered together the servants, indoor
and outdoor staff, the villagers, the tradespeople, the farmers,
and the vicar near the front entrance of the castle. He greeted
them generously, shaking hands, listening to concerns, and
introducing his daughter to those who had not had the pleasure. When everyone quieted, he spoke with candor.

"Welcome, everyone. I'm glad you were able to join me here this beautiful summer afternoon. I know these past weeks have been a shock for you, as they have been for my family, and myself. Whilst we mourned the loss of my father only a year ago, it never occurred to me that we would be dealt such another tragedy in so short a time. Yet here we are, once again mourning the loss of someone we hold dear.

"I know you are all concerned about the future. You're concerned about Hembry Castle and if it will weather this new storm. You're concerned about the village, and you're concerned about your places and your livelihoods. You have every right to be concerned, and if I were in your shoes I would be as well. The reason I gathered you all together is because I want you to know that Hembry Castle will continue as strongly as it ever has. With the loss of my eldest brother, the title, as well as the responsibilities, of the Earl of Staton are now mine. I assure you I intend to keep Hembry on course, to continue its current prosperity and to grow that prosperity into the coming years." He reached out his hand to Daphne and pulled her closer to him. "My daughter, Lady Daphne, will be with me every step of the way, as will the Countess, my mother, who has helped to keep Hembry Castle moving forward for 50 years. I would like to say that nothing will change, but that can never be correct. Things change, circum-stances alter, and it's up to each of us to navigate through the unexpected with all the resilience we can muster. Though I never expected to become Earl, being the second son, I promise each and every one of you that I will work tirelessly day and night to rise to my new challenge with all the fortitude God has seen fit to give me. Thank you, good people of Hembry. God bless you."

The crowd, stunned at first at being addressed so honestly

by their lord and master, burst into applause. Frederick and Daphne walked through the crowd to mingle, and the people, one by one, like synchronized dancers at the London theaters, showed their respect as the men removed their hats and the women curtsied.

"My lord."

"My lord."

"My lady."

"My lord."

Overwhelmed, yet unable to show it, Frederick held out his hand to those closest to him, and the good people of Hembry grasped it willingly.

FOR DAPHNE, little changed. Her father had taken control of Hembry some months before her uncle's death, and whether she was referred to as Miss Daphne or Lady Daphne made little difference to her. She wasn't a different person with an honorary title. After the rush of her presentation and her ball had passed, after the shock of her uncle's death and her father inheriting the title settled, everything in the world became about Edward.

When her father was able to steal some time from Hembry to go to London to see to Daily Observer business (he was getting everything in order so he could officially hand over the editorship to Edward) she went with him. Her grandmother was thrilled, thinking Daphne had gone to participate in the goings-on of Society, perhaps to mingle more with Lord Darges at balls or operas or other soirées. Nothing could have been further from the truth. Daphne kept up with London Society through her father, who gave her the gossip he picked up at the club, tasty tidbits about the fine young ladies and gentlemen who had been guests at Daphne's ball—who was pairing up with whom, who would never pair up with whom. There were already a few engagements, and lo and behold, the ravishing Lady Violet had indeed captured her man, the future earl. Otherwise, all was Edward. A month after her ball his collection of stories, now known as Tales from Southwark, was published by Fergusonandwately. The collection sold well from the day it was released. With the brisk sales, the publishers had already commissioned a new collection, and Edward wasted no time getting to work. It would be hard going for a while, editing the Daily Observer while writing his own stories, but he was used to the long hours, he told Daphne.

Three weeks after Tales from Southwark was released, Frederick hosted a dinner party for Edward at Staton House. True, the family was still in black for the Earl's brother, but Frederick shared the same sentiment about mourning as his father and eldest brother, and he knew Richard would not want them hiding away at Hembry Castle when there was work to be done and lives to live. Fergusonandwately were at the dinner party, drinking the expensive wine and boasting about the many orders Edward's book had already received, as though they alone were responsible for the success. Mr. Ellis stood behind Edward, his butler's guard down enough to beam proudly at anyone who had a nice word to say about his grandson, which was everyone in the room. Mrs. Ellis had come from Hembry as well, and Daphne watched Edward's grandmother loitering near the dining room, close enough to hear the praises heaped upon her Neddie. Once, after Frederick had offered a toast to "an extraordinary young literary talent who very well may be the next Mr. Dickens" she dabbed tears from her eyes with her apron.

The party was well attended. Frederick's friends from the literary world—London editors, authors, and journalists—were there for an introduction to the young writer who had the backing of the Earl of Staton. Everyone wanted a piece of Edward, to shake his hand, to talk to him, to know more about him, to learn about his plans for the future now that he was both an author and the editor of the Daily Observer. Such drive, such talent for such a young man, they said. Five-and-twenty years old, and look at what he's accomplished. Daphne made polite conversation with the wives of the editors while she waited for her turn to speak to Edward. The guests didn't begin to dwindle away until after midnight. After they were alone, Daphne watched Edward slump onto the settee.

"Did you like your party?" she asked.

"I did. It was very generous of your father, and you, to do this for me. Many wonderful things have happened to me since you and your father arrived in England. I can hardly find the words to express my gratitude."

"Papa and I are happy to help you however we can, Edward. You know that."

Edward leaned his head against the back of the settee and closed his eyes. Some chocolate-colored hair fell into his face, and Daphne had to fight the urge to brush it back. She watched his breathing slow, and she wouldn't be surprised if he had dozed off with the long hours he was working. Again, she wondered how Edward felt about her. It was the same confusion she had been having for months. There were still times when he acted as if he couldn't see her enough. He would arrive at Staton House at any time, day or night, with news about how his stories were coming along, or perhaps he just needed to get out of his bachelor's flat for a while, wanting some company to break up the long hours of solitude. In those moments he would talk to her as though she were the only one in the world who understood him, and Daphne thought he must feel more than friendship for her. But there were still times when he would keep his distance, and during those times when he spoke to her it was only in the most superficial manner. They hadn't kissed again since their day in the rain at Hembry Castle. Yes, he had kissed her hand several times, but it wasn't the same, was it? I should ask him once and for all, Daphne thought. I should find out how he feels about me.

Mr. Ellis cleared his throat. "Would you care for some tea, Lady Daphne?"

"No thank you, Ellis. I think your grandson is worn out by the festivities."

"I apologize for his inconsiderateness. He's been working very hard, my lady." The butler prodded his grandson's arm. "Edward?"

Edward sat up. "I wasn't sleeping."

Mr. Ellis peered at his grandson over the top of his spectacles. "Shall I get your hat and coat?"

"You needn't be so formal, Grandfather, but yes, I should be leaving." He held his arm out to Daphne as they stood. "I wasn't sleeping, was I?"

"You were, but don't worry. Your secret is safe with me."

Mr. Ellis returned with Edward's hat and coat. Edward put on his hat and allowed his grandfather to help him with his coat. Daphne walked Edward through the foyer to the front door.

"I wanted to ask you," she said.

"You can ask me anything."

This was the time. She was going to ask him once and for all if she was imagining the warmth she felt from him sometimes. Then Mr. Ellis opened the door, and with the proximity of the butler so near, especially since he was Edward's grandfather, she didn't have the courage.

"What did you want to know?" Edward asked.

"I wanted to ask you about one of your stories. The one about the boy who was raised by his grandparents because his father was a spendthrift and his mother was so angry about the fact that his father was a spendthrift she couldn't stop yelling. Was that about your family? I thought I recognized your grandparents from the way you described them."

"There are pieces of me in all my stories, I reckon. And I owe more to my grandparents than I could ever repay."

Edward nodded at his grandfather, then looked out into the London midnight. The sky was dark and flat, as though there had never been any stars, they were figments of the imagination, and only the moon was real. Edward exhaled and turned his full attention onto Daphne. He stared at her with such intensity she felt heavy under the weight of his scrutiny.

"I know I can make a success of the Daily Observer, even more so than it already is. And I know that if I work hard, very hard, then I can make a success of my books as well."

"I know you can do whatever you set your mind to."

"Then you believe in me?"

"Do you need to ask?"

Edward leaned close to her then, and Daphne was certain he would have kissed her if his grandfather hadn't cleared his throat. Edward nodded at his grandfather, and as he left Daphne wished she had the courage to ask her real question.

FREDERICK OFFICIALLY HANDED the running of the Daily Observer to Edward, though he still had business in London tending to his duties with the House of Lords. Daphne returned to Hembry Castle only to be overrun once again with her grandmother's demands. The day after Daphne returned to the country, Lady Staton joined Daphne in her birdcage bedroom. The Countess stepped close to the wall with the brown tree and ran her hand across the mauve roses.

"The flowers are starting to fade, I'm afraid. Your grandfather had this room painted when we were expecting your father. Your grandfather hoped for a girl since he already had his son and heir, but your father was a boy, and then Jerrold was a boy. After you were born, your grandfather wanted so much for you to live here. He even added little accents he thought a little girl would enjoy."

"I'm here now, and I believe Grandpa knows that."

"It would make him very happy if he did, Daphne." The Countess sat in the Queen Anne chair near the window and held her ear trumpet to her ear. "We have a matter to deal with and I need your help."

"What is it?"

"You have been much asked after since your ball."

"Have I?"

"Lord Darges has been particularly keen. I understand he plans to propose soon."

"To who?"

"To you, silly girl. He's infatuated with you."

"I think he's more infatuated with Papa's fortune, and now I'm sure he's fascinated with the estate."

"He'll be a duke one day, Daphne. He doesn't need your father's estate."

"Whether the future Duke of Norley has his own money or not, he's not for me, Grandma. Even Uncle Richard saw that. The night before he..." Daphne could hardly bring herself to say the words. "The last time I saw him he told me to run in the opposite direction of Lord Darges."

"He didn't understand that a match with Lord Darges

would be ideal for this family. You do realize that your father is getting on in years."

"At all of 46."

"He's no spring chicken, Daphne, that's all I'm saying. You must see that now your father is in the same predicament your uncle was...he needs an heir. There has been talk concerning our family among some unkind people about the circumstances of your uncle's death, so we must work quickly before irreparable damage to our reputation has been done. Your grandfather would roll over in his grave if he could hear the talk about your Uncle Richard."

"Like what?"

"Some are saying he was murdered. Others are saying he deliberately jumped. Your Uncle Richard would never jump into the river. He couldn't swim. And as difficult as he was finding his new position, he would never disgrace the family by taking his own life. Then on top of everything else there's an intruder loitering about the grounds. What if people find out? How would that look?"

"I think Society people would like having a loiterer about. It makes the house seem even more exclusive, like Hembry Castle is so important someone can't leave it alone."

Lady Staton tapped her ear trumpet as she considered. "There may be something to that. For now, we need to find a wife for your father and a husband for you, and we need to do so very soon. We need to make certain you're both settled before the gossip grows vicious. You, young lady, need to be perfectly turned out at every moment. Escott has been formally named your lady's maid. You're not married yet, but I think it's time you had your own maid. You and Escott get along well, I understand?"

"Yes, Grandma, I like her very much. But I don't need as much help..."

"I know, dear, you've told me a hundred times. You're used to doing these things for yourself. I could allow you to slide by a little when your uncle was Earl, but now..." Lady Staton closed her eyes, and when she opened them she couldn't hide her sorrow. "Now things are different. Your father is Earl, and you are an Earl's daughter. I simply cannot allow you to make your own clothing anymore." Lady Staton looked sympathetic, or as close to as she could manage. "I can see this bothers you, Daphne. But you cannot let your emotions get the better of you. True, you are half-American, and that is a weakness, but you are as much your father's daughter as you are your mother's, and I know you have it in you to be strong."

Lady Staton rang the servants' bell and Mr. Ellis appeared.

"Ellis, tell Escott to come at once."

The butler returned a moment later with Pamela by his side. Lady Staton studied Pamela Escott as though she had never seen the young woman before.

"Pamela has been a big help to me," said Daphne.

"She's Escott to you now. Escott, you understand that your new role is maid to Lady Daphne?"

"I do, my lady."

"I'd like you to have Lady Daphne try on the Worth dresses she brought with her from America. I know we're still in mourning for my son," the Countess drew in a breath, "but Lady Daphne will be out of black soon and we need to see that her dresses are ready when she is. They have never fit properly. You can mend them to fit Lady Daphne's form?"

"I can, your ladyship. Miss Rowland taught me."

"All right then. I want Lady Daphne to be the most beautiful woman in the room, whichever room she happens to be in. She has the face for it, the figure for it, and now her clothes must be impeccable and her hair must always be dressed in the latest fashion." Lady Staton held her hands together like a picture frame as though she were a painter studying a form. "Do you understand?"

"I understand, my lady."

"How long do you think it will take?"

"Today and tomorrow for the fittings, and depending on how many dresses there are, the rest of the week to mend."

Lady Staton lowered her ear trumpet. She grunted, which Daphne took as her grandmother being pleased with Pamela Escott. Lady Staton waved her hand to dismiss them. Pamela followed Daphne to her bedroom and they spent the rest of the afternoon fitting the Worth dresses that Daphne thought had already been tailored to perfection.

Daphne couldn't sleep that night. The ghosts are out, murmuring and stomping on the stairs, she thought. She had never noticed the sounds before her uncle's death, though she would hardly be surprised if the old house were haunted. Ten generations of her family had lived there, their essences captured by the portraits on the walls. Since her uncle's death, she had seen his silhouette in the shadows, and she heard his laughter in the whispers of the wind. Sometimes the shadows seemed friendly, but that night Daphne was frightened. She heard the opening and closing of windows, and she heard stairs creaking when there should be silence. She heard the clipped conversation—between two ghouls? She didn't know. After hours of restlessness, she drifted to sleep dreaming of her Uncle Richard.

LADY STATON HAD HER WAY, and the parade of suitors around Hembry Castle had begun. There were eligible young men over to dine, ride, shoot, or simply be in Daphne's way. She didn't know what to make of the young men, especially since she was more unsure of Edward than ever before. He hadn't written lately and he hardly had time to leave London with his work at the Observer and his new collection of stories demanded by Fergusonandwately in half the time he had to write Tales from Southwark. Daphne was dispirited, thinking she would never understand what Edward felt for her. The proximity of the young men didn't help her feel better. She had never been a coquette, like so many of the young women at her ball with their girlish giggles, their fluttering eyelashes, their talking fans, and their coy smiles. She wasn't interested in cultivating the attention of any of the young bachelors. They were nice enough, she was sure, but she didn't want to ride out with them, despite her grandmother's insistence, and she certainly didn't want to marry any of them. When Lord Trevor's eldest son cornered her after luncheon while she was rereading Edward's stories in the rose garden, she slid away as gracefully as possible. When Caspar Bentham followed her into the library she showed him the book she was reading and then left him, and the book, behind.

Edward arrived at Hembry at the beginning of July. Frederick had returned to the country from London, and Edward was coming to seek Frederick's opinion about some difficulties he was having at the Observer. Daphne didn't care why he had come. Maybe she would finally pluck up the courage and ask him about his true feelings once and for all. The morning Edward arrived, Frederick suggested that young Mr. Ellis accompany Daphne on her walk to the Countess' Garden.

"Unchaperoned?" Daphne asked.

"I believe I can trust this young man to do right by my daughter, can I not, Mr. Ellis?"

Edward bowed. "You certainly can, your lordship."

Standing alone with Edward, Daphne felt as though she were near a stranger, one of the young men her grandmother had enticed to Hembry with promises of the hand of the Earl of Staton's daughter. Mr. Ellis opened the door for them, and Daphne led Edward outside where the cloudless sky covered them like a blue smile. They continued in silence down the Countess' Walk, a shady path lined by 100-foot-tall oak trees, and then they arrived in the Countess' Garden. Daphne leaned over the dainty blue forget-me-nots, the lavender asters, the yellow honeysuckles. Edward stood under an oak tree watching her from the distance. His face, usually bursting with expression, was blank. He bent over the purple aubretias, plucked a cluster, and handed them to Daphne.

"Beautiful flowers for a beautiful young lady."

Daphne held the purple petals to her nose to savor the sweet fragrance. They continued down the lane admiring the nasturtiums and the flower sage. After another moment of silence, Edward said, "You've had your hands full, I see. You're like Penelope in The Odyssey fighting off the suitors eager to marry Odysseus' widow. To the victor the spoils."

"There will be no victors here, at least not the kind my grandmother wants."

"Are you certain? I'm sure we can arrange an archery tournament to determine the lucky winner of your hand."

"And who will play the role of my strong, dashing husband who swoops in to save the day?" Daphne stopped near the guelder roses and studied the white blooms. "Do you know Lord Havenham is 71 and has a granddaughter my age?"

"Perhaps he's interested in you as a playmate for his granddaughter."

"Lord Havenham told my grandmother he needs a young wife to keep him young." Daphne shuddered. "As Penelope made herself scarce so she didn't have to see the suitors, so have I."

"I'm not dropping the idea of an archery contest so easily. You'll discover the right man after he strings a bow and arrow."

"Very well. The archery contest is a week from Saturday."

They continued walking, their shoulders nearly touching. Several times they opened their mouths to speak but didn't, so they returned to the Countess' Walk in the same silence that enveloped them during most of their time in the garden. Finally, Daphne said, "Do you have to return to London soon?"

"I leave tomorrow, but I do wish I had more time here. I love it at Hembry. But duty awaits." Edward stepped close to Daphne, close enough that their noses nearly touched. "Will I see you in London?"

"Papa is a peer now and has duties in the House of Lords, so yes, I'll be in London when the Lords are in session. Between us, I don't think I can take much more of my grandmother's meddling. She's frustrated with me because I'm avoiding the young men she's parading around Hembry."

"Whatever happened to the future Duke of Norley? He seemed rather intent at your ball."

"I'm afraid I'll need to turn him down."

Edward stopped walking. "He proposed?"

"He will. At least that's what my grandmother thinks. But I'm afraid I'm going to have to say no. I can't see myself as the future Duchess of Norley. My Uncle Richard warned me to stay away from Lord Darges."

"What did your uncle say?"

"That Lord Darges would never make any woman happy."

"Interesting." Edward looked like his grandfather, his hands clasped behind his back, hunched forward as though searching for something. "I wonder how your uncle knew that."

"They had become friends, my uncle and Lord Darges. I think my Uncle Richard knew that in my heart of hearts, as much as I've come to appreciate Hembry and the people in it, it isn't the life I want."

Edward gazed into Daphne's eyes. Her knees felt weak with the closeness of him.

"What kind of life do you want, Lady Daphne?"

"I want a warm life, a comfortable life surrounded by my friends and family. I want to love my husband with all my heart, and I want him to love me as much in return."

Edward said nothing. He offered his arm, and they returned to the castle in a troubled bubble of silence.

A PREVIOUS ENGAGEMENT

Frederick, Earl of Staton, wandered the ancient hallways of Hembry Castle with his head bowed. He moved with his eyes nearly closed, though it didn't surprise him that he had meandered from the east wing to the west wing and back again without banging into something. He had lived in that house for the first years of his life. Even when he attended Eton, even when he attended Oxford, even when he lived a continent away, he dreamed of Hembry, its curves and ways, its hidden passages, its loose cupboards in the attics, and forgotten floorboards in the scullery. He had never escaped the place, not entirely, and now that he was back, and now that it was his—the curves and ways, the hidden passages, the cupboards and the floorboards—he realized how intertwined he had been with the castle all along. He fled across the Atlantic in quest of a new life, and here he was anyway. We think we're in control of our lives, Frederick thought, but we're not, not really. Life has plans for us beyond our envisionings, plans even we cannot fathom. He laughed, thinking he sounded rather American then. But there it is. We do the best we can, and then life reveals its object for us, and we must either face the path and its challenges head on or burrow ourselves away, pretending we cannot see or hear. That's what Richard had done, poor soul. He couldn't face his life as Earl, so he hid away and excused away, and now Frederick's beloved brother was lost to him forever.

Frederick's philosophical meanderings had been brought on by his second meeting with Mr. Ruckson. After the detective left, Frederick wondered if he was perhaps a suspect in his brother's murder. But he had been at Staton House all that night, and besides, Richard hadn't been murdered. He fell over the bridge. Hadn't he? Frederick realized he needed more answers about that dreadful night. He went to visit John Hough only to be told by a village woman that the doctor had left suddenly without telling anyone. Inside the doctor's cottage were several notes, not about his whereabouts, but about how to tend to the villagers who were still unwell, namely Mrs. Pearson's boy Joseph. The doctor hadn't been himself since Richard's death. No one was surprised. The doctor and Richard had been the greatest of friends for so many years it was strange to see the doctor without Richard by his side. Now Hough had vanished to who-knows-where, and Frederick was uneasy with the news. Hough had been so bewildered when Frederick last saw him over Richard's body in the morgue. He gave his statement, then wept and wheezed like an asthmatic gasping for air. But what if Richard's death wasn't an accident after all?

Lady Staton still grieved, inwardly, for that was the aristocrat's way. Outwardly, she complained about the family's place at the center of Society gossip. "Who killed Richard, Earl of Staton?" was the question on everyone's lips, aristocrats, servants, and villagers alike. Lady Staton wondered aloud if it was better to allow everyone to believe that Richard had been murdered. An accidental death would have made Richard seem careless, and suicides were not treated well, by church, state, or Society. Frederick didn't care what anyone else thought. He only cared that perhaps his beloved eldest brother had been so miserable that jumping to his death from London Bridge seemed the only way out.

Frederick had been surprised by Mr. Ruckson's visit after luncheon. The detective asked the same questions he had before, and Frederick answered patiently.

"As I told you before, Detective Ruckson, there were many people at Staton House the night my brother died. They were coming and going for the ball. Besides, my brother didn't die at Staton House. He was found in the Thames."

"True." Mr. Ruckson stepped closer to Frederick, and Frederick held his breath, overwhelmed by the cigar stench that lingered like a stale halo over the inspector. "Your prospects have certainly improved since your brother's death, wouldn't you say, Lord Staton?"

"Perhaps for someone else. I never wanted this life."

"Is it true you went to America when you were a young man?"

"I moved to New York when I was two-and-twenty and I've only come back to England this past year."

"Is it true that your parents wished often and loudly that you were the heir instead of your eldest brother?"

"People say things when they're frustrated."

"Is it true? That's all I'm asking, Lord Staton. Is it true?"

"It is."

After the detective left, Frederick's stomach felt tight and it was uncomfortable to stand so he crumpled into the wing chair before the hearth. He was tired and didn't want to see anyone, but he couldn't hide as much as he wanted. He had too much to do, and farmers' quarrels to settle, so he went about his day as normally as possible. He knew Daphne would notice any oddities in his manner, and he didn't want to alarm her. Finally, as it neared dinner, he stopped by Daphne's bedroom before going downstairs. He knocked, and when he opened the door Daphne was placing a letter between the pages of a book that lay open on her writing desk. When Daphne saw her father, she turned as pink as her dress.

"And what is that?" Frederick asked.

"A letter from Edward."

"And what does Mr. Edward Ellis have to say?"

"Not much. He's so busy with the newspaper and his own work he hardly has time to write. He said he's been working so hard that yesterday he fell asleep at his desk and his head ended up in his plate alongside his mutton and potatoes. I laughed out loud when I read it." Daphne smiled. "Edward writes such wonderful letters, Papa."

"Yes, he does. Does he write to you often?"

Daphne placed the book on the table near her bed. "Sometimes."

"I see."

"We're just friends, Papa."

Daphne's cheeks were the color of red apples, and Frederick had to restrain a smile. He had liked Edward from their first introduction at the offices of the Observer, and he admired the young man. Edward was clever, observant, and talented in that unfair way that would make you dislike him intensely if he wasn't such a personable young man. No, Frederick decided, I wouldn't mind young Mr. Ellis as a son-in-law at all.

The next afternoon Frederick was lounging in the library reading the newspaper (the Daily Observer, of course) when Daphne found him. Frederick offered his cheek, which his daughter was quick to kiss.

"I was afraid I missed you before you left for London," she said.

"I would never leave without seeing you first. Where have you been all morning, Lady Daphne?"

"I was visiting Mrs. Pearson and Joseph."

"How is the lad?"

"He's sick again. He's so lethargic he can hardly get out of bed, and Mrs. Pearson says he has no appetite. I brought some of Mrs. Graham's scones and clotted cream, and he ate a bit and fell asleep soon after. He's wasting away, Papa, and I don't know what we're going to do without a doctor in Hembry."

"You're right. I can't dillydally any longer." Frederick folded the newspaper and set it on the desk in front of him. "It's why I'm going to London. I've been given a lead about a doctor who might be willing to leave his town practice behind. I'm willing to make it worth his while. I hope this man is as knowledge-able as Hough, but I worry. I doubt I'll ever find anyone with Hough's expertise. I think Hough has read every book written about medicine."

"There's been no word about Mr. Hough?"

"None that I've heard." Through the window Frederick contemplated the slow-moving river as it reflected the radi-ating sunlight. It was a perfect summer day, two pillow-white clouds floating northward, the weather comfortably warm. He saw the river disappear into green in the distance, and he looked to where the stone rotunda pointed its dome toward the sky. A deer meandered past, sniffing the rotunda steps, feasting on the grass, then galloping into the thicket of feathery trees. "You're not worried about the stranger that's been spotted here, are you?"

"I'm not afraid, Papa." Daphne followed her father's gaze to the rotunda. "He hasn't been seen for several weeks, and whoever he is must not mean any harm."

"How do you know that?"

"Because he would have done something by now if he did. When you're in London I know Mr. Ellis is here, along with the other staff. I'm well protected. Maybe the man is lost, lonely, or hungry. Maybe he needs our help."

"My Daphne. I have never met anyone so willing to see the good in others."

"I learned it from you, Papa."

For a moment it seemed as though the bookshelf coughed, and a polite cough it was too. Mr. Ellis stepped out of the shadows.

"Forgive me for interrupting, my lord, but your bags are in the carriage and Cooper recommends leaving as soon as possible so you can meet your train."

Daphne grasped her father's hand. "Don't forget you're going to the Chattaways to dine tonight."

"I haven't forgotten. It will be good to spend time with old Chattaway. I've hardly seen him since we first arrived in England."

Mr. Ellis appeared with Lord Staton's top hat and overcoat, and Daphne helped her father put them on.

"Have a wonderful time with the Chattaways, and tell Christina I'll see her the next time I'm in London, I promise. And, please, make sure you and Mr. Chattaway talk of something other than newspapers or you'll drive the women mad."

"I'm sure we'll find another way to do that."

THAT NIGHT FREDERICK returned to Staton House with a heavy heart. Perhaps I was wrong about Edward and Daphne from the beginning, he thought. Perhaps he hadn't seen Edward's longing glances at his daughter. Perhaps Edward was, as Daphne insisted, simply a friend. But Daphne had fallen for

Edward, of that Frederick was sure. She was too embarrassed, or too unsure, or too afraid, but she was in love. Only now Frederick needed to tell her that the man she loved could never be hers.

Frederick didn't want to wake any of the staff at that late hour so he crept up the stairs in the dark. He didn't know what to do. One part of him wanted to jump on the first train back to Hembry to tell Daphne. She had to know what kind of two-timing double-crosser that Edward Ellis was. Another part of him thought it wasn't any of his business. The final part of him wished he had never returned to England in the first place.

He opened the door to Daphne's bedroom in Staton House, wishing his daughter were there so he could confess to her and comfort her, or she could comfort him, whichever proved more pressing. It was a narrow room, only six feet wide and ten feet across, but the Baroque-style gold moldings on the ceiling added elegance to the space. Frederick sat on the green damask chair near the writing desk and stared at the paper set out neatly alongside pens and ink jars. He wondered if he should telegraph and tell her at once, wait until he returned to Hembry, or say nothing at all. Perhaps Daphne even knew, though Frederick's instinct told him that was not the case.

In the morning, Frederick returned to Hembry since telling his daughter this pressing news became more important than any doctor he might find. He returned to the castle before luncheon, found Daphne, and led her to her bedroom where they might have some privacy. Feesbury, his valet, looked chagrined when his lordship shrugged away any help with his overcoat. The housemaids came in to straighten Lady Daphne's room, but his lordship shooed them away too.

Frederick spoke simply. This was not a time for metaphors and analogies. He repeated what Mitchell Chattaway had said and which had been verified by Miss Chattaway herself, by the entire Chattaway family, in fact. Daphne stared into the hearth for a long time, not moving. Then she shivered and stepped closer to the warmth of the flames. She looked very young, Frederick thought, with the sadness of a child burdened with her first major disappointment when she realized life isn't fair after all.

"I'm so sorry, Daphne. I don't know what to say. Mitchell Chattaway didn't seem to think the information would be surprising to me in any way. He was simply sharing some family news about the engagement of his eldest daughter to a young man I knew. I tried to hide my surprise the best I could, though I'm not sure how well I succeeded. I congratulated Miss Chattaway. After all, there was no point in being angry. If there's an agreement between them there's nothing more to be said."

Daphne's voice quavered. "If anyone made a mistake it was me." She was trembling, though she tried to hide behind a brave smile.

Frederick opened the window and breathed in deeply, hoping to find some breeze outside. He turned to Daphne, who struggled to maintain her composure. "I don't believe young Mr. Ellis is without blame in this. I've seen the way he looks at you. I've seen the way he seeks you out whenever you're near. I saw the two of you dance the day away at Christmas, and I watched you disappear together at your ball. Could we both have been so wrong about him? If he is engaged to Miss Chattaway, which he is, then what would be the point of making you believe...?" Frederick slammed his fist into the windowsill. "No, Daphne. I won't stand for it. I won't be hoodwinked that way. If that young man deliberately wormed his way into my generosity, making me believe he was my friend and more than a friend to you to ensure my assisting his literary ambitions, if he planned to get what he wanted, becoming a successful editor and author while you're cast aside, he has another thing coming!"

"Papa." Daphne's voice was calm. "I haven't been cast aside. He never made any declarations to me. You don't believe Edward planned this, do you?"

"I don't know, my dear, but I'm going to find out."

"What are you going to do?"

"I'm going back to London to give that boy a piece of my mind."

Daphne stood, her hands out toward her father. "No, Papa. Please. When I think back on all our conversations Edward never once, I mean, we did kiss that time near the castle ruins, but..." The dam broke, and no matter how hard she squeezed her eyes or pressed her lips she couldn't stop the waterworks from flowing. She covered her face with her hands and slumped forward.

Frederick took his daughter in his arms and let her cry. "It's all right, my darling. Everything will be fine, you'll see. I'm catching the next train back to London, and I'm going to challenge this rascal face to face. I want to know why he never mentioned this engagement to us. I want to know why he went out of his way to seek you out if he had already spoken out for Miss Chattaway."

"He never came to seek me out, Papa. I happened to be here."

"Happened my eye." His head pounded suddenly, and he thought to ring for some water. "You and Christina are friends, Daphne. She never told you she and Edward were engaged?"

"I knew she was engaged to a journalist, but she never told me his name."

"That didn't strike you as odd?"

"I never thought there was a reason behind it. I thought she was being coy. I realize now I should have made the connection. There were times when I thought Edward had feelings for me, but then there were other times when I thought he didn't. Now I know he didn't. It's my fault. I saw something that wasn't there, maybe because I wanted to see it."

"That is so like you to take the blame upon yourself, my Daphne, but this is not your fault. I cannot put into words how disappointed I am in Edward Ellis. There's more to this story, and I want to know what it is."

Before Daphne could reply, Frederick was gone. He made up his mind, and he would see it through.

MEANWHILE, DOWNSTAIRS
AT HEMBRY CASTLE

*D*inner in the servants' hall was a sight to behold. Miss Rowland, Mr. Feesbury, Pamela, Miss Escott now to the staff, along with Ruth, Jemima, and Colin watched the solo ballet of Henry Horrocks as he landed pirouettes on each leg in its turn while his hands circled arrondi. The elegance of his movements was a stark contrast to the vexation in his voice. Henry pointed at Colin, his feet battu as though the second footman's head were centered on the floorboards and Henry would kick some sense into him with the point of his toes.

"I know you've been in my things. You nicked my letters. From my family, those were."

Colin continued his dinner, nodding after each bite of stew as though it were the greatest meal ever cooked. Henry slammed his fists onto the table on either side of Colin's plate.

"Henry." Miss Rowland dabbed at her mouth with her napkin. "Don't make a fuss. If Colin has been stealing tell Mr. Ellis."

Henry scoffed. "If he's been stealing. He nicked my letters. He knows he did. Colin is the only one in my room."

"When was the last time you saw the letters?" Miss Rowland asked.

"I took them with me to London when we went for Lady Daphne's ball."

"Lady Daphne's ball was weeks ago." Mr. Feesbury shook his balding head. "If the letters were so important you'd think you'd have checked whether or not you had them before now."

Henry slumped forward. He looked like he had been pricked by a pin and the others watched him deflate. "I kept them safe in my book and I brought my book to London and back. I didn't look inside to see if anyone had taken the letters. How would anyone else know they were there?"

"If you had the book at Staton House during the ball anyone could have taken them," said Mr. Feesbury. "It could have been one of those hired hands. I thought one or two of them were on the dodgy side."

"It was Colin!" Henry jumped up and down, an adult-sized child throwing a temper tantrum.

Everyone stood when the Ellises entered. Mr. Ellis pressed his round-rimmed glasses against his nose.

"What, may I ask, is happening? Henry, I can hear you shouting from Mrs. Ellis' sitting room." When no one offered any information, Mr. Ellis tried again. "Ruth, what has happened?"

"Henry thinks Colin stole some letters of his, Mr. Ellis. Henry hasn't seen the letters since London."

The butler and the housekeeper exchanged a curious look. Mrs. Ellis stayed silent, hovering near her husband's shoulder, scanning the faces of the servants standing around the table.

"Henry, Colin, you will join Mrs. Ellis and myself in her

sitting room. The rest of you, finish your meal and attend to your duties. Quickly."

In the housekeeper's sitting room, Mr. and Mrs. Ellis sat in the wing chairs before the hearth while Henry and Colin remained standing.

"Well?" said Mr. Ellis. "Henry, explain yourself."

Henry stared at an Ellis family photograph on the hearth—a sepia-toned picture of their grandson Edward—as he considered his words. He worked his facial muscles, contorting them up and down and side to side, as though searching for some tears to squeeze out from somewhere. "I had letters from home. They're from my pa before he died. I went to look for them today, and they were gone."

"Ruth said you think the letters have been gone since London?" said Mrs. Ellis.

"I didn't think I had to look for them. I thought I knew where they were. They were my personal letters, in my personal book."

"And you're certain you had them in London?"

"Yes."

Mr. Ellis and his wife shared that look again. "I see." The butler's fingers formed a triangle under his chin while he studied the young men before him. "And you, Colin? You have not seen these letters?"

"I have not. What would I want with some of Henry's family letters?"

"You're certain?" asked Mr. Ellis.

"You can check my room if you don't believe me."

Mr. Ellis said nothing, his fingers moving from the triangle under his chin to the arm of his chair where they tapped an impatient tune. "Thank you. You both may go." The young men rushed toward the door. "However, Henry." The footman turned back. "I will have no more of these outbursts in the servants' hall, in the kitchen, in the laundry shed, or in the stables with only the horses to hear. Do you understand?"

"Yes, Mr. Ellis."

Mrs. Ellis watched the footmen escape down the hallway. She slammed the door shut behind them. "Oh, Gussie. How I wanted to tell them we have the letters just to see their faces."

"It's best to keep that quiet for now, Mary."

"I agree." Mrs. Ellis picked up a photograph, this one of Richard, taken a year before his father, the 8th Earl, died. "That dear, sweet boy, trying to live his life the best he could. I can't imagine how he felt once he realized his letters were gone. I wish I could have done more to help him."

"We shielded him as best we could, but once he became Earl he had a destiny bigger than either of us could protect him from."

Augustus Ellis kissed the top of his wife's faded hair, nearly albino white now. He opened the top drawer in her writing desk and pulled out the packet of letters. "Do you think Henry or Colin guessed the author of the love letter?"

"They wouldn't have been able to keep it to themselves if they knew. They could have sold that story for a pretty pound or two, that's for certain." She picked up the letter from the 8th Earl of Staton and spread it on her desk. "It's such a lovely letter. His lordship telling his son and heir that he was proud of him no matter what. What a lovely sentiment for a father to say to his son. I wish…"

"What do you wish, Mary?"

"I wish I had said as much to George. Perhaps things would have turned out differently. Perhaps George would have turned out differently. Now it's too late."

"As long as we have breath in our body we can decide to do things differently. George is a grown man, and he's made his way. He never seemed too eager to find a different path. And look at Edward. He's done so well for himself."

"I'm glad he didn't let George get in his way."

"I think George was Edward's reason for wanting to do more with his life. Edward didn't want to be like his father, and he isn't."

Mr. Ellis sighed. He poured himself some tea from the pot on the round table near the window. He poured a cup for his wife, and they sipped in silence, watching the dark night spread across the sky.

"Do you think his lordship knew?" Mr. Ellis asked. "Richard's father, I mean. Do you think he knew and that's why he told Richard he was proud of him no matter what?"

"That's my guess. And when Richard realized his letters were gone, it must have driven him mad. What would have happened to him, or the family, if the truth was known?" Mrs. Ellis finished her tea and set the cup and saucer on the table. "I think Henry, or Colin, or both, made a connection between the love letter and the message about the baby."

"That would be a logical conclusion, certainly. Then why didn't they sell the letters from that angle? Surely a story about the Earl of Staton's illegitimate child would be worth something."

"Would it? What earl or marquess or duke doesn't have an illegitimate child somewhere? I think the story wasn't worth as much as they thought it would be and that's why they haven't done anything."

Mr. Ellis shook his head. "And Mr. Jerrold?"

"Mr. Jerrold gets clean away with everything as he always has. But he has to live with that crone of a wife, and that's punishment enough for any man." Mrs. Ellis pointed at her husband. "Nothing from you, Augustus Ellis."

"My wife is the very opposite of a crone. I'm the most

fortunate man in the world, as I have been for more than 50 years." The butler kissed his wife's cheek. "So why was Henry so upset about the missing letters suddenly? Why look for them now when he hadn't thought much about them for weeks?"

"I wonder." Mrs. Ellis looked into the hearth flames like a conjuring fortune teller. "Perhaps he realized the letters were worth something after all." Mrs. Ellis poked the dwindling fire awake. "That man who's been spotted loitering around the grounds. Has he been found?"

"Not yet. I admit, I'm baffled. The entire outdoor staff is on alert, so someone should have caught him by now. Why do you ask?"

"I thought maybe he had something to do with Henry's sudden change of heart about the letters."

Mr. Ellis put his hands on his knees and leaned toward his wife. "The fact remains, I must do something. Henry and Colin must go. Whether they stole the letters together, or whether one stole the letters and the other stole the letters from the first one, they both must be gone from this house."

"When will you do it?"

"As soon as I've spoken to his lordship."

"I wish it hadn't come to this, Augustus."

"I know, but what could we have done?"

"There's always something to be done, some way to help."

"I worry, Mary. I worry that his lordship, Richard, I mean, was so upset over the loss of his letters that he..." Mr. Ellis studied the 9th Earl's photograph. "I know he had a hard time after he inherited the title, but I cannot accept that that bright-eyed little boy, with such a keen disposition and so quick to laugh, who used to race through these halls with all joy and abandon, could ever do something so terrible or deliberate."

"There's no reason to think ill thoughts, Augustus. His lordship believes his brother's death was an accident. Everyone else should believe that too."

A knock at the door startled them, and Ruth appeared. "I'm sorry, Mrs. Ellis, but you're needed upstairs."

Mrs. Ellis looked back at her husband as she followed the maid out the door.

THE FOOTMEN'S room was empty. Cramped, windowless, and stale smelling, as though every kitchen odor rose upward, sending only the pleasing odors toward the green baize door and releasing everything else to the attics. There were three beds cramped into a space hardly large enough for two, but since Gregory, the third footman, had left to tend his father's flocks in Aberdeen, there was one less body in the way. The door creaked open, and there was a pause. Yes, it was empty, Henry and Colin were about their tasks in the dining room under Mr. Ellis' watchful eye. Soft shoes shuffled across the wooden floor, a faint jingle with each step like wind chimes in an easy breeze. The room was sparse, the whitewash nearly faded, leaving the walls with a dull sheen. Family photographs lined the chest of drawers shared between the two footmen—parents, brothers, sisters, and one coquette, a young dark-haired beauty, most likely a sweetheart. First one drawer was opened and rummaged through, then the next, then the next. Mattresses were lifted. The jingling stopped. There was nothing to find here. The letters uncovered from the loose floorboard in the attic of Staton House appeared to be all they had. All right then. If there was nothing left to find, then Augustus was right. It was time for action. It was now or never, and never wouldn't do.

IN THE PARADISE

The July sky grew darker and then it was raining, one of those London summer rains that came and went and left the air murkier for it. Frederick waved away Rogers, the driver at Staton House, who chased after him with a second overcoat in an attempt to protect my lord from the whims of the weather, bemoaning the lack of an umbrella.

"It's all right, Rogers." Frederick darted out from under the canopy of the coat. "I'm quite happy walking. It's only a little water."

He outpaced the older Rogers in only four steps, and he heard the driver muttering behind him. Frederick truly didn't mind the rain. It wasn't an angry rain, not yet, and city life continued as it usually did because if life stopped in England when it rained then there would be little life indeed. People darted across the street, some under umbrellas, some pulling their hats closer to their noses, some tugging their coats closer to their ears. The carriages continued on their way, the horses annoyed by the splashes of wet, and the people pressed forward. Frederick was another one of the walking men who pulled his hat down and his coat up. He needed to walk to release the excess energy that had been eating at him since he left Hembry. He couldn't get the image of Daphne, pressing back her tears, wanting so much to be brave, out of his mind. For the longest time she wouldn't admit her feelings, insisting that she admired young Mr. Ellis' determination and diligence. She respected his intelligence and approved of his sense of humor. She admired his talent and especially she loved his stories and she would read them aloud again and again.

Could Edward have hoodwinked them all? Frederick wasn't sure. There was genuine affection between Edward and Daphne, Frederick was sure of it. There was nothing dark or hidden in Edward's manner, at least not that Frederick had seen, to make him think Edward was trying to hurt or take advantage. It didn't make sense. Frederick went over possible scenarios as he walked, trying out various reasons why Edward might have done what he had, leaving Daphne in the dark about his engagement to Miss Chattaway, and not one of those reasons was flattering to Edward.

Frederick arrived at the house on Fetter Lane where Edward lived and knocked at the front door. While he waited he realized the rain was falling harder, pelting his hat like hail. A young girl opened the door.

"Ma," the girl yelled. "It's a man."

"What man?" her mother called back.

The little girl looked at Frederick from his dripping hat to his liquefied shoes. "A wet man."

"My name is Frederick Staton."

"His name is Frederick Staton," called the daughter.

"For heaven's sake, child, let the wet man named Frederick Staton in."

The girl opened the door wider, and Frederick was allowed inside. He took off his hat and coat, which the little girl hung on a peg on the wall, standing on her toes because the peg was taller than she was.

"Excuse me for making you wait in the rain," said the woman, wiping her hands on her apron. "I was getting dinner ready for my boarders."

"Is Mr. Edward Ellis at home?" Frederick asked.

"Mr. Ellis is always at home, sir, when he's not at work. Needs a wife that young man. I says to him, Mr. Ellis, I says, Mr. Ellis, you're a young man at an age when you need a companion, and a female one too, if you understand my meaning."

"I do, indeed." Frederick covered his mouth with his hand, turning his laugh into a cough since he didn't want to offend the proprietor of the boarding house.

"Prudence, run and fetch Mr. Ellis for..."

"His name's Staton," said Prudence.

"Hmm," said the landlady. "Mr. Ellis said he used to work for Lord Staton at the newspaper."

"That would be me."

"You're Lord Staton? Dear me, my lord. Please do come into my humble home." The woman flattened her apron, pressed her hair out of its bun, then bowed, curtsied, and bowed again. "I didn't realize I had the honor of hosting such a personage as yourself in my humble home. Allow me to fetch you a cup of tea. Allow me to dry your clothes. Allow me to..."

Frederick shook his head. "I assure you, I'm only here to speak to Mr. Ellis. Please do return to whatever you were doing."

The landlady ran around Frederick so fast he couldn't keep track of her and his neck hurt with the strain of trying. "But I couldn't have Lord Staton leaving without feeling he was properly attended to, your highness."

Frederick laughed. "I'm not your highness, Mrs..."

"Mrs. Chapman, your majesty. And good of you to ask too."

Her daughter returned downstairs alone. "Mr. Ellis won't come. He won't answer his door."

"Are you certain he's home?" asked Frederick.

"I'm certain, your holiness." Mrs. Chapman flattened her hair with her hand again. "I saw him come in myself, and he had another visitor come by a little while after, another well-dressed man. When the visitor left Mr. Ellis had the wretchedest look about him you ever did see. He wouldn't even answer when I asked him when he wanted his dinner."

"Allow me to try."

Prudence showed Frederick the door on the third floor. Frederick banged on the door with an angry fist. Edward was not getting away so easily.

"Edward! It's Frederick. I need a moment of your time."

There was rustling on the other side. The door creaked open, and Frederick couldn't believe the state of the young man. Edward's hair was sticking out on all sides, pointing north, south, east, and west. His clothes were unkempt, his shirt out of his trousers, black ink smudged over his face, hands, and shirt sleeves, which were rolled up around his elbows. Edward said nothing as he allowed Frederick inside. The young man moaned a mournful tune as he paced the floor, which didn't take long in the cramped quarters. Frederick thanked the little girl and her mother and shut the door in their astonished faces.

"Mitchell Chattaway was just here," Edward said.

"What perfect timing since I'm here to speak to you on that very same subject. I dined with the Chattaways last night, and Mr. Chattaway had some interesting things to say to me concerning you and his eldest daughter." Frederick watched Edward, who was pacing the floor, back and forth, back and forth. Frederick wondered what the tenant on the second floor must be thinking. "So it's true then. You made a promise to Chattaway's daughter. You're engaged."

Edward let out a cry somewhere between frustration and pain. He dropped to the sofa, his head in his hands.

"I asked for Miss Chattaway's hand, but then I met your daughter, and then…" Edward moaned again. "I've never been so confused about anything in all my life." Edward sat on his heels before the Earl. "I want you to know how I feel about your daughter, Lord Staton. I've loved her from the moment I met her."

"Aren't we being formal?"

"I want you to know how serious I am in my love for your daughter."

"You said you were confused."

"I'm not confused by my feelings for Lady Daphne. I'm confused about what to do. I don't know how to get out of the promise I made to Miss Chattaway, but I can't marry her, not now."

"Did you make yourself clear to Chattaway? Did you tell him you're not in love with his daughter?"

"I tried to make him understand. I begged him. I pleaded with him. Christina is a lovely girl. She's sweet natured, and she's kind. She'll find another man far better suited to her than I'd ever be. I told him I was in love with Daphne, and he laughed and said that at no time would the Earl of Staton's daughter marry the grandson of servants. I told him Daphne was different, that you were different, but he wouldn't hear it. He was yelling so loudly I thought the windows would shatter. He threatened to take me to court if I didn't go through with it."

"He has a perfect right to do so."

Poor Edward was so miserable, staring at the window as though he expected to see Mitchell Chattaway flying outside shaking his fists like Jacob Marley rattling his chains at Scrooge. Edward paced again from here to there and back again, a child's yo-yo with Chattaway pulling the string up and down, side to side, anywhere he wanted at his whim. Frederick wanted to feel sorry for Edward. In his heart of hearts he did feel sorry for Edward, yet he was also furious with the young man for toying with Daphne's affections. Daphne, who had fallen in love with this young man. Daphne, with a warm, loving heart who treated everyone around her with kindness. Even when the fact of Edward's betrayal had come to light, she would not say an unkind thing about him, insisting the fault was hers and hers alone. Whether Edward meant to hurt Daphne or not, he did, deeply. Frederick, with his father's love, wanted to fix everything even though it was so much harder to do now she was one-and-twenty. When she was five and she skinned her hand tripping outside he had only to kiss the injured fingers and he could see the pain vanish in her smile. But this was too hard to fix with a kiss or a kind word. Frederick never disliked being Earl of Staton more than he did at that moment. What good was a title if he couldn't help his daughter?

And then Frederick wondered—what could he do? He watched Edward, still swinging from the yo-yo, staggering from side to side, the panic filling his hazel eyes like water rising behind a dam. Frederick thought of Mitchell Chattaway, an easy-going, good-natured man. Frederick guessed that Chattaway was not acting on his own but as an emissary for his wife. Christina Chattaway was a lovely, charming girl, if dreamy-eyed and a little on the quiet side. Yes, she always seemed to be one step behind the rest of the conversation. But she was good-natured like her father and friendly once you got to know her. Daphne and Christina were immediate friends from the moment they met. Did Christina know about

Edward's feelings for Daphne? Frederick suspected she did. Women were astute about such things.

Was it true then? Had Edward been stalling, trying to find a way to break out of his understanding with Christina? Looking at the state of the young man, whose agitated hands were pulling at his chocolate-brown hair with such force Frederick feared the locks would fall in a lump to the floor, he guessed Edward wasn't all right with the way things turned out.

Then Frederick had to consider. More than anything else in this world, he wanted his daughter to be happy. He knew she had been having a hard time since arriving in England. What was supposed to be a short trip to see his ailing father had become a permanent residency, especially now he was Earl. She had been put through the wringer by his mother as much as any wet linen in the laundry room. Frederick pictured Jacinda, the laundress at Hembry Castle when he was a boy. He remembered walking past the servants' entrance, past the stables and the larder to the small building where he'd watch as Jacinda and her assistants soaked the clothing and linens in buckets of soapy water, then flattened them through the wringer. That's what his mother was doing to Daphne—flattening her and wringing out her excess liquid—teaching her how to walk, how to curtsey, how to speak at table, which conversations are appropriate in Society and which are not, desperate to wash away anything about Daphne that didn't fit into the tightly woven fabric of the aristocracy. Frederick had learned such ways from infancy, and the manners were carved into him like engravings into silver. Even after all his time away, the protocol still came naturally to him. It wasn't natural for Daphne, and it was hard for her, remembering all the rules, both spoken and hidden. Daphne was bearing up well enough, she was a strong girl, but Frederick knew she wasn't happy.

Her only joy in England had been Edward, and now it seemed he was gone as well. What can I do, Frederick wondered? How can I fix this for my darling girl?

"Edward?" Edward stopped, his yo-yo string snapped. "Edward, I need to ask you a question. It's rather personal, and of course you're under no obligation to answer. I don't mean to embarrass you."

"I believe I'm beyond embarrassment, Lord Staton. Ask me what you wish."

"Have you ever been alone with Miss Chattaway? I mean, have you..."

"No! Nothing like that. We were never alone for more than a moment or two."

"I don't mean to be boorish, my friend, but it only takes a moment or two."

"I swear to you, Lord Staton..."

"I'm still Frederick, I hope."

"Nothing improper occurred between Christina Chattaway and me. The truth is, I hardly know her. I had been to her family's home for dinner on several occasions when Mr. Chattaway invited me, and Miss Chattaway was sweet natured, and she seemed interested in me and my work. I thought it would be nice to have someone here when I got home or when I had to work late into the night."

"You were lonely. I can understand that. I felt lonely my whole life until I met Daphne's mother. Diana was the first person to understand me."

"That's it exactly! Daphne understands me. She sees me, she sees all of me."

"She certainly didn't see this." Frederick brushed aside his frustration with a shake of his head. He decided that honesty might well be his best policy. "Daphne loves you, Edward."

"Does she? Truly?"

"She loves you so much her heart is breaking." Frederick looked into Edward's eyes. "I need to know what your intentions were toward my daughter, Edward. If you had already made a promise to Miss Chattaway, why did you make Daphne believe you were in love with her?"

"If Daphne believes I'm in love with her it's because I am in love with her. I know I had already promised Miss Chattaway, but when I saw Daphne, from that first time at your father's funeral, something about her spoke to me somewhere inside I didn't even know existed. I think I loved her from that very moment, and the more I knew her, the more I knew her heart, and the more I understood the depths of my feelings for her. But I couldn't speak out because of Miss Chattaway. I kept hoping I would discover a way out of the engagement that would free me without hurting Miss Chattaway."

"I'm afraid there's no way to break off an engagement without hurting the young woman being broken from, especially if that young woman has done nothing to deserve it, which Miss Chattaway has not." Frederick shivered, realizing for the first time since arriving at Edward's he was cold. He stood before the hearth, hands out to absorb the warmth. "If you had not already engaged yourself to Miss Chattaway, your intention toward my daughter would be?"

"I would marry her tomorrow." Edward's voice cracked and his cheeks reddened, from embarrassment more than the heat of the fire, Frederick thought. "I know you're the Earl of Staton now, and I'm the grandson of your servants. I know I have no right to hope, but I love her, Lord Staton. What kind of cruelty is there in the world that I meet Daphne, the woman who has stolen my heart, after I met Miss Chattaway and not before?"

"Perhaps Miss Chattaway will make you happy after all. She

seems a gentle soul. I'm certain she'll do everything in her power to be the wife you wish for."

"Miss Chattaway doesn't have Daphne's spirit or her independence. She doesn't know her mind like Daphne. She doesn't understand me like Daphne." Edward turned away, his cheeks that embarrassed red again, his index finger scratching the air as though he were writing something down. "I know I wish for too much. I know I'm hardly the man your mother would like Daphne to marry."

Frederick laughed. "I wouldn't worry about that. My mother doesn't even like to speak to people who don't keep a carriage." Frederick saw desperation in the young man's eyes, and the last of his frustration dissipated. "Are you telling me the truth, Edward Ellis? Would you marry my daughter if you were no longer tied to Miss Chattaway?"

"Your daughter is the only woman in the world for me."

Frederick sighed. "Very well then. I'll speak to Mitchell Chattaway and see what I can do. I can't promise anything, but I'll try."

Edward dropped to his knees and grabbed Frederick's hands. Frederick pulled Edward to his feet. "Please, son, I'm not the Queen or the Pope. You needn't kiss my ring. I'm doing this for my daughter, but I'm doing this for you too. I can see you love Daphne, and heaven knows she's as much in love with you. If my intervention can help in any way, then I must try. If worse comes to worst, you'll have to break off the engagement knowing the Chattaways would sue you. I can pay any monetary damages the courts require of you, but it's your reputation I'm concerned about. Your career is just getting started. It would be terrible to see your professional life destroyed because of a romantic scandal. Others have been ruined for less. Still, I am the Earl of Staton. That must be worth something."

"Lady Staton won't be happy if there's a scandal."

"We're already on the verge of scandal with my brother's peculiar death. Another one hardly matters. I was never supposed to be the Earl, so no one would be surprised if I muddy things up a bit. I am the wayward, after all."

"Will you go now?" Edward asked.

"Not tonight." Frederick looked at his watch. "I don't want to corner the Chattaways when they're not expecting it, especially not when Mrs. Chattaway will be there chirping into her husband's ear. I'll try to catch Chattaway on his own tomorrow."

Frederick opened the door, sending the landlady and her daughter tumbling down the stairs.

THIS WAS EDWARD ELLIS' life during the summer of 1871: at the offices of the Daily Observer at the crack of dawn, writing, editing, creating layouts, keeping the staff on task, and arguing with the printer. Home after dark to work on his own stories for Fergusonandwately until he was so tired he often woke up with his head on his desk, a crick in his neck, and ink in his hair. Then, at first light, it was back to the offices of the Daily Observer. Certainly, he was thrilled when Tales from Southwark was released. He remembered holding the first copy, warm from the printer's, while he ran across Hyde Park toward Staton House where Daphne waited for him. He waved the book at her, and she rushed down the stairs, across the street, and onto the green expanse of the park, not stopping until she pulled the volume from his grasp, dropped onto the grass, and began to read aloud. She didn't care about her half-mourning lavender dress on the wet grass, she didn't care which fine ladies in which grand carriages and four saw her, she didn't care about anything except Edward and his book.

And then it was back to the grind—back to the Observer, then back home to write until he fell unconscious.

Being busy was a good thing. It kept him from dwelling on the misery that was always lurking one step behind him. He should have been bursting with anticipation. The one thing he had wanted since he read his first Dickens novel—his very own book with his very own words and his very own name on the cover—had happened and all he felt was forlorn because the Chattaways were turning on the pressure for a wedding date. He had to keep thinking of excuses. First, he said he needed a better paying position, which he then received when Frederick officially handed him the editorship. Then, he said he was too busy because he was now the editor of the Observer, which Mr. Chattaway pointed out wasn't the greatest excuse since he, Mr. Chattaway, was an editor and married at the same time, and even had four daughters in the bargain (largely attributed to Mrs. Chattaway). Then Edward said he had to finish writing his story collection, which then was finished, and published, and even sold well. The Chattaways were pleased to point out that Edward now had an extra income from his books, in addition to the larger income from the Observer. Then Edward had to start writing the second collection, not giving himself a moment to breathe after completing Tales from Southwark. That was when the Chattaways became loud in their impatience. Edward's solution? Leaving letters from anyone named Chattaway unopened. But the unopened letters still would have their say, and the Chattaways began to invade Edward's consciousness at all hours of the day and night. The odd thing was he never heard from Christina. The messages, the invitations, and more recently the rebukes, had come from her parents.

Mitchell Chattaway's timing was impeccable. Edward had decided, just that morning, that he would finally put an end to his misery, and the Chattaways'. Mr. Chattaway is a reasonable man, Edward thought. Christina guessed about Daphne months ago, and I told her she was wrong though she was so very right. If I tell Christina the truth now, I believe she would let me go with best wishes because that's the kind of person she is. He would go to the Chattaways after Observer business was done, he would be honest, and open, and tell them what happened—that he had only the most honorable intentions toward Christina when he asked for her hand, but circumstances changed, and now it would be the least honorable thing to marry Christina when he was in love with another. Christina would not be happy married to him, and she deserved all the happiness life could bring her. Edward rehearsed the speech over again until he began writing his words for the Chattaways as the headline for the front page of the Observer (fortunately Tewson, the copy editor, caught it before it went to the printer's). Observer business done for the day, Edward grabbed his coat and hat, headed toward the Chattaways, then thought he should return the trinkets Christina had given him. He didn't mean to seem ungrateful. He only meant to show that they should both move on. He arrived at Fetter Lane, nodded at Mrs. Chapman, patted Prudence on the head, and bounded up the stairs two at a time. He rummaged through his bookcase and grabbed the volume of poetry, then went through his desk drawer for the pens and pen knives Christina had given him. He placed them in a carpetbag and was ready to leave when he heard a knock at his door. There was Mitchell Chattaway, red-faced and red-voiced, yelling about how surprised he was to discover that Lord Staton hadn't known about Edward's engagement to Christina. Why did Edward feel the need to keep the engagement secret from Lord Staton, Mr. Chattaway wanted to know. When Edward gave no reply, Mr. Chattaway let Edward know in no uncertain terms that there was no way out of the engagement without a court case. Edward fell into despair, thinking he would never know joy again. By the time he crawled into bed that night, after Lord Staton's visit, he had glimmers of hope, though he was afraid to grasp those glimmers too tightly for fear they might evaporate before he could close them tight in his hand.

The next day was business as usual. Edward dragged himself from his flat, dodging passers-by and hiding alongside lampposts in case Mitchell Chattaway appeared to make a case of him again. The omnibuses passed, each with its route and color on display: Paragons, Paddingtons, and Favourites represented by red, green, and blue. Occasionally, Edward took the omnibus to Fleet Street, though that morning he walked without his usual interest in the music of city sounds. Where normally he was energized by the industry—the dressmakers and the milliners and the cobblers, the breweries and the clock makers and the jewelers, the shipyards with the fish women and the dock porters and the steamboats floating by—now all passed like specters from scenes from a previous life. He passed identical rows of identical terraced houses with identical window baskets overflowing with identical rhododendrons. He watched the women heading toward Bond Street where they would daydream at the window displays, attend matinees, or partake of tea at one of the new-fangled ladies' teashops. The truth was that Edward didn't want to be out in the world that day. He wanted to stay in bed with a blanket over his head and a bottle of whiskey in his hand.

The day after that Edward again pulled himself out of bed, dressed himself, and walked through the front door at Fetter Lane. He thought back over his conversation with Lord Staton, and he prayed the glimmers of hope were still flickering. He hadn't heard from the Earl since their discussion, and he hoped the silence meant things weren't settled either way. Edward knew how fortunate he was to have a friend in Lord Staton. The Earl could have said, "You shouldn't have made such a rash decision about Miss Chattaway," or "You've made your bed and now you must lie in it," leaving Daphne free to marry whichever willing member of the aristocracy her grand-mother snatched for her. Edward was afraid to allow his thoughts to roam to the one place where he might find some peace—that place where, if Lord Staton's meeting with Mr. Chattaway went well, Edward would be free from his promise to Christina and he could marry the woman he loved. Lord Staton seemed certain that Daphne would marry Edward if he asked. Lord Staton didn't seem at all concerned that he, Edward, was the grandson of the butler and housekeeper. Was it possible?

Edward stopped in his usual place for contemplation, leaning over the Victoria Embankment, staring down into the gray depths of the Thames at high tide as it made its snake-like trail through the heart of London. It was July now, the lumbering fog at bay, the green shrubbery of summer at full bloom. Edward watched the passers-by as he listened to the street vendors call their wares. He thought of Daphne and smiled. All this trouble for an American girl, he thought, and she's worth every moment of it.

Edward knew he had to face the worst that could happen—the Chattaways could refuse to end the engagement. What then? Would he marry Christina for fear of scandal and the loss of his career? Would he end the engagement anyway, come what may? He checked the rising sun and sighed, not wanting to leave this spot where he could think undisturbed. When he arrived at the offices of the Observer, he couldn't concentrate. Later, when the others took a break for their afternoon meal, Edward went outside. It was feeling close in the office and he wiped away the humidity lingering on his temples with his handkerchief. He stepped into the L of Gough Square and saw the flower vendor, the same ruddy-faced man with the same ruddy-faced son, a little taller now, who had given Daphne the flowers. Edward pictured the pile of work on his desk, but he couldn't bring himself to go back inside.

"Edward!"

Edward's knees quivered, the humidity now in his palms, but he faced Lord Staton with his head high. Whatever the news, he would take it like a man. The Earl gestured with his walking stick. "Come with me!" the stick seemed to call, and without asking why, Edward followed Frederick toward Hyde Park. As they reached Park Lane, Edward was certain they were going to Staton House. Lord Staton slowed his pace to explain.

DAPHNE HAD BEEN restless all day, unsure why she was beckoned to Staton House at such short notice. Pamela had packed two bags for her, appearing certain about what Daphne would need when Daphne herself hadn't a clue. When Mrs. Ellis wiped away a tear and bid her a good journey, and when Mr. Ellis bowed to her more deeply than he ever had before, Daphne worried.

"Please, Mrs. Ellis," she pleaded, "you must tell me. Is something wrong with my father?"

"I promise you, Lady Daphne, your father is well. And you will be too."

"Will be?"

Mrs. Ellis wiped away another tear and again bid Daphne a good journey. After Daphne arrived at Staton House, Pamela asked for permission to visit her sister and disappeared. Her father was gone as well, leaving behind a cryptic message

saying he would be home as soon as he could. Her thoughts
turned to Edward and her courage escaped her. She knew her
listlessness came from loving Edward and knowing he
belonged to someone else. Maybe it was better this way, she
thought. She couldn't marry Lord Darges, or any duke's son, or
any earl's son, or any baronet's son, for that matter. The men
she had been introduced to were nice in their own ways, but
they belonged to a world she would never feel comfortable in.
At that moment, with the rain falling, the sky covered in slate-
like clouds, and the house lights not yet lit, the darkness
matched Daphne's state of mind. No one had ever touched her
heart the way Edward had, and she didn't think anyone would
again. It's all right, she thought. She would release him, set him
gently from her heart, and wish him well. And when people
clamored over the great author Edward Ellis, she could say she
knew him once, and he was a fine man indeed.

The front door slammed open and startled her. She heard
hurried steps on the winding staircase, and as she stood her
bedroom door flew open. There he was, Edward, rain-soaked,
treading water onto the Turkish rugs, his hat in his hands, his
chocolate-brown hair matted to his face. Before she could say
anything, he was at her feet, on his knees, taking her hands to
his lips and kissing her fingers. He said words, some beautiful
words that a thoughtful man like Edward would think to say.
When he said, with his heart in his eyes and a lump in his
throat, "My dearest Daphne, would you do me the honor of
becoming my wife?" Daphne sank to her knees beside him and
said yes.

THE INTRUDER

*E*dward arrived at Hembry Castle a fortnight after Daphne and Frederick returned from London. He had to finish some Observer business first, let Tewson know what needed tending to next, and he had to wrap up the story he was working on because Fergusonandwately were going to publish it separately since there was such demand for his work. He was becoming a literary commodity, Edward, and requests for appearances were flooding in. He was still overworked, but he managed to attend a number of the dinners in his honor, and he conducted himself in a gentlemanly way that made the literary establishment take notice. Still, no matter the high sales, no matter the positive critical reviews, no matter the dinners or the speeches, everything was a blur to Edward except thoughts of Daphne.

It had turned out all right in the end. Frederick had pressed his weight as the Earl of Staton in the right way—he wasn't too overbearing while at the same time making Chattaway understand that he would use his family's money, and solicitors, to extricate Edward from this unfortunate situation. Would Chattaway truly be happy for his daughter if she were married to someone who loved another? Thankfully, Chattaway came to see sense. To Edward's surprise he received a letter from Christina, a lovely letter, where she wished him well and reminded him that she had predicted this long ago. As for the scandal, as of yet, a fortnight on, nothing much had happened. Lord Staton predicted the gossip would die away in time, especially once Edward and Daphne were married.

Edward was grateful to be back in the country, back to his fiancée. He walked the winding village roads in Hembry, passed the stone buildings, and nodded at the onlookers, who were even more curious than usual as they glanced in his direction and whispered. Edward doffed his hat and offered good day to everyone, he was in that kind of mood. He made his way up the steep hill and went round to the servants' entrance. As he walked across the small yard with the straggling green sprouts that barely poked above the dirt he watched two giggling maids hurry by, their heads close, their hands in front of their mouths. Edward guessed they, too, were talking about him. He was, after all, the upstart butler's grandson who was marrying Lady Daphne. He thought of Daphne, her full lips pulled into a thin string, looking remarkably like her grandmother, whenever someone referred to her as Lady Daphne. There was never a young woman less inclined to be part of the aristocracy, for which Edward thanked God every day.

He heard the scrambling as the servants went about their business, and no one noticed his knocking. He heard laughing, he heard scolding, he heard a footman whispering things, improper things, most likely, to one of the housemaids. Finally, the two housemaids Edward had seen a moment before opened the door and allowed him to pass. When Lainie

Graham saw Edward in the servants' hall she pointed her accusing wooden spoon at him.

"What are you doing here, young man? You should be upstairs. The fiancé of the daughter of the Earl of Staton shouldn't be hanging around with the likes of him." She pointed her spoon first at the peacock and then at the stairs. "Go on. Upstairs with you."

"Upstairs with whom, Mrs. Graham?" Mr. Ellis pressed his spectacles against his nose as he studied the cook.

"Your grandson is here, Mr. Ellis. I told him he should go upstairs."

"She doesn't want me near Henry," Edward said. "She thinks he'll corrupt me."

"If he hasn't corrupted you by now, I dare say you've survived the worst of it." Mr. Ellis turned to the cook. "Thank you, Mrs. Graham, but as I'm sure you know my grandson is a stubborn one, and if he wants to come downstairs he will come downstairs. He gets his stubbornness from his grandmother, I'm afraid."

"But he's part of the family now," Mrs. Graham said.

"Yes, he'll be part of his lordship's family, but he'll always be part of my family."

"Oh no!" cried Mrs. Graham. "Not you too!"

Daphne smiled at the cook. "Not me too, Mrs. Graham?"

"Lady Daphne in the kitchen!" Mrs. Graham muttered to her wooden spoon as though it were the only one that could hear her. "What would the Countess say if she knew Lady Daphne was in the kitchen?" She dropped her head, too heavy suddenly for her neck. "Lady Daphne in the kitchen..."

"I've been in the kitchen before, Mrs. Graham," Daphne said, though the poor woman didn't seem to hear since she was still speaking to her spoon. Daphne watched the cook with amusement. "I'm afraid I've scandalized Mrs. Graham."

"She'll recover," Mr. Ellis said.

Edward pulled Daphne close and kissed the top of her hair. "Hello to you too."

Daphne laughed, and he loved her even more, as if that were possible. "Yes, hello. I've missed you."

"And I you."

Mrs. Ellis stood in the doorway in the hall, watching her grandson and his fiancée. She beamed with a grandmother's pride, but there was a sadness within her that cast a shadow over the bright joy radiating from the young couple.

"What is it?" Mr. Ellis asked. Mrs. Ellis shook her head and disappeared into her sitting room.

"Should I speak to her?" asked Edward. "Is she upset with me?"

"Not at all. Your grandmother has other troubles on her mind."

"It isn't Father, is it?"

Now it was Mr. Ellis' turn to cast a shadow. Edward exhaled, a puff of frustration, and Daphne took his hand.

"Is there anything I can do?" she asked.

"That is kindness itself, Lady Daphne," said Mr. Ellis, "but I don't see what can be done."

"Would it be too much for you to call me Daphne? We are going to be family."

"It would be too much, Lady Daphne, but I appreciate the sentiment. I'm certain her ladyship wouldn't care for such familiarity."

Edward leaned close to Daphne. He was still getting used to the idea that he could be near her, speak openly to her, and bask in the sweet fragrance of her hair, without worry. "I've been afraid to ask...how is your grandmother taking our engagement?"

"She won't speak to me, which makes life interesting since I live here. Papa said the announcement about our engagement will be in the papers Thursday morning."

"That's when it's scheduled for the Observer."

"Then everyone will know so my grandmother won't have a choice but to accept it."

"Knowing Lady Staton, she might see it as only a temporary setback. I wouldn't be surprised if she brings on a new contingent of suitors to try to tempt you away from the butler's grandson."

Daphne stood on her toes and leaned her face up to Edward's. "There is no one in the world who can tempt me away from the butler's grandson, Edward Ellis."

Edward kissed Daphne's lips. He would have no trouble getting used to having her close.

SUMMER PASSED INTO AUTUMN. Suddenly, it was November, and life at Hembry Castle settled to a pleasant early winter null. The intruder had not been seen for months, and neither had Detective Ruckson or his sergeant son. The detective had been convinced by the lack of evidence to the contrary, and he allowed the initial conclusion that Richard's death was an accident stand. The court of public opinion was still out, however, and the gossipers and naysayers were unwilling to let go of the matter. Packed into the village post office so tightly they hardly had space to expand their abdomens and breathe, villagers rehashed the same theories countless times. When that topic was exhausted, they had a titter or two about the Earl's daughter marrying the grandson of the family's butler and housekeeper. The villagers liked Lady Daphne, and they didn't fault her at all. She was American and didn't know better. There were a few whispered words about how the Countess was allowing her only granddaughter to throw away her life by marrying beneath her. However, the more open-minded among them reminded everyone about Lord Adner's daughter, who had the audacity to elope with a troubadour passing through England on his way to Spain, or from Spain, or was it Australia? Whatever had happened, Lord Adner was doing perfectly well, and Lord Staton and his family would survive too.

On a chilly November afternoon, Daphne found her father at his desk in the library, a thin glimmer of sun reflecting off the river in the distance, leaving a haze filtering through the window.

"What is it, Papa?" Daphne asked.

"I knew being Earl would be hard, but I didn't realize how hard until I took it on."

"Has something happened?"

"Nothing unusual. I suppose the approaching wintertime is making me melancholy. I'm feeling trapped, and I've always hated the feeling of being stuck somewhere and unable to get myself out. I felt trapped here as a boy, so I ran to America to make a life for myself, and now I'm forced to remain with no way out except the grave. Heavens. I'm beginning to sound like Richard."

"Papa." Daphne stepped closer to her father. He had been looking drawn lately, his handsome features weighted down, but she thought it was a passing problem.

"I apologize, Daphne. It's selfish of me to burden you like this."

"That's a very English thing to say. You know you can tell me anything."

"Yes, of course I know that. You see, I knew Richard felt trapped in his role as Earl, and I was selfishly relieved that the title was his destiny and not mine. Now the title is in fact mine, and my instinct to run away has grasped hold of me once again." Frederick saw the time on the clock on his desk and sighed. "I'm afraid I must go. Business to tend to, you know."

Mr. Ellis stood in the doorway. "My lord, do you recall the intruder who was seen around the grounds after your brother's death?"

"Of course. Has he been found?"

"He has. The young man has been camping near the river again. Mr. Harvey was suspicious since it looked like there had been a campfire. He went out especially early this morning and caught the young man still asleep in his blankets."

"Where is he now?" Daphne asked.

"Mr. Harvey took him into his cottage."

"Have you contacted the police?" Frederick asked.

"Not yet. The young man seems confused somehow, as though he doesn't remember who he is. He certainly doesn't remember where he is. He appears to think he's in London, my lord, by the Thames. He keeps stretching out his arms and shouting 'Richard!' as though he sees your brother."

"It sounds like he needs a doctor more than the police," Daphne said.

"I haven't yet contacted the police for that reason, Lady Daphne. The young man appears to be delirious." Mr. Ellis looked at the warming fire. "It's been rather cold the last few nights. Even though he seems to have burned a fire, it couldn't have been very big. The odd thing is, my lord, I believe you know him. He dined here when you first arrived back at Hembry. Mr. David Palmer is his name."

"I remember Mr. Palmer," said Daphne. "He's the one who winked at everyone, isn't he, Papa?"

"I believe you're right. But why on earth would he feel compelled to stay outside in this weather? He should have made himself known."

"I don't believe people knock on the door of Hembry Castle without a previous invitation, my lord."

"That's true enough. Poor fellow." Frederick looked through the window and watched the rain soak the ground outside. "Have you sent for Mr. Wilson?"

"Mrs. Ellis sent for the doctor as soon as we learned of the young man."

"If the doctor thinks Mr. Palmer can be moved, have him brought here. Ask Mrs. Ellis to make up a room for him."

"Very good, my lord."

Frederick dropped onto the sofa. "Blimey. Why do you think Mr. Palmer would camp outside? And why would he claim to see Richard? He was great friends with your uncle. Surely he knows Richard is dead."

"When Mr. Wilson thinks it's all right, we can ask him," Daphne said.

Frederick glanced at the butler standing in the doorway. "Thank you, Ellis." Mr. Ellis didn't move, standing one foot in the shadows, his face in the light. "Yes?"

"My lord, forgive me, but I was wondering. Since the young man seems to be so agitated and drawn to the place where your brother lived, and since he's been spotted several times near the river, perhaps not the one where the body was found, but…"

"Do you think the young man had something to do with my brother's death?" Frederick asked.

"The thought occurred to me. He does seem rather fixated on your brother, my lord."

Daphne looked at her father. "Should we alert the police after all?"

"If there's any possibility this young man was involved in funny business concerning your uncle, I would certainly want the police involved. However, I can't help wondering if we're not bringing more trouble onto our heads by bringing this up when we're not certain what we're dealing with. The young man may simply be grieving, as we all are."

"I beg your pardon, my lord, but I've never had a friend I've grieved to the point where I'd risk sleeping out in the November cold to mourn him."

"You may be right, Ellis. Let's see what this young man has to say for himself."

Mr. Wilson, the new doctor in Hembry, told Lord Staton that young Mr. Palmer could be moved into the castle the next morning. Mrs. Ellis put the visitor in the Green Room with the hunter green furniture, white wainscoting, and Roman busts on the walls. When the doctor told Lord Staton the young man was ready for visitors, Frederick brought Daphne since her gentle manner had proven helpful with those facing illness or other hard times. Daphne hardly recognized the young man she had met at luncheon over a year before. She remembered how he looked then, a finely dressed young man about Edward's age, his long fair hair tucked behind his ears. Yes, he had been agitated even that first time when he couldn't stop winking at everyone. Now he looked lethargic, his eyes no longer winking but wide as though they might never close again. He jumped at every sound, shuddered at every word, and he was so thin Daphne thought he would become as translucent as water if he didn't eat soon. She brought him some of Mrs. Graham's vegetable soup, which he seemed to enjoy during his luncheon at Hembry, but now he would eat nothing. Lord Staton pulled the doctor aside.

"What's wrong with him?" Frederick asked.

"I'm not certain. He caught a chill from sleeping outside in the cold, but he doesn't have a fever. He's been hallucinating, calling to your brother, reaching his hands as though he were trying to pull your brother toward him. Then he sleeps the rest of the day."

"How peculiar." Frederick watched the young man, who was stretched out on his back watching the shadows on the ceiling. "Are you certain it's all right for us to be here? He doesn't look well."

"Your company will do him no harm, and may even do some good. Look."

Daphne cajoled one spoonful of soup into Mr. Palmer's mouth, and then another spoonful, and then another, until he had eaten nearly the whole bowl. As Daphne dabbed the soup from the patient's lips with a napkin, she shuddered. Something at that moment reminded her of the shadows she saw everywhere at night. She thought of the whispers in the corners and the creaking stairs, and then the young man trembled as well. Did he see the shadows too, she wondered? When Mr. Palmer wouldn't accept another spoonful of soup, Frederick sat beside the bed.

"Hello, Mr. Palmer. I hope you're feeling better. I was so sorry to hear you've been unwell. I do wish you had made yourself known instead of sleeping outside in this weather. You would have been most welcome." Mr. Palmer, his fair hair plastered to his forehead, stared at the green wallpaper as though he hadn't heard a word. "I understand you've visited Hembry a few times since my brother's death." Still nothing.

Frederick looked to Daphne for help. Daphne sat on her heels next to her father. "Mr. Palmer, I remember when you joined us for luncheon. I know my Uncle Richard was a good friend of yours. You must miss him very much."

Young Mr. Palmer sat up, his eyes wider, as though he had seen a ghost, which perhaps he had. "Richard! Where are you? Why can't I see you?"

Daphne wanted to weep for the young man. "I'm so sorry,

Mr. Palmer, but my Uncle Richard has died. He..." She was going to let him know how her uncle had fallen over the side of London Bridge, but she decided against it, thinking it might be too much for the fragile young man.

David Palmer grasped Daphne's hands so tightly she flinched. "But I saw him!" He released Daphne from his grip and grabbed Frederick's hands instead. "Mr. Meriwether, I saw him!"

Mr. Wilson was about to speak, but Frederick held up his hand, stopping him.

"I'm so sorry, Mr. Palmer. I truly am. I can hardly believe it myself, but I saw my brother's body after it was pulled from the Thames. Those were his clothes, his watch, his shirt pin. That was the same half-moon scar he received when we were boys. I know this must be difficult for you, but you must be brave. My brother wouldn't want you to mourn him all your days."

"I'm not mourning him. I'm searching for him. I saw him, I tell you, I saw him!"

Daphne covered her face with her hands. The sight of the anguished young man was too much. David Palmer tried to get out of bed, but the doctor pressed him down.

"Not yet, Mr. Palmer. You're not strong enough to be up quite yet." The doctor held the door open. "I'm sorry, Lord Staton, but I think it's best if you and Lady Daphne leave the young man to rest."

"Do you have instructions for us on how to care for Mr. Palmer when you're not here?" Daphne asked. "Mr. Hough used to leave written directions. Writing things down makes it easier for us to remember everything we should be doing."

"If you'd like me to write down the directions, Lady Daphne, I'm happy to do so."

"Thank you, Mr. Wilson."

Daphne followed her father from the Green Room. She stood in the hallway beside him, holding his hand, remembering all too painfully the morning when the Ellises woke them to say her Uncle Richard was gone. Mr. Palmer's torment made her feel as though she had to deal with her beloved uncle's death all over again.

"That poor young man," Frederick said. "I knew he and Richard were friends, but I never would have guessed that Richard's death would touch him so deeply."

"Uncle Richard had many friends, and I'm sure they all miss him, as we do."

Daphne hooked her arm through her father's and they walked from the hallway, leaving the young man time to recover.

A PLAN IS HATCHED

*D*ownstairs the servants buzzed with the news. Lady Daphne to be married to Mr. and Mrs. Ellis' grandson!

"I think it's fitting," said Lainie Graham as she chopped onions for the family's dinner. "They're well suited."

"She has no right to waste her life away like that," said Leslie Rowland, who was waiting for her ladyship's tea. "The daughter of the Earl of Staton ought to marry someone of her rank, or higher."

"Lord Staton moved to America to get away from here," said Pamela. "Why would he want to raise his daughter to know the life he escaped?"

"What did he need to escape from? Was it too much for him, living in this big house with the likes of us to work for him?"

"The likes of us?" Lainie Graham snorted. "What's that supposed to mean?" Mrs. Graham swatted her ever-present wooden spoon at the lady's maid. "You don't know the Ellises' grandson like I do, Miss Rowland. He's a fine lad. Steady, strong. He puts everything in perspective. And he's on his way. He's becoming more famous every day."

"Famous for what? He's the butler's grandson, for Heaven's sake. Whatever happened to the Duke of Norley's heir?"

Mrs. Graham laughed into the poppy seed cake batter. "Lady Daphne had the sense to keep away from him." She poured the batter into the baking dish and slid the baking dish into the oven.

"Lady Daphne should marry Mr. Lowerby," said Jemima. "He'll be a marquess one day."

"Lady Daphne loves Mr. Edward," said Pamela. "Maybe they'll run away to America."

"America?" Miss Rowland scoffed. "What do they have in America we don't have here?"

"I don't think Lady Daphne and Mr. Edward will go to America," Ruth said. "Lady Daphne won't leave her father now he's the Earl. His lordship relies on her. Someone has to help him with his social duties, especially since he doesn't have a wife and her ladyship has all but withdrawn from Society."

"I don't know," said Mrs. Graham, speaking now to the poached eggs. "I don't see Lady Daphne enjoying Society any more than Lord Staton, or his brother or father before him."

"I agree with Mrs. Graham," Pamela said. "Lady Daphne and Mr. Edward are well suited. Anyone can see that."

"Anyone except her ladyship," said Ruth. "She's in quite a state about that engagement. I heard her arguing with his lordship about it this morning."

Miss Rowland's nose reddened as she took the tea tray from one of the kitchen maids. "Why should her ladyship accept the match? Why should Lady Daphne settle for a mere writer when she could have someone far more suitable? Who is this Edward Ellis? Where did he come from?"

"He came from me."

Mr. Ellis glowered in the doorway. The kitchen maids scattered while Jemima, Ruth, and Pamela escaped into the servants' hall. Miss Rowland curtsied at Mr. Ellis as she carried away the tea tray, and Mrs. Graham turned to the bubbling pot on the stove with the concentration of a witch casting a spell over her cauldron. Mr. Ellis heard footsteps coming down the stairs, that creaking third step giving the visitor away. He saw his grandson leaning over the railing.

Edward put on a formal air. "I beg your pardon, Ellis, but might I trouble you for a moment." Mr. Ellis laughed, and Edward followed his grandfather into the servants' hall.

"Where is Grandmother?" Edward asked.

"We have a new maid starting today and your grandmother is showing her around. We needed to replace Miss Escott since she'd been taken as a lady's maid for Lady Daphne. Miss Escott is one fortunate young woman. Hired by his lordship's brother as a housemaid one day and a lady's maid the next. What is it, Edward? You look thoughtful suddenly."

"I was thinking about Lord Staton. I was thinking how his brother's death has wreaked havoc in so many ways."

"More than you know."

"Why, Grandfather. If I didn't know better I'd say you're hiding a secret."

"I hide all the family's secrets. That's how I've held onto my job for over 40 years."

Edward heard his grandmother's keys jingle. "I was thinking about his lordship's problems too," Mrs. Ellis said, "and I have an idea." The butler and the housekeeper exchanged a meaningful glance.

"I don't know, Mary…"

"We should tell him, Augustus. He should know about the child. He's a journalist and he has connections. He might be able to help."

"What child?" Edward asked.

His grandmother shrugged as though the answer were obvious. "The missing child, of course."

Edward leaned forward in his chair, his elbows on his knees, his chin resting on his fists. "Now you have to tell me."

"Come with me." Mrs. Ellis opened the door, saw the hallway deserted, and led her grandson to her sitting room where she explained all in a hushed voice.

DAPHNE SAT before the mirror in her bedroom while Pamela curled her hair. She watched Pamela's reflection as the maid kept dropping pins and apologizing.

"Pamela." Daphne faced the maid. "If you're not feeling well then you should lie down. I can manage myself. My grandmother won't like it, but she's not speaking to me since I became engaged to Edward so her being upset about my hair won't make much difference."

Pamela dropped her face into her hands and sobbed.

"Pamela! What's wrong? Tell me, please."

"I don't think you can help, my lady."

Daphne led Pamela to her bed, and they sat on the pink coverlet beneath the painted tree, her arm around the maid's shoulders. "Won't you tell me what's wrong?"

"If there was anyone in the world I'd speak to it would be you, but I can't speak without betraying your uncle."

Daphne grasped the maid's hands. "He's no longer here to speak for himself, but you can speak for him. What do you know? Please tell me."

"My sister is missing, my lady. And her baby son along with her."

"How do you know they're missing?"

"I haven't heard from her since we were in London."

"That was only two weeks ago."

"My letters have been returned undeliverable."

"Are you sure it wasn't a mistake?"

"I don't think so, my lady. I've been sending her money from my salary. She needs the money, and she wouldn't turn my letters away if she was there to receive them. I've written to her neighbors but they said she's gone and they don't know where she is."

"Do you have any other family? Parents? Siblings?"

"No, my lady. It's just Lucy and me. Our parents died some years ago, and our brother died when we were girls. My sister's gone, my lady, and I don't know where. Where can she be?"

"We'll find her, Pamela, I promise. But what does your sister have to do with my Uncle Richard?"

Daphne handed Pamela her handkerchief, and Pamela pressed it to her eyes. "Did you know that I was hired here because his lordship, your uncle, that is, asked Mrs. Ellis to give me a place?" Daphne nodded. "Your uncle not only helped me, Lady Daphne. He helped my sister. He sent her money every month."

"I'm afraid I'm not following."

"For the child, my lady. Your uncle sent my sister money for the child."

And then Daphne realized. She stared into the pink wall with the stretching branches and mauve roses, the birdcage dangling as if waving in the wind. "Your sister's child...?"

"Is not your uncle's, my lady. Not your uncle the Earl's, I mean."

"The child is my Uncle Jerrold's then." Pamela shrugged, which Daphne took as a sign of agreement. "But it was my Uncle Richard who supported your sister and the child?"

"Yes, my lady. That was the business he had in London that I told you about. He'd go visit my sister and the baby to be certain they had everything they needed. That's why I said he was a good man. He took such an interest. He cared so much, and the baby wasn't even his."

Daphne closed her eyes as she considered everything she heard. "After Richard died, then your sister must have had quite a lot less to live on."

"She had hardly anything, my lady. I always sent her whatever I could from my salary, though it weren't enough to be of much help. When I told Mr. and Mrs. Ellis about my sister's troubles they began sending money too, though it still didn't come close to what she had before. She started falling behind on her accounts, and the baby grew sick."

"Did anyone ask my Uncle Jerrold for help? It is his child."

"My sister asked him, and I asked him too. Mr. Jerrold made it clear that if either of us contacted him again he'd make sure I lost my position here. He said I'd never work again."

Daphne's head hurt suddenly, the pounding inside her skull beating out her Uncle Jerrold's scoundrel name. "I promise you, Pamela, we'll find your sister and the baby. And don't you worry about my Uncle Jerrold. Your position here will never be jeopardized, not as long as my father or I have something to say about it." Daphne looked into the fire in the hearth and sighed. "First Mr. Palmer was found nearly frozen to death by the lake screaming for my Uncle Richard, and now I've learned that my Uncle Jerrold abandoned his own child, leaving my Uncle Richard to handle it all. If it weren't for Edward, I might think there was nothing good left in the world." She kissed the top of Pamela's white cap. "We'll tell my father. He'll know what to do."

MR. ELLIS WATCHED his grandson over the top of his round-rimmed spectacles. "What do you think?"

"I think we need to find the child, though Lord Staton should be told."

"Perhaps we should have told him as soon as we discovered the letters," Mrs. Ellis said, "but we didn't want to upset him, what with everything that's happened. Your grandfather and I sent Pamela's sister whatever we could."

"That's good of you, both of you."

"Not good enough, I'm afraid. It wasn't enough to keep her from her present difficulties." Mr. Ellis shook his head as he cleaned his spectacles with his handkerchief.

After Edward dressed in his dinner suit, he waited in the west wing hallway until Daphne left her room. She looked lovely in her midnight blue velvet dress with pink and gold embroidery, though she could wear a carpetbag and still be the most beautiful girl in the room. Daphne shook her finger at him.

"If my grandmother saw you standing outside my bedroom she'd slap you with her ear trumpet."

Edward took Daphne into his arms. "We're engaged. I can wait for you. I can even kiss you if I like." He kissed her lips and she beamed at him.

"I'd like it if you would kiss me again, Mr. Ellis."

Which he did. It took time before he pulled his lips from hers. When he found some air, he said, "I wanted to catch you before you went down for a reason. I've been talking to my grandparents and I've been informed about some difficulties your family is having."

"Are you referring to my Uncle Jerrold's child?"

"I should have guessed you would know. Who told you?"

"Pamela. She finally confided in me. We can help her, can't we?"

"I'll do everything I can." Edward considered the polished

dark wood floor beneath his feet. "Have you told your father yet?"

"I was going to tell him tonight. But I don't understand why Pamela's sister would disappear with her baby like that. Why didn't she tell Pamela? Who knows where they've gone, or what hardships they're facing? It's so cold outside. It breaks my heart to think of them out there, without shelter, without food."

"There's no reason to think the worst just yet." Edward kissed Daphne's cheek. He couldn't help himself. "Don't worry, Daphne. We'll find them."

DINNER WAS SUBDUED, as dinner had been subdued for some months. Though her ladyship no longer appeared as forlorn as she had those first weeks after Richard's death, she had yet to spring back to her formidable self. She was quiet, so Daphne, Frederick, and Edward remained quiet out of respect. After dinner they met in Mrs. Ellis' sitting room downstairs—Edward, Daphne, Mr. and Mrs. Ellis, his lordship, and Pamela. It would be safest there, Frederick said, since her ladyship may still be lurking about upstairs and they didn't want to cause her any unnecessary pain, especially since they didn't know yet what they were dealing with. In the dark room, lit by two gas lamps and an orange fire crackling in the hearth, the six people huddled close together, whispering though the door was closed and everyone else had turned in for the night.

"There were rumors that your brother, the previous Earl, was seen around London with a young woman and a child," Mrs. Ellis said. "I've heard from other servants from other houses that it's become accepted that he was the father of the child."

"And you know for certain he is not?" Frederick asked.

"Yes, my lord," said Mr. Ellis. "We're quite certain."

"May I ask how you know with such certainty?" Edward looked at his grandparents, their faces long in the shadows from the flickering firelight. "None of us know precisely what his lordship's brother was up to when he would disappear for weeks at a time."

Mrs. Ellis looked at the photograph of Richard on her mantelpiece. "I can say for certain that the 9th Earl was not the baby's father. Mr. Jerrold is."

Frederick leaned his head against the back of the wing chair. He was silent for a long time. Finally, he looked at Pamela. "You know this for certain?"

"Yes, my lord. I know from my sister's lips that the baby's father is Mr. Jerrold."

"My brother Jerrold. The one so worried about propriety, the one determined to maintain the correct order of things, has been decidedly improper himself. And he wasn't even man enough to face up to it. Well well. So how did my brother Richard come to be involved?"

"My sister wrote to your brother the Earl, my lord, asking him for help because Mr. Jerrold had turned his back on her. It was out of the goodness of your brother the Earl's heart that he sent her money and visited her from time to time to make sure all was well."

"My brother Richard always did have a good heart."

"Yes, he did, my lord." Mrs. Ellis removed the packet of letters from her dressing table and showed them to Frederick. "Mr. Ellis saw Colin place these under the floorboards in Staton House. They were stolen by Henry, and we believe Colin then stole them from Henry. The loss of these letters must have caused some worry for your brother when he was Earl."

"We're going to have to do something about that," said

Frederick. He took the letters from Mrs. Ellis and turned them over in his hands. He chose one letter and held it close to his face, squinting as he scanned it in the dark room. "Does anyone know who wrote my brother this love letter?" When no one replied, Frederick studied the letter again. "This hand, I think I know it. It seems familiar somehow, though I can't seem to place it. It's a lovely letter." He showed a stunted smile to the crackling flames. "That's something, I suppose. Richard had love in his life. It makes me glad to know it." He read the second letter and nodded. "Now this I recognize immediately. My father wrote this." He took a moment to read the words. "This is very much like my father, to encourage Richard when no one else would. I wonder why my father felt the need to write such a letter." Frederick handed the letter to Daphne.

"Uncle Richard was always worried about becoming Earl. Maybe Grandpa was telling Uncle Richard he believed he was strong enough to do the job, and that he loved him even if he struggled."

Frederick tapped his chin as he considered. "What about our intruder friend, Mr. Palmer? He may know something, perhaps not about the child, but he knew Richard well. Is it unreasonable to assume he knew more about Richard than he was willing to say?"

"I'm afraid Mr. Palmer has gone, my lord." Mr. Ellis clasped his hands behind his back in his familiar pose. "The doctor informed me that the young man left this morning. Mr. Palmer seemed recovered enough, and the doctor had no authority to make him stay."

"Did he leave any clue about where we might find him?" Edward asked.

"The only thing he said before he left was a message for Lady Daphne. Mr. Palmer said Lady Daphne should say hello to her Uncle Richard."

"Poor man," Daphne said. "I wish he would have stayed longer, Papa. I wish he would have let us help him."

Frederick scanned the letter from Pamela's sister begging for help for her child. He clenched his jaw so tightly Edward could see the knot of muscles in his cheeks. When Frederick finished reading he threw the paper onto Mrs. Ellis' desk. "The fact remains Escott's sister and her sister's child are out there somewhere and we must find them. Even if they've settled elsewhere, we must know they're safe."

Edward turned to Pamela. "Where was your sister living before she disappeared?"

"Near Covent Garden," Pamela answered.

"I'll begin there then. I'll ask a few of the reporters at the Observer to ask around to see if anyone knows anything."

"Edward, know that every resource at Hembry will be made available for their recovery." Frederick turned to the maid. "Escott, may I ask how your sister came to know my brother Jerrold?"

"Lucy was a housemaid at Meriwether Cottage, my lord."

"How convenient. My brother preyed on defenseless girls working in his own home. Jerrold." Frederick spat out the name as though it left a bitter taste in his mouth. "The nerve of him. Lecturing Richard about his wanton ways when Jerrold was the philandering one all along. And Richard, in the goodness of his heart, tried to help by keeping Jerrold's secret, finding Escott a place here, and paying for the child though it wasn't his responsibility. And they call me the wayward."

"Are you going to tell Grandma?" Daphne asked.

"I should. It would serve her right for always favoring Jerrold, encouraging his snobbishness, and making him feel he was the superior one when Richard was the one who needed her support. She spoiled Jerrold when she should have been guiding Richard."

Daphne took Edward's hand. "When will you begin searching for Pamela's sister?"

"I'll return to London in the morning."

"I want to come," Daphne said. "I know London a little now. I can help."

Edward straightened his shoulders and stood tall, the best concerned husband look he could muster. "Daphne, I cannot allow you to come with me. I don't know where in London I may need to go, and some neighborhoods simply aren't safe."

"I'm going, Edward. If Pamela's sister's child is my Uncle Jerrold's, that means the child is my cousin. I'm going to help find them, and that's that." Daphne nodded in a regal manner that would have made her grandmother proud. She led Pamela away with great ceremony.

Frederick laughed. "Edward, you may as well know that you'll be dealing with a firecracker for the rest of your life."

"I'm quite pleased with my firecracker, Lord Staton, I assure you."

Frederick nodded. He stretched his legs, then stood near the hearth, straightening himself into his most regal bearing, an easy task with his height and silver-threaded hair. "Ellis, call Henry and Colin here. I have a few words for them."

"Gladly, my lord."

Edward sat in his grandmother's chair behind the desk and waited—this was going to be quite a scene, better than anything he had seen in the London theaters for some time. In a moment, Mr. Ellis reappeared, his round-framed spectacles as close to the tip of his nose as they could go without falling to the ground, his eyes pulled, his lips tight. It was, Edward thought, the finest impression of a stern schoolmaster he had yet seen from his grandfather. Mr. Ellis allowed Henry and Colin into the room, and both young men stopped on their toes when they saw Lord Staton. The Earl stared at the footmen with a blank expression while the young men hopped from foot to foot, waiting.

"Henry, Colin, I have been informed of the issue regarding letters that were the personal property of my brother, the 9th Earl of Staton. Furthermore, I'm aware that you, Colin, hid the letters at Staton House."

"I did no such thing." If Edward didn't know better he would have believed the indignant footman. Colin would do well as a witness in a court case, Edward mused, or speaking at Parliament.

"I was behind you when you placed the letters under the floorboard," Mr. Ellis said. "And you, Henry, going on about those letters from home that Colin stole from you, yet they weren't your letters at all. They belonged to the 9th Earl. It should not need to be said that we do not abide by such behavior in this house. Would you like to say it, my lord, or shall I?"

"By all means, Ellis, go on."

"Henry Horrocks and Colin Pratt, you are both dismissed. I hope you're able to learn a lesson from this unfortunate event. I hope you'll learn to think beyond your selfishness."

Henry Horrocks stood with his arms crossed before his chest, his eyes darting defiance between Lord Staton and Mr. Ellis. The footman laughed a wicked laugh. "You think you can stop us by dismissing us?" He glared at Lord Staton.

Mr. Ellis stepped toward Henry, but Lord Staton's hand stopped him.

"Let the young man speak, Ellis. I'm most interested in what he has to say."

"It wasn't hard to work out," said Henry. "The 9th Earl had a love letter and a letter from a woman asking for help for her child. The rumors were true then. He had an illegitimate child. I saw the letters, and now they have a use for me, don't they?"

Mr. Ellis clenched his fists, presumably, Edward thought, to stop himself from knocking Henry's skull to the ground. "I believe we've heard enough, my lord. It's time for Henry and Colin to pack for their journey."

"I agree, Ellis. I'm sorry to be the one to remind you, Henry, but you are no longer in possession of the letters. You have no proof of what you say, not only because you no longer have the letters, but because your conclusions are false." Frederick gestured toward the door. "I invite you to bring the story to any newspaper you wish. My future son-in-law here is a journalist, as am I, and we both will tell you that without proof of what you say, you will have a difficult time selling anything to anyone."

Henry turned a smug look onto Edward. "I may not need to do anything to bring this family down, my lord. Looks like that pretty daughter of yours can embarrass the family without any help from me."

Frederick's cheeks broke out in red spots. "Ellis, escort them upstairs. Be certain the carriage is available to drive them away at first light."

"Certainly, my lord."

Henry waved his fist in Frederick's direction. "You haven't heard the last of this."

"I'm sorry to say, Henry, but I believe I have."

When Mr. Ellis returned, he bowed to Lord Staton. "My lord, I apologize. I should have let them go as soon as I knew about the letters."

"No, Ellis. You did the right thing. We needed to have our facts straight before we took action."

"Are you concerned about them selling the story?" Mrs. Ellis asked. "Was that true, that no newspaper would buy their story because they have no proof?"

"That was a lie." Frederick winked at Edward. "Of course, it would be easier for them to sell the story if they still had the letters, but there are plenty of publications out there happy for any hint of scandal no matter the source. It hardly matters if there's proof behind the slander." Frederick slumped back into the chair before the hearth. "If they do succeed in selling the story and furthering the gossip about Richard, the sad truth is it doesn't matter. Richard isn't here to be hurt by their foul words, and the family is already the subject of gossip because of the circumstances of his death. There's also been some talk about the fact that my daughter has become engaged to a young man I highly approve of."

Edward bowed in his seat. "Thank you, Lord Staton."

"Edward, if you don't return to calling me Frederick I'll knock you over the head with my walking stick, I truly will."

"Thank you, Frederick. Now," Edward opened the door, "if you don't mind, I'd like to see my firecracker."

"Away you go, my boy," said Frederick. "Away you go."

THE MISSING CHILD

*J*t took Edward two months to find a starting point in the mystery of the missing child. Christmas passed, New Year 1872 passed, and Edward grew concerned about his ability to find Pamela's family. Looking for a young mother and child in London was worse than trying to find a needle in a haystack. London had hundreds of haystacks and thousands of needles, and no one knew where to begin to find a mother and child down on their luck since there were so many sad souls scraping together some semblance of a life. Edward had started his search near Covent Garden, where Pamela's family lived prior to Richard's death, but the neighbors knew nothing about where Lucy and her child had gone. They cut and run, they did, in the middle of the night, a neighboring woman who smelled suspiciously of burning candles and whiskey told him. The landlord had come for the rent, threatened the young mother if she didn't pay, and then they both were gone to who-knows-where. Edward was down but far from giving up. He enlisted Wellesley and Roberts, both of whom were willingly recruited when they realized an innocent child was involved. The three young men walked into the heart of London with a grainy photograph of Lucy Escott, knocking door to door, asking in public houses, stopping passers-by on the streets. If Pamela's family was in London, Edward was determined to find them, for Daphne's sake, and for the sake of the child.

At first, Edward was able to put Daphne off from accompanying him by going while he was in London on Observer business and Daphne was at Hembry helping her father. Then one day, as February neared, Edward stumbled onto a clue—a young mother who matched Lucy Escott's description and her small child, a son, were spotted living in the slums of the Old Nichol Street Rookery in the East End. They stood out, the man in the pub said, because they were new to the area, the young mother kept to herself, and she didn't seem to fit in with the others, like she had come down in the world and hardly knew what to do with herself. Edward said a silent prayer, hoping the twosome was indeed the missing Escotts (the man in the pub did slur his words, stumbled when he accompanied Edward to the door, and pocketed the change Edward handed him so greedily that how trustworthy a source he was remained to be seen). When Edward told Daphne what he had found, she and Pamela were on the next train to London despite his protests. Frederick wanted to go, as well, but Hembry business detained him, so he sent Daniel, the new footman, and Mr. Ellis with them.

Edward met them at Staton House the next day. Mr. Ellis had Rogers bring the carriage round front, though the butler insisted that Edward should drive them.

"I didn't know I knew how to drive a carriage, Grandfather."

"How hard can it be?" Mr. Ellis asked. "The horses do all the work."

Though he wasn't convinced, Edward relented. Rogers was not so easy. After a stern reminder that Lady Daphne was the Earl's daughter and she wanted young Mr. Ellis to drive them that afternoon (Lady Daphne's wish is law at Staton House, after all), Rogers left the reins of the stately gray carriage in Edward's hands and stomped away. Edward understood his grandfather's concern about Rogers—the driver tended to gossip, as anyone who knew him could tell you—and he didn't want word of their excursion, or the child, getting out.

"I hope I know what I'm doing," Edward said as he turned the reins over in his hands. "More to the point, I hope the horses know what I'm doing."

After a few false starts (the horses would walk three steps under Edward's guidance, stop, look around as though enjoying the sights, whinny, walk another three steps, stop, and continue watching the goings-on at the park, whinny, walk three more steps and stop as though they had gone as far as they would that day) the horses decided they didn't mind Edward at all and they trotted into the street and followed the traffic laws—at least the ones that appealed to them. On their journey they passed Buckingham Palace, Covent Garden, and the City of London before heading toward Bethnal Green and Shoreditch. The further east they drew, the more Daphne felt as though they had traveled to another land where everyone, young and old, poor and poorer, had to toil for scraps to eat and innocuous shelter to protect them from the whimsies of the weather. Edward was able to steer them as far as Spitalfields Market where the roads became too narrow to let the carriage pass. He parked near a pub and handed the reins to a raggedy-looking boy knee-high to the tallest horse who gushed over the shiny coin Daphne placed in his hand. Daphne, Daniel, and Pamela stayed close to Edward as they walked into the chaos. Edward took Daphne's arm and held her so tightly she felt his grip pressing into her skin.

"I don't like this, Daphne. You should have stayed at Staton House. This is no place for you."

"I'm not afraid. I have you and Daniel here, so I'm well protected. I want to see Pamela's sister's baby."

"We don't even know for sure it's my sister, my lady," Pamela said. "We could have come all this way for nothing."

DAPHNE ALLOWED Edward to lead them through the human maze. He kept his eyes on his destination, as though he knew where he were going. There were too many homes, if you wanted to call them that, pressed together with lines of laundry blowing in the wind. There were too many women in rags, hardly protection from the biting winter weather, with too many infants clutched to their chests. Looking at the misery around her, Daphne finally understood what Edward meant when he said that looking for Pamela's family would be like searching for thousands of needles among hundreds of haystacks. She felt as though she had stepped into a Dickens novel, and she was saddened when she saw how true it all was, and what wretchedness poverty brought on. She thought of the quote from A Tale of Two Cities, "A multitude of people and yet solitude," because everywhere around her the people seemed irrevocably alone.

The Old Nichol Street Rookery in the East End of London was one vast slum, a dark maze of rotting streets with every odor and filth, cluttered with disintegrating gray-black tenements with shattered windows. The bite of snow was in the air, and the windows were stopped with newspapers, rags, or whatever else was at hand. It was always night there since sunlight couldn't, or wouldn't, penetrate past the tenements.

No grass grew. Cases of consumption were frequent, and everywhere around her Daphne heard coughing and wheezing. It was a struggle to breathe, for whatever oxygen the smoke-filled air offered. Mortality rates were the highest in the city, and many babies didn't live to see their first birthday. Daphne clutched Pamela's hand and pulled her close.

They continued through the shadowy labyrinth of crumbling tenements, and there were so many people, some talking amongst themselves, others leaning against the buildings, some sitting in the narrow, crooked streets, some huddled together on the stoops so they wouldn't freeze inside the unheated buildings. Edward pressed forward, and Daphne took comfort in his lead. The noises of the slums were rumbling, the peddlers still calling to passers-by, the wives and mothers who needed to feed their hungry families still haggling over prices. Their children needed to eat, now, so they cajoled, begged, or feigned indifference—whichever would enable them to bring home barely enough.

Drivers, either careless or brave, navigated their horse-drawn drays down the narrow lanes, avoiding the elfin boys in suspenders and slouch caps running in the streets, the horses' iron-shod hooves clattering over the cobblestones. They passed tailor shops selling dressmakers' trimmings and second-hand apparel shops with worn-out shoes and jackets hanging in the windows, looking as if they could slide off the hangers and walk away, still holding the shapes of their former owners, still able to speak with eloquence of the sad circumstance that brought a man to sell the clothes off his back. Finally, when they were so far inside the gloom Daphne thought they might never find light again, Edward led them to a tenement where a pitiful sounding baby brawled inside. The stench overwhelmed Daphne and she had to reach toward the wall to steady herself.

"Should I take you back to the carriage, my lady?" It was the first time Daniel had spoken that day, though he had been hovering protectively nearby.

"Perhaps that would be best," Edward said. "Daniel should take you both back to the carriage."

"No, Edward. I want to see."

"Very well then, my firecracker." Edward removed a slip of paper from the pocket in his waistcoat and looked around. "This must be it." He knocked on the door and they heard movement inside. The baby cried louder, but someone, a woman, hushed it. Edward kept knocking. When no one answered the door, he said, in a gentle voice, "Please, we mean you no harm. We know you've come to some difficult times and we wish to help."

Silence. Then a young woman's voice. "I don't have it."

"You don't have what?" Edward asked.

"What you've come for."

"I assure you, I haven't come for anything except to speak to you. My name is Edward Ellis. I'm the fiancé of Lady Daphne Meriwether, daughter of the Earl of Staton, and I'm the grandson of Mr. and Mrs. Ellis, the butler and housekeeper at Hembry Castle. We've been searching for you for some time. I have your sister Pamela with me."

Pamela leaned close to the door. "Lucy? Won't you let me see you?"

Edward heard shuffling, as though furniture were moved aside. The door opened, and a young woman shabby in ragged clothing, her strawberry blond hair barely contained under her cap, her sea-green eyes swollen with tears, held out her arms to Pamela. The young woman was so overcome, and Pamela was so overcome, that the others stepped back and looked away, allowing them privacy for this reunion. Pamela shook her head at the state of her sister.

"Oh, Lucy. Why didn't you tell me?"

"I was so desperate, Pammy. I couldn't ask you or the Ellises for any more money. You've done so much for me already, more than I could ever repay. I received some donations…"

"Donations?" Edward asked.

"Yes, sir. There were times when a messenger would come to my door with money for me. He said it was from a friend. I couldn't guess who might have sent it, I thought it was you, Pammy, and I was so grateful I didn't ask. But then the baby grew sick, and medicines cost so much. I asked Mr. Meriwether for help, but he was so angry. He said that if I contacted you, or the Ellises, or anyone in his lordship's family he'd…" Lucy wept. "How could I burden you, any of you, any more than I had already?"

Pamela wiped away Lucy's tears. "You're no burden. You're my sister."

The baby began brawling and Daphne went into the ramshackle room where a corner had been partitioned off by a tattered bedsheet nailed to the ceiling. Behind the sheet was a two-year-old in rags. Daphne lifted the child from the cold floor and rocked him in her arms.

Lucy led the others inside. She listened as Daphne hummed a lullaby. "He's so sick. The poor babe is so sick."

"He's beautiful," Daphne said. "What is his name?"

"Josiah, my lady."

Daphne clutched the scrawny fingers between hers. "He's so cold. We need to bring him to Staton House. He needs to see Mr. Rallston, our doctor in London."

Pamela brushed her sister's strawberry blond curls from her eyes. "Lucy, did you hear? Lady Daphne is going to bring the baby to her very own doctor."

"I couldn't impose, my lady," Lucy said.

"Your son is my cousin, so you can't say no to me. You'll both stay with us at Staton House."

"But my lady…"

"You should be aware," Edward said, "that Lady Daphne doesn't take no for an answer."

BY THE TIME they arrived back at Staton House, Frederick was there. He had to know if Edward had indeed found Jerrold's child, and as soon as Lucy and baby Josiah entered the room Frederick welcomed them with every kindness. Mr. Rallston was called for, and when the child's ailment was proclaimed to be nothing more than a common cold that should begin healing now that Josiah was out of the damp, they rejoiced. Mr. Ellis poured red wine for everyone. Frederick raised his glass, and the others followed.

"To my brother Richard, who took it upon himself to care for Jerrold's child. I have always known my brother Richard to be a decent man, a caring man, and now I know beyond a shadow of a doubt that it's true. I only wish he were here to see this moment when Josiah was finally allowed to meet his family. I know Richard would have cherished this, and I hope that somehow, some way he knows the good he has done that helped lead to this day."

"To Uncle Richard," Daphne said.

Edward and Daphne joined Frederick by the hearth. "Will you tell Grandma about baby Josiah?" Daphne asked.

"I thought about announcing it over dinner tomorrow night, but I fear that may give her a shock she'll never recover from. What I will do, however, is inform your Uncle Jerrold. And, if I'm in a certain mood, your Aunt Hyacinth."

"What do you think your brother will do?" Edward asked.

"I couldn't say. But I want him to know that I know. I want

him to know that I know that every time he made comments about Richard's wanton way of life he was pointing out the very thing he suffered from himself."

"He certainly has Lady Staton fooled," said Edward.

"I know. And yet I'm afraid I won't have the heart to dissuade her about her youngest son. So often we think we know someone, we know everything about them, every thought they've ever had, every decision they've ever made, but when it comes down to it we realize that we didn't know the first thing about them. Edward, what was that quote from Dickens, about everyone being a mystery to everyone else?"

"A wonderful fact to reflect upon, that every human creature is constituted to be a profound secret and mystery to every other."

"Yes," Frederick said. "That's it. The older I grow the more I realize I don't know anyone else at all, at least not the way I thought I did."

"Maybe a little mystery isn't a bad thing," said Daphne. "Maybe mystery is what keeps us curious about life."

"Who said that?" Frederick asked.

"Edward did." Daphne beamed at her fiancé.

Edward put his arm around Daphne's waist and kissed the top of her gold curls. "I will always be curious about you, Daphne Meriwether." He bowed. "Lady Daphne Meriwether."

Frederick beamed at his daughter like the proud father he was.

THE END

*T*he shadows were about in Hembry again. Footsteps on the curving stairs, whispers in the halls, movements in the breeze. Daphne couldn't sleep that early spring night in April, and instead of being frightened by the sounds she took comfort from them, knowing there were things about life at Hembry she would never understand, and she was all right with that. Ever since she had arrived in England with her father nearly two years before she had been struggling to make sense of life at Hembry. Finally, she realized that it was all right to accept life at Hembry for what it was, a society based on tradition, while accepting herself for who she was. When she thought about everything that nearly kept her apart from Edward, her heart swelled with gratitude and the inconveniences became nothing more than that—inconveniences.

She pulled her shawl over her nightgown, slid her feet into her slippers, and tiptoed downstairs. She was afraid that if she stepped too strongly the old floorboards would creak and wake the entire house. She found her way to the library, her favorite room in the house besides her bedroom, and she sank into the settee in front of the cold hearth which had been put out for the night. She thought about everything she had seen since arriving in England, everyone she had met, most especially Edward. She thought about her losses, her grandfather and her Uncle Richard, and she thought about her gains, most especially Edward. Now she had a new cousin to care for, and now she and Pamela were practically family. She looked around the dark-paneled walls, the floor-to-ceiling bookshelves, the family crest emblazoned on the hearth, and she discovered, perhaps for the first time, that she was comfortable at Hembry Castle. She smiled at a family portrait, an 18th-century ancestor, a young woman wearing a sky-high white wig, a hoop wide enough to hide three people under her salmon-pink dress, and a sweet smile as though she knew she was being watched a century later. Daphne couldn't take her eyes off the portrait, and upon further inspection she saw a young woman who wore different clothing and a different hairstyle, but people haven't changed. Daphne's grandmother had already arranged for a portrait artist to come and paint her father, the Earl, and her, the Earl's daughter, and she wondered who would be studying her portrait in that very room a hundred years in the future. Instead of feeling intimidated, instead of feeling unable to live up to impossibly high standards, Daphne felt as though she understood the young woman in the painting. She wasn't some special being, separated from the rest of humanity by an honorary title. She was a person with the same hopes and dreams as anyone. Did the young woman have a happy life, Daphne wondered? Because that's all anyone wants, no matter which family they're born to, no matter what their circumstances.

It was Lady Staton who helped Daphne understand that.

Grand Lady Staton, perfectly dignified even with an ear trumpet pressed to her head, who carried herself so straight she looked as though she had been born with a curtain rod through her spine, and yet she had crumpled to the floor when her eldest son died like any other mother would have. My grandmother is a person like any other, Daphne thought, with feelings like any other, and the appearance of perfection is merely an affectation. Lady Staton seemed to have softened since Richard's death. She may never be absolutely pleased with Daphne's choice of a husband, but at least her grandmother had finally relented enough to begin accepting it. Lady Staton had even started a conversation with Edward one night over dinner about the state of the newspaper business.

Uncle Jerrold was another matter entirely. The first to point the finger at anyone who seemed to stray from the social norms, and there he was with a child he left to suffer in poverty. Edward had said, and Daphne believed it was true, that whenever people make pronouncements about the morality of others they often have their own morality problems. But all was well on that front too. Lucy and Josiah were living on Hembry grounds, both cared for, both happy. When her father told Uncle Jerrold that Lucy and her child were living in a cottage near the castle, Jerrold took his wife and sons to live in Italy. Which was just as well, Daphne thought. He was the uncle she would never miss.

It was a good thing that Daphne was feeling at home in the vast house. Her father was the Earl of Staton now and he depended on her help. Yes, it was unusual for an earl's daughter to be so involved in the management of the house and village business, but he was the wayward, and she was American, and people, even the fancy ones, let it go for those reasons alone. Yes, it was unusual for an earl's daughter to marry the grandson of the butler and housekeeper, even one growing in fame as a literary talent, but people let that go for the same reasons. She wondered what her life would be like once she was Lady Daphne Ellis. She and Edward had set a date—they would be married in August, just four months away.

She pulled her shawl closer around her shoulders and stood near the cold hearth, staring at the family crest. She remembered the way her Uncle Richard had stared at it the night he died. Daphne went to the shelf where she placed her Uncle Richard's copy of Our Mutual Friend, opened the front cover, and pulled out the letters that had meant so much to him. She was always drawn to the love letter. Yes, Edward sent her love letters all the time, and they were beautiful (leave it to a writer to let you know how much you're loved), yet there was something so pure about the letter written to her uncle. She stared at the words, feeling a shock of recognition. Her father was right. The hand did look familiar. Could it be?

She went upstairs to her room as quickly as she dared, still aware of the centuries-old floorboards and the crickety stairs. Back in her birdcage bedroom, she opened her desk drawer and pulled out her most recent love letter from Edward along with a letter she was writing to her cousin in Connecticut, making sure her American family could come to England for the wedding. At the bottom of the drawer were a few notes about Mrs. Pearson's boy, Joseph, and Mr. Spreang. Daphne compared the notes to her uncle's love letter and she knew. As clearly as she knew Edward loved her, she knew who loved her Uncle Richard. Daphne smiled. Like her father, she was glad to know her uncle had love in his life. She realized she should have made the connection long ago.

After some struggle with the latch, Daphne pushed the heavy window frame up. It had been an angry March, with cold wind and cutting snow, so in April the weather was still nippy. Daphne liked the snap of the air against her face. No wonder Uncle Richard felt so constrained when he became Earl. Now she worried again. Did he see no other way out? Did he jump on purpose after all?

Daphne wondered whether or not she should tell her father about her discovery. She'd talk it over with Edward and decide then. Suddenly, she was so tired. She closed the window, dropped her shawl to the floor, crawled into bed, and fell asleep.

A WEEK later the shadows rattled the walls of the castle again, and again Daphne stayed awake to commiserate with the ghosts. She jumped when she heard a faint tap at her door.

"Daphne?" It was Mrs. Ellis' voice. "Daphne, may I come in?"

It had taken some sweet talking, some cajoling, and a few minor threats, but Daphne had convinced her future grand-parents-in-law to call her by her first name, at least when no one else was around. Daphne opened the door.

"Mrs. Ellis? What's wrong?"

"I need you to come with me to the smoking room, but we must go quickly. We haven't much time."

"Mrs. Ellis…?"

"You'll be glad you came. Trust me."

"Is it Edward?"

"It is not. But I think it's someone you'll be very happy to see."

Daphne followed Mrs. Ellis down the stairs, always on her toes, until they reached the smoking room. Mrs. Ellis opened the door, let Daphne in, and closed the door behind her.

"My dearest Daphne."

Daphne felt her knees go weak at the sight of the form visible only from the flickering light in the hearth. "But how…" She stepped closer, feeling the darkness of the room envelope her, as though she were caught in that middle state between sleeping and wakefulness. "Am I dreaming?"

Richard took Daphne's hands. "You're not dreaming, my most darling niece. I'm here."

"And you're not a ghost?"

Richard laughed. "I'm most certainly not a ghost." He looked at the clock on the mantelpiece. "I don't have long, Daphne. I have to go very soon."

Daphne touched her uncle's face. Was he a figment of her imagination? She had felt the specters around her so often that she wasn't yet convinced that what she saw was real. "How can you be here? Mr. Hough saw you fall off the bridge, and Papa saw your body. Papa took your watch, the one he gave you for your birthday."

"What else did the corpse have?"

"It had…" Daphne closed her eyes as she struggled to remember. "It had your shirt pin."

"Does that sound familiar?"

"Edwin Drood. Edwin's watch and shirt pin were found by the river."

"Good girl. I knew you'd remember."

"Uncle Richard, I still don't understand."

"I didn't fall, my dear, and I didn't jump. The brain sees what it expects to see. Hough's a doctor, remember. He has doctor friends, some of whom are my friends too. It wasn't hard to manage the rest."

"Mr. Hough knew?"

"Not at first. As far as he knew I jumped, and he thought he saw me in the morgue."

"How cruel, Uncle Richard."

"I know, my darling girl, but it had to be done. I needed him to give a convincing account to the police."

"Was Mr. Hough very angry when he found out?"

"Furious, as he had every right to be. But he's since forgiven me."

"I can still hardly believe you're here. How did you ever come up with such a crazy idea?"

Richard smiled in that sly way that made Daphne laugh when she was a girl. She hadn't seen that smile since she arrived in England. "I had some help, you see."

"Our Mutual Friend."

"Yes. And Drood provided that last piece of inspiration. Mr. Dickens would have his flights of fancy."

"But why not tell Papa, or me? You'd hardly recognize Grandma these days, she's so changed."

"I've heard she's more subdued." Richard rubbed his hands together. It grew cold in the room as the fire dwindled away. "I am sorry about that, truly I am, but I'm afraid that had to be done as well. I had to get away from here, Daphne, or I would have gone well and truly mad."

"I understand that, Uncle Richard, I do. But I still don't see why you couldn't at least tell Papa."

"Freddie never wanted the title any more than I did. If he didn't think he was entitled to it, then he might not have taken to it as well as he has. Everything is all right if you think about it. I've taken out the bad Earl and put in the good Earl. Surely that makes up for some of the ills I've caused." He snapped his fingers. "I nearly forgot. This is for you. Consider it a belated engagement present. I knew when I saw you running together in the rain that you and young Mr. Ellis were destined for each other."

Daphne clutched the small box wrapped in silver paper, and she opened it to find a pair of diamond filigree earrings.

"Thank you, Uncle Richard. They're beautiful. But how did you know Edward and I were engaged?"

"Mrs. Ellis told me."

"Mrs. Ellis knew?"

"She did. She even helped in her way."

"Does Edward know? Or Mr. Ellis?"

"They do not. If you ever need help, Mrs. Ellis is the one to call on. Remember that because it may come in handy for you one day." It was nearing dawn and the faintest pink light appeared on the horizon. "I must be gone before anyone sees me."

Daphne grasped his hand. "Where will you go?"

"Who knows? The whole world is open to me now."

"Don't you want to see Papa?"

"I do, but I won't. If you want to tell him, then do. But I say let the Earl be the Earl without any more interference from his exasperating eldest brother. Now I must go."

Richard kissed Daphne's cheek. As he walked through the door he looked back with such contentment she thought once again that she must have been talking to a spirit.

EDWARD FINALLY FOUND time to visit Hembry Castle after being consumed with Observer business, public appearances, and his own writing for more than a month. Daphne told him about her Uncle Richard's revelation even if she hadn't yet told her father. She didn't feel comfortable keeping things from her father, but she wondered if her Uncle Richard was right. Maybe it was best if her father thought the title was rightfully his. Maybe she would tell him another time. Or maybe she wouldn't tell him at all.

Edward was sitting at the desk in the library revising a new story, one about a man who faked his death to live in peace with the person he loves, who remains unknown in the story.

"Isn't that a little close?" Daphne asked after she read it.

"Who's going to know?" Edward looked dreamily through the window to the curve of the river. "It's one of the best things I've written. Everyone deserves their happily ever after, you know, like when Aschenputtel marries her prince."

"Are you my prince?"

"I dare say your grandmother would like me better if I were."

"I like you perfectly fine the way you are."

"Which is all I need."

Daphne grabbed his hand and pulled him toward the door. "Come outside, Edward. You've been stuck at that desk all day. Walk with me. The rose garden has bloomed and it's beautiful."

She led him through the house, out the front door, past the river to the rose garden that caught her attention when she first arrived at the great house. "I think this is where I began to love Hembry." She looked at the castle on the hill. "I wasn't sure what to think when I first saw it. It's beautiful, but it's so big, and I didn't think it would ever feel like home. But it does now. I have my home, and I have you. I don't need anything else."

"If you only knew how many nights I lie awake longing to hear those words come from your beautiful lips, how many times I prayed we could be together somehow, some way, then you would know how full my heart feels right now."

As Edward kissed Daphne it began to rain. They laughed, then dashed across the parkland to the mock castle where they kissed that first time, also in the rain. They stopped under the stone archway and clasped hands. Perhaps they kissed again.

"Do you still complain about how much it rains in England?" Edward asked.

"Not anymore." Daphne threw her arms around Edward's neck. "I didn't know then."

"What didn't you know?"

"How much joy could be had when it rained at Hembry Castle."

<u>The End of Book One</u>

AUTHOR'S NOTES

This novel, *When It Rained at Hembry Castle*, was 20 years in the making. While I always loved the idea of writing a story set in Victorian England, the concept was put aside while I pursued other projects. Finally, my other projects completed, I was able to focus my attention on this idea I had been kicking around for nearly two decades. The places of Staton and Hembry exist only in my imagination (and hopefully now in your imagination too).

Thank you as always to my wonderful readers from all over the world. You are more appreciated than you know.

As I have said before, my historical fiction stands on the shoulders of historians who do the heavy lifting of researching the eras I write about. Here are some of the books that were helpful to me as I wrote *When It Rained at Hembry Castle—Up and Down Stairs: The History of the Country House Servant* by Jeremy Musson; *What Jane Austen Ate and Charles Dickens Knew* by Daniel Pool; *How To Be a Victorian: A Dusk-to-Dawn Guide to Victorian Life* by Ruth Goodman (one of my favorite historians

—she lives what she studies); *The Victorian City: Everyday Life in Dickens' London* and *Inside the Victorian Home: A Portrait of Domestic Life in Victorian England* by Judith Flanders; and *The Writer's Guide to Everyday Life in Regency and Victorian England From 1811-1901* by Kristine Hughes.

ABOUT THE AUTHOR

Meredith Allard is an award-winning author known for the bestselling *Loving Husband Trilogy* and the Victorian novel *When It Rained at Hembry Castle*, which IndieReader named a Best Historical Novel. Her prequel, *Down Salem Way*, earned the B.R.A.G. Medallion and was a semi-finalist for the Chaucer Award in Early Historical Fiction.

A recognized authority on the craft, Meredith is the author of *Painting the Past: A Guide for Writing Historical Fiction*, a #1 Amazon New Release in Authorship and Creativity Self-Help. For over twenty years, she has mentored writers of all ages, helping them find their voices while honing her own signature blend of meticulous research and haunting prose.

When she isn't unearthing the secrets of the past, she can be found in the hills of Southern Nevada with her cats and a cup of coffee.

Join Meredith online at www.meredithallard.com for her weekly blog posts and monthly newsletter.

BOOKS BY MEREDITH ALLARD

www.ingramcontent.com/pod-product-compliance
Lightning Source LLC
Chambersburg PA
CBHW050534260626
47157CB00002B/290